ASHLEY BELL

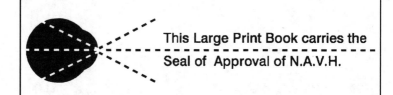

This Large Print Book carries the
Seal of Approval of N.A.V.H.

ASHLEY BELL

DEAN KOONTZ

LARGE PRINT PRESS
A part of Gale, Cengage Learning

GALE
CENGAGE Learning·

Farmington Hills, Mich • San Francisco • New York • Waterville, Maine
Meriden, Conn • Mason, Ohio • Chicago

GALE
CENGAGE Learning·

LIBRARY OF CONGRESS CATALOGING-IN-PUBLICATION DATA

Names: Koontz, Dean R. (Dean Ray), 1945-
Title: Ashley Bell / by Dean Koontz.
Description: Waterville, Maine : Thorndike Press, 2015. | Series: Thorndike
  Press large print core
Identifiers: LCCN 2015040067 | ISBN 9781410484956 (hardback) | ISBN
  1410484955 (hardcover)
Subjects: LCSH: Young women—California—Fiction. | Suspense fiction. |
  Mystery fiction. | Large type books. | BISAC: FICTION / Suspense.
Classification: LCC PS3561.O55 A94 2015 | DDC 813/.54—dc23
LC record available at http://lccn.loc.gov/2015040067

ISBN 13: 978-1-59413-905-5 (pbk.)
ISBN 10: 1-59413-905-9 (pbk.)

Published in 2016 by arrangement with Bantam Books, an imprint of Random House, a division of Penguin Random House LLC

Printed in the United States of America
1 2 3 4 5 6 7 20 19 18 17 16

With much affection,
this book is dedicated to
Susan (Allison) Cathers,
my sister from another mother.
Thank you for thirty years
of kindness and excellence.

She . . .

Hears the song in the egg of a bird.
— James Dickey, *Sleeping Out at Easter*

■ ■ ■ ■

1
THE WOMAN WHO INTENDED TO MARRY A HERO

■ ■ ■ ■

1
THE GIRL WHOSE MIND WAS ALWAYS SPINNING

The year that Bibi Blair turned ten, which was twelve years before Death came calling on her, the sky was a grim vault of sorrow nearly every day from January through mid-March, and the angels cried down flood after flood upon Southern California. That was how she described it in her diary: a sorrowing sky, the days and nights washed by the grief of angels, though she didn't speculate on the cause of their celestial distress.

Even then, she was writing short stories in addition to keeping a diary. That rainy winter, her simple narratives were all about a dog named Jasper whose cruel master had abandoned him on a storm-swept beach south of San Francisco. In each of those little fictions, Jasper, a gray-and-black mongrel, found a new home. But at the end of every tale, his haven proved impermanent for one reason or another. Determined to keep his spirits high, good Jasper traveled southward, hundreds of miles, in search of his forever home.

Bibi was a happy child, a stranger to melancholy; therefore, it seemed odd to her then — and for years after — that she should write multiple woeful episodes about a lonely, beleaguered mutt whose search for love was never more than briefly fulfilled. Understanding didn't come to her until after her twenty-second birthday.

In one sense, everyone is a magpie. Bibi was one, but she didn't know it then. Much time would pass before she recognized some truths that she had hidden away in her magpie heart.

The magpie, a bird with striking pied plumage and a long tail, often hoards objects that strike it as significant: buttons, bits of string, twists of ribbon, colorful beads, fragments of broken glass. Having concealed these treasures from the world, the magpie builds a new nest the following year and forgets where its trove is located; therefore, having hidden its collection even from itself, the bird starts a new one.

People hide truths about themselves from themselves. Such self-deception is a coping mechanism, and to one extent or another, most people begin deceiving themselves when they're children.

That sodden winter when she was ten, Bibi lived with her parents in a small bungalow in Corona del Mar, a picturesque neighborhood of Newport Beach. Although they were just three blocks from the Pacific, they had no ocean view. The first Saturday in April, she was home alone, sitting in a rocking chair on the front porch of the quaint shingled house as warm rain streamed straight down through the palm trees and the ficuses, as it sizzled on the blacktop like hot oil on a griddle.

She was not a child who lazed around. Her mind remained always busy, spinning. She had a yellow lined tablet and a collection of pencils with which she was composing yet another installment in the saga of lonesome Jasper. Movement at the periphery of her vision caused her to look up, whereupon she discovered a soaked and weary dog ascending the sidewalk from the distant sea.

At ten, her sense of wonder had not been worn thin; and she sensed that a surprising turn of events was about to occur. In the grip of an agreeable expectation, she put down the tablet and the pencil, rose from the chair, and went to the head of the porch steps.

The dog looked nothing like the lonely mongrel in her stories. The bedraggled golden retriever halted where the bungalow walkway met the public sidewalk. Girl and beast regarded each other. She called to him, "Here, boy, here." He needed to be coaxed, but eventually he approached the porch and climbed the steps. Bibi stooped to his level to peer into his eyes, which were as golden as his coat. "You stink." The retriever yawned, as if his stinkiness was old news to him.

He wore a cracked and filthy leather collar. No license tag dangled from it. There wasn't one of those name-and-phone-number plates riveted to it, which a responsible owner should have provided.

Bibi led the dog off the porch, through the rain, around the side of the house, into a brick-paved thirty-foot-square courtyard flanked by stuccoed privacy walls along the property lines to the east and west. To the south stood a two-car garage that opened onto an alleyway. Exterior steps rose to a small balcony and an apartment above the garage. Bibi avoided glancing up at those windows.

She told the retriever to wait on the back porch while she went into the house. He surprised her by being there when she returned with two beach towels, shampoo, a hair dryer, and a hairbrush. He ran with her across the courtyard, out of the rain and into the garage.

After she turned on the lights, after she took the stained and mud-crusted collar from around his neck, she saw something that she had not previously noticed. She considered dropping the collar in the garbage can, burying it under other trash, but she knew that would be wrong. Instead, she opened a drawer in the cabinet beside her father's workbench, took one of several chamois cloths from his supply, and wrapped the collar in it.

A sound issued from the apartment overhead, a brief hard clatter. Startled, Bibi looked at the garage ceiling, where the open four-by-six joists were festooned with spider architecture.

She thought she heard a low and anguished voice, too. After listening intently for half a minute, she told herself that she must have imagined it.

Between two of the joists, backlit by a bare dust-coated bulb in a white ceramic socket, a fat spider danced from string to string, plucking from its silken harp a music beyond human hearing.

Bibi thought of Charlotte the spider, who saved Wilbur the pig, her friend, in E. B. White's book *Charlotte's Web*. For a moment, Bibi was all but unaware of the garage as an image rose in her mind and became more real to her than reality:

Hundreds of tiny young spiders, Charlotte's offspring fresh from her egg sac many weeks after her sad death, standing on their heads and pointing their spinnerets at the sky, letting loose small clouds of fine silk. The clouds form into miniature balloons, and the baby spiders become airborne. Wilbur the pig is overcome with wonder and delight, but also with sadness, while he watches the aerial armada sail away

15

to far places, wishing them well but sorry to be deprived of this last connection to his lost friend Charlotte. . . .

With a thin whine and soft bark, the dog brought Bibi back to the reality of the garage.

Later, after the retriever had been washed and dried and brushed, during a break in the rain, Bibi took him into the house. When she showed him the small bedroom that was hers, she said, "If Mom and Dad don't blow their tops when they see you, then you'll sleep here with me."

The dog watched with interest as Bibi dragged a cardboard box out of the closet. It contained books that wouldn't fit on the already heavily laden shelves flanking her bed. She rearranged the volumes to create a hollow into which she inserted the chamois-wrapped collar before returning the box to the closet.

"Your name is Olaf," she informed the retriever, and he reacted to this christening by wagging his tail. "Olaf. Someday, I'll tell you why."

In time, Bibi forgot about the collar because she wanted to forget. Nine years would pass before she discovered it at the bottom of that box of books. And when she found it, she folded the chamois around it once more and sought a new place in which to conceal it.

2

ANOTHER PERFECT DAY IN PARADISE

That second Tuesday in March, with its terrible revelations and the sudden threat of death, would have been the beginning of the end for some people, but Bibi Blair, now twenty-two, would eventually call it Day One.

She woke at dawn and stood at the bedroom window, yawning and watching the still-submerged sun announce its approach with banners of coral-pink light, until at last it surfaced and cruised westward. She liked sunrises. Beginnings. Each day started with such promise. Anything good could happen. For Bibi the word *disappointment* was reserved for evenings, and only if the day had truly, totally sucked. She was an optimist. Her mother had once said that, given lemons, Bibi wouldn't make lemonade; she would make limoncello.

Silhouetted against the morning blue, the distant mountains seemed to be ramparts protecting the magic kingdom of Orange County from the ugliness and disorder that plagued so much of the world these days.

Across the California flatlands, the tree-lined street grids and numerous parks of south county's planned communities promised a smooth and tidy life of infinite charms.

Bibi needed more than a mere promise. At twenty-two, she had big dreams, though she didn't call them dreams, because dreams were wish-upon-a-star fantasies that rarely came true. Consequently, she called them *expectations*. She had great expectations, and she could see the means by which she would surely fulfill them.

Sometimes she was able to imagine her future so clearly that it almost seemed as if she had already lived it and was now remembering. To achieve your goals, imagination was almost as important as hard work. You couldn't win the prize if you couldn't imagine what it was and where it might be found.

Staring at the mountains, Bibi thought of the man she would marry, the love of her life now half a world away in a place of blood and treachery. She refused to fear too much for him. He could take care of himself in any circumstances. He was not a fairy-tale hero but a real one, and the woman who would be his wife had an obligation to be as stoic as he was about the risks he faced.

"Love you, Paxton," she murmured, as she often did, as if that declaration were a charm that would protect him regardless of how many thousands of miles separated them.

After showering and dressing for the day, after snaring the newspaper from the doorstep, she went into the kitchen just as her programmed coffee machine drizzled the sixth cup into the Pyrex pot. The blend she preferred was fragrant and so rich in caffeine that the fumes alone would cure narcolepsy.

The vintage dinette chairs featured chrome-plated steel legs and seats upholstered in black vinyl. Very 1950s. She liked the '50s. The world hadn't gone crazy yet. As she sat at a chromed table with a red Formica top, paging through the newspaper, she drank her first coffee of the day, which she called her "wind-me-up cup."

To compete in an age when electronic media delivered the news long before it appeared in print, the publisher of this paper chose to spend only a few pages on major world and national events in order to reserve space for long human-interest stories involving county residents. As a novelist, Bibi approved. Like good fiction, the best history books were less about big events than about the people whose lives were affected by forces beyond their control. However, for every story about a wife fighting indifferent government bureaucrats to get adequate care for her war-disabled husband, there was another story about someone who acquired an enormous collection of weird hats or who was crusading to be allowed to marry his pet parrot.

Like her first cup, her second coffee was black, and Bibi drank it as she ate a chocolate croissant. In spite of all the propaganda, she didn't believe that oceans of coffee or a diet rich in butter and eggs was unhealthy. She ate what she wanted, almost in a spirit of defiance, remaining trim and healthy. She had one life, and she meant to live it, bacon and all.

As she ate a second croissant, she got a bite that tasted as rancid as spoiled milk. She spat it onto her plate and wiped her tongue with a napkin.

The bakery she frequented had always been reliable. She could see nothing wrong with the wad of pastry that she had spit out. She sniffed the croissant, but it smelled all right. No visible foreign substance tainted it.

Tentatively, she took another bite. It tasted fine. Or did it? Maybe the faintest trace of . . . something. She put down the croissant. She had lost her appetite.

That day's newspaper was thick with weird-hat collectors and the like. She put it aside. Carrying a third cup of coffee, she went to her office in the larger of the apartment's two bedrooms.

At her computer, when she retrieved the unfinished short story she'd been writing on and off for a few weeks, she stared for a while at her byline: *Bibi Blair.*

Her parents had named her Bibi, not because they were cruel or indifferent to the travails of a child saddled with an unusual name, but because they were lighthearted to a fault. Bibi, pronounced *Beebee,* came from the Old French *beubelot,* meaning toy or bauble. She was no one's toy. Never had been, never would be.

Another name derived from *beubelot* was Bubbles. That would have been worse. She would have had to change Bubbles to something less frivolous or otherwise become a pole dancer.

By her sixteenth birthday, she was accustomed to her name. By the time she was twenty, she thought Bibi Blair had a quirky sort of distinction. Nevertheless, sometimes she wondered if she would be taken seriously, as a writer, with such a name.

She scrolled down the page from the byline and stopped at the second paragraph, where she saw a sentence that needed revision. When she began to type, her right hand served her well, but the left fumbled over the keys, scattering random letters across the screen.

Her surprise turned to alarm when she realized that she could not feel the keys beneath her spasming fingers. The sense of touch had deserted them.

Bewildered, she raised the traitorous hand,

flexed the fingers, saw them move, but couldn't *feel* them moving.

Although coffee had entirely rinsed away the rancid taste that earlier had spoiled her enjoyment of the second croissant, the same foulness filled her mouth again. She grimaced in disgust and, with her right hand, reached for the coffee. The rim of the cup rattled against her teeth, but the brew once more washed her tongue clean.

Her left hand slipped off the keyboard, onto her lap. For a moment, she couldn't move it, and in panic she thought, *Paralysis.*

Suddenly a tingling filled the hand, the arm, not that vibratile numbness that followed a sharp blow to the elbow, but a crawling sensation, as if ants were swarming through flesh and bone. As she rolled her chair away from the desk and got to her feet, the tingling spread through the entire left side of her body, from scalp to foot.

Although Bibi didn't know what was happening to her, she sensed that she was in mortal peril. She said, "But I'm only twenty-two."

3
THE SALON

Nancy Blair always booked the earliest appointment at Heather Jorgenson's six-chair salon in Newport Beach because it was her considered opinion that even the best stylists, like Heather, did less dependable work as the day wore on. Nancy would no sooner have her hair cut in the afternoon than she would schedule an after-dinner face-lift.

Not that she needed plastic surgery. At forty-eight, she looked thirty-eight. At worst thirty-nine. Her husband — Murphy, known to all as Murph — said that if she ever let a cosmetic surgeon mess with her face, he would still love her, but he'd start calling her Cruella de Vil, after the stretched-tight villainess in *101 Dalmatians.*

She had great hair, too, thick and dark, without a fleck of gray. She got it cut every three weeks because she liked to maintain a precise look.

Her daughter, Bibi, had the same luxurious dark-brown hair, almost black, but Bibi wore hers long. The dear girl was always gently pressing her mother to move on from the short and shaggy style. But Nancy was a doer, a goer, always on the run, and she didn't have the patience for the endless fussing that was required to look good with a longer do.

After wetting Nancy's hair with a spray bottle, Heather said, "I read Bibi's novel, *The Blind Man's Lamp*. I really liked it."

"Oh, honey, my daughter has more talent in one pinkie than most other writers have in their fingers and their thumbs." Even as she made that declaration with unabashed pride, Nancy realized that it was less than eloquent, even a little silly. Whatever the source of Bibi's talent for language, it hadn't come with her mother's genes.

"It should have been a bestseller," Heather said.

"She'll get there. If that's what she wants. I don't know if it is. I mean, she shares everything with me, but she's guarded about her writing, what she wants. A mysterious girl in some ways. Bibi was mysterious even as a child. She was like eight when she made up these stories about a community of intelligent mice that lived in tunnels under our bungalow. Ridiculous stories, but she could almost make you believe them. In fact, we thought for a while *she* believed in those damn mice. We almost got her therapy. But we realized that she was just Bibi being Bibi, born to tell stories."

As an ardent consumer of magazines that chronicled the lives of celebrities in plenty of photos and minimal prose, Heather perhaps had not heard Nancy after the third sentence of that long ramble. "But, gee, why wouldn't she want to be a bestseller — and *famous*?"

"Maybe she does. But it's not why she writes. She writes because she has to. She says her imagination is like a boiler that's all the time building up too much pressure. If she doesn't let out some of the steam every day, it'll explode and blow off her head."

"Wow." Heather's face in the mirror, above Nancy's face, loomed wide-eyed and chipmunky. She was a cute girl. She would have been even cuter if she'd had her upper incisors brought into line with braces.

"Bibi doesn't mean that literally, of course. Her head isn't going to explode any more than there were intelligent mice living under our bungalow back in the day."

Heather's insistent teeth lent a comic quality to her expression of concern. She was adorable.

Murph had once declared that if a girl was cute enough, some men found an overbite sexy. Ever since, Nancy had been wary of any attractive woman in her husband's life who needed orthodontal work. Murph had never met Heather. If Nancy had anything to say

25

about it, he never would. Not that he cheated. He didn't. He wouldn't. Maybe he didn't believe that his wife would castrate him with bolt cutters, as she'd sworn she would, but he was smart enough to know that the consequences of infidelity would be ugly.

"Close your eyes," Heather said, and Nancy closed them, and the spray bottle of water made a spritzing sound. Then a little fragrant mousse. Then a final blow-dry and shaping with a brush.

When her hair was done, it was perfect, as always. Heather was such a talented cutter, she wouldn't refer to herself as a beautician or a hairstylist. Her card identified her as a *coiffeuse,* and that little pretension, so Newport Beach, was in her case justified.

Nancy paid and tipped. She was assuring her *coiffeuse* that she would pass along the good review of *The Blind Man's Lamp* to the author when she was interrupted by her phone's current ringtone — a few bars of that old Bobby McFerrin song "Don't Worry, Be Happy." She checked the caller ID, took the call, and said, "Bibi, baby."

As if from beyond some barrier more formidable than distance, Bibi said, "Mom, something's wrong with me."

4
SEARCHING FOR THE SILVER LINING

Bibi was sitting in a living-room armchair, her purse on her lap, trying to dispatch the creepy head-to-foot tingling sensation with positive thinking, when her mother burst into the apartment as if she were leading a style-police SWAT team intent on ferreting out people wearing unimaginative coordinated ensembles. Nancy looked splendidly eclectic in a supple-as-cloth black-leather sports-jacket-cut men's coat from St. Croix, an intricately patterned ecru top by Louis Vuitton, black Mavi jeans with subtle and carefully crafted areas of wear, and black-and-red athletic shoes by some designer whose name Bibi could not recall.

She didn't share her mother's obsession with fashion, as her off-brand jeans and long-sleeved T-shirt attested.

As Nancy crossed the room toward the armchair, a rush of words spilled from her. "You're pale, you're positively gray, oh, my God, you look terrible."

"I do not, Mom. I look normal, which spooks me worse than if I were stone-gray with bleeding eyes. How can I look normal and have these symptoms?"

"I'm going to call nine-one-one."

"No, you're not," Bibi said firmly. "I'm not going to make a spectacle of myself." Using her good right hand, she pushed herself up from the chair. "Just drive me to the hospital ER."

Nancy looked at her daughter as she might have regarded some pathetic truck-stricken creature lying crippled at the side of a highway. Her eyes blurred with tears.

"Don't you dare, Mother. Don't you cry at me." Bibi indicated a small drawstring bag beside the armchair. "Can you get that for me? It's pajamas, toothbrush, overnight things in case I have to stay till tomorrow. No way I'm going to wear one of those tie-in-the-back hospital gowns with my butt hanging out."

Her voice as quivery as aspic, Nancy said, "I love you so much."

"I love you, too, Mom." Bibi started toward the door. "Come on, now. I'm not afraid. Not much. You always say, 'It'll be what it'll be.' Say it, so live it. Let's go."

"But if you've had a stroke, we should call nine-one-one. Every minute matters."

"I haven't had a stroke."

Hurrying ahead of her daughter, opening

the door but blocking the exit, Nancy said, "On the phone, you told me your left side is paralyzed —"

"Not paralyzed. Tingling. As if fifty cell phones, set on mute, were taped to my body, vibrating all at once. And my left hand is a little weak. That's all."

"Sounds like a stroke. How do you know it isn't?"

"It's not a stroke. My speech isn't slurred. My vision's okay. No headache. No confusion. *And I'm only twenty-two, damn it.*"

Nancy's expression softened from anxious dread to what might have been chagrin as she realized that she was alarming rather than assisting her daughter. "Okay. Yes, you're right. I'll drive you."

The third-floor apartments opened onto a covered balcony, and Bibi kept her right hand on the railing as they moved toward the north end. A pleasantly cool day. Songbirds celebrating. In the courtyard, the palms and ferns rustled faintly in the mild breeze. Phantom silvery fish of sunlight schooled back and forth across the water in the swimming pool, and the simple scene was profoundly beautiful as it had never appeared to her before.

When they came to the end of the balcony, Nancy said, "Honey, are you sure you can do stairs?"

The open iron staircase featured pebbled-concrete treads. The symmetry of the stairs, the grace with which they descended to the courtyard, qualified them as sculpture. Bibi had not previously seen the stairs as art; the prospect of perhaps never seeing them again must have given her this new perspective.

"Yeah, I can do stairs," Bibi impatiently assured her mother. "I just can't *dance* down them."

She negotiated flight after flight without a serious incident, except that three times her left foot did not move when it should have, and she needed to drag it from one tread to the next.

In the parking lot, as they approached a BMW with vanity license plates that announced TOP AGENT, Nancy started for the front passenger door, evidently remembered that coddling was not wanted, and hurried around to the driver's side of the vehicle.

To Bibi's relief, she found that getting into the car was no more difficult than boarding the gently rocking gondola of a Ferris wheel.

Starting the engine, Nancy said, "Buckle up, sweetie."

"I am buckled up, Mother." Hearing herself, she felt like an adolescent, dependent and a little whiny, and she loathed being either of those things. "I'm buckled."

"Oh. You are. Yes, of course you are."

Nancy exited the parking lot without coming to a full stop, turned right on the street, and accelerated to get through a nearby intersection before the traffic light changed.

"It would be ironic," Bibi said, "if you killed us trying to get to a hospital."

"Never had an accident, honey. Only one ticket, and that was in a totally fraudulent, tricked-up speed trap. The cop was a real smog monster, a mean-eyed kak who wouldn't know glassout conditions from mushburgers."

Surfer lingo. A smog monster was an inlander. A kak was a dick. Glassout was when the ocean flowed unruffled, perfect for surfing, and mushburgers were the kind of waves that made surfers think about leaving the water for a skateboard.

Sometimes it was difficult for Bibi to keep in mind that her mother had long ago been a surfer girl supreme, riding tubes, taking the drop with the best of them. Nancy still loved the sun-baked sand and the surf. From time to time, she paddled out and caught some waves. But of the words that defined her now, *surfer* was not as high on the list as it had once been. These days, other than when she was on the beach, surfspeak crept into her vocabulary only when she had a beef about one authority figure or another.

She concentrated on the traffic, no tears in her eyes anymore, jaw set, brow creased, checking out the rearview mirror, the side mirrors, switching lanes more often than usual, totally into the task, as she otherwise was only when she went after a real-estate listing or thought that a property sale might be on the verge of closing.

"Oh, crap." Bibi snatched a few tissues from the console box and spat into them twice, without effect.

"What is it, what're you doing?"

"That disgusting taste."

"What taste?"

"Like spoiled milk, rancid butter. It comes and goes."

"Since when?"

"Since . . . this started."

"You said your only symptoms were the weak hand, the tingling."

"I don't think it's a symptom."

"It's a symptom," her mother declared.

In the distance, the hospital towered over other structures, and at the sight of it, Bibi acknowledged to herself that she was more afraid than she had wanted to admit. The architecture was unexceptional, bland, and yet the closer they drew to the place, the more sinister it appeared.

"There's always a silver lining," she assured herself.

Her mother sounded anxious and dubious: "Is there?"

"For a writer, there always is. Everything is material. We need new material for our stories."

Nancy accelerated through a yellow traffic light and turned off the street into the medical complex. "It'll be what it'll be," she said, almost to herself, as if those words were magical, each of them an abraxas that would ward off evil.

"Please don't say that to me again," Bibi requested, more sharply than she intended. "Not ever again. You're always saying it, and I don't want to hear it anymore."

Following an ER sign that directed them off the main loop and to the left, Nancy glanced at her daughter. "All right. Whatever you want, honey."

Bibi at once regretted snapping at her mother. "I'm sorry. So sorry." The first two words came out all right. But she heard the distortion in the last two, which sounded like *show sharry.*

As they pulled to a stop in front of the emergency entrance, Bibi admitted to herself the reason she hadn't called 911: She possessed a writer's well-honed understanding of story construction. Perhaps from the moment that her left hand had failed to engage the computer keyboard as she directed it, and surely from the moment the tingling had begun, she'd known where this was going, where it had to go, which was into a dark place. Every life was a story, after all, or a collection of stories, and not all of them tapered gracefully to a happy ending. She had always assumed her life would be a tale of happiness, that she would *craft* it as such, and during the onset of her symptoms, she had been reluctant to consider that her assumption might be naïve.

5
PET THE CAT

Although spring heat hadn't yet reliably settled over the Southern California coast, Murphy Blair went to work that morning wearing sandals, boardshorts, a black T-shirt, and a blue-and-black plaid Pendleton shirt worn open, with the sleeves rolled up. His shock of sandy-brown hair was shot through with blond streaks, legitimate sun bleaching, not bottle-born, because even on low-Fahrenheit days, he found the sun for a few hours. He was walking proof that, with sufficient obsession and contempt for melanoma, a summer tan could be maintained year-round.

His shop, Pet the Cat, was on Balboa Peninsula, the land mass that sheltered Newport Harbor from the ocean, in the vicinity of the first of two piers. The name of the store referred to the motion that surfers made when they were crouched on their boards, stroking the air or water as if to smooth their way through a section.

The display windows were full of surfboards and bitchin' shirts like Mowgli tees, Wellen tees, Billabong, Aloha, Reyn Spooner. Murph sold everything from Otis eyewear with mineral-glass lenses to Surf Siders shoes, from wetsuits to Stance socks featuring patterns based on the art of surfing champion John John Florence.

At fifty, Murph lived his work, worked to play, played to live. When he arrived at Pet the Cat, the door was unlocked, the lights were on, and Pogo was standing behind the counter, intently reading the instruction pamphlet for Search, the GPS surf watch by Rip Curl.

Glancing up at his boss, Pogo said, "I'm gonna get one of these here for damn sure."

Three years earlier, he escaped high school with a perfect two-point grade average and foiled his parents' attempt to force him onto a college track. He lived frugally with two other surf rats, Mike and Nate, in a studio apartment above a thrift shop in nearby Costa Mesa, and drove a primer-gray thirty-year-old Honda that looked as though it was good for nothing more than being a target car in a monster-truck demolition derby.

Sometimes an underachieving wanker took refuge in the surfing culture and remained largely or entirely womanless until he died with his last Social Security check uncashed. For two reasons, Pogo didn't have that problem. First, he was a wave king, fearless and graceful on the board, eager to master even the huge monoliths that had come with Hurricane Marie, admired for his style and heart. He might have been a champion if he'd possessed enough ambition to participate in competitions. Second, he was so gorgeous that when he passed, women tracked him as if their heads were attached to their necks with ball-bearing swivel hinges.

"You gonna give me the usual discount on this?" Pogo asked, indicating the GPS surf watch.

Murph said, "Sure, all right."

"Twelve weekly payments, zero interest?"

"What am I — a charity? It's not that expensive."

"Eight weeks?"

Murph sighed. "Okay, why not." He pointed at the flat blank screen of the large TV on the wall behind the counter, which should have been running vintage Billabong surf videos to lend atmosphere to the shop. "Tell me that's not on the fritz."

"It's not. I just sort of forgot about it. Sorry, bro."

"Bro, huh? Do you love me like a brother, Pogo?"

"Totally, bro. My real brother, Clyde, he's a brainiac stockbroker, might as well be from Mars."

"His name's Brandon. What's with this Clyde?"

Pogo winked. "You'll figure it out."

Murph took a deep breath. "You want the shop to prosper?"

As he fired up the Billabong videos, Pogo said, "Sure, yeah, I want you to rule the scene, bro."

"Then you'd help my business a lot if you went to work at some other surf shop."

Pogo grinned. "I'd be crushed if I thought you meant that. But, see, I get your dry wit. You should do stand-up."

"Yeah, I'm a riot."

"No, really. Bonnie thinks you're hilarious, too."

"Bonnie, your nose-to-grindstone sister who works her butt off to keep that restaurant afloat? Oh. I see. Bonnie and Clyde. Anyway, she's another brainiac. You mean you and her share a sense of humor?"

Pogo sighed. "Hey, when I say 'brainiac,' I don't use the term pejoratively. I have lots in common with my twin siblings."

" 'Pejoratively,' huh? Sometimes you give yourself away, Pogo." Murph's cell phone rang, and he checked the caller ID. Nancy. He said, "What's up, sugar?"

A chill climbed his spine and found his heart as his wife said, "I'm scared, baby. I'm afraid Bibi's had a stroke."

6

THE FRIGHTENING PACE
OF EXAMINATION

On a Tuesday morning, the ER wasn't as busy as it would be on the 7:00-P.M.-to-3:00-A.M. shift. The night would bring those injured by drunk drivers, victims of muggers, battered wives, and all manner of aggressive or hallucinating druggies sliding along the razor's edge of an overdose. When Bibi arrived with her mother, only five people were in the waiting room, none of them bleeding profusely.

At the moment, the triage nurse was actually an emergency-care technician named Manuel Rivera, a short, stocky man in hospital blues. He checked her pulse and took her blood pressure as he listened to her recite her symptoms.

Bibi slurred a few words, but for the most part her speech was clear. She felt better and safer, being in a hospital, until Manuel's sweet face, almost a Buddha face, darkened with worry and he guided her to a wheelchair. With apparent urgency, he rolled her through a pair of automatic doors into the ER ahead of the other people who were waiting for treatment.

Each emergency-room bay was a cubicle with a gray vinyl-tile floor and three pale-blue walls and one glass wall that faced the hallway. Toward the head of the bed stood a heart monitor and other equipment, awaiting use.

Nancy settled in one of the two chairs for visitors, holding her and Bibi's purses, hands clutching them as if she anticipated a robbery attempt, though it wasn't a purse snatcher that she feared.

Manuel lowered the power bed and assisted Bibi to sit on the edge. "Unless you feel dizzy, don't lie down yet," he instructed.

He rolled the wheelchair into the hallway, where he met a tall athletic-looking man in scrubs, evidently a physician. The doctor wheeled before him a portable computer station designed to be used while the operator remained standing, into which he entered details regarding the preliminary diagnosis and treatment of each patient he attended.

"Are you all right, baby?" Nancy asked.

"Yes, Mom. I'm okay. I'm going to be fine."

"Do you need anything? Water? Do you need water?"

Bibi's mouth kept flooding with saliva, as if she were about to throw up, but she swallowed it and kept her breakfast down. The last thing she wanted was water.

In the hallway, after Manuel spoke with the tall man for a moment, the latter came into the cubicle and introduced himself as Dr. Armand Barsamian. His calm demeanor and confident manner would have reassured Bibi under other circumstances.

While he checked her eyes with an ophthalmoscope, he asked a few questions — her name, date of birth, Social Security number — and she realized that he wanted to ascertain whether or not her memory had been affected by whatever was happening to her.

"We need to get a CT scan of the brain," Dr. Barsamian said. "If this is a stroke, the quicker we identify the cause — thrombosis, hemorrhage — and determine treatment, the more likely you'll fully recover."

Already an orderly with a gurney had appeared in the doorway. The physician helped Bibi lie upon it.

As she was wheeled away, her mother stood in the hall, looking bereft, as though she half expected never to see her daughter again. The orderly turned a corner, and Bibi lost sight of her mom.

On the second floor, the room containing the CT scanner felt chilly. She didn't ask for a blanket. Superstitiously, she felt that the more stoic she remained, the better the outcome of the test.

She transferred from the gurney to the

scanner table.

The orderly stepped out of the room as a nurse appeared with a tray on which were arranged a rubber-tube tourniquet, a foil packet containing a disposable cloth saturated with antibacterial solution, and a hypodermic needle containing a contrast medium that would make blood vessels and abnormalities of the brain show up more clearly.

"Are you okay, dear?"

"Thank you, yes. I'm okay."

After the nurse departed, the unseen CT technician spoke to Bibi through an intercom from an adjacent chamber, explaining how the procedure would progress. The woman had a gentle girlish voice with the faint trace of a Japanese accent, so that when Bibi closed her eyes, a scene more vivid than the CT room formed around her. . . .

A flagstone path leads to a red moon gate entwined with dazzling white chrysanthemums. Beyond lies a teahouse sheltered by cherry trees in blossom, a scattering of their pale petals gracing the dark stone underfoot. Inside, geishas in silk kimonos wear their long black hair twisted up in elaborate arrangements held in place by ivory pins carved in the shape of dragonflies.

A sliding cradle in the table moved Bibi backward, headfirst, into the aperture of the scanner, rousing her from that teahouse of the mind. The procedure was completed so quickly that she wondered if it had been done correctly, though she knew that the hospital staff's competence was the least of her concerns.

She was frightened by the speed with which they had handled her case since she had entered the ER waiting room. She would have no hope of peace until they arrived at a diagnosis. Nevertheless, the faster they worked, the more she felt as though she were sliding down a chute, accelerating, into an abyss.

7

THE POWER OF COOKIES

Olaf, the stray golden retriever that wandered out of the rainstorm, had been with the Blair family for less than a week when he settled into the habit of climbing the stairs to the apartment above the garage. He enjoyed lounging on the small balcony that contained a pair of rocking chairs. He rested his chin on the bottom rail of the white-painted balustrade, peering between the balusters and into the courtyard behind the bungalow, as if he were a prince contentedly surveying his domain.

Each time she discovered him up there, young Bibi called him down, at first in a whisper that she was certain he could hear, because dogs had better hearing than did human beings. Although he watched her as she stood below, Olaf always pretended to be deaf to her entreaties. When she raised her voice to a stage whisper, he still failed to come to her, though the soft thumping of his tail against the balcony floor proved that he understood her commands.

44

She dared not climb the stairs to take the dog by the collar and escort him down. Once on the balcony, she would be only a few feet from the front door of the apartment. Too close.

Frustrated, Bibi paced the courtyard, glancing up repeatedly at Olaf but never at any of the three windows. The sun made mirrors of those panes of glass, so that she couldn't see anyone even if he might be standing inside, watching. Nevertheless, she did not rest her gaze directly on any window.

She went into the bungalow and, from a tin in the pantry, took two of the carob cookies that the retriever couldn't resist. In the courtyard once more, she held a treat in each hand, arms raised above her head, letting Olaf smell his delicious reward for obedience. She knew that he caught the carob scent, for even from the courtyard she could see his wet black nose twitching between the balusters.

The cookies had always worked before, but not this time. After a few minutes, Bibi retreated to the back porch of the bungalow and sat on a wicker sofa with thick cushions upholstered in a palm-leaf pattern.

Olaf liked to lie there beside her, his head in her lap, while she stroked his face, scratched his chest, and rubbed his tummy. The porch roof blocked her view of the apartment windows, but she could just still see the lower part of the balcony railing and the dog with his snout between two balusters. He was watching her, all right.

Bibi brought one of the carob treats to her nose, smelled it, and decided that it would not be offensive to the human tongue. She bit the cookie in half and chewed. It didn't taste bad, but it didn't taste fabulous, either. Carob was supposed to have a flavor much like that of chocolate, which dogs couldn't eat, but it would never put Hershey out of business.

From his perch on the apartment balcony, Olaf had seen half of his treat brazenly consumed. His chin no longer rested on the bottom rail of the balustrade. His snout poked between two balusters a foot below the top rail, which meant that he'd gotten to his feet.

Bibi waved the remaining half of the cookie back and forth in front of her nose, back and forth, raising her voice to express her unqualified approval of that delicacy. "Mmmmm, mmmmm, mmmmm."

Olaf bolted down the stairs from the balcony, across the brick courtyard, and onto the porch. He bounded onto the sofa, landing with such force that the wicker crackled and creaked in protest.

"Good boy," said Bibi.

With his soft mouth, he took the half cookie from between her thumb and forefinger. She fed him the second cookie whole, and while he chewed it with noisy pleasure, she said, "Don't go up there again. Stay away from the apartment. It's a bad place. It's terrible. *It's evil.*"

After he finished licking his chops, the dog regarded her with what she took to be solemn consideration, his pupils wide there in the shadows of the porch, his golden irises seeming to glow with an inner light.

8
HAMMERED AND
FULLY PROSECUTED

Nancy told herself to chill out, gel, to sideslip through the moment, ride out the chop, to just sit in one of the visitor chairs and wait for Bibi to be brought back from the CT scan. But even when she had been an adolescent surf mongrel learning the water, she had never been a Barbie with the placidity of a doll. When on a board, she had always wanted to shred the waves, tear them up, and when the waves were mushing and the land had more appeal than the ocean, she had always nonetheless pumped through the day with her usual energy.

And so when Murph turned the corner from the first ER hallway into the second, Nancy was pacing back and forth outside the cubicle from which Bibi had been wheeled away on a gurney. She didn't see him immediately, but intuited his arrival by the way a couple of nurses did double takes and smiled invitingly and whispered to each other. Even at fifty, Murphy looked like Don

Johnson in the actor's *Miami Vice* days, and if he had wanted other women, they would have been hanging off him like remora, those fish that, with powerful suckers, attached themselves to sharks.

Murph still wore a black T-shirt, a Pendleton with the sleeves rolled up, and boardshorts, but in respect for the hospital, he had stepped out of sandals and into a pair of black Surf Siders with blue laces, worn without socks. Newport Beach was one of the few places in the country where a guy dressed like Murph would not seem out of place in a hospital or, for that matter, in a church.

He put his arms around Nancy, and she returned his hug, and for a moment neither of them spoke. Didn't need to speak. Needed only to cling to each other.

When they pulled back from the embrace and were just holding hands, Murph said, "Where is she?"

"They took her for a CAT scan. I thought they would have brought her back by now. I don't know why they haven't. It shouldn't take so long — should it?"

"Are you okay?"

"I feel like I've been hammered, fully prosecuted," she said, both terms surfer lingo for wiping out and getting brutally thrashed by a killer wave.

"How's Bibi doing?" he asked.

"You know her. She copes. Whatever's happening to her, she's already thinking what she'll do once she's gotten through it, if maybe it's good material for a story."

Rolling his mobile computer station before him, Dr. Barsamian, the chief ER physician during the current shift, approached them with the news that Bibi had been admitted to the hospital following her CT scan. "She's in Room 456."

The doctor's eyes were as black as kalamata olives. If in fact he knew something horrific about Bibi's condition, Nancy could read nothing in his gaze.

"The CT scan seems to have been inconclusive," Barsamian said. "They'll want to do more testing."

In the elevator, on the way from the first floor to the fourth, Nancy suffered a disturbing moment of sensory confusion. Although the position-indicator light on the directory above the doors went from 1 to 2, then to 3, she could have sworn that the cab was not ascending, that it was descending into whatever might occupy the building's two subterranean levels, that they were being cabled and counterweighted down into some enduring darkness from which there would be no return.

When the light moved to the 4 on the directory and the doors of the cab slid open, her anxiety did not abate. Room 456 was to the right. When she and Murph got there, the door stood open. The room contained two unoccupied beds, the sheets fresh and taut and tucked.

Bibi's drawstring bag stood on the nightstand beside the bed that was nearer to the window. When Nancy peered into it, she saw a toothbrush, toothpaste, and other items, but no pajamas.

Each bed came with a narrow closet. One of them proved empty. In the other hung Bibi's jeans and long-sleeved T-shirt. Her shoes stood side by side on the closet floor, her socks stuffed in them.

With the squeak of rubber-soled shoes and the scent of soap, a young blond woman in blue scrubs entered the room. The nurse looked too young to be credentialed, as if she might be just fifteen and playing hospital.

"They told us our daughter would be here," Murph said.

"You must be Mr. and Mrs. Blair. They've taken Bibi for tests."

"What tests?" Nancy asked.

"An MRI, blood work, the usual."

"None of this is usual to us," Nancy said, trying for a light tone of voice and failing.

"She'll be all right. It's nothing intrusive. She's doing fine."

The much-too-young nurse's reassurances sounded as hollow as a politician's promises.

"She'll be a while. You might want to go

down to the cafeteria for lunch. You'll have the time."

After the nurse left, Nancy and Murph stood for a moment in bewilderment, looking around the room as though they had just now been teleported into it by an act of sorcery.

"Cafeteria?" he asked.

Nancy shook her head. "I'm not hungry."

"I was thinking coffee."

"Hospitals ought to have bars."

"You never drink before five-thirty."

"I feel like starting."

She turned toward the window and then, with a sudden thought, turned away from it. "We need to tell Paxton."

Murph shook his head. "We can't. Not now. Don't you remember? His team is on a blackout mission. No way to reach them."

"There's got to be a way!" Nancy protested.

"If we tried and Bibi found out, she'd want our scalps. Even though they're not married yet, she's getting more like him each day, tough-minded and committed to the way things are in that life."

Nancy knew he was right. "Who would have thought it would be her we'd have to worry about instead of him?"

She switched on the TV. None of the programs was entertaining. All of them seemed intolerably frivolous. The news inspired despair.

They went down to the cafeteria for coffee.

9
INTO THE TUNNEL OF FATE

Later, Bibi would be told that the CT scan had been inconclusive but suggestive, that her doctors would have preferred a stroke to what was now suspected. Having eliminated the possibility of embolism or hemorrhage, they proceeded with a growing concern that they refrained from sharing with her. Their smiles were masks, not because they wished to deceive her, but because physicians, no less than their patients, live to hope.

Later, too, she would learn that if embolism and hemorrhage were ruled out, her best chance of a full recovery might be a diagnosis of brain abscess, which was a pus-filled cavity surrounded by inflamed tissue. This life-threatening condition could be treated with antibiotics and corticosteroids. Often surgery proved unnecessary.

They drew blood for a culture. They took chest X rays. They hooked her up for an EEG that lasted almost an hour, to study the electrical activity of her brain.

By the time she was gurneyed to another room for an MRI, Bibi felt as though she had run a marathon up countless flights of stairs. She wasn't merely tired but *fatigued*. Such weariness couldn't be the result of what little physical activity the day had entailed. She assumed that her growing exhaustion was yet another symptom of her illness, like the head-to-foot tingling along her left side, the rancid taste that came and went, and the weakness in her left hand.

She had no appetite for lunch, and they had offered her only water. Perhaps fasting was required for some of the tests. Or maybe they were anxious to gather all the information required for an urgently needed diagnosis.

Because the MRI machine was an enclosed tunnel only slightly greater in diameter than a human body, a nurse asked, "Are you claustrophobic?"

"No," Bibi said, refusing a mild sedative as she lay on the table that would carry her into the ominous cylinder.

She refused to admit even the possibility of such a weakness. She wasn't a wimp, never had been, never would be. She admired toughness, fortitude, determination.

Instead, she accepted earbuds that allowed her to listen to music and a handheld device with which she could signal the equipment operator if she became distressed.

Her time in the machine would be lengthy.

Modern MRI technology allowed scans with highly specific purposes. A functional MRI would provide measurements of nerve-cell activity in the brain. Magnetic-resonance angiography could assess heart function and blood-vessel flow throughout the body. Magnetic-resonance spectrography would provide detailed analysis of chemical changes in the brain caused by a variety of afflictions.

The music proved to be wordless, mellow orchestral versions of songs she couldn't quite identify. From time to time, the machine made thumping noises audible through the music, as if the technician needed to spur the MRI along with hammer blows. Bibi felt her heart laboring. The signaling device grew slippery in her sweaty hand.

She closed her eyes and tried to distract herself with thoughts of Paxton Thorpe. A beautiful man in every way: his body and face, his eyes, his heart and mind. She'd met him more than two years earlier. Five months ago, she had accepted his proposal. Just as her name had meaning, so did his: Paxton meant *town of peace,* which was ironic, considering that he was a kick-ass Navy SEAL. Pax was currently on a full-silence mission with his team, going somewhere to do something to bad people who no doubt deserved even worse than they were going to get. The team would be operating in blackout mode for maybe a week or ten days. No phone calls. No tweets. No way for him to be told what was happening to his fiancée.

She missed him desperately. He said that she was the touchstone by which he would, at the end of his life, measure whether he had been a good man or not, fool's gold or the real thing. She already knew the answer: *the real thing.* He was her rock, and she wanted him now, but she was already steeped in the stoic code of the military and refused to be reduced to tears by his absence. In fact, sometimes she thought she must have been a military wife in a previous life, for the mind-set of one came so naturally to her.

As the humming machine knocked and thumped, saliva suddenly filled Bibi's mouth. As before, this suggestion of impending regurgitation wasn't accompanied by nausea, and the threat passed.

In her mind's ear, she heard her mother say, *It'll be what it'll be.* Those five words were Nancy and Murphy's mantra, their concession to the ways of nature and fate. Bibi loved them as much as any child loved her parents, but their understanding of the world's true nature did not match hers. She would concede nothing to fate. Nothing.

10
THE KIND OF GIRL SHE IS

By four o'clock that afternoon, Dr. Sanjay Chandra had become the principal physician in charge of Bibi's case.

Nancy liked him on sight, but for the strangest reason. In her childhood, she'd been enchanted by a book about a gingerbread cookie that came to life. In the illustrations, the cookie, whose name was Cookie, had not been as dark as gingerbread, but instead a warm shade of cinnamon, with a lovely smooth round face and chocolate-drop eyes. If the book hadn't been at least forty years old, about the same age as the physician, she might have thought that the artist had known him and that he'd been the inspiration for the look of the storybook character. Dr. Chandra possessed a sweet, musical voice, as you might expect that a cookie-come-to-life should have, and his manner was likewise pleasing.

After the array of tests she endured, Bibi had been returned to her hospital room in a state of exhaustion. In spite of her concern about her condition, she wanted only to sleep before dinner. She had passed out as if she'd mainlined a sedative.

Dr. Chandra didn't want to disturb her, and indeed he preferred to wait until the following day to sit with her and discuss what the tests had revealed, after he had more time to review the results. But although Bibi was twenty-two, no longer a ward of her parents, the doctor wished to speak with them first, and at once, "to determine," as he put it, "the kind of girl she is."

Nancy and Murph sat with him at a table in the break room, at the north end of the fourth floor, where at the moment none of the staff was taking a break. The vending machines hummed softly, as though mulling over some grave decision, and the unforgiving glare of the fluorescent lights did not inspire serenity.

"I've told Bibi only that time is needed to review all the test results, to reach a diagnosis and design a course of treatment," Dr. Chandra said. "I'll meet with her at ten tomorrow morning. It is always a concern to me that my diagnosis and prognosis are presented to my patient in as comforting a manner as possible. I have found that it helps to have a sense, in advance, of the person's psychology and personality."

Nancy didn't like the sound of this. Good

news didn't require the careful tailoring of the words with which it would be delivered. She might have said as much, except that suddenly she didn't trust herself to speak.

"Bibi is an exceptional girl," Murph said. Perhaps no one else but Nancy could have detected the strain in his voice. He looked only at the doctor, as if to meet his wife's eyes would undo him. "She's smart, a lot smarter than me. She'll know if you're putting even the slightest shine on the truth. That'll upset her. She'll want to hear it blunt and plain, not prettied up. She's tougher than she looks."

Murph began to tell the physician about the death of Olaf, the golden retriever, who had passed away almost six years earlier, a few months after Bibi's sixteenth birthday. At first Nancy was surprised that her husband would think this story had any relevance to the moment. As she listened, however, she realized that it perfectly answered Dr. Chandra's question about the kind of girl Bibi was.

The physician did not interrupt, only nodded a few times, as though he had no other patient but Bibi for whom to prepare.

When Murph finished telling of Olaf's death, Nancy dared to ask a question, throughout which her voice trembled. "Dr. Chandra . . . what kind of doctor are you? I mean . . . what's your specialty?"

He met her eyes directly, as though he assumed that she shared her daughter's indomitable and stoic nature. "I'm an oncologist, Mrs. Blair. With an additional specialty in surgical oncology."

"Cancer," Nancy said, the word issuing from her with such a note of dread that it might have been a synonym for *death.*

His dark-chocolate eyes were warm and sympathetic, and in them she saw what seemed to be sorrow. "Though I really do need to review the test results more closely, I feel certain we are dealing here with gliomatosis cerebri. It originates in the connective cells of the brain and infiltrates quickly, deeply into surrounding tissue."

"What causes it?" Murph asked.

"We don't know. Scientists have had little chance to study the disease. It's exceedingly rare. We see no more than a hundred cases a year in the entire United States."

Nancy realized that she had come forward in her chair and that she was holding the edge of the table with both hands, as though to anchor herself against some great approaching turbulence.

"You'll remove the tumor," Murph said, making of those words a hopeful statement rather than a question.

After a hesitation, the oncologist said, "This tumor isn't localized like those in other forms of cancer. It has a spiderweblike pattern, filmy threads across more than one frontal lobe. It can be difficult to detect. The boundaries of the malignancy are hard to define. In certain cases, primarily in young children, surgery may be an option, but seldom a good one."

Perhaps consoled and given hope by the fact that the glioma was not easily detected, Murph said, "Then you treat it how — with chemo, radiation?"

"Often, yes. That's why I want to study Bibi's test results more closely before deciding what we might do to extend her life."

Although she gripped the table tighter than ever, Nancy felt as if she were floating away on a tide of despair as real as any flood waters. "Extend her life?"

There were lustrous depths in the physician's eyes, and in those depths coiled a knowledge that suddenly she didn't want him to share with them.

Dr. Chandra looked down at the table, at Murph, at Nancy once more, and said almost in a whisper, "It pains me to tell you that there is no cure. Survival time from diagnosis averages one year."

Nancy could not breathe. Could not or didn't wish to breathe.

"But with chemo and radiation?" Murph asked. "What then?"

The oncologist's compassion was so evident, his sympathy so tender, that though Nancy irrationally wanted to hate him for what he revealed next, she could not muster

61

even anger. "One year is *with* chemo and radiation," Sanjay Chandra said. "And your daughter's cancer is already very advanced."

11
A Time When She Believed in Magic

After she woke from her nap, Bibi freshened up in the bathroom. Her face in the mirror surprised her. Sparkle in the eyes. Color in the cheeks and lips without benefit of makeup. She continued to look better than she felt, to the extent that she might have been staring not at a looking glass but into a parallel dimension where another, healthier Bibi Blair lived without a serious concern.

Having developed an appetite, she made her way back to bed to wait for the return of her parents and for dinner. The tingling along the left side of her body had grown less intense. The weakness in her left hand diminished, and not once did she find herself dragging her left foot. In the past few hours, she hadn't suffered a recurrence of the foul taste.

She knew better than to conclude that the subsidence of her symptoms meant her affliction, whatever its cause, must be temporary. In spite of all its myriad wonders and its exquisite beauty, this world was a hard place;

the comforts and joys that it offered, all the sublime moments, were purchased by days of quiet anxiety, by anguish, and by suffering. Such was the world that humanity had made for itself. Thus far in her life, she had enjoyed much more bliss than melancholy, more success than adversity, and she had for some time known that eventually she, like everyone, would have to walk through a fire of one kind or another. As long as she had a chance of coming out the other end intact, she would spare everyone her complaints, and she would not waste energy wishing for a magical resolution to this current plight.

For a while in Bibi's childhood, she had believed in magic. A popular series of novels about young wizards mesmerized her, though certain other books had an even greater impact. Also, a few events in her life had suggested otherworldly presences, both light and dark. The dog, Olaf, came to her as if by magic, just when she needed him. And both before and after the golden retriever's arrival, there had been incidents in the apartment above the garage that had seemed supernatural in nature.

Those experiences were long past, and time tended to cloud the shine on everything that had been wondrous in childhood. When she recalled those events, the once-shimmering mystery of them was now tarnished silver, and it became possible to suppose that there were logical explanations for what had happened back then.

When the dinner tray arrived at 5:15, she found the meal to be at such odds with the conventional image of hospital food that it almost renewed her belief in magic. A thick slice of meatloaf, creamy mashed potatoes, a little disposable foam thermos of hot gravy, mixed vegetables that didn't taste as if they came out of a can . . . She tucked the paper napkin in the neck of her pajama top and ate with the enthusiasm of a hardworking lumberjack.

She was relishing the cherry cobbler and hot coffee when her parents at last returned. They were like two clever imposters, formed out of the goop inside an extraterrestrial seed pod, alike in every physical detail to the real Nancy and Murphy, but not quite able to get their attitudes and mannerisms correct. They smiled too much, and none of their smiles seemed genuine. All of Bibi's life, her mom and dad had been blithe spirits. Now they seemed to be wired to bomb timers.

She wondered if they knew something that she didn't. Probably not. Most likely, her hospitalization and disturbing symptoms were more than enough to leave Nancy and Murphy as unsettled as they were now. *Go with the flow* always proved to be a philosophy that worked only until the flow washed you up against a crisis so large it blocked the stream. The dears were at the moment both adrift and stranded.

Anyway, if they did know something bad, Bibi didn't want to hear it from them. They would divulge it with too much emotion, and *she* would have to console *them.* When she met with Dr. Chandra in the morning, she wanted a calm environment and a clear head. Whatever was wrong with her, she would need to *think,* to understand her options. She would need to find the right door out of this dark place or, if her situation was more dire than she now knew, slip through the eye of Death's needle and away before he sewed her into a shroud.

When it became clear that her parents might hesitate to leave when visiting hours ended, Bibi pretended to be falling asleep even as the hospital bed held her in a sitting position. They were at last set in motion by the lubrication of kisses, hugs, and re-assurances.

Bibi missed them the moment they left the room, but she didn't call them back. Alone, she took the drawstring bag from the night-stand and from it retrieved a small spiral-bound notebook and a pen. She wasn't in the mood to read the paperback that she had brought, and the TV had no appeal. Instead, in neat cursive, she recorded the events of the day, with special attention to everything that she had felt and thought with each unsettling development. What most intrigued her, for reasons she could not quite define, was that she had harkened back more than once to those years in the Corona del Mar bungalow, when as a young girl she had believed in magic.

12

FOOTSTEPS OF A MAN UNSEEN

Early on a Sunday morning in February of that rainy winter, six weeks before the dog came dripping and nameless along the sidewalk from the sea, Bibi Blair took one of the spare keys to the apartment off a Peg-Board in the pantry, quietly left the kitchen, and eased the door shut as she stepped onto the back porch of the bungalow.

Her parents were sleeping late, which they often did on this first morning of the week. Nancy had no open houses to oversee, as she did on some Sundays. And in this off-season, Pet the Cat welcomed shoppers only Monday through Saturday. They had been out well past midnight with friends, leaving Bibi in the care of Chastity Brickle, an insufferably self-absorbed fifteen-year-old babysitter who had no doubt already — and more than once — failed to live up to her first name. They would not stir for another couple of hours.

Rain had fallen before dawn. Now the low gray sky looked more like ashes than like a scrubwoman's sodden rags. Bibi didn't bother

68

with an umbrella but quickly wended her way among the puddles in the brick-paved court-yard, to the garage at the back of the property.

At the top of the open stairs, standing on the balcony, she looked back and down upon the bungalow, half expecting to be caught. Her mom and dad were unaware that she spent time in the apartment, and although there was nothing shameful in what she was doing, she preferred that they never learned about those visits.

The front door opened on a small kitchen. Blue Formica counters. Blue-and-gray speckled linoleum floor. A dinette table and two chairs. Last year's wall calendar revealed the page for November. Although the digital clock on the microwave oven glowed with the correct time, the refrigerator did not hum, having been turned off weeks ago. The air was still and cool and faintly musty.

Bibi never turned on the lights, lest they reveal her presence even in the daytime, which they would have done on this dim morning. Although lacking blinds, the two kitchen windows admitted only gray light as feeble as misted moonglow.

In the center of the table stood the round, narrow-necked white vase, from which had often flowered a few roses or carnations. The vase stood empty, its glaze softly radiant in the gloom, as though it might be a milky crystal ball placed there for a pending séance.

She stood staring at the floor beside the first chair, where the dead body had been found. All the blood had been cleaned up long ago, but Bibi thought — imagined? — that the faintest trace of it remained on the air, a cruel smell. She wrinkled her nose in repugnance.

This place had no charm anymore, and after these visits, she felt sad and unsettled. Sometimes bad dreams followed. Yet she kept returning. She didn't fully understand what drew her there. She would never find anything to make sense of what had happened. *It just was what it was,* her parents said, and of course they were right.

In addition to the kitchen, the apartment included a living room and bedroom, both furnished, plus a bath and a walk-in closet. She usually toured the entire place, alert and observant, and yet as if she were half in a dream state, seeking she knew not what. On this occasion, however, as she crossed the kitchen toward the living-room door, which stood slightly ajar, she halted at the thump of footsteps elsewhere in the apartment.

Both the bedroom and the living room featured hardwood floors that were less than half covered with area carpets. The tread sounded like that of a large man, and a few floorboards creaked under weight, not with every step taken, but often enough to confirm that these were indeed footsteps in the apartment rather than a noise from outside.

In spite of the fact that she had been the one who found the body back in the day, Bibi was not at first alarmed, only intrigued. Just then she realized that she had been coming here in expectation of some encounter. What the nature of that encounter might be, she could not say even now, but she had anticipated it, and here it was.

Louder, louder grew the footsteps. Definitely in the living room now. Slowly approaching the door to the kitchen.

Fear found Bibi then. Fear, but not blind fright, not panic. She backed past the table, toward the balcony from which she had entered.

The portentous footsteps of a man unseen stopped at the living-room threshold. The ensuing silence shared the character of certain silences in disturbing dreams: those hushes that settle on the scene as if, after a suitable pause, the curtain will close and the sleeper arise, though in fact it always proves to be instead the quiet just prior to the final shock that wakes the dreamer, gasping.

The faintest scraping-ticking arose as the knuckles of the hinge leafs turned against pivot pins in need of oil, and the door swung ever so slowly into the kitchen, toward Bibi. It blocked her view of whoever stood on the threshold.

Remembering the blood and ghastly eyes

71

of the November corpse, she bolted. She had no awareness of escaping, however, until she found herself crashing down the last steps into the brick courtyard.

She looked up the stairs. No one there. Above, the door to the apartment was closed. She must have thrown it shut as she departed.

For a while, as the spent sky sluggishly refilled its reservoir with laden clouds drawn off the ocean, Bibi watched the apartment's two kitchen windows. No face appeared at either. No suggestion of movement stirred through the gloom beyond those panes.

Eventually, she retreated to the wicker sofa on the back porch of the bungalow, where she had left a paperback and the notebook in which she composed the stories about Jasper, the lonely dog.

Later, her father appeared, ready to make his weekly inspection of the garage apartment, to check for roof leaks and other problems.

"Dad." When he looked back at her from the bottom of the porch steps, she said, "Be careful."

He frowned. "Careful of what?"

"I don't know. Maybe I heard someone up there."

As larky as ever, he said, "Maybe that raccoon got down through the attic again. He's damn well gonna pay rent this time."

When he returned ten minutes later, he had

found neither the raccoon nor any other uninvited lodger.

As the sky gathered rain to spend, young Bibi retreated to her room to write a Jasper story. Two weeks passed before she dared to return to the apartment.

13
YOUNG AGAIN IN GRIEF

On the drive home from the hospital, through the alien night, Murph and Nancy shared an awful, solemn silence. The mutual quiet became so oppressive, so suffocating, that several times one or the other tried to slash it away with words, but both were rendered incoherent and emotionally bewildered by the loss that seemed to lie in their future. The unthinkable loss.

With greater success in retail and real estate, they had moved from the bungalow three years earlier, into a two-story pale-yellow stucco house with sleek modern lines. They still lived in that part of Corona del Mar known as the Village, no longer three blocks short of the Pacific but only one and a half. From the roof deck, from one upstairs room, and from the front terrace on the ground floor, they had an angled view of the ocean that lay beyond the end of the east-west street.

Murph had been proud that two surf rats

— as he still thought of himself and Nancy — could remain in touch with their beach roots and nevertheless earn a major piece of the California dream. That night, however, the house meant nothing to him, and in fact it seemed cold and unfamiliar, as if by mistake they had let themselves into a residence owned by strangers.

He and Nancy had always been understanding of each other, always available to each other, uncannily in sync in all circumstances. He assumed they would sit together at the kitchen table, the lights low, maybe in candlelight, and together work their way through the horror and the pain of what had befallen them.

As it turned out, neither of them was ready for that. As if the shock, still building force hour by hour, had not only cast them off their moorings, but also had washed them far back in time, both chose to revert to the coping mechanisms of their youth. No doubt they would come together soon, but not yet.

Nancy went into the ground-floor powder bath, snared the box of Kleenex from the counter, dropped the lid of the toilet with a bang, and sat down as from her came the most wretched sounds of grief that Murphy had ever heard issue from anyone. When he spoke to her and tried to enter the half bath, she said, "No, not now, nooo," and pushed the door shut in his face.

Feeling helpless, useless, he stood listening to her despairing sobs, to the thin shrill animal sounds of utter desolation that tore from her between desperate ragged breaths. She sounded like a child, racked as much by fear as by misery. Her heartbreak sharpened his own until he could not stand to listen to her a moment longer.

If Nancy reverted to childhood in her grief, Murphy fell back into the angry rebellion of adolescence. He took a six-pack of cold beer from the refrigerator and carried it up to the roof deck. He wanted to punch someone, anyone, just punch and punch until he was exhausted and his knuckles were swollen. He wanted someone to pay — to suffer and be chastened — for the unfairness of Bibi's cancer. But there was no one to hold responsible, nor anyone to comfort him, not in a world where what will be will be. Instead, he sat in a redwood lounge chair, opened the first can of Budweiser, and chugged it as he stared over his neighbors' roofs, over the few lights along the last width of the bluff, stared out into the vast night sea, which lay black under a moonless sky, black under a higher blackness salted with icy stars, its presence confirmed only by the rhythmic rumble of the breakers punishing the shore. Halfway through the second beer, he began to cry. Weeping only fueled his anger, and the angrier he became, the harder he wept.

He wished they had gotten another dog after Olaf died. Dogs needed no words to console you. Dogs were the ultimate practitioners of the therapy of touch. Dogs knew and accepted the hard realities of life that human beings could not acknowledge until those obvious truths were exhaustively described with words, and even then there was often more bitter acknowledgment than humble acceptance.

Dogless, perhaps soon to be childless, after only two beers, Murphy felt lost. If he had tried to go downstairs to his wife at that moment, he would not have been surprised if he'd been unable to find his way off the roof deck.

With a crisp metallic sound, the ring-pull peeled open the third can.

14
SHE SAT UP, SAT UP, SAT UP IN BED

The dream that came to Bibi the first night in the hospital was one that she'd been having on and off for more than twelve years, since before Olaf, the dog, had found his way to her:

She is ten years old, asleep in her bedroom at the rear of the bungalow in Corona del Mar. She does not thrash or whimper, but across her softly illumined young face pass tormented expressions.

Abruptly she sits up in bed, though this awakening is part of the dream in which she still resides. In response to three shrieks of a night bird, she throws back the covers and steps to the window.

In the courtyard, lit by only the grin of a Cheshire moon, two mysterious robed and hooded figures, tall and shambling, carry a rolled rug, moving toward the garage apartment. Visibility is poor, but Bibi intuits deformities in their limbs and spines.

When she realizes that the rug is in fact a

corpse wrapped in a shroud, she knows they must be returning the dead man to the place of his demise. As though it feels the weight of her stare, one of the bearers of the body turns its head to look at Bibi where she stands at the window. She expects a dimly visible skull within the hood, the classic countenance of Death, but a worse revelation awaits her. The night brightens somewhat, as if an immense solar flare has bloomed on the farther side of the planet, reflecting fiercely off the crescent moon. The hood keeps more secrets than the better light reveals. But before the intruder turns away from her, she sees something that she cannot abide; the glimpse so terrifies her that she does not — cannot, will not — carry the image with her into the waking world, but instead confines it to the world of sleep, forgotten or at least repressed.

For the second time in the dream, young Bibi sits up in bed, breathless, trembling, chilled to the marrow. When she switches on the lamp, she discovers the shrouded burden that the hooded creatures had been carrying. The wrapped figure sits in a corner chair, for the moment still. Then it squirms in the confining shroud — and speaks.

The third time Bibi sat up in bed, she was awake and no longer a child. By repetition, the nightmare had lost much of its power years earlier. She no longer cried out on waking or trembled. But the skin creped on the back of her neck, and a thin sweat cooled her brow.

As on other such occasions, a rough voice followed Bibi from the dream, speaking words out of context: *". . . is everything."*

The voice was always the same one, but it did not repeat the same words every time. Sometimes he said, "supreme master" or "so sadly to seek," or "the word was," or scraps even more mystifying.

The other hospital bed remained empty. She was alone.

The ambient glow of the suburban sprawl laid a yellow faux frost on the window. Above her headboard, the lamp by which she'd written her impressions of the day was at its lowest setting, bright enough only to allow proper care when the nurse looked in on the patient.

The dream, which had been frequent when Bibi was ten, occurred less often as the decade passed. Now it came once or twice a year.

In the early days, she'd thought it might be predictive. But it was a dark fantasy that could never unfold in the real world.

Entering adolescence, she sometimes brooded about the persistent dream's possible symbolic content. Because it recurred so often back then, she also wondered if she might be disturbed, psychologically unbalanced, as in crazy-waiting-to-happen. But no.

No, that was the worst kind of young-adult-novel hokum: tragic young girl hiding her tri-polar psycho-paranoid true-werewolf nature from the world and from herself until she has a breakdown the very day before she would have been voted the Most Popular Girl in Ninth Grade and would have been kissed by the cutest bad-boy rebel in school. Even at that young age, she was remarkably self-possessed, confident of her right to be in the world and her ability to make her way on her own terms.

Now she dismissed the dream for what it surely always had been: nothing more than proof that finding the body by the dinette table had been traumatic — the abundance of blood, the blind and drooling eyes, the mouth gaping in a silent cry.

The bedside clock read 3:49 A.M. In little more than six hours, she would receive a diagnosis from her physician. She had no reason to fear Dr. Sanjay Chandra, just as she had no reason to fear the bearers of the dead in a dream. There were no boogeymen. She would be well, all would be well, all manner of things would be well.

Reclining once more, her head upon her pillow, she closed her eyes. She told herself where she would be a day from now, a week from now, a year. Soon she slept again, and this time her sleep was not sullied by a nightmare.

When the seizure struck Bibi, her body spasmed on the bed, and from her throat issued thick wordless grunts. The episode was mild and brief, however, and it did not wake her.

15
ONE MOMENT OF TRUTH
AMONG MANY

Room 456 had three chairs for visitors. They were cheap and only as comfortable as they had to be for the name *chairs* to apply.

Dr. Sanjay Chandra didn't want to loom over Bibi as she lay in bed, reporting on her health from a superior height. He placed two chairs by the window, and they sat facing each other, with blue sky and scattered white clouds to Bibi's right, as if she were receiving this news in the foyer of Heaven.

In spite of wearing a white lab coat over iron-gray suit pants, a pale-blue shirt, and a blue tie, and although he had arrived carrying an ultrathin laptop with which he could evidently access all Bibi's test results, Dr. Chandra had none of the intimidating presence that was natural to some physicians and cultivated by others. Soft-spoken, with an air of serenity that suggested that he had made peace with this world of endless frustrations and with his own ambition, he seemed less like a doctor than like a counselor of the troubled.

In preparation for this meeting, Bibi had taken a shower, brushed her long, dark hair, applied makeup, and donned a sapphire-blue silk robe over her pajamas. If the physician had bad news to deliver, she intended to receive it with style, to appear in no way pitiable or in the least defeated.

The diagnosis proved to be bad indeed, her prognosis even worse. A year to live. A year of decline and suffering.

She knew now why Dr. Chandra had wanted to speak to her alone. Neither her mother nor her father possessed the emotional fortitude to watch her receive this news. Her reaction, no matter how stoic, would have undone them, and Bibi would have been too concerned about them to remain focused on her options as single-mindedly as she must.

With the gentleness and compassion of a caring chaplain in a death-row conference with a condemned man, Dr. Chandra explained why Bibi was without good options. Her cancer was far advanced. Even caught early, gliomatosis cerebri was too dispersed in the brain for surgery to be a permanent solution. At this stage, chemotherapy and radiation would gain her little time, if any. "And the side effects will make the days ahead harder, Bibi. Much harder, I'm afraid."

"No offense," she said, "but what about a

second opinion?"

"I asked Dr. Beryl Chemerinski to provide one. She is a highly respected surgical oncologist at another hospital, with no connection to me. She concurs with my conclusions. I wish she didn't. You can do chemo and radiation nevertheless. Only you can make that decision."

She met his eyes for the longest time. He didn't look away. At last she said, "I guess they call this the moment of truth."

"I believe in truth, Bibi. And I know you do, as well."

She looked down at her hands. She made them into fists. The left one would not close tight. "I want to fight it. Chemo, whatever. One year to live, huh? Really just one year? We'll see."

16
A MEMORY INEXPLICABLE
IN THESE CIRCUMSTANCES

After Dr. Sanjay Chandra departed, before
Nancy arrived with Murphy, Bibi sat with
her notebook and pen in one of the chairs by
the hospital-room window, to record her
thoughts and feelings while they were fresh.
She was anxious, but not in the grip of dread.
Not yet. The news had been a hard blow;
however, she regarded it not as a calamity,
but as a summons to action. Often her
notebook provided a refuge from the world,
and with it she seemed to step out of time,
into a place where she had the leisure to
reflect on her impressions and emotions
before acting on them. This time-out frequently saved her from doing and saying
things that she would have regretted.

As she settled into the chair, her attention
was drawn beyond the window, to a flock of
large seagulls. The hospital lay only a few
blocks from the ocean. The birds soared,
plunged, soared again, each to its own intentions, exhilarated by the gift of flight, their

joy as clearly expressed as any messages ever printed on the heavens by the skywriting planes that advertised to summer beach crowds.

Into her mind came a memory of gulls on a December morning when she was eighteen. She was crossing the university campus to visit Dr. Solange St. Croix, who with an email had called her to a student-teacher conference. The gulls were joyful then, too, but if she thought they were an omen foretelling a rewarding meeting with the professor, Bibi was soon disappointed, left confused, embarrassed. . . .

In spite of heavy competition, Bibi had earned one of the few places in the university's renowned and exclusive creative-writing program. Some of its graduates had over the years become bestselling novelists and literary stars. For three months, she had diligently honed her craft, until her work had caught the eye of Dr. St. Croix, whom some called the holy mother of the writing program.

The professor's office décor set new standards for minimalism. One desk, cold steel except for a black-granite top. Two chairs. The visitor's seat featured wafer-thin blue cushions that ensured discomfort if one lingered past fifteen minutes. To the left of the long window stood a narrow bookcase with eight shelves, all half empty, as if to suggest that from the entire history of literature, only a few volumes merited inclusion in this collection. On the desk were only a laptop, currently closed, and beside it the printout of an essay that bore Bibi's name on the cover page.

Dr. St. Croix — tall, thin, attractive in spite of herself — wore her graying hair in a bun long out of style and dressed as severely as a grieving widow. Her default image was of a cool, composed, and brilliant writing guru. She could be warm and funny, but she paid out her smiles sparingly, revealing her wit when least expected, thereby magnifying its effect. Now her eyes shone as cold and blue as the chemical gel in a refreezable ice pack. Her smile had flatlined.

Bibi knew that she was in trouble, but she didn't know why.

"Miss Blair," St. Croix said, "I understand you have expressed to other students some uncertainty about the value of being here."

Dismayed to hear her perhaps naïve concern expressed in those words, she said, "No, not at all. I've learned so much already."

"You worry that the system of inspiration at the core of this program is a confining set of rules, that to an extent it encourages disparate voices to sound alike."

"Someone has exaggerated my concern, Dr. St. Croix. It's just a small thing that I think about. It's natural to have little doubts."

"Our system of inspiration is not a set of rules, Miss Blair."

"No. Of course it's not."

"We don't press upon our students either a way of thinking or a rigid set of values."

Bibi doubted that was true, but she kept silent.

"If you think in fact we do just that," Solange St. Croix said, "then you have a fine excuse to drop out, one that even exasperated parents might have to accept as reasonable and ethical."

Bibi half thought she hadn't heard correctly. "Drop out?"

With undisguised contempt, the professor indicated the four-page manuscript. "How reckless of you to write about me."

The recent assignment had been to choose someone in the writing program, student or instructor, someone you knew but whose residence — whether dorm room or apartment or home — you had never visited, and then to create as vividly as possible a credible living environment that grew from what you had observed about that person.

"But, Dr. St. Croix, you put yourself forward as a subject."

"And you know perfectly well it's not what you've written that is outrageous. It's what you've *done*."

"I don't understand. What have I done?"

Bibi recoiled when she saw that her claim

of puzzlement angered Solange St. Croix beyond all reason. The woman's posture was that of righteous indignation. Something worse than vexation and barely less than wrath drew her face into leaner lines.

"What you think is clever, Miss Blair, is only low cunning. I have no patience for you. I won't dignify your behavior by discussing it." Her face flushed, and she seemed no less embarrassed than she was furious. "If you don't drop out, I will see that you're expelled, which will complicate any academic future you may have and be a stain on you as a writer, in the unlikely event you have a future as one."

Even then, people didn't push Bibi around without consequences. She stood up for herself when she was in the right. She leaned in to trouble. She was likewise practical, however, and she knew that she was out-gunned in this inexplicable conflict. If she stayed, she would be struggling forward with a sworn enemy who was the founder of the writing program. She had no future here. Besides, while it was true that she had learned much in the past few months, it was also true that she entertained serious doubts about the program.

When Bibi reached for her manuscript, Solange St. Croix drew it back. "This is my evidence. Now get out."

■ ■ ■ ■

Beyond the hospital window, the seagulls sailed westward in a loose formation and out of sight.

Bibi didn't know why the birds triggered the memory of Dr. St. Croix instead of recalling to mind one of the hundreds of memorable experiences she'd had involving surfing and the beach, where gulls were omnipresent. Unless perhaps it was blind hope that had made the link between then and now. Leaving the writing program had turned out to be a good thing, had led to her becoming a published author much faster than otherwise would have been the case. And so perhaps death from brain cancer was no more inevitable than had been the ruination of her writing career.

That made a kind of sense. But she knew intuitively that it was not the correct explanation.

She never had figured out what had so incensed the professor. And now she wondered if the offense of which she had never been properly accused was in some mysterious way related to the death by brain cancer that she now faced.

17
IN THE HOURS
BEFORE THE CRISIS

Bibi was sitting on the edge of her bed, making a list in the spiral-bound notebook, when her parents arrived with the intention of lifting her spirits as best they could, although they did not succeed in this. The moment that they walked through the door, the stricken look in their eyes was poorly synchronized with their smiles.

They didn't fail her; they never could. Only she could keep her spirits up. Anyway, she wasn't depressed, certainly not despairing. She didn't have time for that. Or the inclination. Even as grim as it sounded, her prognosis was a challenge, and the only reasonable way to respond to a challenge was to rise to it.

She was still the girl whose mind was always spinning, and now it spun out tasks for her mother, which she added to the list in the notebook. "They're keeping me here until tomorrow, maybe even till the day after. Dr. Chandra needs to do a few more tests to plan a course of chemo and radiation. The choice is mine, and I'm going to fight. I need you to go to my apartment, bring my laptop. I'm going to research the crap out of this. I need changes of underwear. And socks. My feet get cold. Some of my nice soft towels. The ones here are scratchy. And all my vitamins. My iPod with the headphones. I'll have to use headphones in here." Because she maintained a post-office box, she needed her mail to be collected and brought to her. She described a few other errands as she appended them to the list, and then she tore off two pages and handed them to her mother.

Grateful to have something to do other than dwell on his daughter's situation, Murphy said, "We'll split up the work, Nancy. You take the apartment stuff. I'll do the other running around."

Bibi said, "No, Dad. Let Mom take care of it. You get back to business."

He looked perplexed, as if he had forgotten that he was anything other than her father. "What business?"

"The one Pogo is this very minute running into the ground."

He shook his head. "But I can't —"

"You can. You must. If I'm going to devote all my time to this battle, I won't be writing. My income will dry up. Mom's commissions will probably go to hell while we're fighting this. You'll have to support me as if I were ten years old again. You have to, Daddy."

Hugs and kisses. Declarations of love. Clumsily expressed covenants to face the future together with resolution, to win in spite of the terrible odds. And then her parents were gone.

After using the bathroom, while washing her hands at the sink, Bibi studied her reflection in the mirror — until her vision blurred and one face became two, smeary and distorted. Vision problems were a symptom of gliomatosis cerebri. She gripped the sink with both hands, taking slow deep breaths, wondering if she would go blind. Not yet. Her vision cleared.

18
SOMETHING BAD AND SOMETHING WORSE

Bibi took her lunch by the window. She ate every bite. Other than surgery, treatments for cancer often caused prolonged bouts of nausea and a depressed appetite. She needed to forget about being svelte and pack on several pounds of reserves to get her through the coming battle. She supposed that eventually she should shave her head instead of waiting for her hair to fall out in a mangy fashion. The more she took control of her appearance, the better.

Poor Paxton would come home from war to find that his fiancée had morphed into a bald sumo wrestler. Well, he said he would always love her, through the bad times no less than the good, and she believed him. If she had him all wrong — which she didn't, but if she did — then she was better off knowing the truth sooner than later. The only plus to having brain cancer might be that it provided the ultimate test of your guy's true intentions. Given a choice between putting herself through gliomatosis cerebri and putting Paxton through a lie-detector test, she would of course have chosen the latter; but she hadn't been given a choice.

A perky blond volunteer in a candy-striper uniform, smelling of a lemony perfume, came to collect the lunch tray. Bibi arranged for the girl to go to the cafeteria and buy a supply of PowerBars in various flavors. "I want to look like John Goodman by next week."

"Who's John Goodman?"

"A large actor. He played Roseanne Barr's husband on TV."

"Oh, yeah. He's in lots of movies. He's cute."

A nurse arrived to get a urine sample. A phlebotomist drew five vials of blood. A woman "from legal" had papers to be signed.

Bibi engaged in only minimal small talk with them, though for most of her life she had been a fountain of words. Everything in this world amazed and fascinated her — from the fragile beauty of a lily to the mysteries of quantum mechanics — and she usually had to share her wonder or burst. Being named Bibi had encouraged her to chatter away because, even as a child, she had been determined to impress upon everyone that, in spite of her name, she wasn't a toy, not frivolous, but a keen observer of the world, a philosopher by the time she graduated from the potty chair. She had never been for long struck speechless — until she received a diagnosis of brain cancer.

Her mother returned at five o'clock with everything that Bibi had requested, and her father phoned minutes later to say that the three of them should have dinner together in her room, not hospital food, but whatever outrageous high-calorie fat-rich takeout she wanted. Cheeseburgers and milk shakes. Burritos. Four-cheese pizza. Anything, anything.

"No, Dad. Mom's exhausted." Nancy began to protest, but Bibi raised one hand to quiet her. "You both are. These two days have been hard on all of us. You and Mom have dinner, just the two of you, with a good bottle of wine. I'm okay. I'm not going anywhere. I just want to do some research on my laptop while I eat, then early to bed. I hardly slept last night. I'll ask for a sedative. I want to be dreaming about a certain Navy SEAL by seven o'clock at the latest."

To get Nancy out of the room and off to dinner, Bibi had to escort her along the hallway to the elevators. Alert for any tendency of her left foot to drag, determined not to become Quasimodo with boobs, she walked with her shoulders back and her head up.

"What about the tingling?" her mother asked. "The fifty-cellphones-on-mute head-to-foot thing?"

"It's quieter. And I haven't had that rancid

taste all day."

"Baby, I can see your left hand's still weak."

"So I'll use the other one to scratch my butt."

In the elevator alcove, the doors to one of the cabs slid open. Nancy didn't get aboard. "This is so wrong. I can't just leave."

As the doors started to slide shut, Bibi blocked them. "Mom, we have to stay as normal as possible. The three of us can't group-hug twenty-four/seven. We'll melt down if we do."

When Nancy tried to speak, she couldn't. Her mouth trembled.

Bibi kissed her mother's cheek. "You're a sweetie. Now go. Eat too much. Drink too much. Live, Mom. *Live.* I sure intend to."

In her hospital room again, she sat at the small table by the window and used her laptop to learn about anticancer and cyto-toxic drugs. Alkylating agents. Nitrosoureas. Antimetabolites. Mitotic inhibitors. At least her disease was enhancing her vocabulary.

As the March afternoon dressed itself in scarlet to approach the evening, a nurses' aide brought a dinner tray. Suitable reading with dinner did not include an article about the side effects of chemo. As she ate, Bibi watched amusing dog videos on YouTube.

The bad thing happened when she got up from her chair to wash her hands. A sudden pain of migraine intensity split her skull.

She almost dropped to her knees. She staggered, made her way onto the bed, and pressed the call button for a nurse.

Sudden headaches could be a symptom of gliomatosis cerebri, a consequence of pressure on the brain; however, they usually occurred in the morning. The tests she'd undergone the previous day had not revealed excess cerebrospinal fluid. "No hydrocephalus," the doctor had said. Maybe that had changed.

Having raised the upper half of the bed, she sat with both hands clasped to her skull and imagined that she could feel the bone itself deforming with each throb. The nurse arrived, asked a few questions, and returned with aspirin plus another pill. Bibi didn't ask about the second medication, just swallowed it with a long drink of water.

"I'll keep checking on you," the nurse promised. "Now rest."

When the woman left, Bibi twice tried to recline, but both times she panicked when a vivid sense of falling overcame her. More than a mere feeling, it was an absolute conviction that she would tumble backward into a bottomless void, as if she were sitting on the brink of eternity. Besides, the very act of leaning backward as much as an inch or two intensified her headache. Even knowing that the inclined bed would prevent her from so much as lying full-length on her back, she made no third attempt. Sitting forward, head hung, eyes closed, she wrapped her arms around her torso as if to anchor herself.

To her surprise, in five minutes or less, the pain began to diminish. Aspirin didn't work that quickly. Evidently, she owed her relief to the second medication.

When she opened her eyes, red radiance bathed everything, and she at first thought that she must be having vision problems again. Then she realized that none of the lights were on and that the room, previously brightened by only sunshine, was now illuminated by the sunset, which had melted the sky into a fire-shot river of molten glass slowly flowing west and away.

She reached for the lamp control that was clipped to the bedrail. The oval dimmer switch felt *wrong* in her fingers, felt soft and scaly, as if she had gripped the head of a living reptile, and the pale cord wriggled in protest. She dropped the switch and watched with astonishment as her suddenly stiff-fingered hand pecked at the air like a bird pecking at a tree trunk to feed on crawling insects, pecked violently, pecked and pecked, and she could not control it.

Seizure, she thought, and as if confirming her own diagnosis, she grunted and mewled like an animal, and made thin hacking sounds in the back of her throat.

The stiffness in her hand spread up the arm, through her body, and she fell backward against the inclined mattress, which stopped her, but she didn't feel as if she had been stopped. The brink she had feared earlier was there, and she was overcome by a sensation of plunging into a void, down and down, plummeting, although the hospital room shimmering with crimson light did not recede, which it should have if she were really doing an Alice down a rabbit hole.

Several glossy spots of darkness appeared in her field of vision, floating like fat beads of black oil in the red radiance, first fewer than a dozen, then scores, then hundreds. As all light vanished and the glistening blackness flooded over her, she tried to cry out for help, but like all drowned girls before her, she had no voice.

19

IF ONLY IT WERE JUST A GHOST

Two weeks after fleeing from the apartment above the garage, four weeks before Olaf padded into her life, on another sleep-in Sunday for her parents, young Bibi rose and dressed while the last defenses of the night barely held off the advancing dawn. She tucked two granola bars into the pockets of her fleece-lined denim jacket and, as the morning spread its flamingo-pink wings across the east, she walked two and a half blocks to the park along Ocean Avenue.

She sat on a bench at Inspiration Point to watch the breaking surf and the dark sea as mottled green-greenblack as watermelon skin. From that perch, she sometimes imagined herself to be one of a pirate crew sailing on violent tides, or else a whale so big that she feared nothing in her shadowed watery world. This morning, she imagined life after death, not as it might be in Heaven, but as it might be here and now, in this world, if such things as ghosts were real.

After finishing the first granola bar and

deciding not to linger long enough to eat the second, she returned home. If she was a girl of action, a girl of unshakeable intentions, like the girls whom she most admired in the books that she most enjoyed reading, she could no longer shrink from the mystery that demanded her attention.

By the alley gate, she let herself into the courtyard between garage and bungalow. Climbed the stairs. Hesitated on the balcony.

Two weeks earlier, the gray wet day had been appropriate to séances and conjurings — and to unsettling encounters with restless spirits. Under this bright and lively sky, with the warbling and clear, short whistles of meadowlarks celebrating the recent dawn, being in the mood for Pooh was easier than being in the mood for Poe.

Nevertheless, Bibi stood at the door, staring through the four panes in its upper half, studying the kitchen before she dared to enter. There was no corpse apparent either on the floor or standing grim and moon-eyed in expectation of her. She went inside.

On this brighter morning, the kitchen seemed to be a benign if not entirely welcoming place, until Bibi noticed the one change since her previous visit. On the table, the spherical white vase, which had held no flowers before, not for months, now contained three withered roses. The once-green sepals of the flowers' receptacles were brown, and the petals were mostly brown as well, with few remaining traces of red coloring. Some petals had fallen to the table, where they lay as curled and crisp as the shells of dead beetles.

The sere and shriveled roses looked as if they had been here longer than two weeks. They were so thoroughly dehydrated that they might have been in the vase since November.

She should have left the apartment; but she could not. Unlike many other ten-year-old girls, she did not dream of being a princess or a pop star. She wanted to be plucky, intrepid, and lionhearted. Stalwart. Valiant. Superman and Supergirl had no appeal for her; everything was too easy for them and other invulnerable superheroes, without genuine danger. Bibi knew that life could never be that way. Every surfer surfed with sharks unseen and swam with the risk of riptides. Death was real. You had to face that truth if you were ever to grow up. She wanted no caped costume with an *S* upon her chest. But she would have been proud to wear a sweater with a small embroidered *V* — a *V* for *valiant* — though only if by her actions she earned it.

Therefore, rather than retreat from the mystery of the roses, she moved past the table toward the living-room door, which stood open, as she had left it two weeks earlier.

Someone — something — had pushed it inward before she'd fled. As on that day, the door blocked her view of the threshold, where someone had been standing.

She felt confident that no one would be standing there now.

As she approached the door, she heard footsteps on a creaking hardwood floor, as she had heard them on her other visit. She halted, listening, but then realized the footsteps were moving away from her.

Lionhearted girls seldom retreated when they were threatened, and they never turned tail and ran without good reason. When she passed the door and reached the threshold, trembling more than she would have liked, no one waited there.

She saw a door swinging shut at the farther end of the living room. It closed with a bang and rattle.

None of the furniture had been removed. After what had happened here, Nancy and Murphy didn't want another tenant. Eventually they would dispose of the furniture, sell it or give it away to Goodwill.

Rather than proceed to the bedroom, Bibi considered sitting on the edge of an armchair to await developments. Sometimes, patiently waiting to see what happened next was much wiser than making it happen, which was one of the differences between truly smart girls in smart books and airheaded girls in witless books.

After a hesitation, as a weakness crept into her legs and her mouth went almost as dry as the flowers in the kitchen, shame made her cross the living room. You were either plucky or not, stalwart or not, and the lionhearted didn't make excuses in the quick of things, when you either gave it or you didn't.

She halted at the bedroom door. Trying not to hear the rapid knocking of her heart, she listened for what sounds might come from the next room. She cocked her head to the left, to the right, and when her gaze drifted lower, she saw the blood on the doorknob. Red. Glistening. Wet. A single drop slid off the knob and fell to the floorboards in what seemed like slow motion.

Valiant girls were more than spunky and resolute. They were also wary, heedful, and prudent. And they knew with clearheaded certainty when it was wise to act upon those virtues. She didn't bolt, but she backed slowly away from the bedroom. She turned and walked across the living room, quietly through the kitchen, out of the apartment. After she locked the door, she needed to hold the handrail as she made her way down to the courtyard.

On the back porch of the bungalow, sitting on the wicker sofa, Bibi reviewed events, a thousand threads of thought spinning through the loom of her young mind, weaving a strange fabric. She wouldn't tell her parents what had happened. They would find no flowers or blood in the apartment, just as her father had found no intruder two weeks earlier. Besides, Bibi sensed there was something she knew that she didn't know she knew, an elusive understanding that, if she could arrive at it, would make sense of everything.

The morning grew mild, but Bibi remained cold to her bones.

20
A CONDITION OF COMPLETE SIMPLICITY

Bibi realized she was awake when she heard the nurse talking with a nurses' aide. She wasn't able to open her eyes or speak. She could only listen. One said, "She's exhausted, poor thing." The other took her pulse, seemed to be satisfied, and let go of her wrist. Bibi realized that she was breathing shallowly, making a sound like a soft snore. They must think she was asleep. No one witnessed the violent seizure when it felled her earlier. They pulled the sheet and blanket up to her neck. She tried to tell them it wasn't sleep that held her quiet, but something worse. The words formed in her mind, not in her mouth. She heard the nurse and the aide leaving, then a mortal silence.

She lay mute and blind and limp, unable to be sure whether she was lying on her back, on her chest, or on her side. No muscle in her body would respond to her command. A remembered fragment of verse came to her, its source for the moment forgotten: *A condi-*

tion of complete simplicity. She was indeed in a condition of complete simplicity, and although she should have been frightened, she was not. Valiant girl she would be, as she had been for so long, plucky and intrepid and stalwart. Lionhearted.

A condition of complete simplicity / (Costing not less than everything) . . .

With the second line of verse, she recalled the source: *Little Gidding* by T. S. Eliot.

She took some comfort from the fact that though her body seemed to have seceded from her soul, her mind remained clear and still part of her kingdom. Fragments of other Eliot lines came to her:

Quick now, here, now . . . At the still point . . . Neither from nor towards . . . Where past and future are gathered . . .

Bibi drifted away once more into a nothingness that might have been a more solemn oblivion than mere sleep.

Later she revived in a panic, acutely aware of the severe decline in her condition. Paralysis. Blindness. Her tongue cinched into a knot that would not allow her the grace of words. She had gone downhill faster than rhyming Jill after she tripped over the idiot Jack. Suddenly the Big Question was whether chemo and radiation made any sense in her case, or whether the better course of treatment, the more humane course, would be to give her a box of morphine lollipops and let her suck her way out of this world in some hospice run by kindly nuns. Valiant girl or not, she wanted to cry for herself, but if she wept, she could not feel the heat of tears or the tracks they made down her face.

She woke again in the night, and this time she could open her eyes and see by the dimmed lamp above her bed. The orientation of her body became obvious to her, as well: She was lying on her right side, facing the first — still empty — bed, and the door at the farther end of the room.

That door opened and a man entered, backlit by the hall light as he approached. Even when the door eased shut behind him, closing off the light, he remained a silhouette. Bibi saw the leash as he arrived between the beds. Earlier someone had put down the railing. The dog stood on its back legs, forepaws on the mattress, favoring Bibi with the fabled smile of its breed: a golden retriever. Perhaps more than any other breed, goldens had unique faces, and although for a moment she thought that this was Olaf, it was not.

This was just some Good Samaritan with a therapy dog named Brandy or Oscar or whatever. These days, hospitals were veritable dog parks, with hordes of well-meaning people trying to make the sick and the depressed get with the uplift program. She

110

had seen others like these two since being admitted as the poster girl for aggressive tumor maturation, and they were all sweet, the people and the dogs, though she declined their determined efforts to help her find the giggles in gliomatosis.

Her left hand lay palm-down upon the mattress. She could see it but not move it.

The dog began to lick her hand, and at first she couldn't feel that canine caress. Soon, however, her sense of touch returned, and the warm wet tongue working between her fingers filled her with a wild hope. To her surprise, she broke her paralysis, moved the hand, and repeatedly smoothed the fur on the retriever's noble head.

As she petted the dog, their eyes met. She knew that hers were dark and unrevealing, but the retriever's were so gold and luminous and deep that its gaze stirred something within her. That lustrous stare awakened the slumbering child that Bibi had once been, the easily enchanted girl who, in recognition of inevitable adulthood, had taken a page from the book of bears and had hibernated through a long winter.

When the dog dropped from the bed, Bibi said, "No, please," but the visitors moved away.

At the door, as he opened it just wide enough to slip out into the hall, the man turned to look back, still just the outline of a man, and said, "Endeavor to live the life. . . ."

Bibi had heard those words before, although in her current condition she could not quite remember when.

Alone in the near dark, she could not decide if something extraordinary had happened or if she had hallucinated the encounter.

She flexed her left hand, which was still moist with the dog's saliva. She could feel her body to all its extremities. She wiggled her toes. When she tried to roll onto her back, she had no difficulty doing so.

As a great weariness descended, she wondered if she was awake or dreaming. In the absence of the loving dog, whether or not it had been real, a bleak sense of isolation pierced her, and she felt alone and lost. Her voice shamed her for the misery it revealed. Valiant girls did not so boldly disclose the distress of mind and heart, but it was all there in his name when she spoke it — "Paxton, Pax. Oh, Pax, where are you?" — and then a wave of darkness washed her into sleep or something like it.

21
Half a World Away from Home

The head-shed — senior commander — planners called it Operation Firewalk. They had an endless supply of colorful names for special-ops missions, some of them literary, which proved they had gotten a well-rounded education at Annapolis. There would be no firewalk, no doves from scarves, no lady sawn in half, no other illusions that made magicians' audiences applaud, just a street-level strike that should be, to the bad guys, as unexpected as an earthquake.

Paxton Thorpe and three guys on his team had come down from the cold hills in the night, having taken two days to make their way from the insertion point, where the helicopter left them, to the outskirts of the town. Had they been dropped closer, the helo noise would have been an announcement no less revealing than if they had been preceded by a bluegrass band on a flatbed truck draped with red-white-and-blue bunting. They wouldn't have been able to cross the open ground and enter those streets without being cut down.

Surrounding the town were fields once tilled, now fallow. The last planting had never been harvested. Months of searing heat and stinging cold and skirling winds had threshed the crops and withered the remaining stems into finely chopped straw and dust, all of it so soft that it produced little sound underfoot. Depending on where he stepped, Pax caught a musty scent that reminded him of the feed bins and hayloft in the barn on the Texas ranch where he had been raised.

The moon had risen in daylight and had set behind the mountains before midnight. Under feeble starlight tens of thousands and even millions of years old, the four men relied on night-vision goggles.

As far as the world was concerned, this place ahead of them was a ghost town. If you believed in spirits, you would want to pass on by, because here the hauntings, if there were any, would surely be horrific. The remote town had been established above a rare aquifer in otherwise barren territory, and the citizens tapped the deeply stored water to transform the surrounding fields into productive farmland. For a few generations, people had lived here in rural peace, unschooled and mostly happy in their ignorance. And then the barbarians arrived in a fleet of stolen military vehicles, bearing rocket-propelled grenades and automatic carbines. Perhaps six hundred residents were killed in the taking of the town, half the population, and the flag of the conquerors — black with a red slash — flew on every street by the second day. After the prettier women endured gang rape and dismemberment, the remaining citizens — men, women, children — were executed in the following three days. Bodies were stacked by the hundreds in pyres, sprayed with gasoline, and set afire. On the sixth day after the invasion, the killers took down their flags and left. They had wanted nothing in that settlement, only its destruction.

Savages though they were, they nevertheless filmed the massacre and made a recruitment video that spoke to the souls of like-minded radicals everywhere. It had found an eager audience on the Internet.

Seventeen months after the massacre, Lead Petty Officer Paxton Thorpe and three warriors, three friends, three of the finest men he'd ever known — Danny, Gibb, and Perry — were on the hunt for big game where, only a week earlier, no targets were thought to exist. Some in the American media called their primary target the Ghost, which lent him an air of glamor — intentionally or not. Pax and his guys called their quarry Flaming Asshole, FA for short.

Back in the day, FA had led the assault on this village, but that was not the only crime for which he was currently sought. It seemed unlikely that he would return to such a place of slaughter, far from the comforts of civilization that terrorist leaders now felt to be their right, far from most of his multitude of admirers. But the head sheds had intel that they found convincing, and they were far more often right than wrong.

They were in a nation not worthy of that designation, but at least it was not currently an active supporter of terrorists or colluding with anyone against the United States. And its wrecked economy could not support a military adequate to regularly patrol most of its territory. Pax and his men had gotten in without an encounter, but now it might be fan-and-feces time.

The town contained more than two hundred buildings, mostly one and two stories, none higher than three, some of stone, many of mud bricks covered with stucco, crudely constructed, as if no engineer existed in this country with more than a medieval education. A third of the structures had been reduced to rubble in the assault, and the remaining were damaged to one degree or another. If FA and six of his most trusted allies were holed up here, they would most likely secret themselves in a central building, so that no matter from which point of the compass a hostile force might arrive, they would have plenty of warning that a search of the town had commenced.

Intel suggested that a three-story building at the northwest corner of the burg offered an ideal observation post. The team's attention needed to be focused only east and south for some sound or sign of habitation. The roof had a parapet behind which they could remain hidden, conducting surveillance with two periscopic cameras.

As Paxton, Danny, Gibb, and Perry came quietly out of the fields to the back of the building, they passed the horned skeletons of what might have been three goats, which regarded them with hollow sockets as deep as caves. The savages who killed the people of the town had also shot the livestock, leaving the animals to rot where they fell.

The back door had long ago been broken down. They cleared the rooms as though they expected resistance, but found no one. The walls were bullet-pocked. Spent cartridges littered the floors; also chunks of plaster and broken crockery and what might have been bits of skull bones with streamers of human hair attached. Debris-strewn stairs led to the flat roof. The four-foot-high parapet was as described. In the liquid dark of the arid night, they dared to stand, surveying the ghost town to the south and east, looking for the smallest of lights, whether mundane or supernatural, finding neither.

Having arrived safely, they slept two at a

time, the other two always alert and listening, watching. Every sound would travel far into the hush of the dead town, and therefore they said nothing to one another. They had been through so much together that none of them needed conversation to know what the others must be thinking.

They remained on the roof after sunrise, when the chill of night only half relented, though they stayed below the parapet. They would not execute a search on foot until they had given their quarry and his men twenty-four hours to inadvertently reveal their location. They had their periscopic cameras, their ears, and patience.

Nothing had happened by 4:00 P.M., when Pax raided his MREs for beef jerky, chicken-noodle slop, and a PowerBar. He ate sitting on the roof, his back against the parapet wall. He wore body armor, but his MOLLE-style web system with all the gear attached was a separate rig that could be taken off and set aside. His pistol lay on the roof a mere foot from him: a Sig Sauer P220 chambered for .45 caliber.

Abruptly Bibi came into his mind with such force that, startled, he almost bit his lip along with the half-eaten PowerBar. He thought of his singular girl often every day, but this unbidden image of her lovely face bloomed vividly in his mind's eye, as no memory had ever pressed itself upon him before. He recognized the moment: he and Bibi standup paddleboarding side by side in Newport Harbor on a sunny summer day. She'd said something funny, and his comeback had cracked her up so much that she had almost fallen off her board.

The vision of her face, prettily contorted in laughter, so lifted his spirits that he tried to hold on to it, to freeze-frame the recollection in all its astonishingly sharp and poignant detail. But memory wanes even as it waxes; she faded and could be summoned back only in a less intense manifestation.

Paxton glanced at his G-Shock watch. 4:14 P.M. local time. That would be 4:14 A.M. where Bibi lived half a world away. She should be home in bed, sound asleep. Worry wound its way through him, not just the usual worries he sometimes had when he thought about Bibi, but a deep disquiet unique to this moment. He wondered if he had gone on a blackout operation at the worst possible time.

22
WHAT THE HELL
JUST HAPPENED?

This time, stilting in silence, the robed and hooded bearers of the dead convey the corpse along a hospital corridor where the roof and ceiling have been scalped away, allowing moonlight to bathe the scene. They enter Bibi's room, and the face of one so shocks and horrifies, as always before, that she rebels against consideration of it and sits up in bed, sits up and wakes not from the dream, but from one dream scene to another. Gone are Death's two henchmen, or whatever they might be. In one of the chairs by the window, in the red radiance of a sunset, sits the corpse cocooned in a white shroud glowing with the reflection of the burning sky. The fabric masking its face stretches, and a shallow concavity appears as its mouth opens. From it comes the voice that she knows well: "The forms . . . the forms . . . things unknown." Frightened of hearing more, she sits up once again, but this time not in another dream scene, this time —

— in the real hospital room.

Morning had come with a difference in it.

The tingling in her left side had completely relented, head to foot. Not one prickle, tickle, shiver, no static in the nerve paths.

Sitting in bed, she flexed her left hand, which had at times seemed to be the instrument of another Bibi than her, some other self who wished to use it to her own — and different — purposes. Now she had full control of it once more. No weakness. She closed it into a fist, and though her fist was small, she liked the look of it.

No headache. No dizziness. No foul taste.

With an exhilarating quickness, she said, "Peter Piper picked a peck of pickled peppers. She sells seashells by the seashore." Each word escaped her perfectly formed, without a slur or slip of tongue.

She put down one of the safety railings and sat on the edge of the bed, where for a moment she hesitated, warning herself that the cessation of symptoms didn't mean that she was somehow cured. If she dared to cry out in wonder and celebration, her voice might trigger an abrupt collapse into her previous condition. But no. That was pure and foolish superstition. There were not three goddesses of destiny as the ancient Greeks had believed, no sisters spinning and measuring out and cutting the thread of each life, who might take offense at her delight in having escaped the fate of cancer. She got out of bed and into her slippers, walked the room, walked it and then did a silly little dance, and in each case her left foot, just like her right, performed as she demanded without a moment of stiffness or a misstep.

Through the doorway came a nurse, Petronella, whose hair was pulled tight and braided at the back. She'd been on duty the previous day and proved to be an efficient and confident woman who had seen everything that anyone in her career could expect to see and who seemed never to have been for a moment unsettled or caught unaware by any of it. Her chocolate-brown face warmed now with surprise and amusement as she stopped just inside the threshold and said, "Girl, what's gotten into you this morning?"

"I can dance," Bibi said as she performed a modest soft-shoe number.

"Maybe you can," the nurse said, "but I'll wait to see the evidence."

Bibi laughed and clapped her hands three times quickly. "No funky left foot, no tingling head to toe, no nothing. Peter Piper picked a peck of pickled peppers — perfectly pronounced, Petronella. I'm not sick anymore."

The nurse's smile first froze and then melted. With pity in her eyes and sympathy in her voice, she said, "Things come and go, then they come again, child. It's best to stay real with that."

Bibi shook her head. "It's true. It's real. I

don't know what the hell just happened, but something sure did. I can feel it through and through. Clean. Healthy. I need to talk to Dr. Chandra. He needs to see me. We've got to take another look at this."

23

SHE JUST CAN'T
LEAVE IT ALONE

After another two-week reprieve from temptation: the Sunday-morning quiet, the sunless day fogbound and chilly, the key in the lock, the creak of the hinges, the white vase on the table without flowers this time, the open inner door, the living-room threshold, the living room itself, the closed bedroom door. If the blood on the doorknob had been real on her previous visit, someone had wiped the brass clean in the meantime.

Sometimes Bibi did not understand herself. She wasn't a foolish girl, yet she had returned. She knew that she was no coward, that she didn't need to test her courage, but here she stood. She remained convinced that the dead didn't come back, and yet she wondered. Worst of all, she understood that it would not be a good thing if one of them *did* find a way back into the world of the living; nonetheless, a part of her kind of, sort of, undeniably yearned to have just such an encounter, supposing of course that it turned out to be magical in the best possible way.

She worried that she might have dark impulses. She knew about dark impulses because she'd read about them in novels. She read at a tenth-grade level, five grades above her station, which led her to believe that she must be well informed about compulsions, fixations, obsessions, manias, and morbid drives. Such dark impulses could be of the mind or the heart. She was certain that she was not insane; and so she hoped that whatever dark impulses she had were of the heart, and were therefore not particularly dangerous.

Valiant girls routinely did brave things or else they lost their chance to be above the herd. Thereafter they became sad, timid women, washed-out wallflowers, pitiful drudges condemned to drab lives in gray rooms. Bibi had been boogie-boarding since the age of seven, full-on surfing for almost a year now, and she had no intention of becoming a would-have-been, had-been, washed-up, washed-out loser either now or fifty years from now.

You had to drop in from the peak, shoot the curl, tear it up when the surf was off the Richter. No fear. That was the difference between a true surf rat and a goob, a spleet, a wilma, and a wanker. Valiant girls could never be goobs, spleets, wilmas, or wankers.

She turned the knob and opened the bedroom door.

Everything remained pretty much as it had been back when the apartment was occupied. The bed had been stripped of its spread, blanket, and sheets, leaving only a mattress cover, and the pillows had been put away in a linen closet. Otherwise, nothing had changed.

Like a ghost sea, like high tide as high as it might have been a million years earlier, thick fog pressed at the two windows, and only a murky drowned light found its way inside. Because the bedroom lay at the back of the apartment, the lamps that Bibi turned on could not have been seen from the bungalow even if there had been no fog.

The bathroom stood open, but the walk-in closet door was closed.

She surprised herself by knocking on it.

No response.

She thought, *Drop in from the peak, rip it, don't hair-out.*

She opened the door, turned on the light. Valiant girls didn't believe in boogeymen, and there wasn't one waiting for her.

A pull rope hung from a ceiling trap door. She knew that if she yanked on the rope, the trap would come open on sturdy hinges and springs, and a segmented ladder would unfold from the back of it.

For the first time during this visit, she heard noises that she hadn't made. They came from the attic.

She considered the rope, but, somewhat to

her chagrin, she did not at once reach up for it.

Someone must have pushed hard on the trap door from above, for it swung open and the springs sang like an annoyed cat. The ladder unfolded to the closet floor.

Peering into the gloom above, Bibi said, "Captain? Are you up there, Captain?"

24

HOW SWEET IT WOULD BE
IF IT COULD BE TRUE

This time, the MRI machine seemed not in the least ominous, not a tunnel of doom, but instead a passageway to resurrection. Bibi didn't need the earbuds that she had required previously, didn't want the music, because her racing thoughts were music of a better kind, the equivalent of up-tempo jazz full of sizzle and sparkle, thoughts shot through with amazement, astonishment, wonder, and not a little awe. The impossible had happened. She knew. *She knew.* She didn't need to wait for the test results. She *felt* the truth of remission in her bones, in every part of her healthy body. They said that gliomatosis cerebri never went into remission. Until now. Let them do it all again: the functional MRI, magnetic-resonance angiography, magnetic-resonance spectrography. They would find nothing. Not even one cluster of cancer cells. Her joyfully spinning thoughts repeatedly spun back to the incredible mystery at the heart of this new chance at life, to the unfathomed reason for her reprieve, a puzzle that challenged the writer in her to understand the hidden story.

After the MRI, they wanted to repeat certain other tests. She could tell by their expressions that they were thunderstruck by the results they had thus far seen. None of them was rash enough to tell her that the impossible had happened, not yet, not before they were absolutely sure, but Bibi knew. She *knew.*

Mira Hernandez was young to be the head of nursing in such a large hospital. She appeared to be no older than forty, a pretty woman with glossy sable hair, wide-set eyes as black as the fur of a Halloween cat, and full lips, the bottom one of which she kept chewing as she listened while Bibi answered her questions.

Nurse Hernandez sat in a chair by the window, the one in which Dr. Sanjay Chandra had sat the previous day, when he had delivered the dreadful prognosis. Bibi sat facing the nurse in what she now thought of as her lucky chair. In fact, every item in the room now seemed to be a lucky something: the lucky table between them, the lucky bed, the lucky TV that she had never turned on, her lucky silk robe, her lucky slippers.

"I need you to help me understand," said Nurse Hernandez. "You think the golden retriever cured you?"

"No. Maybe. Hell, I don't know. The dog had something to do with what's happened. It *must* have. Listen, I'm not saying it's a miracle dog. What would that mean, anyway, 'miracle dog'? Sounds ridiculous. But the dog and the man who brought him — they must know something. Don't you think so? I think so. Well, the man might know something. The dog wouldn't necessarily know. Who knows what dogs know? And even if the dog knew something, it wouldn't be able to tell us what it knew, because dogs can't talk. So we need to talk to the man."

Nurse Hernandez regarded Bibi in silence for a moment and then said, "You seem to be agitated."

"No. Not agitated. I'm hyper. *Good* hyper. Hyped up. Wouldn't you be, too, if you were riddled with brain cancer one day and free of it the next?"

The nurse didn't want to encourage false hope. "Let's not get ahead of the doctors, Bibi."

"See, the thing is, I had a huge seizure last evening, when no one was here. I thought I was dying. Passed out. Later I woke when a nurse checked on me. She figured I was asleep. But I was paralyzed, and I couldn't speak, and it was awful. I knew I was nearly gone, almost out of here, worm food. The next time I woke, it was the dog. After the dog, I wasn't paralyzed anymore, I could talk.

And this morning, when I woke like *this*" — she made a fist of her previously weak left hand and pumped it in the air — "I knew something good had happened, the biggest good thing possible."

As nice as she might be, as patient as she was, Nurse Hernandez nevertheless looked as if she wanted to say, *But that's the point — it isn't possible.* Instead, after typing a note on her laptop, she said, "See, my problem is . . . we don't allow any therapy dogs in the hospital after visiting hours. There weren't any here last night."

"There was *one*," Bibi insisted cheerily. "A beautiful golden."

"Are you sure you couldn't have dreamed it or hallucinated it?"

"My hand was warm and sticky with dog drool."

"Okay, well, so the man with the dog — what did he look like?"

"He was backlit, just a silhouette, and then in shadows."

"What was the dog's name? Do you remember?"

"I don't know. The owner didn't say."

"The first thing they usually do is introduce the dog."

"Maybe usually, but not this time."

After the nurse typed on her laptop again, she looked up and smiled, but there was a look of misgiving in her eyes when she said,

"I'm sorry. I don't mean this to sound like a police interrogation, Bibi. I really do want to understand if . . ."

"If it turns out I'm cured? It's okay. You can say it. You won't be encouraging false hope. I am cured. You think I'm hyper now? Just wait till Dr. Chandra tells me there's no cancer. I'll be bouncing off the walls. That's the kid in me. Most people can't wait to leave kid-hood behind. But I keep the kid in my heart, you know, and once in a while she gets out. It's a writer thing. The past is material. You never want to forget it, how it was, how it felt."

Nurse Hernandez listened with interest, as if she didn't think Bibi was just babbling. When she could get a word in, she said, "What did this man with the golden retriever say to you?"

"Nothing. Until he was going out the door with the dog. Then he looked back and said, 'Endeavor to live the life.' "

The nurse frowned. "What did he mean by that? It sounds . . . I don't know. It sounds odd, kind of formal. Don't you think?"

Bibi shrugged. "Probably he just meant that I should get on with my life." She had heard those words before but couldn't remember when or where. She wondered why she failed to tell Mira Hernandez that she had heard those words before.

Suddenly she had a girl-detective thought

that pleased her. "What about security cameras? They usually store their video for thirty days. If you review it from last night and see this guy and his dog, then you'll know I wasn't dreaming."

25

CAPTAIN? ARE YOU UP THERE, CAPTAIN?

When the ladder folded out of the ceiling to the floor of the walk-in closet, Bibi knew that an invitation had been issued, but she hesitated to accept it. In spite of the rigid geometry of the ladder, something about the way it zigzagged downward in segments made her think of a snake.

As she stared up into the attic, the darkness above retreated, although not entirely, when a string of bare bulbs brightened the upper realm from gable to gable.

This second invitation failed to encourage her to ascend in search of the captain.

She had called him Captain because at one time he had been a captain in the United States Marine Corps. He'd had many colorful adventures in times of war and times of peace, and Bibi had enjoyed his stories no matter how often she cajoled him into repeating them. He'd held other jobs after leaving the corps, and he'd been the tenant in the apartment above the garage for five years — until she found him dead in the kitchen, lying in so much blood that he seemed to be afloat.

Captain was a man of courage and integrity and honor. She had always been safe in his company. He would never have harmed her. He would have died for her.

If the captain was in the attic, even if he had come back from a place where dead heroes went for eternity, surely she had no reason to fear him. Valiant girls did not discourage — and certainly did not defeat — themselves by abandoning reason and indulging superstition with all its irrational fears.

"Captain?" she asked again. "Are you up there, Captain?"

In answer came the sweet ringing of bells. Rather, it was the ringing of a single special bell that sounded like three. The captain had brought it back from Vietnam many years earlier, a souvenir of his days in a wearying and misfought war.

Beautifully crafted of silver, the size of a wineglass, the bell housed an ingenious mechanism. The three clappers were suspended so that they operated simultaneously and yet didn't interfere with one another's arcs. The first clapper struck the waist of the bell. The second summoned sound from the hip of the classically shaped silver, the third from the lip. The three notes were different but complementary, and together they produced a most pleasant musical ringing.

Before the war, before the gray pall of communism, Vietnam had been a land of enchantment, with unique myths and much exotic lore. By its appealing music, the bell suggested the magical nature of the country's history. The memory of the elegant shape and glimmer of the silver form, the unison notes — each an octave apart from the one below it — and her profound affection for the man who had owned this bell at last drew Bibi up the ladder.

Upon his death, Captain had no siblings or children in far-flung places for whom his charming little collection of souvenirs needed to be accounted and forwarded. Nancy said all those items were Bibi's if she wanted them, and she wanted them very much. The sight of his humble treasures, however, sharpened her grief. Back in November, less than three months earlier, her mother had helped her pack them away for the day when the sting of Captain's death had been dulled by time.

Although she mourned him no less than she had on the day that she found his corpse, she entered the attic with a tentative gladness equal to her intense curiosity, which would not be quenched. Particleboard provided a floor, and the raftered space rose high enough for an adult to stand erect everywhere except near the eaves. Upon Bibi's arrival, the ringing stopped.

At the periphery of vision, movement caught her attention. She looked up to see what, for an alarming moment, appeared to be lazily billowing smoke, evidence of a smoldering fire. But those fumes were only slithers of mist seeping through the screen that covered the attic vents, as though the ocean of fog outside possessed curiosity about the contents of the houses currently submerged in it.

Little of the room's copious contents had been the property of the captain; most belonged to Nancy and Murphy. Bibi had forgotten where in the aisles of stacked boxes the bell and other items had been tucked away.

Sans bell, in the small soundless exhalations of fog, the silence pooled so deep that Bibi felt as if she were in a cellar rather than an attic. She might have thought that she had imagined the silvery ringing if the ladder and the lights hadn't been proof of another presence.

Because the one-inch particleboard had been securely screwed to the joists, rather than nailed, her feet found no creaks in it as she moved along the center line of the attic, looking left and right into the aisles of shelving and free-stacked goods. The captain had provided the labor to replace the old rotting plywood flooring, one of a number of small jobs that he did for free, to prove his value as a tenant, although no one felt it needed to be proved. That was just Captain's way: always wanting to be useful.

When she reached the next-to-last aisle at the east end of the attic, Bibi discovered a presence, perhaps the one who for some weeks she had been seeking with both yearning and misgiving. He — or someone — stood at the back of the aisle, ten feet from her, in the shadows past the fall of light.

The apprehension that she had overcome before, that she felt was unworthy of her, flowered again, a black-petaled fright that severely tested her image of herself. Valiant girl? Or was she just another uncertain and confused kid pretending to be mature and brave, self-deceived by the fake-out she pulled on everyone else?

"Captain?" she said softly.

The presence moved toward her, into the light.

She realized then that madness and sanity were two worlds separated from each other by no more than a single step.

26
PEOPLE OF SINISTER INTENTIONS

When Nurse Hernandez returned to Bibi's room, she brought with her the chief of security for the hospital, whom she introduced as Chubb Coy. Whether Chubb was his real name or a nickname, he lived up to it. Pleasantly rounded rather than markedly fat, he moved with the lithe and supple ease of a dancer, which was peculiar to certain amply padded people. His last name was less appropriate than his first, because he was neither taciturn nor shy.

Mira Hernandez powered the unoccupied first bed to its maximum height, and Mr. Coy opened his laptop on the mattress. Bibi stood with them as Mr. Coy tapped into the hospital's video files from the night just passed.

"Aren't any security cameras in patients' rooms," he said, "or in other areas where their privacy has to be protected. Frivolous lawsuits already jack up medical costs. Costs would go through the roof if everybody's grandma won a million bucks in court because she'd been humiliated being filmed while she used a bedpan."

In a gently chastising tone, Nurse Hernandez said, "Of course, maintaining patient privacy is important for much better and more important reasons than defending against legal action."

Mr. Coy in no way indicated that he realized he'd been quietly admonished for his frankness. "The stairwells are all monitored. And the public elevators. But not the elevators the staff use to move patients around. We monitor all the hallways. If a patient steps out of a room with his hospital gown untied in back and then wants ten million bucks 'cause Security had to look at his pathetic bare butt, well, so we have to go to court and hope there's maybe at least a couple sane people on the jury. Not that I'd bet on it."

Nurse Hernandez looked past her associate and smiled at Bibi, and Bibi returned the smile reassuringly.

Mr. Coy said, "Here's the main east-west fourth-floor hallway, just outside your room. The time's at the bottom."

The digital clock on the screen read 4:01 A.M. As the seconds flashed past and 4:01 turned to 4:02, a golden retriever appeared at the side of a man in a hoodie. The guy kept his head lowered as if to prevent the camera from capturing his face. He pushed open a door on the left and followed the dog through it.

"Mr. Hoodie just went into your room," said Chubb Coy. He fast-forwarded the video. "Then he comes out three minutes later, at four-oh-five. There he is. He and the dog leave how they came, by the elevator."

"Just like I told you," Bibi said to Mira Hernandez.

The nurse shook her head. "Wait."

Turning away from the laptop, face-to-face with Bibi, Mr. Coy said, "Here's the problem. At that time of night, we're locked up except for the main lobby entrance and through the ER receiving area. There's no video of that guy or his dog using one of those, either coming or going."

"Some other door that was supposed to be locked must have been open," Bibi suggested.

"Not a chance. We run a tight operation. Here's another thing — it so happens the camera in the elevator he used goes on the blink at three-fifty, ten minutes before he sashays on scene, so there's no video of him and the dog in the elevator, either coming up or going down. The camera in the ground-floor elevator alcove *is* working, but it never shows Mr. Hoodie either boarding the cab or getting out of it later."

Bibi looked at the laptop screen, where video from the previous night showed the corridor after the mysterious visitor's departure. "I don't understand."

"Me neither," Chubb Coy said. "It's stupid to think he and the dog boarded the elevator mid-floor, coming through the hatch in the ceiling of the cab. No way, José. So did you recognize the guy?"

Bibi met the security chief's eyes. They were gray flecked with blue, a steely contrast to the round amiable face in which they were set. "Recognize him from the video? But he didn't show his face."

"From his posture, his walk, the dog?"

"No. I didn't recognize him."

"Whatever he was up to," Chubb Coy said, "it wasn't good."

"Well, I don't know, but somehow I'm cured."

"The doctors confirmed that?"

"Dr. Chandra is meeting with me this afternoon."

"I hope you had a miracle, I really do," Coy said, although he clearly had his doubts. "But, see, I was a real cop before this. I've known a bunch of bad guys. People that act like Mr. Hoodie . . . you can bet the rent money, they've got sinister intentions."

27

WHAT SHE DID WHEN SHE DIDN'T GO INSANE

Bibi did not remember turning away from the presence in the attic, but the next thing she knew, she was descending the ladder to the floor of the walk-in closet. At the bottom, when she looked up, she saw that the lights had been extinguished in the high room.

Panic had not seized her. She was in the grip of something else, perhaps shock, that rendered her half numb to all sensation. Her mind wasn't spinning at the moment; instead each smallest impression and sentiment twitched to the next as if a pair of lever-wrench pliers in her brain were ratcheting them along in a futile attempt to restore her usual flow of thoughts.

She hesitated at the foot of the ladder, breath held, expecting someone to come into view above, uplit by the closet light. But when no one appeared, she gave the lowest segment of the ladder the hard push required to start it folding back into the ceiling. The ladder drew the trap door shut behind it, and the pull rope swayed back and forth like a pendulum.

She did not remember passing through the bedroom or the living room, but she became aware of being in the kitchen, standing at the dinette table, staring at the white vase. It had been empty when she entered the apartment. Now it contained three fresh scarlet roses.

As she descended the stairs from the balcony, thick fog flowed behind her and billowed around her as if it were the train of a magnificent white dress. In the courtyard, she could barely see the bricks underfoot, and the bungalow seemed to drift like a ghost ship on a shrouded sea, its lines visible but its substance unconvincing.

When she went into the house, her parents were still sleeping. Bibi retreated to her room, took off her shoes. Without removing her clothes, she slipped under the covers.

Something more had happened in the apartment attic than she had the fortitude to contemplate. She pushed away the memory of what had occurred, for it was both too frightening and too sad to bear, a weight no girl of ten — perhaps of any age — could carry for an hour, let alone for a lifetime. Better to put down that burden and let time bear it away.

She slept without rest, a sleep of denial and forgetting.

Her mother woke her. "Hey, sleepyhead. Get a move on. We're going to brunch and

144

then the movies."

With the covers pulled to her chin, Bibi said, "I don't want to. I stayed up all night reading." That was a lie, but not a mortal one. "You go without me. There's leftover chicken in the fridge. I'll make a big sandwich."

Picking up a book from the nightstand, where at least one novel remained always near at hand, Nancy read the title: "*The Secret War in the Garden.* Pretty thrilling, huh?"

"Mmmmm," Bibi agreed.

Imagining themselves to be free spirits, footloose children of Nature, her parents encouraged their daughter to be independent and self-directing. She would never be chastised for staying up most of the night, either to read or to watch one stupid thing or another on television.

"The movie's supposed to be totally funny," Nancy said. "It's the new Adam Sandler."

Insisting on her exhaustion by keeping her eyes shut and her face in a sort of slack pout, by speaking with weary exasperation, Bibi said, "He's not funny."

"You're too old for Adam Sandler, huh?"

"Decades."

"My daughter, the fifth-grade sophisticate. Well, all right. But don't hit the surf alone."

"I never do. And it's too cold, anyway."

She remained in bed for fifteen minutes after her parents left, to be certain they were gone.

A short while later, as she sat at the kitchen table, finishing a breakfast of chocolate milk and Eggo waffles smeared with peanut butter, she began to tremble and then to shake uncontrollably, as if the hinges of her bones had come loose every one and all at once. She didn't ask herself why the shaking. She didn't want to know why. It wasn't about a ghost, either real or imagined. Ghosts couldn't harm her. Even if it had been a real ghost in the attic, she would most likely never see another. Ghosts didn't swoop up every day, from all around, like sparrows and meadowlarks taking wing. If something else happened in the high room, some moment of insight or even revelation, it had been of so little importance that it had evaporated from memory while she'd slept, before her mother woke her. She insisted that she just had a chill. That was all. That was enough to explain the shakes.

Leaving the last few bites of the meal on her plate, she went into the living room, where the gas fireplace featured an electronic ignition; she switched it on with a remote control. Hands thrust in the pockets of her jeans, she stood at the hearth, basking in the heat, staring into the blue-and-yellow flames that leaped around the ceramic logs. Sometimes she liked to search for animals and faces in the shapen clouds of a summer day. Flames were too quick and fluid for the eye

146

to glimpse the suggestion of any presence other than fire, and that was a good thing.

When the shakes passed, she decided to walk to the park along Ocean Avenue and sit on the bench at Inspiration Point, even if the fog still largely obscured the Pacific. The sea always calmed her, even just the scent of it and the soothing sound of waves dashing against rocks and splashing across the sand. But as she stepped onto the front porch, even before she pulled the door shut, an unexpected flood of tears spilled from her. She was not a girl who wept in front of others, and she retreated into the bungalow.

She didn't wish to understand this bitter emotion any more than she had cared to analyze the cause of her shaking. She wanted only to stop crying, to shut off the flow before it might wash into view a reason for this grief, if it was grief, or this dread, if it was dread. When she realized that the tears might be as persistent as the shakes, she ran for the only medicine that reliably cured any bout of unpleasant feelings: a book.

Although her mother thought that Bibi had stayed up all night reading *The Secret War in the Garden,* which was the third young-adult novel in a beloved fantasy series, she had not yet begun the story. Now she snatched the book off her nightstand, hurried with it to the living room, switched on a floor lamp, dropped into an armchair, and sought refuge in the tale: *The first rumors of war came from the field mice, who traveled daily between the garden behind the Jensen house and the world below, which was far larger than our world and still unknown to most people, though known to certain children.*

At first, as Bibi read, she wiped her tear-streaked face with the sleeves of her sweatshirt. Soon, however, the blurred print became clear, and her eyes stopped sabotaging storytime.

And so it was that hour by hour, day by day, she moved away from the disturbing knowledge that she needed to put behind her. The eerie and unsettling experience in the attic became about nothing more than an apparition or hallucination. She rejected the revelation that had been part of the incident, cut it from the cloth of memory and sewed shut the hole it left — or thought she did.

She read books and wrote stories about Jasper, a black-and-gray dog who had been abandoned by his owner and sought a new home along the coast of California. A couple of weeks later, when a golden retriever came to her out of the rain, she kept him and named him Olaf. As kids do, she made a confidant of her dog and told him all her secrets — as she knew them. She told him about Captain, how wonderful he had been. She told Olaf that the apartment above the garage was an evil place, but she didn't tell him why.

28
A VISIT FROM THE DOCTOR

Bibi had folded the pajamas and the robe into her drawstring bag and had donned the jeans and long-sleeved T-shirt she'd been wearing when Nancy had brought her to the hospital. This was an expression of confidence in her belief that the brain cancer had gone into remission, that the glioma hadn't merely shrunk but had vanished.

When Dr. Sanjay Chandra entered the room, Bibi was pacing not to work off a bad case of nerves, but with impatience to get back into the world and reclaim her life. He halted at the sight of her, and his expression was so solemn that something caught in her throat, as if she had tried to swallow a large bite of meat without chewing it, though she hadn't eaten anything.

What appeared to be solemnity, or even distress at the news he had to deliver, proved to be awe. "Nothing in my years of practice, nothing in my *life,* has prepared me for this. I'm not able to explain it, Bibi. It's not possible, but you are entirely free of cancer."

The previous day, Nancy had said that Dr. Chandra reminded her of Cookie, the ginger-bread cookie that had come to life in an old children's book that she had shared when Bibi was five years old. The resemblance owed more to Nancy's sense of whimsy than to fact, and it certainly wasn't so pronounced that some snarky magazine would pair Dr. Chandra's and Cookie's photographs in a "Separated at Birth" feature. However, everything about the physician — his boyish face, chocolate-drop eyes, musical voice, humility, and charm — made her want to like him. Upon his confirmation of remission, she *loved* the man. She flew to him like a child into the arms of an adored father.

"Thank you, thank you, thank you," she gushed, exhilarated even as she was embar-rassed by her exhilaration.

He returned her embrace and then held her at arm's length, his hands on her shoulders, smiling broadly and shaking his head slowly, as if marveling at her. "The first diagnosis was not mistaken. You did have gliomatosis cerebri."

"I'm sure I did. I know I did."

"Other tumors can break down and be absorbed, and the remission can be surpris-ingly quick. It's not common, but it does oc-cur. Except with *this* cancer. Never with this hateful thing. I'll want to see you for follow-

151

up. Quite a lot of follow-up."

"Of course."

"Oncologists specializing in gliomas will want to study you."

"Study me? I don't know about that. I don't think so."

"What is it about you that made the impossible possible? Is it genetic? A quirk in your body chemistry? A higher-functioning immune system? Studying you might save uncountable lives."

She felt irresponsible for having shied from the prospect of being studied. "Well, if you put it that way . . ."

"I do. I put it that way." He released her shoulders. His happy expression was infused with wonder again. "Yesterday, when I said you had at most a year to live, you said, 'We'll see.' Do you remember?"

"Yes."

"It's almost as if you knew then that you'd go home today."

29
THE POISON-IVY
ITCH OF INTUITION

Because Nancy and Murphy were coming for a long visit at four o'clock, Bibi hadn't called to tell them what had happened in the night or that her death sentence had been miraculously commuted. Although she'd *known* that her health had been restored, she hadn't wanted to pop the champagne cork with them, figuratively speaking, until she had Dr. Chandra's confirmation. Besides, she wanted to see their surprise, their disbelief, their joy when they walked through the door and saw her in street clothes, her former glow restored.

Fifteen minutes before Bibi's parents were due, Chubb Coy, chief of security, peered through the open door. His pale-blue shirt with epaulets looked fresh, and his dark-blue slacks still held a sharp crease. He said, "Got a minute?"

Rising from a chair by the window, Bibi said, "Suddenly, I have millions of minutes."

Failing to match her smile, Coy entered the

room. "Since I spoke to you last, we've quick-scanned the parking-lot video for the past twenty-four hours. No Mr. Hoodie. No golden retriever. Seems they didn't drive here or walk, and I'm not a guy who believes in crap like teleportation. What about you? You believe in teleportation?"

"What? No. Of course not."

"So I asked myself, did they come here more than a day ago and hide out in the building? Are they still hiding in the building?"

"Why would they do that?" she asked.

"Damn if I know." He shrugged and looked bewildered, pretending for a moment to be without suspicion. "So we searched the place, end to end. Nada. Zip." He walked past her to stare out the window. Head tipped back. Pondering the sky. "It makes me feel stupid, you know? So I kept looking at the same scrap of video till I noticed something weird. Want to guess what it was?"

"I have no idea."

Still at the window with his back to her, Chubb Coy said, "When the guy and the dog come along, they pass two other people going the opposite direction. A nurse. Then an orderly. Neither one glances at Mr. Hoodie. Kind of peculiar, huh? That hour, the hoodie, and not even a glance? But stranger still, here's this beautiful dog at four in the morning, and they don't glance at it, either. People

154

see a beautiful dog, they stare, they smile. Most want to pet it, ask the owner its name. They're off-duty now, the nurse and the orderly, so I called them. Both swear there wasn't a dog. They're adamant. They never passed a dog in the hallway. You know what I'm wondering now?"

"I don't have a clue," Bibi said. "I'm sure you'll tell me."

He turned from the window to face her. "I don't know how it's possible, but just about anything is these days, when it comes to fiddling with digital recordings, sound or image. So I'm wondering if some hacker breached our security archives, somehow inserted Mr. Hoodie and the dog in our video, made them be where they never were."

Perplexed, Bibi said, "Who'd go to all that trouble? And why?"

Instead of answering her, Chubb Coy said, "Watching it about a hundred times, I still can't see any technical giveaway. The guy and the dog register with the same clarity as the nurse and orderly. The light plays off them exactly as it does other people in the scene. But I'm no expert. A first-rate techie specialist, an analyst with the right credentials, should be able to prove it's a fraud."

"Except for one thing you seem to have forgotten," Bibi reminded him. "I saw them. The man, the dog. They came into my room. The dog stood on its hind feet, put its front paws on my bed. Those lovely luminous gold eyes. It licked my hand." She held up her left hand, as though a residue of case-closing golden-retriever DNA might still be found between her fingers.

The security chief's blue-flecked steel-gray eyes were to him as scalpels to a surgeon. Direct and sharp and intent on cutting through all deception, his gaze seemed to flense her with exquisite delicacy, peeling away the layers of her image in a search for the most artful chicanery, some subtle telltale, that would put the lie to everything he'd been told.

"These days," he said in a dead-flat voice from which he took care to bleed all inflection, "I may be just a glorified mall cop, in a somewhat more respectable environment, but I was once the real thing, and I still have good gumshoe instincts."

Regarding him with growing amazement and uneasiness, Bibi asked, "What are you saying?"

"I'm not saying anything, Miss Blair."

"That I'm some kind of suspect?"

He raised his eyebrows and widened his eyes in an unconvincing pretense of surprise, as if she had misinterpreted what he'd said and had leaped to a conclusion about his intentions that astonished him.

"What am I supposed to have done?" she asked, not with offense or anger, but with a kind of amused bafflement. "Faked the remission of my cancer? Tricked the MRI machine? Deceived all my doctors? Does any of that make sense?"

If the irrepressible joy she felt as a result of her recovery had not been still so fresh in Bibi's heart, the security chief's smug smile would have ticked her off.

"That old cop intuition, Miss Blair, it's like poison ivy. It just itches and itches, you can't ignore it, so you have to scratch it real good to get relief."

With those words, which Bibi took to be a promise or even a threat, Chubb Coy headed for the door.

She said, "Try some calamine lotion. It has a funny smell and it's lady-pink, but it relieves the itching."

Without glancing back, Coy left the room.

The soft laugh that escaped Bibi had only a slight nervous edge. She said, "Looney-Toon."

30
PROUD COLLECTOR OF
10,000 HEADS

Throughout the morning and the afternoon of their first day on the roof of the three-story building, the four members of the SEAL team used periscopic cameras with nonreflective zoom lenses to scan the dead village without much risk that sunlight, flaring off the glass, would betray their presence. The images transmitted to the display screens were crisp, clear, and tedious. When the sun moved west but not directly behind Paxton and his men, they were bold enough to poke just their heads above the parapet to study the townscape: a drab gray-and-sand-brown hodgepodge of characterless structures, bullet-pocked stucco, cracked and crumbling concrete, and iron security gates hanging useless from broken hinges, strewn through with rubble.

Their target, the Ghost, whose name was Abdullah al-Ghazali, was holed up somewhere in these grim ruins, and he had with him six acolytes, all true believers, two of them possibly women. He had chosen to hide in this town, whose population he had slaughtered seventeen months earlier, perhaps because he thought it was the last place anyone would look for him, but perhaps because the atmosphere of an abattoir appealed to the bastard, surrounded as he was with memories of vicious cruelties and abhorrent violence, which he found delectable. Paxton had studied the culture that produced such men, but a lifetime of study would not help him understand why they became death-loving haters of everything the rest of humanity held dear.

An equal-opportunity terrorist who murdered not only Jews and Christians and Hindus and those who had no faith, Abdullah al-Ghazali also butchered Arab tribes other than his own, Muslims he considered less than pure. He claimed to have taken — or ordered taken — the lives of ten thousand people, and most experts thought he had undercounted.

He usually moved with impunity through countries impressed by his barbarism, but not since the past October. In spite of Homeland Security and no-fly lists and surveillance of every transportation system coast to coast, he had gotten into the States, activated ten sleeper cells, planned two attacks — led one — on shopping malls, and murdered 317 people. Most of his associates had been killed or arrested, but he had escaped the United States, only to find that he was now too hot to be welcomed in those kingdoms and fake democracies that had once provided him with rent-free villas when he needed them.

Pax, Danny, Gibb, and Perry had been sent to provide justice, which in this case did not require a judge and jury. Now that they were in town, they were eager to do the job and go home, impatient with the need to conceal their presence until the targets revealed themselves, instead of boldly going on the search.

Later in the afternoon, only half a block away, a man appeared on the flat, railed roof of a two-story building on the farther side of the street. Although he was dressed in gray to match the concrete around him, his camouflage was pathetic. A pair of binoculars hung around his neck. The SEALs at once put down their field glasses and ducked out of sight.

Perry raised a camera on its stick, so that it barely cleared the parapet wall. The instrument was so small, there was little danger that the watchman would spot it. Perry and Pax lay with the display between them, watching an enhanced image of the terrorist. Not Abdullah. One of his butt-kissers. The guy lit a cigarette and took two draws before raising his binoculars to survey this jumping-off place that he and his companions used as their rats' nest.

Having put up a second camera, Gibb and Danny huddled over that display. Four men scoping the scene, analyzing the smoker's behavior, were better than two. Each might see a crucial detail that the others missed. For starters, Pax figured the six targets must feel safe if one surfaced only periodically to perform a cursory surveillance of the town. Maybe their edge had worn off because they were doing good dope, which, among their teetotaling kind, was a common indulgence. Mass murder was stressful. They had to chill out *somehow,* after all.

Three hundred seventeen shoppers. Ten thousand victims. Back when Muammar Qadhafi had ruled Libya, the Ghost had done an American-TV interview from a villa there, in which he'd said — in addition to the usual propagandist rant — that he possessed a small collection of severed heads in one of his residences. The heads, he declared in his taunting manner, were much like books on a shelf, each one a story. He wished that he had a library large enough to hold ten thousand.

Throughout the day, Pax had thought often about Bibi, worried about her, wondered about the vivid image of her that had thrust into his mind the night before. Now she receded to a back corner of his thoughts.

A job needed to be done. He and his guys

would do it as well as it could be done and with considerable satisfaction.

31
CRAZY WHEN YOU LEAST EXPECT IT

Nancy and Murphy didn't know whether to laugh or cry, and as usual when torn by conflicting emotions, they succumbed to both, switching back and forth, and back again, from tears of joy to tears that watered a large garden of what-might-have-happened fears. They made such a spectacle of themselves in the hospital room that a nurse stepped in and politely asked them to remember, please, that the other patients needed peace and quiet.

As soon as Bibi had the discharge papers, her parents shepherded her along the corridor, into the elevator, down to the lobby, out to the parking lot, both of them often talking at the same time. They had a thousand questions, and they wanted to hear everything that had happened, but they weren't able to stop themselves from interrupting her with hugs and kisses and exclamations of relief, some in surfer lingo — "epic, foffing, totally sacred, just a pure glasshouse pipe of a day, stylin' " — which for the first time sounded wrong coming from them, as though their daughter's flirtation with Death had made them desperate to be young again.

Dinner had to be special, celebratory, a night to be remembered forever, an amped-up commemoration of the impossible become possible. Bibi knew too well what that meant: the best combination Mexican-and-burger joint in town, where cheese came on everything and the spices were hot hot hot, too many bottles of icy Corona, too many shots of tequila. But she went along with the plan because she was hungry, happy, still afloat on wonder, and because she loved her mom and dad. They were always sweet, always amusing, and they weren't alcoholics, only special-occasion drunks once a month or so.

During the dinner, Nancy whispered in Murphy's ear and left the table for ten minutes. When she returned, giggling, Murphy whispered in Nancy's ear. Then *he* went away for ten minutes. They were clearly conspiring at something, and Bibi half dreaded what it might be. They were generous and thoughtful, but a surfeit of emotion and too much booze could be a wicked combination that motivated them every so often to drop upon their daughter a wildly inappropriate gift.

To observe the publication of Bibi's first

novel, they had presented her with an illegal tiger cub, which seemed reasonable to them because one of the big cats was a featured player in the book. Of course, she'd contacted animal-welfare authorities, pretended to have found the cub in the park, and made sure that the little fellow went to a first-rate refuge for exotic animals.

She didn't want another tiger or, God forbid, an elephant, but she said nothing because nothing she said would stop them once they had agreed on a "perfect gift." Her parents could hit you with crazy when you least expected it.

Bibi had drunk little beer and no tequila while convincing Nancy and Murphy that she was keeping pace with them. Now she insisted they couldn't drive her to her apartment; she would take them home and, in the morning, return their BMW. They snuggled in the backseat as if they were teenagers.

At the house in Corona del Mar, their attempt to disentangle and clamber out of the car was worthy of Ringling Bros.' finest trying to exit a joke vehicle the size of a riding lawnmower. Nancy paused in that performance to say, "When you get home, angel girl, just go with it."

"Go with what?"

Grinning, her dad said, "You'll see."

"Oh, no. I didn't think it would be tonight."

"It's just what you need," Murphy assured her.

"What I need, Dad, is a hot bath and bed."

"Her name's Calida Butterfly."

"Whose name?"

He closed the door and bent down with Nancy to grin at Bibi through the front passenger window. The two of them waved and blew kisses, as though she hadn't been dying just the day before, as if she were eighteen and going off to college. *It'll be what it'll be,* and it had turned out to be some kind of miracle. Even if the good twist might be impossible, inexplicable, Nancy and Murphy would by morning have put all the recent stress and worry behind them, would waste no psychic energy on wondering why or what if. They would grab their boards and hit the beach, so to speak, and respect fate by giving no thought to it until they were slammed by the next thing that would be whatever it would be.

On the drive to her apartment, Bibi repeatedly reminded herself that, having had her ticket taken away and torn up as she waited on the banks of the River Styx, she should be grateful for every breath and accept every annoyance and frustration with patience. Easier said than done when someone named Calida Butterfly was apparently waiting for you with just what you needed.

She parked in one of the two spots reserved

for her apartment and switched off the headlights, but not the engine. She considered putting down the power windows an inch, to provide ventilation, and sleeping in the car. That was a childish impulse. She hadn't been a child even through much of her childhood. She shut off the engine, but took no satisfaction in her maturity.

In the apartment-complex courtyard, in the expectant stillness of the night, the palms and ferns were as motionless as plants in a diorama. Ribbons of steam rose and withered from the heated, eerily illuminated pool, and a young man as sleek as a trout swam laps so effortlessly that his arms sliced from the water only a quiet *slish-slish-slish.*

Carrying her drawstring bag and laptop, Bibi climbed the open iron staircase to the long balcony that served the third-floor units. When she came to the door of her apartment, she found it open wide. Beyond the threshold and the shallow foyer, extravagant bouquets of red and white roses dressed the living room, as if a wedding would soon commence, and all the shimmering light issued from candles in glass cups that crowded every surface not occupied by flower vases.

As Bibi hesitated in the foyer, a woman stepped into view from the right. She wore flat-soled white shoes, white slacks, and a short-sleeved white blouse. She might have been taken for a physical therapist or a dental assistant except for the blue-silk sash that she wore as a belt, the gold-star-on-blue-field silk scarf at her throat, dangling silver earrings, each ear with three hoops of different sizes, and enough expensive-looking bracelets and finger rings to stock a jewelry store. She was an Amazon. Five foot ten. Maybe six feet. Formidable but feminine, with a face reminiscent of Greta Garbo if Greta Garbo had looked a little more like Nicole Kidman. She was about forty, with clear, smooth skin, blond hair cut in a pageboy, and eyes that were blue or green or silver-gray depending on how the quivering candlelight revealed them.

In a voice both slightly husky and melodious, she said, "I am Calida Butterfly. Welcome to this first day of your new life."

Except that her parents were more traditional in some things than they believed themselves to be, except that their beloved and otherwise libertarian surf culture didn't have much patience for woman-woman or man-man romance, Bibi might have thought that their gift to her would turn out to be her first lesbian experience.

But of course it was far different from that. She was about to learn why she had survived brain cancer.

■ ■ ■ ■ ■

2
GIRL WITH
A MISSION,
GIRL ON THE RUN

■ ■ ■ ■ ■

32
SOLANGE ST. CROIX AND THE BUTTERFLY EFFECT

Calida Butterfly traveled with a folding massage table and a small ostrich-skin suitcase. Featuring two compartments, the case could be opened from either side. Half of it contained the lotions, oils, and items related to massage. The other half held things she needed for her second occupation, which she had declined to reveal until she completed working on Bibi's tense, knotted muscles.

"If you're thinking about what comes next," Calida had said, "you're not getting the full effect of the massage."

"If I'm *wondering* about what comes next and why you're being so mysterious," Bibi had replied, "that won't relax me, either."

"The writer that you are, I guess you're used to being a kind of dictator, telling the characters in your stories what to do."

"It doesn't work that way."

"Good. It doesn't work that way with me, either." Taking off her rings and bracelets, she said, "Now you lie down and be a good girl."

Holding a towel across her breasts, wearing only panties, Bibi had done as she was told. Her embarrassment passed quickly because of Calida's brusque yet reassuring manner. An uneasiness remained, but she couldn't identify a cause; maybe it was a lingering effect of the cancer scare, the residue of concerns that need no longer worry her.

The table had a cutout for her face, so that she was looking at her living-room carpet, where reflections of candlelight flowed and wimpled almost like water. "Did you bring all the candles and roses?" Bibi asked as she waited for the massage to begin.

"Heavens, no. Your parents asked me to have them delivered at the last minute. I can get anything done on a two-hour notice."

"How do you manage that?"

"I have sources. Proprietary information. Now shush."

Calida switched on an iPod. Israel Kamakawiwo'ole, whose voice was one of the warmest ever recorded, began to sing a soothing medley of "Somewhere Over the Rainbow" and "What a Wonderful World."

"How did you get in here?"

"Your mom has a spare key, right? She put it in an envelope and left it with the hostess at the restaurant. I picked it up."

About five seconds after the first touch, Bibi

realized that Calida Butterfly had magic hands. "Where did you learn this?"

"Do you ever shut up, girl? You be quiet and just float."

"Float where?"

"Anywhere, nowhere. Quiet now, or I'll tape your mouth shut."

"You wouldn't."

"Don't test me. I'm not your ordinary masseuse."

In spite of the faintest uneasiness, Bibi got with the program. The candlelight purling and undulating on the carpet proved hypnotic.

Just as she began to float, she wondered if the woman massaging her was in fact Calida Butterfly. Someone could have disabled the real Calida, or even killed her, taking her place in order to . . .

To what? No. Such a twist was a novelist's conceit, and not a good one. Bad thriller plotting. Or a movie with shrieking violins and the latest scream queen channeling a young Jamie Lee Curtis.

The rippling, curling candlelight. The music. Calida's magic hands. Soon Bibi was floating again, floating anywhere, nowhere.

Somewhere. Gelson's supermarket. An express checkout lane. Seven months after she had dropped out of the university.

Bibi was puzzled that memories involving Dr. Solange St. Croix — such old news, after all — should trouble her twice in two days.

That afternoon three years earlier, she stopped at the market for a head of lettuce, a few ripe but firm tomatoes, radishes, and celery. Carrying everything in a handbasket, she recognized her former professor standing last in line for the express checkout.

Her first inclination was to retreat, explore a few aisles even though she needed nothing more, waste enough time for the holy mother of the university writing program to make her purchases and leave. The encounter she'd had with the woman in that minimalist office with the half-empty bookshelves had left, however, an enduring sore spot on Bibi's ego. She always stood up for herself, never pigheadedly, never without good reason; but on that occasion, she had backed down with uncharacteristic wimpiness, shocked and confused and unsettled by the professor's inexplicable fury. If she withdrew now, hiding out in the bakery department, she would suffer a second blow to her self-respect, this one more deserved than the first.

To be honest, there was another consideration. In the seven months since leaving the university, living with her parents, she'd written six short stories. Three had been accepted for publication: by *The Antioch Review,* by *Granta,* and by *Prairie Schooner.* Such prolific production and acceptance were remarkable for a writer not yet nineteen. In one of the smaller rooms of her heart, Bibi harbored the unworthy desire to share her success with her former professor.

She stood in line behind her target, telling herself not to force the moment, to wait for the woman to notice her. She wouldn't take a snarky tone when disclosing her good fortune. Striving to sound sincere, she would *thank* the professor for all she had learned in those three months, as if being harried out of the university had been a valuable service, had awakened her to her faults, and had brought her to her literary senses. She would be so convincingly humble and ingenuous that Solange St. Croix would be left speechless.

The professor's handbasket contained nine items, and when her turn came at the checkout conveyor belt, she turned to her left to unload her purchases. She saw Bibi from the corner of her eye and turned to face her with an almost comical expression of astonishment.

The woman seemed to be wearing the same outfit as on the day in her office when she'd breathed fire, a tailored but drab pantsuit and a blouse the gray-green of dead seaweed. Her graying hair was still in a bun, her face without makeup, and her blue eyes were cold enough to freeze her opponent in a smackdown with the mythical Medusa.

Before Bibi could get out a word, the professor said, "You bold little bitch," spraying spittle with the *B*'s, and her face contorted with what seemed to be both anger and fear. "Following me, stalking me." Before Bibi could deny the charge, the woman rushed on: "I'll call the police on you, don't think I won't, I'll get a restraining order, you crazy c— !" In the river of invective that followed, she used the c-word, the t-word, the f-word more than once, and it was impossible to tell whether rage or genuine terror scored higher on her emotional Richter scale. "Get this girl away from me, someone help me, *get her away from me.*"

Three shoppers had stepped into line behind Bibi, making retreat a clumsier bit of business than she would have liked. Maybe they knew who the esteemed professor was or maybe she looked so unthreatening and widowlike that, in spite of her foul language, they were inclined to sympathize with her. On the other hand, customers and clerks and aproned bagboys stared at Bibi, *gaped* at her, as if she'd committed an offense against the helpless older lady that, although witnessed by none of them, must have been malicious in the extreme. With St. Croix still asking for help and warning everyone about her dangerous assailant, Bibi made her way among the shoppers in line behind her and turned left, crossing the front of the store. Rattled as she rarely was, mortified, she didn't know where she was going — that is until she put down her handbasket of vegetables on a display of Coca-Cola, said "Excuse me" to a young mother and child with whom she collided, and headed for the nearest exit.

So much for floating.

"You tensed up all of a sudden," said Calida Butterfly.

"Just a bad memory."

"Men," said the masseuse, making a wrong assumption. "Nothing we can do about them except shoot them, if it was legal."

Bibi hadn't gone back to Gelson's for a year, although it was her favorite market. Even to this day, she imagined an employee now and then recognized her and, to be safe, kept out of her way.

She hadn't seen Dr. Solange St. Croix since. Hoped never to see her again. With no slightest clue to puzzle out the reason for the professor's bizarre behavior, Bibi had decided it must be early-onset Alzheimer's.

A draft stirred the candle flames for a while, and fluttering cascades of soft amber light spilled across the room, which smelled sweetly of roses. Bibi took slow, deep breaths and exhaled through the face hole in the massage table.

"That's better," Calida said, "much better." A few minutes later, she said, "We're done with this part, kid. Now let's find out why you were spared from brain cancer."

33
WAITING FOR THE WRONG
PEOPLE TO SHOW UP

Fully dressed, feeling pleasantly wrung-out, Bibi opened a chilled bottle of chardonnay, poured two servings, and brought the glasses to the chrome dinette table with the red Formica top.

Calida Butterfly had moved some of the candles from the living room and distributed them on the table and countertops to provide the proper mood for the second thing that she had been hired to do.

Laying her ostrich-skin suitcase on one of the chrome-and-black-vinyl chairs, Calida said, "Do you know what divination is?"

"Predicting the future," Bibi said.

"Not entirely. It's also a tool for uncovering hidden knowledge by supernatural means."

"What hidden knowledge?"

"Any hidden knowledge," Calida said, as she opened the half of her suitcase that didn't contain items related to massage therapy.

"I don't believe in prognostication, all that stuff."

Calida wasn't offended. She said cheerily, "Well, the way it works is, you don't have to believe in it for it to be true."

Bibi saw, among other things in the bag, a Sig Sauer P220 or maybe a P226. She recognized the weapon because the P226, chambered for nine-millimeter ammunition, was the standard pistol issued to SEALs. Paxton had purchased his own P220, because it was chambered for .45 caliber and more likely to knock a bad guy down hard in close combat. The two guns looked all but identical.

Bibi had her own P226, which Paxton had taught her to use. An engagement gift.

The uneasiness about Calida, which Bibi had shaken off, now crept up on her once more. "Why the gun?"

Calida took the pistol from the suitcase and put it on the table. "Divination creates the psychic equivalent of seismic waves, shock waves. The vast majority of people can't feel them or don't realize what they're feeling. But certain people can feel them — and sometimes locate the source."

"What certain people?"

"The wrong people. That's all you need to know. Mostly they let me alone. They've learned better than to mess with Calida Butterfly."

Because eccentric people and the details of their obsessions were good material for fiction, Bibi was genuinely interested when she asked, "Do you have silver bullets in the gun?"

Taking from the suitcase a bottle of rubbing alcohol, a small roll of inch-wide gauze, and a self-dispensing roll of adhesive tape, Calida said, "Didn't figure you for the kind of writer who would leap to a cliché. Good old American ammo will do the job."

Bibi settled into one of the chairs, holding her wineglass in both hands. "What's your real name?"

"Calida Butterfly, believe it or not."

"I'll buy the Calida, but who were you before Butterfly?"

"Okay, you've got me, I am caught, revealed. Before I was Calida Butterfly, I was of course Calida Caterpillar."

The masseuse-diviner placed a small packet, twice the size of a matchbook, beside the rubbing alcohol and then turned to rummage in the suitcase once more. Bibi reached across the table, picked up this newest item: a seamstress's kit of needles in a variety of sizes.

Replacing the packet where she'd found it, she said, "What are you going to sew?"

"Flesh."

That answer required another question, but Bibi didn't ask it. A session of fortune-telling, though pointless, had seemed to promise a little fun. But moment by moment, the weirdness mounted and the mood grew darker.

181

Nancy and Murphy had gotten involved with some strange people over the years, but most of them were harmless surf dudes who had been clamshelled, prosecuted, and thoroughly rinse-cycled by so many monster waves that their common sense had been washed out of them. Calida didn't seem crazy in a dangerous way, but she didn't seem to be as tightly wound as a new spool of thread, either.

The last things the woman took from her bag were a folded white-cotton cloth, a silver bowl, and a flannel sack with contents that rattled softly when she put it down.

"I didn't know my parents were into this. I mean, they never want to think about the future. You know — 'It'll be what it'll be.' "

Calida sat, picked up her glass, and poured half the wine down her throat as if she had no interest in the taste of it. "Like I said, divination isn't only fortune-telling."

"Oh, that's right. It's also for uncovering hidden knowledge by supernatural means. What knowledge did Mom and Dad want uncovered?"

"You're a nice kid, but you're nosy. I would no more divulge my experiences with other clients than a priest would tell you what someone said in confession."

Bibi felt rebuked, but to no degree embarrassed. "When did you go into this divination business?"

Rather than answer, Calida finished the rest

of her chardonnay in one long swallow. She put down the empty glass and met Bibi's stare and seemed to want to see how long her client could tolerate silence between them. Candlelight ceaselessly fingered her face, as if trying to lift the shadows that veiled part of it. Earlier, the color of her eyes had seemed to fluctuate, depending on the angle at which the light entered them, but now they were a steady green — and striated in such a way that they reminded Bibi of the eyes of the tiger cub that her parents had given her.

After picking up the bottle and refilling her wineglass, Calida at last answered the question. "I started twenty-seven years ago. I was sixteen. My mother taught me."

"What's your mother's name?"

"Thalia. Thalia Butterfly."

"Butterfly and Butterfly. So it's a two-diviner practice, like mother-daughter attorneys or something."

"My mother died twelve years ago, and it wasn't an easy death."

Although Bibi didn't know what to believe, she nonetheless felt bad for having been flippant. "I'm sorry. What happened?"

"One night, after a session like this, the wrong people showed up. They tortured and then dismembered her. If you think that's just a story, you can check it out online. The crime was never solved."

34
THE I OF THE NEEDLE

Astragalomancy was a method of divining the future or learning hidden knowledge by rolling dice. A ceromancer dropped melted wax into cold water and interpreted the figures thus produced. Halomancy required the reading of the shapes made by casting a handful of salt on a flat surface. A necromancer sought answers by communicating with the dead.

When Calida pulled the drawstring on the small flannel bag and spilled the familiar lettered tiles onto the dinette table, she said, "My mother devised and perfected the occult art of Scrabblemancy."

Bibi almost laughed, but then she remembered the brutal murder and dismemberment that could be researched online. She swallowed the laugh and washed it down with a sip of wine to conceal how close she had come to giving offense. Even in such vain and silly pursuits as divination, you could unwittingly encounter a sociopath and become the object of her wrath. In fact, the more fruitless and outré the subject of your interest, the more likely it might be that those without a moral compass and with a taste for violence, empty and wandering in search of convictions, might cross your path. Besides, she didn't want to hurt Calida's feelings.

"We are told that in the beginning was the word," Calida said, "and that the world — the entire universe — was *spoken* into existence. My mother speculated that the best material with which a diviner could work would be words, not human entrails or lines in your palm or a handful of salt cast on a table, but words. And if words existed before matter of any kind, before suns and worlds and seas and human beings and fortune-tellers . . . well, then an alphabet must have existed even earlier, so that words could be formed. Therefore letters are more fundamental and powerful than anything else a diviner could use to force the secrets of the universe into view. Now I'm going to ask you a question, Bibi Blair, and you must answer truthfully, frankly, because I'll conduct the session in different ways depending on your response. Does Scrabblemancy make sense to you — *not* do you believe it will work, but does it make sense, and to what degree?"

When Calida leaned in to the table, tilting her head toward Bibi, her blond hair shimmered forward and flared slightly to each side of her face, like golden wings, and her eyes were disconcerting in their hawkish intensity and predatory focus. As much as Bibi wanted to like the woman, moments such as this made her feel as though they had been born on different worlds and could never fully relate to each other.

"Does the theory make sense, and to what degree?" Calida repeated in a whisper, and in the glass cups on the table, candles popped and hissed as the flames found impurities in the wicks, as if the melting wax were speaking in sympathy with the diviner.

"It makes a little sense, I mean, in the context of divination," Bibi said, striving to be truthful without being dismissive. "But I'm more interested in things being spoken into existence than I could ever possibly be in using the occult to discover hidden knowledge."

"What if things spoken into existence, who spoke them and why, is the same thing as hidden knowledge?"

"But I don't believe they are," Bibi replied.

The hawk-eyed diviner seemed to search the depth of Bibi's eyes as a real hawk, gliding in its gyre, would scrutinize a meadow far below, seeking a mouse to hunt down and snatch up. Then she sat back in her chair, and the wings of flaxen hair closed against her face, once more curtaining her ears. She drank from the refilled glass, again finishing half the wine in one long swallow.

When she put down the glass, she said, "Did you lock the front door when you came in?"

Bibi nodded. "Yes."

"Is there a second door?"

"No."

"Are the windows locked?"

"Yes."

"Then let's begin and finish quickly. The less time we're at it, the safer we'll be."

As the diviner swiped the Scrabble tiles off the table and into the silver bowl, rings sparkling with candlelight, Bibi sipped the wine and savored it, considering whether her parents would be insulted if she refused the second part of their gift and sent this woman away.

Calida returned the bowl to the table. From the seamstress's packet, she selected the largest needle, held it in a candle flame, and then placed it on the folded white-cotton cloth. She removed the cap from the rubbing alcohol, stuck the thumb of her left hand into the bottle, let it soak for a minute, and then screwed the cap on once more.

When the diviner picked up the two-inch needle with her right hand, Bibi said, "You're not serious."

As she began speaking softly in a language that Bibi didn't recognize, Calida thrust the needle through the plump pad of her own thumb, not through the nail but behind it. The crown with its eye protruded from one side of the thumb, the gleaming point from the other, and about a third of the shank could not be seen because it was buried in the flesh.

"Why the hell did you do that?" Bibi demanded as blood oozed from the entrance and exit wounds and dripped onto the cotton cloth.

Calida spoke a few more words in the arcane language and then, through clenched teeth, hissed in distress before answering: "Your skepticism prevents you from being involved enough for this to work. So I have to be more intently focused to compensate for your doubt. Nothing focuses the mind quite like pain."

"This is nuts."

"If you keep up your useless commentary," the diviner warned, "I'll have to put a second needle through the meat of my palm."

"Not if we stop this right now." Bibi pushed her chair back from the table.

Calida grimaced. "We've begun the session. We must complete it, close the door I've opened. Or those psychic shock waves I mentioned earlier won't stop. They're a beacon. An irresistible summons. You'll have visitors you do not want."

Bibi's skepticism wasn't absolute. The piercing needle and the blood argued for

Calida's sincerity, if not for her sanity. After a hesitation, Bibi sat. She pulled her chair closer to the table.

Her mother and father had not become strangers to her because of their interest in divination and this bizarre gift. The fullness of her love hadn't diminished whatsoever. Her comfortable image of them, however, was evidently an inadequate likeness, and her long-held assumptions about their interior lives now seemed deficient, immature, if not naïve.

Stirring her right hand through the wooden tiles in the silver bowl, Calida seemed to speak to an invisible presence. "I bleed for answers. I cannot be denied. Attend me." To Bibi, she said, "How many letters should I draw?"

"I don't know. How would I know?"

"You've got to participate, girl. *How many letters?*"

Bibi looked at the kitchen window above the sink and was only somewhat relieved to see that indeed it had been locked. "Eleven," she said, though she had no reason why that number and not another. "Eleven letters."

35
A World and a Half Away

Paxton and Danny didn't believe in ghosts. Perry allowed for the possibility, but never expected to see one. Only Gibb was as certain of the reality of unmoored spirits as he was of the existence of the air he breathed, for his mother, who had raised him alone, sometimes saw his dead father walking in the fields behind their house or standing under the oak tree in the yard, or sitting on the porch, smiling and translucent. On those occasions, she said it made sense that dear Harry would decline to move on as souls should, considering that he had loved her and Gibb as no man had ever before loved his wife and son. Gibb never glimpsed the apparition, though he yearned to see it. He knew it must be real, because his mother never lied; and each time she saw the wraith, she grew luminous with delight.

Yet none of the four SEALs, including open-minded Perry and true-believing Gibb, felt that this town in the barren outback of

Hell might be haunted. If anyplace in the world should have made you feel that it lay aswarm with otherworldly presences, it should have been this doomed village. But perhaps the cruelties visited upon these people had been so demonic and vicious, the murders committed with such cold-blooded pleasure and violence, that the many victims had been killed twice, in body and in spirit, and had no choice of either an afterlife or a lingering haunt.

At 3:00 A.M., when the SEALs had left their surveillance post on the roof, moving into the narrow streets with a stealth that only ghosts could have matched, the town seemed never to have supported life, to have been forever as dead as any crater on the airless moon that shed now only a quarter of its potential light. The dwellings were crammed together, each walled from its neighbors, curiously isolated in proximity to the others, segregated, crude and sullen-looking places, lacking any sense of comfort or community, each family a separate tribe on its own speck of an archipelago, so that no aura of history adhered to the structures, either. Nor did they serve even as monuments to those who had once inhabited them.

Pax wondered if this deadest of dead places would be the death of him, but he didn't dwell on the thought. Difficult as it might be for civilians to believe, a battle-hardened

SEAL valued his life less than the lives of his buddies, less even than his honor, which was the only attitude to have if you wanted to win a war.

They had split into two teams and had circuitously approached the target house by using the streets that paralleled the one onto which it faced. Pax and Perry entered, from behind, a damaged building that stood across from what might be Abdullah al-Ghazali's nest. They took fifteen minutes to ease through the walled and debris-strewn backyard and through the ruined interior to the front door, which had been blown off in an attack seventeen months earlier.

Crouching just inside the doorway, they studied the house across the street from this closer vantage point, wearing night-vision gear, and confirmed what they had seen previously with periscopic cameras and binoculars. The structure was intact except for pockmarks and divots chipped out by bullets, all the windows protected by exterior metal shutters. Instead of mud bricks plastered over with stucco, the house appeared to be more modern, constructed of reinforced concrete, not an uncommon preference in a country where unending sectarian and tribal warfare once fought with rifles had long ago escalated to machine guns and rocket-propelled grenades.

At 5:11 A.M., the mission-specific satellite

phone in Paxton's jacket pocket vibrated. The caller could be only Perry, who with Gibb had taken up a position on the roof of the building to the east of the target house, with a view of its backyard.

Perry spoke softly. "Faint interior light, leaking around a shutter. Just now."

This served to confirm that the cigarette smoker on the roof, seen the previous afternoon, had not merely used the house as an observation platform, but had taken shelter there, perhaps with the mass murderer Abdullah al-Ghazali.

Pax and his guys would not move against the house until full daylight, and even then they would wait as long as the situation supported a delay, hoping for some indication that the smoker was not the sole occupant. If the seven terrorists were spread out in, say, three widely separated houses, an attack on one would alert those quartered in the other two, and the element of surprise would be lost. In that event, the odds of nailing al-Ghazali himself were not as good as they ought to be. Regardless, the assault would occur during the coming day; a further delay was too risky.

From somewhere in the waning night came the eerie cry of that desert wild cat called a caracal, and Paxton tensed.

36

SCRABBLEMANCY

Crazy as it was, with the pierced thumb and the blood and the tiger-eyed blond Amazon, with candle wicks popping and hissing, with salamanders of candlelight chasing their own lithe shadows across the tabletop, with the fragrance of roses rising with ever greater — and somehow funereal — intensity from the next room, and with the threat of unknown enemies gathering in the night to home in on psychic waves that Bibi could in no way detect, she nonetheless found her disbelief suspended. For the moment, Calida Butterfly had a presence, an air of authority, that would make the most committed skeptic doubt his own doubt.

The diviner stirred her right hand through the wood tiles that filled the silver bowl, neither watching to see what letters her fingers plucked from that alphabet soup nor trying to discern them by a Braille-reader's touch.

"I command the secret knowledge regarding Bibi's cancer cure," she said, her husky yet musical voice conveying an intolerance for resistance from whatever occult power she meant to interrogate. "I bleed for answers. I can't be denied. Attend me. Why was Bibi Blair spared from gliomatosis cerebri?"

She dropped four tiles upon the table, and they clicked like dice, and then two more, and three, and a final two. Some tiles were facedown, and she turned them over. She arranged them from A to V and had this: A, A, E, E, F, I, L, O, S, T, V. She lined them up on the table so that if she turned to her left and Bibi to her right, both could read them.

From eleven letters, even if there were duplicates, many words could be formed. Although Bibi made no move to organize the tiles, she saw LEAVE, LEAF, FAST, FEAST, SOFT, SOLVE, FLOAT, SOLE. . . .

Calida fingered four letters out of the lineup — EVIL — which didn't improve Bibi's mood.

"We must use all eleven of them to find the true message," the diviner explained. First she spelled out A FATE SO EVIL and studied it for a moment, but then said, "No. That's not an answer. At most, it's a half-assed threat."

"Threat? Who's threatening you? Or is it me being threatened?"

Rather than answer either question, Calida rearranged some of the letters to spell EAST EVIL OAF. "Off to a false start," she said. "*Evil* isn't the key word."

A quiet but growing urgency in Calida's manner. A puzzling continued intensification of the fragrance of roses until an odor of floral rot seemed to underlie their perfume . . . A quickening of the pulse-and-flitter of the many candle flames, so that the table swam with silverfish of light and phantom moths beat their soundless, insubstantial wings against the walls . . . Bibi began to feel that she was slowly — then more rapidly — succumbing to a fever not born of physical illness, a fever of unreason as dangerous as any infection.

On the table, FOIL A TEASE made no sense, and it left one letter unused.

VIA LEAST FOE was likewise without clear meaning.

Suddenly Bibi saw what the diviner did not, and reached out to spell TO SAVE A LIFE.

"That's it," Calida loudly declared, with no slightest note of uncertainty. "Kid, you're a natural for this, intuitive. The client never sees the message. They sit like toads, waiting for me to feed them flies."

Bibi said, "Let me get this straight. So I was spared from cancer to save my life. I sort of already knew that."

"No, girl, that's not what it says. You can read the words, but I can read the words *and* their intended meaning. You were spared from cancer so that you could save the life of *someone else.*"

Bibi didn't at once buy into that interpretation. Save from what, when, where, why? She wasn't an adventurer, not a superhero — she hated tights and capes — not a woman of action unless the action was on the written page.

"Who?" she asked. "Save who?"

"That's what we ask next."

Not quite ready to pose the question, the diviner picked up her glass and quickly swallowed the remaining wine.

Bibi realized now that the chardonnay was either to help Calida cope with the pain of the needle piercing her thumb or to boost her courage, or perhaps both.

Stirring her right hand in the silver bowl full of tiles, the diviner said, "I bleed for answers. I can't be —"

Before the woman could finish, Bibi's smartphone, lying on the table, issued a call tone that imitated the antique ring of a rotary-dial telephone. She glanced at the screen and said, "There's no caller ID. Ignore it."

Failure to take the call clearly alarmed Calida. "No! If you don't answer it, we won't know if it's *them.*"

"Them who?"

"The wrong people!" Her candle-glitter stare no longer seemed to be that of a diviner confident that she had her foot on the throat of whatever supernatural entity she had been

consulting. "Answer it, for God's sake."

Further disquieted, Bibi took the call. "Hello?"

A man said, "Top agent?"

"Huh? Who is this?"

"What does that mean — top agent?"

"I don't know what you're talking about."

"Why play dumb? It's the license plate on your car."

"Oh. Not my car. My mother's. Who is this?"

The caller hung up.

"Some guy," Bibi told Calida. "I drove Mom's car home. He wants to know what the vanity plate means."

Calida's worried frown folded some of the youth out of her face. "Doesn't sound like one of them."

"Whether it's one of them or not, he must have seen me when I drove home. Or he's in the parking lot right now. Everything's sort of sliding, isn't it?"

"Sliding? What do you mean?"

"Downhill, over the edge, into chaos," Bibi said, and wondered why her usual self-possession seemed to be failing her.

Well, she hadn't prepared herself for a world with these sudden new and strange dimensions. She had prepared herself to write stories for *The Antioch Review,* for *Granta,* for *Prairie Schooner,* to publish a first novel with Random House. She didn't possess the emotional and psychological flexibility to deal easily with sudden inexplicable cancer cures and the supernatural consequences that followed them.

Calida looked at her oddly. "Everything is always sliding. Life is an avalanche, kid, and you know that as well as I do. Sometimes a slow and more enjoyable kind of sliding, sometimes wild. I read your novel. It's in there — the avalanche. Get your skis on, girl, and ride the snow wave. Don't let it wipe you out."

"Yeah, well, right now I feel like a spleet."

"A what?"

"A goob, a wanker, a wilma." She picked up her half-full glass. She pulled a Calida and finished the chardonnay in one long swallow.

"To save a life," the diviner said, reading the tiles on the table. "Now let's find out whose."

37
EVERY MAMA'S BABIES
GOT TO PEE

The shriek of the caracal in the night had worried Pax because he thought it might be the work of a mimic. When two shrieks followed and seemed to originate in a far different place from the first, his concern increased. If he and his guys were known to be in town, maybe they were being stalked by agents of some local warlord, signaling readiness to one another in the language of caracals.

There were caracals in the Middle East, though their numbers were much lower than in Africa and Asia. Iranians had once trained those cats to hunt birds. Although caracals weighed as much as forty pounds, they could leap straight up as high as seven or eight feet, biting and battering down eight or ten birds at once from a low-flying flock.

Pax and Danny had stood ready, awaiting another cat cry to judge its authenticity, MK12s in hand, wishing the guns pumped out a more damaging caliber. Yet time had passed, and the dawn had come without incident. Sometimes a caracal was nothing more than a caracal.

As the first hours of light brought no wind, only a deepening quiet, Paxton hoped for some telltale to confirm that more than one of the terrorists resided in the shuttered house. At 8:47, his satellite phone vibrated.

Perry called from his position, with Gibb, on the roof of a two-story building east of the target house. He spoke in hardly more than a murmur. "One male. Not the smoker. Backyard. Two buckets."

"Say again — buckets?"

"Carrying buckets." After a pause, Perry said, "Back gate. Into the street. Moving south."

"Weapon?" Paxton asked.

"Drop-leg holster."

If the terrorist hadn't been armed, and if he had ventured far enough from the target house, they might have tried to capture him for interrogation. But one shot would alert the other bad guys — and, if intel was correct, bad girls.

"Probably night soil," Perry said.

He was a fan of historical fiction, especially novels of war and seafaring set in the eighteenth century. Occasionally he used antiquated words, not pretentiously, not even consciously, but because they had become part of his vocabulary.

"Clarify — night soil," Paxton said.

"Shit," Perry replied, which was pretty much what Pax thought he'd meant.

Like most small- to medium-size settlements in this blighted country, the town was in some respects medieval. No sewage system. No septic tanks. No indoor plumbing except, in a few cases, a hand pump in the kitchen sink, tapping a private well. There would be an open-air communal latrine just beyond the last buildings, basically ditches and a series of baffles, where people relieved themselves or to which they carried their products. It would be situated to ensure that the prevailing winds more often than not carried the stink away from the town, which meant in this case to the south and west.

Perhaps the personal-hygiene standards of Abdullah al-Ghazali forbade the dumping of their waste in a far corner of the backyard. More likely, they periodically disposed of it in the communal latrine because the stench it produced and the cloud of flies it drew would identify their hideout as surely as if they had raised over the house one of their black-and-red flags.

Into his phone, Pax said, "One bucket for men, one for women?"

"Honorable modesty," Perry agreed, and he terminated the call.

Short of knocking on Abdullah's door and pretending to be from the Census Bureau, they were not going to get any better confirmation that all seven terrorists were in the house. The buckets were superb intel.

In the deep shadows, just inside the doorway of the building that faced the terrorists' haven, Paxton and Danny began quietly to set up the Carl Gustav M4 recoilless rifle, an antitank weapon that was also effective as a bunker-buster.

38
GIVE DEATH A KISS

Bibi was wired. Not on chardonnay. Wired on the weirdness of it all. Cranked up by a feeling of impending violence. Like the air pressure before the first lightning flash of a storm so strong that it might spawn the mother of all tornadoes.

Apparently some weird guy lurked in the parking lot, obsessing over the meaning of the vanity plates on Nancy's sedan. And evidently a nameless presence stalked the kitchen, because the smell of rotting roses had become a stink, because the candle flames were undulating three or four inches above the lips of the cups that contained them, and because the room had suddenly grown chilly. The wall clock and her wrist-watch had stopped, their sweep hands no longer wiping away the seconds, and the digital clock on the microwave had gone dark, as if something that lived outside of time had stepped into this world and brought its clock-less ambience with it. Perhaps the psychic-wave detectors, a.k.a. "the wrong people" — whoever or whatever they might be — were already on their way to Bibi's apartment to beat her to death or suck her blood, or steal her soul, whatever the hell they did to those cretins who were foolish enough to think that a little divination session over the kitchen table would be harmless, gosh, perhaps even fun.

Twenty-four hours earlier, Bibi would not have taken any of this seriously, for she had been a highly efficient, driven autodidact who had taught herself at least two college degrees' worth of knowledge, a levelheaded realist who enjoyed fantasizing, yes, but who always knew *precisely* where the borderline was between the real world and false interpretations of it. She'd had a keen eye for the too-bright, too-fuzzy worlds of idealists and for the too-dark, too-complicated versions of reality concocted by paranoids. Now the borders seemed to have been erased or at least blurred, and for the first time in her life, she felt that among things a modern woman needed, a gun was no less essential than a smartphone.

"I need a gun," she declared, and though the words sounded alien to her nature, she knew that she spoke the truth.

Calida's pistol lay on the table, but she pulled it closer to her, beyond Bibi's reach, as if she didn't rule out the possibility that her client meant to shoot her, the messenger.

"I don't need yours. I have one," Bibi said. "Paxton insisted on it. But I keep it in a box in the closet."

When Bibi started to get up from her chair, Calida said sharply, "Sit down. We have to finish this, and quickly."

With her right hand, the diviner stirred the loose tiles in the silver bowl. "I bleed for answers. I cannot be denied. Attend me." The air grew chillier. To Bibi, she said, "The name of the person you're meant to save. How many letters?"

"I don't know."

"You *do* know. You just don't know you know. *How many letters?*"

Bibi guessed, "Ten."

After Calida plucked the tiles from the bowl, she placed them side by side in alphabetical order: A, B, E, E, H, L, L, L, S, Y.

Seeing names in that mess was harder than seeing words, but after a moment, the diviner spelled out SALLY BHEEL. "Know anyone with that name?"

"No."

"It isn't necessarily someone you know."

Calida rearranged the tiles into SHELLY ABLE.

"This is ridiculous," Bibi said, but she couldn't deny the room had gone so cold that her breath and the diviner's smoked from them.

206

As before, Bibi suddenly saw what Calida did not, moved the tiles around, and formed the name ASHLEY BELL. As she slid the last two letters into place, she heard the silver bell with the three tiny clappers that Captain had brought back from Vietnam, and although their ringing was clear and sweet and undeniable, she knew that she heard them only in memory.

As if Calida were a curious cat and Bibi were a ball of string in need of unraveling to reveal the wild secret at its center, the diviner watched her client intently, waiting for the best moment to snatch up a frayed end and run. "The name is familiar to you."

Bibi shook her head. "No."

"I can see it is."

"No. But I'll admit it resonates."

"Resonates," the diviner said, wanting something more specific.

"It's so euphonic, it makes you want to know the person who goes by it, to see if she's as pleasant as her name."

"She or he. It could be either."

"It's a she," Bibi said with immediate conviction.

"How can you be so sure?"

Bibi frowned. "I don't know. I just am."

"You not only have to find her. You have to save her."

As Bibi stared at the name, it had half drawn her into a trance, as though each of the ten letters must be a syllable in a sorcer-er's spell. Now she shivered and looked up at the diviner and said, "Save her from what? Should you ask — and draw more letters?"

"No. We're running out of time. We've been too long at this."

Bibi realized that warmth had returned to the kitchen and that the clocks were working once more, as was her wristwatch. "I need to know why she's in trouble — or will be. Where she lives. What she looks like. I have a thousand questions."

A mewl as thin as a paper cut escaped Calida as she extracted the needle from her flesh. She pressed her bleeding thumb against the bloodstained cotton cloth. "We only get so many answers for free. And then they begin to cost us dearly, word by word. Now peel off a few three-inch strips of that adhe-sive tape for me."

Producing the first strip with the dispenser's built-in cutter, Bibi said, "Cost us what?"

Hurriedly winding the gauze around and around her thumb, keeping it tight to stanch the bleeding, Calida said, "Time. Our allot-ted time. Days, then weeks, then months, our lives melting away fast from the farther end — and then we pay with something worse."

"What could be worse than losing part of your life?"

"Losing the capacity for passion and hope, being left alive but with no emotions other than bitterness and despair." She held out her thumb so that Bibi could apply the length of tape. "No additional answers we might get would be worth the cost."

The roses in the living room smelled sweet again. The flames had stopped leaping violently above the rims of the clear-glass cups. The fluttering reflections of candlelight on the tabletop and the walls no longer reminded her of swarming insects.

The air of impending violence should have diminished.

It had not.

While the diviner hastily used three more strips of tape to encase the gauze, Bibi came further to her senses, much as the once-cold room had returned to warmth. "I can't do this."

Glancing at the clock, displeased by the time, Calida said, "Can't do what?"

"Save a life. Whoever she is. Wherever she is. It's crazy on the face of it."

"Of course you can do it, the kind of girl you are. Besides, you have no choice now."

"I might end up doing more harm than good. I'm planning to marry a hero, but I'm not one myself. I mean, I don't think I'm a coward, but I don't have the *skills.*"

Pouring the Scrabble tiles from the bowl into the flannel sack, returning the sack and the bowl to the ostrich-skin suitcase, Calida said, "You asked why you were spared from cancer. You were told. If you're not prepared to do it now, there's a terrible price to pay."

"More harm than good," Bibi repeated. "It could end up with this Bell woman dead — and me, too."

Getting to her feet, closing the suitcase, Calida said, "You've already been on a date with Death and survived. If he shows up again, kiss him and tell him he has to wait. Make it a good kiss. Put some tongue in it. Now grab your gun, girlfriend, and let's get the hell out of here."

"What? No." Bibi yawned and stretched. "I'm exhausted. I'm going to bed."

Calida regarded her as if she had just announced that she would lie down in a cauldron of boiling oil. "If you stay here ten more minutes, you're dead. Maybe five."

"But this is my apartment."

"Not anymore. Not after what we just did here, which drew their attention. Now the apartment is *theirs.* And no lock will keep them out."

39
LOVE CALL AND WAR CRY

Assuming that Abdullah al-Ghazali and his associates were heavily armed and ready to die a martyr's death, it would be suicide to blow down the door and fight the seven of them room by room. And seven would be the number, because the women would not be bystanders. If intel had their identities right, these two mothers — mothers in more than one sense of the word — had with enthusiasm provided four of their young children for service as human bombs. This spec op was the science-fiction-movie equivalent of a bug hunt, for which the sole hope of success would be the ruthless application of maximum force.

The Carl Gustav M4 recoilless rifle weighed fifteen pounds, four less than the M3, and had an overall length of thirty-seven inches. The ammunition was heavy, but considering the nature of all possible targets in the ghost town, none of which could be defined as a true bunker, merely aboveground buildings often of dubious construction, they had chosen to bring only four rounds. To compensate for this extra weight, which would complicate an overland trek, they carried less ammo for their rifles and pared their gear down where possible.

Two men were required to operate the weapon, one to fire it and the other to load. Paxton would fire, and Danny would load; and they agreed to launch not from the doorway of the abandoned house but from a long-ago-shattered front window. Some guys called the Carl Gustav the Carl Johnson, a surname used as slang for the male sex organ, and others called it the Goose, but whatever its name, the launcher was more effective than Thor's hammer, with a range of more than 1,300 meters. Abdullah's current residence stood little more than twenty feet away; a blowback of debris would be significant. Firing over the windowsill from a kneeling position, they could duck their heads after launch and hope that most of the trash flung in their direction would rattle harmlessly off the walls that surrounded the window opening.

After they both put on double ear protection, Danny arranged the four rounds on the floor, under the window. Kneeling, Pax shouldered the Gustav. Danny opened the Venturi lock, a handle that moved the hinged breech to one side for loading, and inserted the first round.

The roof of the two-story building across the street from the rear of Abdullah's rathole provided a high mud-brick parapet with cutouts fitted with widely spaced iron bars, an ideal setup for a sniper. Perry and Gibb lay at different crenellations, watching the back of the house and the street.

In the quiet of the morning, the empty buckets, swinging from their handles, squeaked as the murderer returned from the community latrine. He let himself through the rear gate and crossed the yard, a rectangle of cracked and littered concrete. Someone had been watching for him. The door opened. He went inside.

Perry called the one number programmed into his satellite phone, and when the connection was made, he said, "Everyone's safe at home."

Given the short range to target, Pax didn't need either the 3× optical sight or the fitted-iron sights. The impact explosion at once rocked the morning, while blowback junk rattled-pocked-pinged against the front wall of their house and whistled through the window over their heads simultaneously, or so it seemed, with the blast. There were the smells of concrete dust and hot gases from the Gustav, and Danny sneezed as he opened the Venturi lock to load the second round.

A Carl Gustav round could slam through steel-reinforced concrete as if through cheese, and the overpressure from the explosion tended to screw up most of a building's interior. From their roof position across the street, Perry and Gibb were not able to see what happened to the front of the house, but the entire structure quaked and swayed and deformed, and two exterior shutters on the back windows blew off, clanging across the concrete yard, as spikes of window glass bounced and splintered on the pavement.

At most twenty seconds after the building was slammed, the back door flew open, and two men staggered out, disoriented and no doubt half deaf. The night-soil manager drew the pistol from his drop-leg holster, and the new guy carried a fully automatic carbine with an extended magazine, maybe an Uzi. Gibb needed one shot to take out the would-be Scarface, a second to ensure the kill, and Perry dropped the other terrorist, sparing him from further latrine duty.

Following the second round from the Gustav, the house resembled a set from a Transformers movie after a robot had stomped through it. Pax was prepared to use the remaining two rounds, and Danny loaded one. But the building swayed as though constructed of pudding and crashed in upon itself, clouds of dust billowing into the street.

They tore off their ear protection, snatched up the MK12s, ventured outside as the air slowly cleared. Approaching the target house, they were cautious, though the chance of anyone within having survived seemed nil. Perry and Gibb came in from the street to the east, which was when Pax learned that two had been sniped, leaving five under the rubble.

Time now to call in the carrier-based helo to extract the team, though the task remaining would not be easy. The point was to prove you could not kill 317 Americans and live long enough to brag about it to your grandchildren. They needed to find al-Ghazali, photograph his face or what remained of it, and take a tissue sample for DNA. Otherwise, some anonymous Internet-savvy bonehead would fake proof that he was al-Ghazali, and 31 percent of Americans would believe him.

Pax started to call for the helo when Bibi's face bloomed so vividly in his mind's eye that the ruins of the ghost town ceased to exist for a moment. If previously he'd suspected she was in trouble, he knew it now. This was battleground intuition on steroids — and more than intuition. He had to wrap the op, ditch this cesspool country, and call Bibi as soon as the blackout rule no longer applied, when they were at sea, aboard the aircraft carrier.

40
DOWNHILL, OVER THE EDGE, INTO CHAOS

Calida Butterfly was a whirlpool, a vortex of dark energy that could not be resisted, so that Bibi was caught up in the woman's fear, felt it swirling through her. So convincing was the diviner's anxiety, so distraught the series of expressions that tortured her face, it proved impossible quite to believe that she could be a fraud with criminal intent. And there had been too many bizarre occurrences to dismiss her as a delusional paranoid. Something extraordinary was happening, about to happen, approaching fast, and the prudent course seemed to be to get out of its way before it arrived.

In the bedroom closet, as Bibi opened the shoebox and retrieved the holster with the Sig Sauer P226, Calida said, "I'll leave my massage table. It'll slow me down. I'll get it later, next week, whenever. Can you *hurry*, kid? Come on, *come on!*"

Bibi shrugged into the shoulder rig, adjusted it, pulled a blazer off a hanger, and slipped into it. The pistol already held a full magazine. She glanced at herself in the closet-door mirror. The gun didn't show under the coat. Her reflection did not quite resemble the one to which she was accustomed: hair kind of wild, windblown on a night without wind; strangeness swimming in the dark pools of her eyes; hard edges in her face that she hadn't seen before. She thought she looked like a desperado. Or a perfect idiot.

In the living room, as Calida snatched up her suitcase, Bibi grabbed her purse and laptop. "Damn it, why did Mom and Dad sic you on me?"

"Not their fault. They couldn't know. Nothing like this ever happened when I did them."

"Nothing like what?"

"The disgusting rotten smell, the cold from nowhere, the weird candle crap, the clocks. The wrong people coming."

Following the woman to the front door, Bibi said, "I figured stuff like that *always* happened."

"Never happened to me before."

"Never?" Bibi pulled shut the door. She fumbled with the key to engage the deadbolt. "But you're the diviner, the big kahuna."

Hastening along the balcony toward the stairs, Calida said, "It happened to my mother sometimes. She warned me about it, but maybe I didn't take her seriously enough."

"Wait up." Bibi hurried after the blonde. "Didn't take her seriously? Really? I mean, *really*? Your mother, who was tortured and dismembered?"

"No need for the snarky tone, kid. Sometimes you can be pretty damn insensitive."

The long-legged Scrabblemancer bounded down the stairs two at a time, her footfalls hammering reverberant groans from the ironwork. In vanilla-white slacks and top, flamboyant sash and scarf, multiple hoop earrings, and a glittering trove of finger rings, she might have been a glamorous fugitive from a 1950s movie comedy about a Las Vegas showgirl on the run from the Mob.

Nimble and agile, Bibi plummeted after her, risking a bad fall, but proving, if there had been any doubt, the symptoms of gliomatosis cerebri were gone without a trace. "Hey, you know, sometimes you can be damn frustrating."

"Better than snarky."

"I wasn't snarky."

"Ear of the beholder," Calida said as she came off the last flight of stairs and made her way between the row of sun loungers and the glimmering pool, where the trout-swift young man had earlier been swimming laps.

Sprinting to close the gap between them, Bibi reached with her left hand and snared the expensive-looking gold-star-on-blue-field silk scarf that trailed behind Calida, hoping to use it to ransom a few answers from the panicked diviner. The exquisite scarf was not merely wrapped around the woman's throat, however, but was instead loosely knotted, which called before the court the laws of physics, in particular those that dealt with motion, action, and reaction. With a choking sound, Calida Butterfly abruptly ceased forward motion and dropped her ostrich-skin suitcase to clutch at the strangling silk, simultaneously staggering backward two steps and colliding with Bibi, whose forward speed was at that instant decisively checked. For a moment they wheeled around each other like the gimbal mountings of a gyroscope, but though one of the functions of a gyroscope was to maintain equilibrium, they were not able to maintain theirs. They teetered together on the pool coping, a mere degree of tilt away from a wet plunge. When Bibi thought to let go of the scarf, the forces of Nature, which had been cunningly engineered to make amusing fools of human beings in most circumstances, at once rebalanced themselves, thereby casting both women off balance. Calida fell to her knees on the pavement, while Bibi tottered backward and dropped hard into a sitting position on one of the sun loungers.

The Amazon diviner had progressed from fear and anger to terror and rage. She acted on the latter as she thrust to her feet, cursing

Bibi and the Thorpe children that she hadn't yet produced. "Get away from me, stay away from me, you insane crazy bitch."

As Calida turned toward her dropped suitcase, Bibi said, "Crazy bitch? Me? *Me? Meeeee?* I was just having the best day of my life, that's all, *free of cancer,* then you show up and . . ."

But she abandoned that line of response. She loathed the whine in her voice, did not want to paint herself as a victim. Valiant girls did not whine. They never played the victim even if there were benefits to be had from inhabiting that role, which there were, huge benefits, which was why everyone wanted to be a victim these days.

Half of Calida's custom-crafted two-sided suitcase had fallen open when she dropped it, spilling the silver bowl and some of the other items that she used for divination. She stooped to repack with urgency.

Bibi rose from the lounge chair. "Look, maybe I am crazy, running from my apartment because you say someone's coming — someone or something — I don't even know who or what or why, crazy for buying in to this Ashley Bell thing, but here I am. So tell me how to find her. Tell me who these *wrong people* are."

Turning to face her, suitcase in hand, Calida said bleakly, "Oh, you'll know them."

Because the apartment complex catered to young professionals, most of them single, thought had been given even to the lighting in the courtyard. In the service of romance, or whatever the hippest of the cool called it these days, the tall bronze lamps and every fixture used in the landscape lighting produced a calculated radiance — a candescence, resplendence — that flattered every face, that buttered an appealing sheen of health on the skin of every limb and curve that might be revealed.

In this well-schemed, computed, designed light, Calida remained as pale as bleached flour. Oppressed by fear, she had a face that appeared sliced-bread flat, incapable of offering any expression other than dread. "You'll know them when you see them."

"What're we going to do?" Bibi asked.

"*We* aren't doing anything. I don't want to be anywhere near you. Not now. Not ever. What *I'm* going to do is run. Run and hide."

With that, she turned away and hurried toward the parking lot, all of her bejeweled and silk-scarfed glamor gone, now just one more desperate woman overwhelmed by the madness of the world.

41

SIX YEARS EARLIER
THE WARRIOR OLAF AND HIS VALKYRIE

For six happy years, the foundling Olaf had been an exemplary companion: as pure of heart, as noble, as joyful, as loving as any dog who had ever lived. He had walked out of the rain to become his beloved girl's best friend, and he had kept faithfully at her side through every mood and circumstance, taking to the sea and surfboard as enthusiastically as she did.

When he first showed symptoms, the cancer had already spread from his spleen to his liver and heart. Dr. John Kerman called it "hemangiosarcoma." Although Bibi was a lover of language, that was a word she would hate for the rest of her life, as if it were not merely a word, but also one of the names of Evil. Neither chemo nor radiation would extend the dog's life. The veterinarian estimated that Olaf had a week — at most two weeks — to live.

Bibi gave her cherished friend all the affection that could be squeezed into so little time, fed him all of his favorite treats and some that he'd never tasted before. She took him on easy walks, not where she determined, but where he seemed to want to go. They sat on the bench at Inspiration Point for hours, watching the sea in all its serenity and all its tossing glory, while she shared with the golden retriever every confidence, as always she had.

Her mother and father were not surprised by Bibi's devotion, but they did not expect that her commitment to Olaf's comfort in his last days would extend to participation in the act of euthanasia. The moment might arrive when the cancer, thus far largely painless, would begin to work its agony in the flesh. With human beings, a natural death was a death with dignity. But animals were innocents, and as their stewards, people owed them mercy. Bibi decided not only that Olaf must not suffer, but also that he must not be in the least afraid when the moment came to put him down. The dog liked his vet, but he didn't like needles and became anxious at the sight of them. Only his trusted mistress, so precious to him, might inject him without causing him so much as a moment of fear.

Dr. John Kerman was a good man, extending every kindness and courtesy to people and animals alike, but he did not at first think it wise to grant young Bibi's request to administer the mortal drugs herself. Although mature for her age, she was nevertheless only sixteen. Soon, however, she convinced him that she was up to the task both emotionally and intellectually. During that week, each time he had a dog to be anesthetized for teeth cleaning or other procedures, Dr. Kerman welcomed the girl into his surgery to observe how a catheter was placed in a leg vein. She also attended two emergency euthanasia sessions, observing solemnly — and wept only later, at home. Using green grapes and hypodermic syringes, she practiced the carefully angled insertion of a needle.

On the morning of the tenth day after they had been given Olaf's prognosis, the dog came to a crisis, suffering a sudden weakness in his legs. His breathing became labored, and he began whimpering in distress. John Kerman arrived at the bungalow with his medical kit, confirmed that the moment had come, and on the nightstand in Bibi's bedroom, he placed the instruments that she would need.

Murph carried Olaf to the bed, and for a few minutes, they left the girl alone with the retriever, that she might look into his eyes and whisper endearments to him and promise him that they would meet again one day in a world without death.

When Bibi was ready, the vet returned to stand to one side and watch, prepared to intervene if the girl lost her courage or if she appeared to be about to make a mistake of procedure. Nancy and Murph got onto the bed with Olaf, to hold and stroke and reassure him.

The dog exhibited none of his usual fear at the sight of the needles, but watched his mistress's hands with interest. They were delicate but strong and steady hands. Once the catheter had been placed in the femoral artery of the left rear leg and taped in place, Bibi inserted the needle in an ampule of sedative and expertly drew the required dose. Through the catheter port, she slowly administered the injection. Dr. Kerman's preferred two-step technique was not to put the dog down in a sudden hard fall, but first to bring on sleep in a gentle fashion. As the barbiturate flowed from the barrel of the syringe into the vein, Bibi looked into Olaf's eyes and watched as they clouded with weariness and fluttered shut to enjoy his last rest. When the dog was deeply asleep and certain not to feel even the barest moment of panic when his cardiac muscles stuttered, Bibi used the second needle to inject the drug that stopped his noble heart.

On the drive to the pet cemetery with her mom and dad, Bibi sat in the backseat, holding the blanket-wrapped body of Olaf in her lap.

The Power-Pak II Cremation System was housed in a garagelike building behind the pet-cemetery offices. Usually, if the family wished to wait during the cremation, they did so in the visitors' lounge in the front building. After watching Olaf's body be placed alone in the cremator — Bibi insisted his ashes must not be mingled with those of other animals — Nancy and Murph preferred to wait in the lounge, where there were magazines, a television, and coffee. Bibi remained in the back building, perched on a chair in one corner, watching the hulking cremator, sitting witness to her companion's voyage through fire. More than two hours later, when the ashes were presented to her in a small urn, the bronze was warm in her cupped hands.

The Vikings believed that fallen warriors were conveyed to Valhalla by beautiful maidens known as Valkyries. On the bench at Inspiration Point, on beach walks, and elsewhere, Bibi sometimes had explained to Olaf that the world was a battleground, that in a sense, every man and woman was a warrior, which was part of Captain's philosophy that he shared with her in the years before Olaf had come along. Everyone struggled; everyone fought the good fight — or raised arms against those who fought it. "You're a warrior, too," she said, and the retriever always looked at her as though with understanding. "Dogs try to do what's right. Most of them, anyway. And dogs suffer. They're tormented and starved and abused by people unworthy of them. Who knows what you endured before you found me? My furry warrior."

That afternoon, leaving the crematorium, she was Olaf's Valkyrie, although she could not take him to Valhalla, only home to the bungalow and to her bedroom, where she holed up for three awful days, felled by grief, unable to talk to anyone, not even to her mom and dad.

In the meeting with Nancy and Murph, when he had delivered the news of Bibi's brain cancer, Dr. Sanjay Chandra had wanted to know what kind of girl Bibi was, her psychology and personality, so that he could determine how best to share with her the diagnosis.

Murph had said, *Bibi is an exceptional girl. She's smart. . . . She'll know if you're putting even the slightest shine on the truth. . . . She'll want to hear it blunt and plain. . . . She's tougher than she looks.*

When those words had not adequately conveyed the kind of girl she was, Olaf's euthanasia was the story that Murph had then shared with the physician.

42

THE BOOK OF LEAPING PANTHER AND GAZELLE

Bibi watched Calida Butterfly fleeing the courtyard until the woman disappeared into the parking lot and the night.

Amped on adrenaline, apprehension, and the mystery of all things, Bibi glanced at her wristwatch — 10:04. Looking up at the third-floor balcony, she thought of her bed. Under the currents of energizing fright and amazement that kept her mind spinning, she felt a deep weariness that, given a chance, would surge up and overwhelm. The unfinished wine in the bottle of chardonnay might be just the key to open the door to dreamland. Would she really be at risk in that cozy haven where she had for years locked out the world and all its temptations, all its frustrations, to create worlds of her own? Calida said yes, said run, said hide. But the name Calida wasn't a synonym for *truth.* When Bibi had left the apartment, the roses had been as beautiful and fragrant as when she'd first come home, not rotting as she thought they were while she'd been mesmerized by Calida at the kitchen table. Here in the fresh air and normalcy of the California night, she could half convince herself that nothing of the recent events had been as strange as it had seemed at the time.

Half convinced was not convinced enough. Heart still beating too fast, too hard, she picked up the purse that she'd dropped when she collided with the diviner, slung it over her left shoulder. Carrying her laptop in her right hand, she started toward the parking lot.

An object lying in a fan of trembling palm-frond shadows and lamplight caught her attention. She scooped up a small hardcover book that must have fallen out of Calida's suitcase with the other divination gear. Bound in high-quality tan cloth, the volume featured two inlaid, stylized Art Deco figures crafted of intricately stained and engraved leather; they were depicted back to back, in profile — a panther leaping toward the spine, a gazelle leaping toward the right. There was neither a title nor an author's name.

From nearby came the deep, hoarse, trumpeting cry of a great blue heron, startling Bibi. She surveyed the sky, certain she had heard the bird's flight call low overhead. Except for a distant police helicopter thumping through the cool night, nothing plied the heavens. A bird the size of the heron — four feet tall with a six-foot wingspan — could not be overlooked in motion. When the cry came again, louder and more protracted than before, it seemed to be not a common expression out of nature, but from out of time, a mystical alarm meant to shake her awake from her indecision. Hoping to be gone before the wrong people showed up, she ran out of the courtyard and into the parking lot.

43

THREE DAYS IN A LOCKED ROOM

The story that Murphy had told Dr. Sanjay Chandra ended with the cremation of Olaf and with Bibi's retreat into her bedroom, where she remained for three days alone with the urn that contained the dog's ashes. This seemed to be the natural end point of the tale, but there was another scene known only to the girl. Perhaps it did not qualify as a fully developed scene, only as a coda; no one but Bibi could know the extent and complexity of it.

In any other family, a sixteen-year-old girl would not have been able to sequester herself in her locked bedroom for three full days, feeding on a supply of apples, cheese-and-peanut-butter crackers, and dry-roasted almonds. When her parents were asleep, she ventured out to snatch sodas and bottled water from the refrigerator. She refused to respond to questions addressed to her through the door, though after the first few hours, her parents granted her the consideration of silence.

Her mother and father had always loved her deeply and without reservation, had always wanted the best for her, but their love had not been twined with expectations. They had not given her guidance regarding anything more than the rules of the household. Never had they suggested that any endeavor or aspiration was better than anything else she might be doing or wish to achieve. Their politics, to the extent that they had any, were libertarian, and their love for their daughter grew in a libertarian garden. If their attitudes in this matter had been different, the family might have been a place of unceasing argument and tension, for even by the time that Bibi was six or seven, she had ideas about some subjects that were different from her parents' positions on those issues.

Often in her childhood, relatives and others had commented on her quiet nature and reserve (by which they intended to imply that she seemed shy or, worse than shy, aloof), had observed that she was unusually assured and self-reliant for her age (by which they meant that she struck them as being peculiar and suspicious), had noted always with well-meant concern that she took everything perhaps too seriously, that she engaged in every activity — whether reading books or surfing, or competitive skateboarding, or learning to play the clarinet — with a disturbing intensity (by which they wished to warn that she had the potential for obsessive-compulsive disorder), and had remarked in a tone of praise characterized by uneasiness that she might be some kind of genius or prodigy, or at least gifted (by which they avoided saying that they found her a bit weird). Nancy and Murphy understood that, in one sense at least, an alien lived with them, an otherworldly but benign creature who loved them but did not understand key things about them, such as the it'll-be-what-it'll-be doctrine that stood central to their creed; and they were cool with their daughter's difference.

Therefore, with the urn containing Olaf's ashes always near at hand, Bibi spent three days in solitude, though she was never lonely and certainly not bored. At her small corner desk, in her armchair, and often sitting up in bed, she wept with grief and wrote for hours at a stretch. Sometimes she made entries in her spiral-bound diary, at other times composed fiction in a large lined yellow tablet, her meticulous cursive script never faltering, regardless of the length of those sessions.

Frequently in the past, she had written while in a condition of infatuation — with ideas, with language, with storytelling — when, for an hour or two at a time, she had neither the desire nor the will to look up from the page. Alone with Olaf's ashes, this infatuation was shot through with desperation, energized despair, as never before. Her primary motivation during those three days was to argue herself out of some bad ideas, one in particular, compared to which mere suicide would have been preferable.

She exhausted herself with writing, so that it seemed when she crashed, she should have had no imagination left to craft stories in her sleep. But her dreams swelled with wild adventure, threat, and mystery. She dreamed repeatedly — but not exclusively — of the tall and monkish figures in a variety of settings and scenarios. When those menacing phantasms turned toward her, she erupted from the nightmare every time, certain that she would have died in her sleep if she had glimpsed more than the pale moonlit suggestion of their horrific faces.

On the third day, she remembered a trick of forgetting that the captain taught her. In more than one war, Captain had seen things — the bloody aftermath of human viciousness, outrages from the darkest end of the spectrum of cruelty — that disturbed his sleep night after night, that left him despondent. He could not bear to live with the memories. The trick of forgetting had been revealed to him by a Gypsy or a Vietnamese shaman, or by an Iraqi version of a voodooist. The captain could not remember the identity of his benefactor, no doubt because for some good reason he had used the magic procedure to forget that person, too. Anyway, what you needed to do first was write the hated memory or the reckless desire or the evil intention on a slip of paper; the trick worked for more than the disposal of garbage memories. Then you said six words that had great power, said them with sincerity, with all your heart. After you had spoken that incantation, you put the slip of paper in an ashtray or a bowl, and you set it afire. Or you scissored the paper into tiny pieces and flushed them down a toilet. Or buried them in a graveyard. If you recited those magic words with humility, and if you were entirely truthful with yourself when you claimed to want forgetfulness, you would receive it.

Bibi forgot. Not forever, as it turned out, but for years, she forgot the bad idea that she had written on the slip of paper, the thing she had wanted to do — had almost done — that would have ruined her life. Her sharp grief remained, but her fear was lifted from her with the memory. She slept without dreams that night and on the following day returned to family life.

That was the third time that she had used the captain's method of forgetting. She as yet had no memory of the first and second.

44
ADJUSTING TO PARANOIA

In the lot behind the apartments, the parked vehicles and the thick posts supporting the roofs of the open-air carports provided cover for anyone who might have bad intentions. At the very least, Bibi expected the guy who brooded over the meaning of vanity license plates.

She walked directly to her Ford Explorer, which was parked beside Nancy's BMW. Step by step, she surveyed the night for a suspicious malingerer, ready to drop the laptop and draw the pistol from her shoulder rig to warn him off. She reached her SUV without being assaulted and, in the driver's seat, at once locked the doors.

She felt foolish for wondering if the Explorer would explode when she switched on the engine, and of course it did not. Whatever real-life drama she had been thrown into, it thus far had been free of mafia-movie clichés.

Just as she pulled out of the lot and turned left, headlights flared behind her, glaring off her rearview mirror. A sedan followed her into the street. When she turned right at the first intersection, so did the other vehicle. After two more turns, she had no doubt that she was being tailed.

Might this be one of them — *one of the mysterious Wrong People?* she wondered, capitalizing the term for the first time. No. Common sense argued that adversaries with paranormal abilities, which the Wrong People evidently possessed, wouldn't need to resort to standard private-investigator techniques, shadowing her the same way that a PI would conduct surveillance of a wife suspected of adultery.

There was only one means by which to identify the follower in the sedan, but Bibi hesitated to plunge into a confrontation. She was grateful to Paxton for encouraging her to get a firearm and teaching her how to use it, but the difficult truth was that acquiring a gun, with expert knowledge of its function, was not adequate preparation for pointing it at another person and squeezing the trigger. For five minutes she drove a random route, brooding about options. The tail fell back and moved closer and fell back again, even allowing another car to come between them and provide him with cover, but he didn't fade away as she hoped he might.

At last she became sufficiently agitated to force the issue. She drove to Pacific Coast

Highway, to an area that boasted a wealth of trendy restaurants and nightspots, ensuring a flood of traffic and enough witnesses to make her feel safe. She timed her approach to an intersection and stopped first in line as the controlling light turned red. The stalker-on-wheels was two vehicles behind her, mostly blocked from view by a Cadillac Escalade. She put the Explorer in park, set the brake, and got out.

As she strode past the Escalade, which sparkled with a surfeit of aftermarket gew-gaws, the man behind the wheel flashed her a scowl and a what-the-hell gesture, powering down his window to say gratuitously, "You don't own the road, bitch." In a mood, she drew one finger across her throat, as if threatening to slash his, and left him to worry that he had insulted a violent lunatic.

The stalker slouched in a black Lexus. Even through a windshield half cataracted by reflections from a streetlamp, the identity of the driver was as apparent as it was surprising: Chubb Coy. The head of hospital security. Who had all but accused Bibi of lying about the middle-of-the-night visit by the man with the therapy dog. Chubb Coy sat like a humorless Mr. Toad behind the wheel of the Lexus, his old cop intuition no doubt itching like poison ivy.

The moment he saw Bibi coming, Coy wheeled the Lexus to his left, nearly clipping her with the front bumper, and crossed the double yellow lines into the southbound lanes. To a chorus of car horns and shrieking brakes, he completed a 180-degree turn and accelerated into the night.

45

No Haven from Her Enemies

Bibi Blair trembled violently when she got behind the wheel of the Explorer and pulled shut the driver's door. The cause of her shakes was not primarily fear, although fear was part of it. Anger, yes, all right. Coy's offensive invasion of her privacy angered her, but she was smoldering, not hot. The principal cause of her distress was indignation, shock and displeasure at the intrusion of massive unreason into the workings of the world, resentment at the sudden tangle of narrative lines in her life, which she had spent so many years crafting into a tight and comfortable linear story. The whole Calida business made no sense: opening a door to Somewhere Else, to a cold and smelly rotten-flower elsewhere in which dwelt hostile and inhuman powers. The hoodie-wearing Good Samaritan and therapy dog who were visible to some cameras but not to others. Now Chubb Coy and his itchy intuition. Trailing her through the night. Far beyond the limits of his authority, which extended only as far as the hospital grounds. In retrospect, she was pretty sure it had been Coy's voice on the phone, asking about TOP AGENT. He had come into her life before Calida Butterfly, before the divination session that supposedly had invited the supernatural upon her, before Bibi had even heard about the Wrong People, and yet common sense insisted that each weirdness was linked to the others.

The driver of the Escalade behind her pressed hard on his horn the instant the light changed, having gotten in touch once more with his essential rudeness, now that Bibi turned out not to be a violent psychopath.

A few minutes later, on a residential street lined with massive old sycamores gone leaf-less at winter's end, she parked at the curb to think. She turned off the headlights but not the engine, because she felt safer if she remained able to rocket away from the curb at an instant's notice.

Think. Since everything had gone screwy in her apartment, she had been reacting with animal emotion to events, instead of with her usual calm and consideration. She had been playing by *their* rules, the Silly-Putty rules of crazy people. Now she realized that by doing so, she had contributed to the momentum of the insanity. *Think.* The unreal and flat-out seemingly impossible things that had hap-pened would have logical explanations if she thought about them enough, and the threats that seemed to be rising all around her would then either diminish or even evaporate altogether. *Think.*

Her phone rang. The caller ID indicated that Bibi was phoning herself. So they were mocking her. Clever bastards. Whatever else the Wrong People might be, they were apparently techno wizards.

She answered with minimal commitment. "Yeah?"

A man with a silken, subtly seductive voice said, "Hello, Bibi. Have you found Ashley Bell yet?"

She told herself that by participating in a conversation, she would be playing by their rules, but if she terminated the call, she stood no chance of learning anything useful. She said, "Who is this?"

"My surname at birth was Faulkner."

From that peculiar reply, Bibi inferred that obfuscation and evasion would define his style, but she played along. "Any relation to the writer?"

"I'm delighted to say no. I hate most books and bookish people, so I changed my name. I am now — and have been for a long time — known as Birkenau Terezin." He spelled it for her. "Friends call me Birk."

She doubted that such a name appeared in any Orange County phone book, on the voter rolls, or in the property-tax records. "What can I do for you, Mr. Terezin?"

"I'm standing now in your apartment."

She did not take the bait.

"If I may say so," Terezin continued, "you have taste, but lack the means to afford fine things. The result is an earnest but tacky attempt at interior design. Your parents have resources. Why didn't you reach into their pockets?"

"Their money is theirs. I'll make my own."

"Maybe you will, maybe you won't. We have found the two hundred forty-eight pages of the novel you're currently writing, which we're taking, along with your computer. We will destroy both."

Bibi glanced at the laptop lying on the passenger seat. The 248 pages were duplicated in its memory.

"We'll also get the laptop," Terezin said.

Bibi wouldn't give him the satisfaction of reacting to that lame attempt to make her think he could read her mind.

"And if you should copy the pages onto a flash drive, we'll get that as well. And smash it."

On the sidewalk, a man approached through pools of lamplight and lakes of sycamore darkness. He was walking a German shepherd.

To her caller, Bibi said, "What do you want from me?"

"Only to kill you."

Man and dog passed the Explorer. She watched them recede in the passenger-side mirror.

Terezin continued, "I'd rather it wasn't something as common as a bullet to the head. Too banal for a writer whose short stories have appeared in such esteemed magazines. Death by a thousand stab wounds would be nice, especially if we used a thousand sharpened pencils and left you bristling like a porcupine."

The response that occurred to her was straight out of a low-rent TV drama, so she remained mute.

"We believe in justice, Bibi. Don't you think all living things deserve justice?"

"You do," she said.

"Cancer cells are alive, Bibi. Did you ever stop to think about that? They are so enthusiastic about life, they grow far faster than normal cells. A tumor is a living thing. It deserves justice."

"I haven't done anything to you," she said, being careful not to whine and thereby suggest weakness.

"You *offended* me. You deeply offended *us* when you allowed your ignorant masseuse to demand answers. Why was Bibi Blair spared from cancer? The answer is simple, as simple as this — so that she could die another way."

Bibi had no hope that conversing reasonably with a homicidal fanatic would convert him to clear thinking, and there was a chance that she would stoke the fires of his madness and make him more dangerous than he already was.

Neither could she survive by hanging up on him and pretending that he didn't exist. She went to the quick of it and said, "Who is Ashley Bell?"

The worm of condescension, turning in his voice, was almost as loud as his words. "You aren't taking this pathetic quest seriously, are you?"

"Why do you care if I am or I'm not?"

Rather than answer her, Terezin said, "To us, you're just a worm, a pissant, something we step on without noticing. You don't have a hope of finding her. We'll find you first and put an end to this. Did you know, lovely Bibi, that every smartphone is also a GPS? Everywhere you go, the traitorous phone reports your whereabouts in real time."

She knew this, of course, but never imagined that she might be quarry.

"Anyone who has the right connections with the police or with certain tech companies can find you at any moment of any day. And anyone with the ability to hack their systems can find you, too, my lovely pissant."

The phone felt *alive* in her hand.

"And your three-year-old Ford Explorer," Terezin said, "bought without your parents' money, a proud statement of your independence — of course it has a GPS. You can be followed by satellite anywhere you go. And by the way, if you go to Mom and Dad for help, we'll kill them, too."

She switched off the phone and dropped it on the floor, but she knew that wasn't good enough. Its perpetual signal would still locate her. Although she killed the engine of the SUV, that wouldn't be good enough, either.

She zippered open her purse, crammed into it the slim book with panther and gazelle, zippered it shut, and grabbed her laptop and, with it, the sole remaining 248 pages of her unfinished novel. She threw open the door and got out of the Explorer.

By abandoning the phone and the Ford, she would be conceding a possibility to the impossible. If she believed that the Wrong People could find her by such traditional means as high technology, it seemed she also had to accept that, when Calida held a divination session, these same people were alerted to the practice by the psychic equivalent of seismic waves that they could follow back to the source.

Headlights appeared three blocks to the west, ice-white and flaring strangely through the sentinel sycamores, as if this were the witchy light emanating from an extraterrestrial craft, stretching the bare-limb shadows until they broke. When Bibi pivoted at the sound of an engine, she encountered more headlights two blocks to the east, as an immense SUV rounded the corner with the menace of a vehicle packed full of CIA assassins. The moment seemed too genre-movie to be taken seriously, but many of the least credible movie villains of the past few decades had in recent years manifested in the real world, as over-the-top as any sociopath portrayed by any scenery-chewing actor. To run west or east might be to flee into the jaws of a pincer, and to go north would require dashing across the street in full view.

Left with no viable alternative, after the briefest hesitation, Bibi accepted the fact of this new dark and unfathomed world in which she found herself. She ran across the sidewalk, onto the front lawn of a shingle-sided house with dormered roof, white trim, deep front porch, and windows glimmering like the panes of a candled lantern. This was a place where you took refuge after a long and dispiriting day, where you could always go home again. But it was no home to her, and she suspected that if she attempted to take refuge there, her knock would bring to the door Chubb Coy or the once-named Faulkner now known as Birkenau Terezin, or someone more surprising and even more hostile. She raced alongside the residence, through the outfall of light from the windows, into the black night of the backyard, no destination yet in mind, driven by an instinct

that promised safety only in perpetual motion.

■ ■ ■ ■

3
FROM TIME TO TIME
THE WORLD
GOES MAD

■ ■ ■ ■

46
WHERE SHE WENT WHEN SHE COULDN'T GO HOME AGAIN

Phone discarded, vehicle abandoned, clinging to the laptop not for its inherent value or its function, but for the 248 pages that existed nowhere except in its memory, Bibi Blair entered the backyard of the shingled house, wondering if she might be running from a twisted equivalent of the police detective in *Les Misérables* or from a variant of the robot assassin in *The Terminator,* as if it mattered a damn whether her ordeal conformed to classic fiction or to pop art.

From the street came the bark of brakes but no crash. Either an accident had been averted or two vehicles were disgorging pursuers. The property was encircled by one of those stucco-coated concrete-block privacy walls that Californians called a fence. At the rear of the lot, Bibi put her purse and computer on top of the fence. She got a two-hand grip on the bricks that capped the stuccoed blocks, and climbed into another backyard.

Having retrieved laptop and purse, she set

out past a swimming pool dimly revealed by the quarter moon, circulation pump rumbling.

In the passage between the dark residence and the property fence, a bicycle with a front-mounted cargo basket leaned against the house. Bibi put the laptop and purse in the basket and wheeled the bike into the street. She boarded it and pedaled westward, adding theft to the crime of trespass. Glancing back, she saw no one and dared to believe that they would not discover she had nabbed the bicycle.

If bad men actually were pursuing her on foot, and if they returned to their SUVs to conduct a wider search, she would be dead when they caught her on the street. Their type wouldn't be afraid to risk a four-wheel-drive execution in public.

Right away, she needed to get down from the hills and out of sight over the Balboa Peninsula bridge, so they wouldn't know which way she'd gone. When she reached Newport Boulevard, she swung left past the hospital, leaning hard into the turn to shorten the arc and maintain speed. Out of the turn, onto a straightaway. All downhill from there to the peninsula. Three lanes, little traffic at the moment. If there was a bike lane, she had no interest, preferring the wide, clear pavement. Stones and sticks and junk ended up in the bike lane, all kinds of crap that, at high speed, could send you wobble-wheeled into an embankment or jack your ride out from under you. Leaning forward, head low, slicing through the cool night air. Going faster than she had ever ridden a bicycle before. Passing some of the cars and trucks, all of the drivers staying wide of her when they realized that she was among them. She would have been exhilarated if she hadn't been expecting the Wrong People to ram her from behind.

She was anxious about encountering the police, too. A bicycle didn't belong in the center of the boulevard. She wasn't wearing a helmet, as the law required. And she was carrying a concealed weapon. She had a permit for it, but if there was a misunderstanding . . .

Before she quite realized it, the harbor glimmered to her left, and she was crossing the bridge. She raced down the final slope to the flats of the peninsula. Here land was in such short supply and so valuable, the seriously wealthy and the merely well-to-do lived in fabulous waterfront houses on postage-stamp properties, within shouting distance of older funky beach cottages rented by groups of surf rats working short-hour low-wage zombie jobs to preserve most of their time for tearing up epic waves or wiping out, either way, because all that mattered was *being there.*

Tentacled fog felt its way slowly, blindly off the sea and through the streets, breathing a cold dew on Bibi's face. She left the bicycle in an alley behind a block of businesses, closed at that hour, and continued on foot to the nearer of two piers.

As Thursday waned, traffic was light. For a place of such tight-packed structures and dense population, Balboa Peninsula felt lonely just then. It was easy to believe that an unaccompanied woman might vanish between one block and the next, never to be seen again.

As the fog married the land to the sea, passing traffic made Bibi think of submersibles plying the ocean through a sunken city, though one with humbler architecture than Atlantis. By the time she reached the vicinity of the pier, where faux-antique iron lamps silvered the mist, she seemed to be the only person in sight.

For emergencies, she had a key to Pet the Cat. Just inside the front door, during the alarm system's one-minute delay, she entered the code with the keypad. Spaced throughout to inconvenience thieves, security lamps provided more than enough light for Bibi to reach the stairs in the back-left corner of the shop.

The store occupied two commercial units. Her dad also leased the rooms above, which otherwise would have been rented as an apartment. He used half that upper space to store merchandise, and the other half served as his office, complete with a kitchenette and a cramped bathroom with shower.

In addition to a desk and filing cabinets, the office contained a comfortable sofa and two armchairs. On the walls hung five framed, mint posters for *The Endless Summer.* Her dad would not sell even one.

After turning on a desk lamp, Bibi closed the louvered shutters, which were tight enough to allow only a little light to escape.

When she sat in the office chair where her father had sat, she felt safe for the first time since she'd fled her apartment. Beside the desk lamp stood a framed photograph of Bibi and her mother.

She so wanted to call them. But she remembered Terezin's threat. If she went to her parents for help, he would kill them, too.

She wondered what the police would say if she approached them with her bizarre story. Would they invoke the danger-to-herself-and-others law and remand her for a psychiatric evaluation? For the moment, at least, the usual authorities were of no use to her.

She opened her laptop and plugged it in. On the desk stood a mug holding a selection of pens and pencils. She opened a desk drawer in search of a tablet or notepad.

Among the items in the drawer was a silver bowl containing a One-Zip plastic bag full of Scrabble tiles. She stared at it for a while before she picked it up.

■ ■ ■ ■

The online phone directory for Orange County included numerous people named Bell, but Bibi could not find an Ashley. There might be a spouse or daughter named Ashley not included in the listing, but to find her would require calling every number or visiting every address where one was provided. And there were surely other Bells who had unlisted numbers. The task was too daunting. She needed to think of a smarter, quicker way to conduct the search.

She googled Ashley Bell and found a number of them in states from Washington to Florida, but none in Orange County, which made her doubt her assumption that this person must be a local. She discovered photos of some of the Ashleys on Facebook — males and females — but she experienced no frisson of connection when she studied their faces.

During all this, she kept glancing at the bowl full of lettered tiles. It wasn't the same bowl that Calida had used. And the Amazon's tiles had been in a flannel bag, not a One-Zip.

So . . . questions. If Scrabblemancy was just a lark to Murphy and Nancy, why would he want his own gear? Had an amusement grown into an obsession? But assuming that

Calida wasn't a fraud, that she was a gifted diviner, the gear itself was of no use to people without her power. Did Murphy fancy himself some kind of medium?

That seemed absurd. People who made it to fifty by coasting happily along on an it'll-be-what-it'll-be mantra, whose relationship with fate was guided by a don't-ask-don't-tell mentality, who never exhibited a passing interest in philosophical issues, who lived for work and surf and surfers' simple pleasures, didn't abruptly become occultists any more than they became true-believing Jehovah's Witnesses, passing out pamphlets door to door. And if her father had gone over the edge, her mother had gone with him, because in a fundamental way, each had always been the other; perhaps their foremost saving grace was their commitment to each other, deep and unshakeable. If anything, Nancy would be less likely than Murphy to become a seeker of hidden knowledge. She was top agent, hard-nosed flogger of dream homes and fixer-uppers, a surfer babe who insisted on shag-cut hair because it saved her X number of minutes each day that could better be spent on maintaining a tan and catching some waves, drinker of tequila shots and beer, eater of jalapeños and habaneros, and all but certainly more enthusiastic in her marriage bed than her daughter cared to contemplate. Nancy was far too earthy to be floated off her feet by the helium of occult pursuits. And if not Nancy, then never Murphy. Divination with Scrabble tiles could be no more to them than a party game.

After working awhile longer with the computer, Bibi took a break to use the bathroom. On the vanity, beside the sink, she found a bottle of alcohol, a packet of seamstress's needles, and a white-cotton cloth crusted with old bloodstains and damp with new ones.

47
NIGHT VISITORS

Bibi would make no assumptions about her mom and dad, neither about their interest in the occult nor anything else. She loved them and she trusted them. The silver bowl, the lettered tiles, and the blood evidence could not possibly mean what they seemed to mean. She pushed it all to the back of her mind, until some simple explanation asserted itself, which was sure to happen, some sudden understanding that presented an entirely different interpretation of the facts, some answer so blazingly obvious that she would feel stupid for not having grasped it immediately upon finding the items in the bathroom.

Exhausted after an eventful day, she got a cold bottle of beer from the office refrigerator and sat in an armchair. Maybe the beer would chill her in the good sense of the word and help her catch a few hours of sleep.

Having stopped speculating about Nancy and Murphy, she brooded now about the person whose life she was supposed to save as payment for her cancer going into remission. She repeatedly reviewed what Terezin had said on the phone. His confidence that he would kill Bibi before she got close to Ashley did not come solely from his assessment of Bibi as an easy target. The logical thing to infer was that he knew Ashley Bell's whereabouts, and therefore he knew how hard it would be for Bibi to find her. Which seemed to point to one of two possibilities. First, maybe Ashley Bell was one of them, one of the Wrong People, and capable of using paranormal means to remain hidden if she did not want to be found. Second, and more likely, she was their prisoner, held for the usual wicked reasons . . . or for some purpose uniquely horrifying. If that proved to be the case, Bibi would have to descend through several levels of their homemade Hell to free her.

To free her.

To save Ashley Bell.

At her kitchen table with Calida, Bibi had insisted that she possessed neither the passion nor the skills to become the comic-book rescuer of people she didn't even know. Yet now she contemplated that very task. Something had changed. Not necessarily for the better. Perhaps she hadn't gained confidence in her skills, hadn't discovered in herself a greater depth of courage than she had believed existed; perhaps instead she was finding it easier to accept unreason than to resist it.

She set the empty beer bottle on the small round table beside the armchair and closed her eyes. Fatigued to the point at which the mere idea of lifting her arms from the arms of the chair was itself physically tiring, she nevertheless doubted that she would sleep. Her tumbling thoughts had no capacity for exhaustion. From as far back as she could remember, she had been the girl whose mind was always spinning. In sleep, of course, that mental wheel still turned, and it spun forth a thread of dreams. . . .

If the tall robed-and-hooded figures appeared in her dreams that night, they were among presences and occurrences that she didn't later remember. The sheet-wrapped corpse that played supporting roles in her occasional nightmares, that clearly wanted to be center stage, sat now in several scenes in different places, prevented by its bound condition from a more active performance. Its immobility was curious, considering that anything should be possible in a dream; the cadaver could have split out of its cocoon at the whim of the dreamer's mind, could have shown its face and wounds as it capered or threatened or strode the stage in a solemn soliloquy. Instead, it appeared in her hospital room as it had been before, in a chair near the window, its shroud colored by a blazing sunset, and it spoke through its fabric mask: *"The forms . . . the forms . . . things unknown."* Or it sat beside her on the wicker sofa, on the bungalow porch, struggling unsuccessfully to press a hand through the cotton sheeting to touch her, whispering, *". . . supreme master . . ."* and *". . . must be truth . . ."* and *". . . nothing . . . nothing at all. . . ."* Or she opened a door and found the wrapped corpse standing at the threshold as it said, *". . . forces of nature. . . ."*

As weary as Bibi was, slumped there in the office armchair, her encounters with the corpse were not fearsome enough to break the hold of sleep. But later, a more harrowing nightmare had its way with her, more harrowing because it was more than just a dream. . . .

She is young, not quite six, alone in her bed, where night presses at the bungalow windows. The only light is dim and largely confined to that farther corner of the room where a Mickey Mouse night-light has been plugged in to a wall outlet. Bibi is a small child, but not afraid of the dark. She has been as much embarrassed as amused by Mickey glowing over there in his yellow shoes and red pants, with his big silly smile. Her parents bought the little five-watt lamp a week earlier because they decided that all children needed reassurance in the dark. Well, Bibi is a child, but not a baby. She is so done with being a baby. Stupid Mickey watching over her is like being told she is still a baby and always will be a baby. Some nights she gets out of bed and unplugs the stupid glowing mouse. She doesn't want to hurt her parents' feelings. They mean well. Which is why she hasn't thrown Mickey away or put him in the bathroom where maybe he wouldn't upset her so much. She really, really, really doesn't want him here. Until this night. Now she is grateful that she is not in total darkness.

She lies on her back in bed, the covers pulled up to her chin, listening intently, waiting for the thing to move. From time to time, it crawls or creeps, or slides, or does whatever the heck it does to get around. But then it goes quiet for a while, as if it's thinking what to do next, thinking about what it wants and how to get it. This has been going on for more than an hour.

Earlier, before the bad thing started to happen, there were the voices and music of the TV, turned low in the living room, which had been nice. If there were those sounds now, Bibi would feel much braver than she does. But the house is quiet, so that when the thing decides to start moving again, there is nothing else she can listen to other than the little noises it makes. This wouldn't be so bad if it were a mouse like Mickey, scurrying around, making mouse sounds. Then she would get out of bed and try to win its trust, catch it gently and carry it outside to let it go free. Mouse sounds were cute, and a mouse would be scared, not dangerous, just frightened. This is not a mouse, however, and she doesn't think it is afraid.

She doesn't want to scream or call for help. That is total baby behavior. And if her mom and dad come running, maybe they won't find anything. Then they will tease her forever and ever. Something is here in the bedroom with her, for sure, but maybe only she can see and hear it. That's how it sometimes is in stories and on TV. And there is another worry. Maybe her parents *will* see and hear it. And maybe it will hurt them. If it hurts them, that will be Bibi's fault. Instead of screaming, she wishes the thing away, and every time it becomes quiet, she thinks it is gone. But it is not gone. Aunt Edith, who sometimes visits from Arizona, says if wishes were fishes, no one would go hungry, but Bibi wishes anyway, uselessly, hopelessly.

In addition to wishing the terrible thing away, she wishes that the captain already lived in the apartment above the garage, so she could run to him and get his help. He won't move in for a long time, until two weeks after her sixth birthday. She hasn't met him yet. She doesn't even know the captain exists. But dreams have no respect for the proper order of past, present, and future. As she dreams of the very young Bibi, adult Bibi would love nothing better than to have the captain in her present-day life as well as in her life on this long-past night of terror in her bungalow room.

When next the quiet ends, she hears the thing questing along a wall. The distinctive rattle of the cord from the nightstand lamp suggests that it is finding its way to her. She turns her head to the right, dreading that she will see the thing ascend into view, hardly more than two feet from her face. But the lamp cord ceases rattling between wall and nightstand, as the thing explores farther. This time, when it falls silent, it is without doubt under her bed.

If she wanted to scream now, she could not. She breathes, but has no breath to cry out. If she wanted to run, she could not. Her heart beats fast and hard, she is vital and acutely alive, it beats fast then faster, hard then harder, but it beats her into a strange submission, a kind of paralysis, in which the cardiac lub-dub sounds to her like two words relentlessly repeated: my fault, my fault, my fault. . . .

Quiet pools throughout the bungalow bedroom. The quiet is a drowning weight, fathoms of ocean pressing down. A deep stillness heavy with expectation, in which Bibi can almost hear the thing's thoughts, its needing and wanting and feverish scheming.

Perhaps its silent progress was a matter of stealth or maybe the blankets muffled what sounds it made, for she didn't realize that it was in bed with her until, under the covers, it touched her left foot.

Bibi erupted from the office armchair, flung to her feet by the touch of the malignant creature in the dream. Wild-eyed, gasping, she looked around, half expecting to see dream and reality become one and herself no longer alone or safe. She was cold to her bones and so emotionally wrung out that she felt hollow.

The reason for the nightmare's singular effect did not escape her. Of all her dreams, this was the only one that was also a memory. Although she had long forgotten, she remembered now that she had been there for real, in that place and on that night — and the crawling thing she so feared had been there, too.

48

EXTRACTION

Paxton expected a medium-lift helicopter with a two-man crew to extract them. When the monster Sea Dragon clattered down the sky and landed west of the town — no street was wide enough to accommodate its seventy-nine-foot-diameter rotor — he realized that new orders had modified the mission. He and his guys arrived in the meadow as the last of the three big turboshaft engines died, the rotary wing wheezed to a stop, and the final flush of downdraft threw dust and chaff in their faces.

In addition to two pilots and an aircrewman, the helo carried two demolition specialists, two search-and-rescue specialists, four Marines to defend the craft when it was on the ground, and a ton of equipment.

Marines were always welcome, even if their presence meant that a firefight previously thought unlikely might now be expected. Most concerning was that the Sea Dragon, used primarily for mine-sweeping operations, was dressed for assault-support with a ramp-mounted GAU-21 .50-caliber machine gun.

Marine Corporal Ned Sivert, with a straightforward manner and an amused contempt for standard-issue politicians, which had been raised into him in Heflin, Alabama, succinctly explained the new situation: "Some shit-for-brains White House aide, lookin' for glory, leaked just enough so the local drag-ass military could decide to ride in here and make themselves an incident if they want to bad enough."

"Then we should get out twice as fast," Pax said.

"Yessir, you'd think so. But some plain-clothes general in the West Wing now wants al-Ghazali's body, not just a smidge of DNA and a picture for the scrapbook. Fact is, he wants all seven bodies."

"At the last minute? Why?"

"I never ask why of my betters. They might tell me, and I might see as how I'm workin' for even bigger fools than I thought."

Among the equipment on the helo were two gas-powered portable generators, compressors, hydraulic jacks, and large inflatable bags of tough material that could lift thousand-pound slabs of concrete rubble.

"We'll be going home in a flying morgue," Pax said.

Gibb, whose mother sometimes saw his father's spirit lingering around their property

270

in Georgia, who himself believed in ghosts and hauntings, said, "No big deal, Pax. Valiant boys like us don't spook easy."

Pax smiled. "Valiant boys never spook. They do the spooking."

"Won't always be true," Gibb said. "But mostly."

49

THE MAN WHO BORROWED
THE NAMES OF DEATH

Bibi tweaked open one of the slats in a
window shutter and stared out at the sidewalk
and the pier parking lot, where the fog
sparkled like diamond dust in the glow of the
streetlamps. She stood there until she felt
sure that Pet the Cat was not under observation, until she stopped trembling.

She recalled now. . . .

The memory of the crawling intruder in
her bedroom had inspired a repetitive nightmare that had tormented her for eight
months, until she was six months short of
her seventh birthday. Then, for the first time,
she used the captain's magical technique for
shedding memories so distressing that they
poisoned your life. On an index card, with
the captain's help, she had written a description of the events in her room on that bleak
night when Mickey Mouse had failed to keep
the boogeyman at bay, not just what it had
been but how and why it had happened.
Holding the card in a pair of tongs, repeating

the six magic words that Captain taught her, she set it afire with a candle flame. When the captain swept up the ashes with his hands and blew them from his hands into the trash compactor, the unwanted memory was blown from her mind.

This slate-wiping trick was a childish device, nothing but a wishing-away, no more magical than were the paper and the fire. But she had wanted so desperately and intensely for it to work that it had worked for many years. Bibi didn't understand the psychology of repressed memories. Maybe she didn't want to understand, because if she had deceived herself in this fashion, perhaps she was not, after all, the bring-it-on-I-can-take-anything girl that she had always believed she was.

More than fifteen years after burning that memory in the candle flame — and more than sixteen years since the creepy encounter had occurred — the extraordinary stress of this strange night had brought the dormant memory back into flower. But it had not restored to her all the details of the repressed experience. That long-ago night, she had known what crawled the room and creeped beneath her bed. She had seen it then. But she could not see it now in her mind's eye.

Maybe sooner than later, the full truth would come back to her. Although if it did, she might wish that it never had.

What she could see clearly now was that some extraordinary event in her past must be related to the remission of her cancer and to all that had occurred since Calida Butterfly had begun to pull Scrabble tiles from that silver bowl. In the dream that was a memory, maybe the crawling thing in her bedroom had in fact been a horror and far beyond ordinary human experience, but perhaps calling it a *thing* was a way of clouding the truth, an attempt to evade what had actually happened by transforming the threat into a harmless cliché, into the generic monster of all nightmares. She tried to force recollection, to expand the most crucial moments in the dream, but for the time being, no more details could be recovered.

By the time her tremors stopped, it was 4:04 A.M. She returned to her father's desk, searched the drawers, found a pack of unused flash drives, and made two copies of the 248-page manuscript that was on her laptop. She crawled into the kneehole and, with Scotch tape, securely fixed one flash drive to the underside of the desktop. She slipped the other one into a pocket of her jeans.

She took a shower in the small bathroom adjacent to her father's office and then put on again the clothes she had been wearing since she'd fled her apartment.

Hungry, she searched the refrigerator in the kitchenette, but found nothing that she wanted to eat except a pint of dark-chocolate ice cream with peanut-butter swirl. Not a healthy breakfast by any standard. So what? If the supernatural insisted on weaving its web through her life, denying her the solace of pure reason — then to hell with such reasonable things as low-fat diets and exercise regimens.

While she ate, she sat at her father's desk, searching the address book on his computer. Violating his privacy disconcerted her, so that more than once she hesitated to continue. But her future was at stake, if not her life. Her embarrassment never matured into shame, and she searched for the four names that were thus far most central to her dilemma. She found a phone number and address for Calida Butterfly. When she could not find an entry for Ashley Bell or Birkenau Terezin, or Chubb Coy, she was relieved. To have found any of them — especially all of them — would have forced her to question not just the judgment but the reliability of her parents, which would have been painful in the extreme.

Online, she googled Birkenau Terezin. Although she did not find a man with that name, she found two places with a history of evil.

Terezin proved to be a town in the Czech Republic, which seventy-five years earlier had been called Theresienstadt and had been part of German-occupied Bohemia. The Nazis had ejected the seven thousand residents of Terezin in order to use the town as a Jewish ghetto, where as many as fifty-eight thousand were forced to live at one time and where more than one hundred fifty thousand passed through during the war years. They lived there only temporarily, because Terezin was a transport center to which Jews were taken from all over Czechoslovakia and from which they would be conveyed to various death camps as the gas chambers and furnaces could accommodate them. One of the camps to which they were transported by the tens of thousands was Auschwitz-Birkenau.

She wondered what kind of man so hated books and bookish people that he would trade the name Faulkner for names that were synonymous with cruelty and death.

Halfway through the pint of ice cream, she realized that she had forgotten something when she'd been searching her dad's address book. Bibi returned to it and, with a pang of remorse for suddenly being such a doubting daughter, typed in FAULKNER. The directory popped to KELSEY FAULKNER, complete with a local address and phone number.

50

FOG AND THE FOG OF TIME

With the desk light turned off, Bibi felt her way to the window and used the tilt rod to open the louvers on one half of the shutter. She stood staring out at the lamplit fog that still drifted onshore like the ghost of some poisonous sea that had existed billions of years earlier, before the current healthy sea had formed.

With no one to turn to, she would have to be her own detective. And she was as certain as she had ever been about anything that she had little time to wrap the case. The Wrong People were searching for her, and she sensed that their numbers might be daunting, that they were not just a cult of a dozen or two dozen deranged individuals, but were more like a battalion — or an army. Whether they sought her by ordinary or paranormal means didn't matter; either way, when they found her, they would kill her — and for reasons she still didn't quite understand.

If Bibi was right about Ashley Bell, that she

was a prisoner of these people, held for God knew what purpose, then it would be necessary to find them in order to find her. For that detective work, she needed wheels, and she thought she knew where to get them. But she had to wait for a more reasonable hour, at least seven o'clock, before making the call.

Fog could paint mystery on the most mundane scene. Now when she thought of Pax in some hellhole unknown to her, the mist also painted the night with melancholy. Sorrow was a degree of sadness that she dared not indulge; it would sap her will and strength. As much as she yearned for Pax, she could not dwell on him.

She thought of another foggy night, when she had been six years old for just two weeks, the evening of the day when Captain had moved into the rooms above the garage. He was the only important newcomer in Bibi's life until, four years later, Olaf came to live with her.

Previously the apartment had been rented by a twenty-something woman, Hadley Rogers, who was busy with a career in art, not as a painter or instructor, but as a dealer or broker or agent, whatever. She had not been a meaningful presence in young Bibi's life, seen most often flitting down the stairs to her Corvette in the carport. Miss Rogers seemed puzzled by children, as if she wasn't entirely sure of their origin or purpose. She seemed less substantial than a real person, more like an animated painting of a person.

Captain, on the other hand, was obviously real and important. Tall, rugged-looking, with thick white hair, he was attentive and polite to everyone, even children. Bibi had accompanied her mother when the captain had been shown the apartment, and by the end of the tour, she liked him and knew she would always and forever like him. In spite of his scarred hands and two missing fingers, though his face was weather-beaten and his eyes were as sad as those of a bloodhound, Captain was glamorous; she just knew he had a lot of good stories to tell.

That night, after the fog had laid siege to Corona del Mar, Bibi couldn't fall asleep. After a while, she slipped out of bed and went to get a glass of milk. As she approached the kitchen, where her parents were at the table, talking over mugs of coffee and Kahlua, she heard her mother say something that warned her to step to the side of the doorway, be silent, and listen.

"I'm thinking it's a mistake. This has a bad vibe."

Murphy said, "Well, I'm not getting any vibe, good or bad. I'm vibeless, babe."

"I'm serious, Murph."

"Yeah, I figured that out an hour ago."

"Who moves into a place with just two suitcases and a duffel bag?"

"They were big suitcases. Anyway, it's a furnished apartment."

"People still have boxes and boxes of personal belongings."

"You're making yourself crazy for no reason."

"What about Bibi?"

"Listen to yourself, babe. He's not a child molester."

"I didn't say that. Don't put words in my mouth. But he's not like Hadley, hardly home. He's going to be up there all the time. He'll be an influence. She was instantly fascinated with him."

"Retirees do tend to be more homebodies than hot young girls climbing the art-world ladder."

"You think Hadley is hot?" Nancy asked.

"Not by my standards, not even lukewarm. But I have a lot of empathy. I can see the world through other guys' eyes."

"You might need to, if I poke out *your* eyes."

"Here you are threatening your own husband, and you think maybe some worn-out, worn-down geezer with eight fingers is a problem."

Nancy laughed softly. "I just don't want any bad influences in Bibi's life."

"Then we'll have to move to Florida or somewhere, because right now your sister Edith is just across the border in Arizona."

Young Bibi had gone back to bed without

milk and worried herself to sleep, afraid that the exotic and interesting captain would soon be gone, replaced by another bland and boring Hadley.

She need not have lost sleep. Captain lived above the garage for more than four wonderful years, until that terrible day of blood and death.

Now, standing at the window in her father's office, Bibi saw what might have been dawn light refracting through the fog, faintly pinking it. She looked at the radiant dial of her watch. Almost time to call Pogo.

51
THUNDER CRUSHER

At 7:05, using the phone on her father's desk, Bibi called Pogo. She expected to wake him, but he sounded as sharp as a shark's tooth when he answered on the second ring: "Tell me."

"I thought you knew it all."

"Hey, Beebs. You never call me."

"Don't mom me, bro." She asked about the surf rats with whom he shared an apartment: "How are Mike and Nate?"

"Still in bed. Probably abusing themselves."

"I'm surprised you sound so together at this hour."

"I was gonna catch a few before work," he said, meaning a few waves, "but I wake up and it's like milk soup. You've got to have a guide dog to surf this. Anyway, you had me scared, Beebs."

"You mean the cancer thing."

"Sounded too tough even for you."

"But here I am. Clean and ready to tear it up."

"You've always torn it up."

"This has nothing to do with cancer. That's totally yesterday. But I need some help, Pogo."

"Why else do I exist?"

"That old Honda of yours. Does it have GPS?"

"Hell, Beebs, it hardly even has brakes."

"Could I borrow it?"

"Sure."

"Don't you want to know why?"

"Why would I need to know why?"

"I might want it for a few days."

"I've got friends with cars. I've got a skateboard. I'm cool."

"Listen, this isn't the boss's daughter working you."

"Hey, no, you and me grew up together, Beebs. Anyway, I don't think of Murph as my boss."

"He's aware of that. I'd appreciate it if you don't say anything to him about this."

"Not a word. When you want the car?"

"The sooner the better. I'm at the store."

"I'll be there in like twenty minutes."

"You're the real thing, Pogo."

"Beebs?"

"Yeah?"

"You catch a bad wave or something?"

"A real thunder crusher," she said.

"Maybe you need more help from me than just the car."

"If I do, I'll let you know, sweet boy."

After she terminated the call, Bibi opened her purse and took from it the book with the panther and gazelle on the cover. There was no title or author's name on the spine, either, and no text on the back. When she opened the book and thumbed through it, the pages were blank. Or they appeared to be blank until faint gray lines of cursive script rippled across the paper, flowing as fluidly as water, gone before she could read a word. She paged through it more slowly, and twice again words appeared, shimmering as if seen through a film of purling water, but rinsed away before they could be read.

She examined the binding. There was no space for electronics or batteries to be concealed within the spine. It was just a book. But not just.

52
GOING HOME WITH THE DEAD

With more than fourteen thousand combined horsepower, the three General Electric engines produced a confidence-building shriek, and the huge rotary wing thumped the air like a heavyweight boxer's fists pounding the crap out of a punching bag. SEALs and Marines and associated Navy men left the ghost town and headed out-country in the last two hours of light, at an air speed of 150 knots.

As the deck vibrated under them, the seven dead terrorists were restless in their body bags. Restless as they had been in life. Good men and women sought calm, peace, time for reflection. Evil people were eternally restive, intractable, always eager for more thrills, which were the same few thrills endlessly repeated, because the evil were unimaginative, acting on feelings rather than reason. Forever agitated, they were unaware that the cause of their fury was the confining narrowness of the worldview they crafted for themselves, its *emptiness.* There would never be an end to them — and always a need for men and women willing to resist them at whatever cost.

Just before sunset, without incident en route, they touched down on the aircraft carrier, much to Paxton's relief. There would be a debriefing, after which he expected to call Bibi in California, where it was morning. That expectation was deflated three minutes after they debarked from the helo. Washington wanted all team members to maintain silence with the outside world for at least another eight hours, for reasons that they did not feel obliged to share.

53
WALK THE BOARD, DUDETTE

When headlights tunneled the fog in the parking lot and the primer-gray Honda glided to the curb like a ghost-driven spirit car, Bibi stepped out the front door of Pet the Cat.

Because the heater took a long time to warm up, Pogo left the engine running and came around the front of the car to Bibi. "You've got that surf-goddess look going more than ever."

"Maybe cancer was good for me."

She knew that she was pretty enough, but not fall-down gorgeous or anything. On the other hand, Pogo made most of the male models in the big fashion magazines look as if they were trying out for roles as orcs in a possible sequel to the *Lord of the Rings* movies. He seemed oblivious of his physical perfection, even when girls were throwing themselves at him in such numbers and with such insistence that the air became scintillant with the fragrance of estrogen. It sometimes seemed to Bibi that if Pogo's appearance meant anything at all to him, it was largely an embarrassment. But they truly had grown up together, as he had said earlier, and going to bed with him was as unthinkable as going to bed with a brother, if she'd had one. Two years older than Pogo, Bibi had taught him how to take the drop (how to slide down the face of a wave immediately after catching it), how to pull a rollover to get through white water, how to perform a roundhouse cutback, and other moves, when he was a preadolescent surf mongrel, before he surpassed her skill level. His good looks might have mattered to her when she was a preteen and early teenager. Then it had been a power trip to have the full attention of the boy that all the other girls most wanted. But now and for some years, what she loved about Pogo was his spirit, his humility, his tender heart.

He kissed her on the cheek and looked her in the eyes and said, "Who're you hiding out from?"

"That's not the way it is."

In a staring contest, neither one of them would ever be the first to look away.

Pogo decided not to make it a contest. He surveyed the lonely mist-soaked morning, as the distant foghorn sounded at the mouth of Newport Harbor. "Just so you know where to get help when you're finally not too stubborn to ask for it."

"I know where," she assured him.

He opened the passenger door and took from the seat a bag of breakfast staples from McDonald's and a paperback novel.

After Bibi put her laptop and purse on the seat, she closed the door and said, "You don't hide the books anymore."

"Doesn't matter if my folks find out I can read. I already escaped college."

"You've always known what you wanted. Doesn't it sometimes scare you that years from now, it'll turn out not to have been enough?"

"The past is past, Beebs. The future is just an illusion. All we have is now."

Indicating the McDonald's bag, she said, "I don't want that to get cold. But I have a couple questions."

He gestured toward the store. "There's a microwave inside. This stuff heats okay."

She could smell the faint exhaust fumes as the Honda tailpipe pumped faux fog into the real stuff. "Has Dad ever mentioned someone named Calida Butterfly?"

After a hesitation, Pogo said, "She comes here. Tall woman, blond, jingles with jewelry when she walks."

"Comes here to the store? How often?"

"A couple times a month."

"I look at her," Bibi said, "I don't think boardhead."

"She's totally an inlander, not even a wish-was surfer. She comes to see Murph."

"What about?"

"Beats me. They go up to his office." She met his eyes, he read her instantly, and he said, "That's not how it is, Beebs. They aren't humping up there."

It hurt her to ask, but she asked, "How do you know?"

"I don't *know,* but I know. They go back a long way, but the vibe isn't sex."

"When did this start?"

"Maybe a year and a half ago."

Continuing to pour in from the sea, the morning fog defied the sun. But there must have been some clearing inland, because jets were taking off from John Wayne Airport, the dragon roar of their engines speaking down through the fog as if from some Jurassic otherwhere.

"What about a guy named Kelsey Faulkner?"

Pogo considered, shook his head. "Never heard of him."

"Birkenau Terezin?"

"That's a name? Sounds like some kind of rash."

"Ashley Bell?"

"I knew another Ashley once. Ashley Scudder. She traded surfing for corporate finance."

"Must be some who do both, corporate-finance surfers."

"Not many."

"I better go, you better microwave," Bibi said.

When she kissed him on the cheek, he hugged her fiercely. With his head on her shoulder, his face averted, he said, "When Murph called from the hospital Tuesday to say about the cancer, I closed the store, turned out the lights. Sat behind the counter and cried for an hour. Didn't think I was gonna stop. Don't make me cry again, Beebs."

"I won't," she promised, and when he looked at her, she lightly pinched the tip of his perfect nose. "Thanks for the wheels."

"Whatever thunder crusher you're riding," he said, "just walk the board the way you do so well."

To maintain control of a board, a surfer walked back and forth on it, shifting her body weight.

Bibi went around the Honda, opened the driver's door, and looked across the roof at Pogo. With an affection so profound that she could never have found the words to describe it in a novel, she smiled and said, "Dude."

He returned her smile. "Dudette. Walk the board, dudette."

54

A TASTE OF THE CATERPILLAR'S MUSHROOM?

Because Pogo enjoyed tinkering with cars more than attending college but less than surfing, the Honda drove better than it looked. The well-tuned engine offered good takeoff from a stop and plenty of power for hills. In spite of the joke he had made about the brakes, they were in good working order.

Calida Butterfly lived in Costa Mesa, in a neighborhood that had once been middle-class, had fallen into decline, but had begun to come back strong before the crash of 2008. In the current economic malaise, gentrification had stalled, leaving newer semi-custom two-story homes next door to fifty-year-old ranch-style residences, some well kept and some not. Seventy-year-old bungalows were in the mix, too, this one stucco and that one clapboard, most of them in need of new paint and repairs. Some properties were landscaped and neatly kept, but here and there were weedy yards and overgrown shrubs, and bare dirt scattered with gravel.

The biggest pluses of the neighborhood were its future if the country ever got back on a vigorous growth path and the massive old trees that spread sheltering limbs over the streets, an eclectic urban forest of podocarpus, oaks, carrotwood, stone pines, and more.

Bibi parked across the street from — and a hundred feet west of — Calida's place, in the enrobing indigo shade of a California live oak. The fog had retreated somewhat from this area, although a scrim still stirred close to the ground, like a lingering poison gas that had been shelled into the neighborhood by an enemy army.

The masseuse-diviner's house stood on a lot and a half, a well-maintained two-story bungalow with touches of Craftsman style. Bibi had been watching the place less than five minutes when the segmented garage door rose and a silver Range Rover rolled down the driveway, turned east into the street, and motored away, roiling the low fog in its wake. She had never before seen what Calida drove and didn't know if this might be it. Distance and the vehicle's tinted windows prevented her from identifying the occupants.

She hadn't been sure if she'd come here to have a face-to-face with Calida or to nose around. The departure of the Rover helped her make up her mind. Nose around.

Preferring not to be encumbered by a purse, she tucked it under the driver's seat.

She locked the doors of the Honda and boldly crossed the street to the house, the small oval leaves of the live oak, dead and dry, crunching underfoot like beetle shells. When no one answered the doorbell, she rang it again, with the same result.

Without any furtive behavior, as though she had every right to be there, Bibi went around the side of the house, through a gate that stood ajar, past a patio shaded by a wisteria-entwined arbor, into the backyard, where a property wall screened her from the neighbors.

Her attention was drawn at once to an unexpected structure: a quaint decorative greenhouse of white-painted wood and glass, about twenty feet by thirty, set at the back of the property. This was such an unlikely discovery that she felt compelled to investigate it.

Four statues cast in terra-cotta, representing the four seasons, stood on plinths, two on each side of the approach to the building. The entire quartet — not just winter — looked threatening, as if they had been crafted in a place and a century that had never known a day of good weather.

There wasn't much point in locking a house of glass containing nothing of value, and Bibi found the south door open. She stepped into a warm and moist enclave of exotic plants, most of them growing in trays of fecund-smelling soil set upon tall tables flanking narrow work aisles. There were no orchids or anthuriums or other species grown solely for their flowers. All appeared to be herbs. But only a few were the herbs that people used in their kitchens. She recognized basil, mint, chicory, fennel, rosemary, tarragon, and thyme. But there must have been a double score of other thriving varieties unknown to her. Some of the tables featured a bottom tier, where sunlight never directly reached, and in those still pools of wine-dark shadows were fungi — toadstools and puffballs and molds — that looked unhealthy, maybe even lethal.

Wandering through the greenhouse, Bibi thought of Lewis Carroll's Wonderland and the hookah-smoking caterpillar that had offered Alice pieces of this mushroom and that. Although she had accepted the reality of the events in her kitchen the previous night — the sudden plunge in the room temperature, the strange behavior of the candle flames and clocks, the stench of rotting roses where the only roses were in fact fresh and fragrant — perhaps she should consider the possibility that a part of what she had experienced might have been related to the effects of some hallucinogen distilled from one of these plants. It could have been slipped into her glass of chardonnay when she wasn't looking.

She turned a corner and, on one of the

tables, discovered a wire cage about a yard long and two feet wide, occupied by fifteen or twenty mice in various shades of brown and gray. The rodents were busy feasting at small bowls of food and water, coming and going from shallow burrows in coagulated masses of damp shredded newsprint, grooming, defecating, and copulating. Granted that mice were by nature nervous creatures, this community nonetheless seemed unusually jittery, fidgeting from end to end of the cage, twitching in alarm when others of their kind unintentionally stepped on their tails, ceaselessly surveying their domain with eyes as dark and liquid as beads of motor oil.

Movement drew Bibi's attention to the concrete floor, where a possible explanation for the mice's agitation slithered to her feet: a snake, and then another, and a third.

55
THE PHOTOGRAPH

Bibi saw at once that the squirming serpents on the greenhouse floor were not rattlesnakes and that each was different from the others. Never having had the slightest interest in herpetology, she could neither identify them nor tell if they were deadly. She assumed they couldn't be venomous, because Calida wouldn't let them roam free if they were dangerous.

Of course, with what they believed to be cold and unassailable logic, people made assumptions all the time that got them killed. And Bibi had so recently promised Pogo that she would not give him another reason to cry. So she backed slowly away from the sinuous trio, dreading that she might step on a fourth behind her, ready to turn and sprint if one of them began coiling to strike.

Perhaps the snakes had been interested in her only because she might have been Calida come to feed them mice. As she retreated, they did not follow. Two glided silently beneath the table on which stood the cage of rodents. The third twined around a table leg and oozed upward to inspect the various nervous entrées that might be selected for dinner.

Bibi's breath escaped her in a sigh of relief when she stepped outside and closed the greenhouse door.

At least she had learned something in return for the risk she had taken: Calida's occult interests exceeded Scrabblemancy. Whether the murdered mother, too, had been a woman with numerous cabalistic pursuits or whether Calida had added new lines of business to her mom's basic enterprise, the masseuse seemed to be seriously twisted, maybe fully wacked.

In either case, Bibi had to go into the main house. Considered as a preview, the greenhouse suggested that essential information would be found in the bungalow.

She tried the kitchen door, but it was locked. She hadn't seen a sign warning that the house was protected by an alarm company. But she was loath to break a pane of glass. For the novel that she had been writing, she had researched burglary, speaking with detectives in the robbery detail and with a convicted criminal serving time for a score of offenses. She had learned that in some jurisdictions, you needed to force entry *and* steal something to be guilty of burglary. If you did neither, merely trespassed, you were at most guilty of the lesser charge of house-breaking.

That she should be calculating the legal consequences of her criminal activity, committing a crime rather than contemplating it, was disturbing. Well, screw it. She had no choice. The cops didn't help you with complaints of supernatural harassment, and it was likely that *some* Wrong People were on the police force, too. The thing to keep in mind was that, two days earlier, Death had not just been on her doorstep but had been ringing her bell and knocking and calling for her to come out and play. Whatever trouble she got into now would be, by comparison, as sweet and smooth as pudding.

Among the many interesting things she learned when researching burglary was that a surprising number of people were diligent about locking potential points of entrance on the ground floor but were careless regarding second-story windows and sometimes even balcony doors.

At each end of the wisteria-entwined arbor that shaded the back patio, the vertical members were made of two-by-twos and appeared strong enough to serve as ladder rungs. She chose the end where the wisteria grew thinner. Assuring herself that this was less dangerous than surfing, since there were no sharks in the arbor, she climbed to the top with an agility that gratified her. She might have spent the last few years being more of a desk-bound writer than she would have preferred, but she hadn't gone soft yet.

Four double-hung windows overlooked the arbor and the backyard. The third proved to be unlocked. Bibi slid up the lower sash. When no alarm sounded, she climbed over the sill, leaving the window open in case she needed to make a hasty exit.

Sneak thief, even minus the theft, still wasn't a title that made her feel dashingly romantic, certainly not proud. She almost drew the pistol from her shoulder rig, to search the house at the ready, but that seemed stupid. She had no experience of a job like this. Her nerves were tripwire tight. If she turned a corner and encountered Calida — or, worse yet, a total innocent — she might squeeze the trigger in startled reaction. Instead, she went naked, or so it seemed, wondering why she had never thought it essential to earn a black belt in one martial art or another.

She had entered what seemed to be the master bedroom, which looked more ordinary than she might have expected. Neatly made bed with dust ruffle. Reproductions of California plein-air paintings. No zodiac carpet, no black candles in polished-bone holders, no weird totem hanging on the wall behind the bed. No snakes. The door to the walk-in closet stood open, and the clothes were hung in an orderly fashion.

Although she had risked a housebreaking conviction to come here, Bibi had no intention of pawing through Calida's dresser drawers in search of secrets, which would probably turn out to be about things that had nothing to do with her and that were in one way or another pathetic, as most bedroom-kept secrets were. She suspected that if anything important waited to be found in this house, it would be grotesque or at least singular. She would recognize it the instant she opened a door or crossed a threshold.

The maple floor of the upstairs hallway talked back underfoot. She could do nothing to silence it. Staying close to a wall didn't lessen the noise. Proceeding quickly caused no greater disturbance than stepping slowly and cautiously.

Beyond the hall bath were two rooms, the first peculiar but not helpful. No furniture whatsoever. Nothing hanging on the walls. The windows had been blacked out by fitting them with mirrors. She glimpsed her reflection and didn't like the way she looked. Anxious, small, uncertain. In the center of the pale maple floor, in neat black letters an inch high, had been painted THALIA. The name of Calida's mother. If you could believe anything the diviner said, Thalia had been cruelly tortured and dismembered by the

Wrong People, twelve years earlier. Most likely not in this house. Somewhere else. This room, with the name on the floor, didn't feel like either a marker of the crime or a shrine to the victim. For reasons that Bibi couldn't specify, the chamber felt as if it had been established for the purpose of communication, although with whom or what, she could not say.

Across the hall from the empty room lay an office. A corner desk held a computer and two printers, the second for color work, all the equipment dark and silent. More plein-air paintings. A rosewood sideboard along one wall. In the center of the space stood a round worktable attended by a single chair.

She had found the grotesque, the singular, the something.

On the table stood the silver bowl filled with lettered tiles. In addition, two lines of tiles had been arranged on the table, as though Calida had returned to the inquiry that had begun in Bibi's kitchen the night before. The first line read ASHLEY BELL. The line below it was an address: ELEVEN MOON-RISE WAY.

Beside the bowl lay a sheet of high-quality photographic paper of the kind used in a color printer. When Bibi turned it over, she was staring at a lovely girl of perhaps thirteen. Champagne-yellow hair. Wide-spaced violet eyes the shade of certain hyacinths. It was mostly a head shot, from the shoulders up. The girl wore a white blouse with a crisp white collar, and across that garment were written five words: *Calida, this is Ashley Bell.*

56
OUT OF CHAOS, CONVICTION

This girl. This Ashley Bell. Her face beautiful. Her expression serene. But in that serenity, Bibi saw a hard-won composure, a mask meant to deny the photographer his subject's true emotions, which were fear and anger. She warned herself that she might be reading into the photo a scenario from her imagination. Maybe the girl was just bored or trying for one of those vacuous expressions that models were encouraged to assume for the haute-couture magazines these days. But no. For Bibi, the proof could be seen in that remarkable stare. If the colors in the picture were true to life, those enchanting reddish-blue eyes were as limpid as distilled water and revealed a profoundly observant and quick mind. They were wide-set eyes but also as wide open as they could be without furrowing her forehead, as if she meant to belie the apparent tranquillity of her face, or as though the photographer or something else beyond the camera disquieted her.

In addition, Bibi perceived in the girl a tenderness and vulnerability that inspired sympathy, a kindredness that she could not — or would not — explain to herself. This reaction, this sense of equivalence, hit her with such force that it changed everything.

Until now, the search for Ashley Bell, such as it was, had been to a degree unreal, a game without rules, a joke quest without many laughs. It might even be a hoax involving a cleverly staged, phony divination session enhanced by hallucinogens, perpetrated by a group of crazies whose motivation was likely forever to elude a sane person. To this point, Bibi had played this dangerous game as though she exclusively stood at the center of it, focus and sole target. Because of the girl's appearance and demeanor, which were at once radiantly ethereal and as real as stone, Bibi's perception changed. She was the paladin, the white knight, and a secondary target only because she would act to save the girl. Ashley Bell was the primary target of the Wrong People and the focus of all that would happen hereafter. In surfing terms, Ashley was the grommet, the trainee surf mongrel, and Bibi was the stylin' waverider who had to save her from being mortally prosecuted by a series of storm-generated behemoths.

Reality had finally resolved out of the chaos of the last twelve hours. It had bitten hard, infecting Bibi with conviction.

Ashley Bell was real. And in desperate trouble. The people who threatened her were in some way weirdly gifted and beyond the reach of the law. Also well organized. Also homicidal.

Calida had printed out a picture of Ashley that someone had emailed to her as an attached JPEG. It would be helpful to know the source of the photograph. Maybe she had printed the email, too.

Like any house, this one produced noises separate from those its people generated. Creaks and ticks and soft groans of expansion, contraction, and subsidence. A series of these caused Bibi to freeze and listen intently, but silence and a guarded sense of safety settled after the building finished complaining about gravity.

She looked through desk drawers for the email. Nothing. An electric shredder fed the waste can, which contained mostly quarter-inch-wide ribbons of paper suitable for celebrating a welcome-home parade of astronauts returning from the moon, but otherwise useless. The remaining contents did not include the email.

She suspected that she'd already spent too much time in the house. Exploring Calida's computer might be interesting, but it would also require a reckless delay.

Carrying the photograph in her left hand, keeping her right free to reach beneath her blazer to the pistol, Bibi descended the stairs through a stillness that no tread disrupted. She passed also through a lens of morning gold admitted by a skylight, in which particles of dust not evident elsewhere were revealed revolving around one another, as though she had been given a glimpse of the otherwise invisible atomic structure of the world.

The ground-floor rooms were without eccentricity, furnished as normally as those in any house. But when she got to the kitchen, she found the aftermath of a visit by the Wrong People. The dinette table had been jammed into one corner; the chairs stood upon it. A heavy-duty white-plastic tarp, fixed to the floor with blue painter's tape, protected the glazed Mexican tiles. A few stained rags had been left on the tarp; but there was not much blood. Apparently, they killed her in such a way as to avoid a mess, possibly by strangulation. Then the amputations had been performed postmortem, both to minimize the need for cleanup and to ensure there would be no shrill screams to alarm the neighbors. The body had been removed, perhaps in the Range Rover and for disposal, but the ten fingers, each sporting a flashy ring, were on a counter near the refrigerator, lined up neatly on a plate, as if they were petits fours to be served with afternoon tea.

Human cruelty could disgust Bibi, but not shock her. She wasted no time reeling from the hideous sight or wondering for what purpose the fingers had been kept. She understood at once the urgent message the scene conveyed: The cleanup was not finished; either those who had left in the Range Rover would return or another crew would soon arrive to complete the job.

As she started across the kitchen, she heard a vehicle in the driveway and the muffled clatter of the rising garage door.

■ ■ ■ ■

4
PUTTING THE PIECES
TOGETHER AT
THE RISK OF
FALLING APART

■ ■ ■ ■

57

BREAKFAST WITH A
SIDE OF SURPRISE

When she heard the roll-up door rising in the garage, Bibi reached under her blazer, to the holstered pistol, wondering if she would be able to get the drop on whoever might be coming, disarm and restrain and interrogate them. If there was only one of them, the answer was probably not. If two, the answer was definitely not. If more than two, they would butcher her into more pieces than they evidently had rendered Calida. Courage and steadfastness were not enough when you were up against a crew of sociopaths and you weighed 110 pounds on a fat day and your gun had only a ten-round magazine and you weren't self-deluded. She didn't hesitate even long enough for the garage door to finish its ascent, fled the kitchen, went directly to the living room and out the front door.

She stayed away from the east end of the porch, where the driveway led past the house to the garage. Avoiding the steps as well, she hurried to the west end of the porch, vaulted over the railing, and landed on her feet. She raced across the front lawn, across the street, and took refuge in Pogo's Honda, in the deep shadows under the live oak.

She put the photograph of Ashley on the dashboard and extracted her purse from under the driver's seat. If she could sound genuinely horrified and panicked, which shouldn't be a problem, a call to 911 might bring the police to Calida's house while someone remained there to be arrested. *Bloody rags. Severed fingers. Murder.* If that wasn't enough to bring out Costa Mesa's finest, they must be busy filming a reality-TV show. Only as she zippered open the handbag did she recall that she no longer had her phone. She had abandoned it — and its GPS — with her Explorer, the previous night.

If she got out of the car and screamed, trying to rouse the neighbors, she would accomplish nothing except to alert the murderers to her presence and provide them an opportunity to see what she was driving these days. She sat stewing in frustration for a minute or two, but she gained nothing from that, either. When she drove away, she hung a U-turn, heading west, to avoid passing the house.

Instead of sustaining her, a half pint of ice cream before dawn had led to a sugar crash. She went directly to a Norm's restaurant, the ultimate working man's eatery, because the food was pretty good and reliable, but also because she had a hunch that the Wrong People wouldn't be seen in a Norm's even if they were starving to death and it was the last source of nourishment on the planet. During their short telephone conversation, Birkenau — "Call me Birk" — Terezin had sounded like a snob and a narcissist. His associates were likely to be of the same cloth; power-trippers put a low value on humility. When your enemies were elitist snarky boys, one way you could go off the grid was to eat at Norm's and buy your clothes at Kmart.

The hostess put her in a small booth at the back of the room, and Bibi chose to sit facing away from most of the other customers. More than food, she wanted coffee. Her thoughts were fuzzy from too little sleep and too much weirdness. She needed to clear her head. The pleasant and efficient waitress brought a second cup of strong black brew with Bibi's order of fried eggs, bacon, and hash browns, which promised to grease her thought processes for hours.

In movies, people on the run from killers, having recently seen the severed fingers of a corpse, did not take time out for breakfast. They didn't take time out for the bathroom, either, or to think about how little life and movies resembled each other.

With a pen and a small notebook that she carried in her purse, she made a note to that effect, which she headlined REMEMBER FOR NOVEL: MOVIES AND LIFE. While she ate, her intention was to make a list of things she needed to buy and to do in order to stay off the grid as much as possible, but she wasn't surprised that she should also be jotting down ideas for her fiction. After all, she wasn't always running for her life and trying to save the life of another, though she *was* always a writer.

Okay, she needed a disposable cell phone. Although it didn't have the smartphone features she might need, it couldn't be traced to her and wouldn't make her vulnerable to GPS bloodhounds. And if they still sold those electronic GPS maps, which wouldn't have any link to another device known to be owned by her, she could use one.

She found herself making another note off the subject, this one regarding the three occasions that she had used Captain's trick to forget unwanted memories. They had been spread over ten years. She headlined the list IMPORTANT!

The first time had been when, with Captain's help and a candle flame, she had burned to ashes the incident of the crawling thing. She'd been five years and ten months old when the creature terrorized her, six and a half when she took steps to forget it.

The second time, she was ten, and the captain had been dead about four months.

She burned the memory of what happened in the attic above his apartment, which still remained beyond recollection. In that instance, she had not even written the memory on paper, but had merely stood before the ceramic logs in the bungalow's living-room fireplace and had offered the memory to the gas flames.

As Bibi composed her list with salient details, Norm's resonated with conversations, clinking cutlery, rattling china and glassware, and background music that she could not identify and that soon she did not hear. With her concentration came a silence broken not even by the sounds of her eating, for she heard nothing now other than the whisper of pen on paper.

The third time, she had been sixteen, half crazy over the loss of Olaf, confused and distraught and bitter and angry, when to her had come a most hideous idea, an intention so loathsome that she could hardly believe it had originated in her own mind; and though the plan that began to form was so out of character, she knew that the temptation to implement it would be irresistible. Had she acted on that idea, she would have ruined her life and the lives of her parents. And so she wrote it on a page of a notebook, tore it out, and fed the page to flames in the fireplace, taking no chance that offering it without committing it to writing would work as it had worked before.

In those three forgotten moments were the roots of her current troubles. What had crawled the floor of her bedroom? What happened in that spidered attic where fog quested through the vents? To ease the unendurable pressure of her emotions in the wake of the dog's cremation, what abomination had obsessed her, what violence or outrage had she feared committing so much that it must be burned out of her memory?

She was surprised that she had finished eating. As she put her fork down on the empty plate, the sounds and pleasing aromas of the establishment seeped back into her awareness.

There in the ordinariness of Norm's restaurant, Bibi wondered about the extraordinary nature of her secret self. Proof seemed to be mounting that a singular darkness gathered in her heart, though she saw herself as a child of sea and sand, of ocean breeze and summer light. She knew that few people ever completely — or even largely — understood themselves. And yet she had assumed that she was one of the enlightened few, that she could read herself from first page to last and grasp every nuance of Bibi Blair.

After she assured the waitress that she wanted nothing else, Bibi left a tip, picked up the check with the intention of paying at the cashier's station, and rose from the booth. As she slung her purse over her shoulder and turned, she saw Chubb Coy at the farther end of the busy restaurant, having breakfast in a booth by the big front windows. The hospital security chief had no evident interest in her, apparently didn't even know she was there. His attention was focused entirely on his pancakes and his breakfast companion, Solange St. Croix, holy mother of the university writing program.

58
OFF THE GRID

Whether Chubb Coy and Dr. St. Croix were Wrong People or were compatriots of another kind, conspiring for their own purposes, the professor seemed to regard Norm's with the disdain that Bibi imagined Terezin and his pals would hold toward any restaurant lacking white tablecloths and designer china. Before her stood only an untouched glass of water. Her expression was more sour than usual, and she sat with the shoulders-back rigidity and lifted chin of a stern advocate of temperance who found herself unaccountably in a tavern. Her apparent contempt was not directed at Coy, as he plowed through his pancakes, for the two of them were engaged in animated conversation that seemed to amuse rather than offend him.

Before they might take notice of her, Bibi turned away from them, sat down, and fished enough money out of her purse to pay the entire bill, which she left on the table with the tip. At the back of the room were double portholed doors to the kitchen, and she headed for them as though she had legitimate business with someone on the staff, her face averted from Chubb Coy and his date.

Cooks and other staffers looked up in surprise, less because she didn't belong there than because she had slammed through the doors with the energy of someone bent on lodging a loud complaint. When she started to make her way through prep aisles, past the griddles and grills and ovens, someone asked what she wanted, and someone else tried to give her directions to the women's restroom. She saw the distant back door and waved them away, saying, "Air, need some air," as though the dining room behind her had abruptly become a vacuum.

In the parking lot, after she moved the Honda to have a clear view of the entrance to the restaurant, Bibi slouched behind the steering wheel and wished that she had a baseball cap. Twenty minutes later, Coy and the professor came outside and stood talking for a minute before shaking hands and parting. He went to his black Lexus, and she got into a Mercedes.

Starting the engine, Bibi figured she should follow one or the other, but then decided not to bother with either. Being a former cop, Chubb Coy would spot a tail in minutes. Wherever the professor was going, it was unlikely to be as revelatory as finding her here with this man. That they knew each other was enough to convince Bibi that they were in league against her and that she had been a topic — if not *the* topic — of their meeting. If later she needed to have a few words with Solange St. Croix, she knew where to find the bitch.

After the Lexus and the Mercedes were out of sight, Bibi sat for a while, thinking about coincidences. She didn't believe in them. Could they have known where to find her? Could they have wanted to be seen? Could they be all-knowing masters of the universe in human form? "For God's sake, Beebs," she said, "you're losing it." Even if they knew what kind of car she was driving now, which they didn't, they couldn't have known she would be going to Norm's until she got there. Anyway, she was certain she hadn't been followed. But she still didn't believe in coincidences.

From Norm's, she went to three different branches of her bank and withdrew two hundred dollars from each ATM, bringing her supply of cash to $814. At a big-box store, she purchased a disposable cell phone and an electronic map with GPS. She also bought a baseball cap and a pair of sunglasses in case she again needed to disguise herself a little.

In the parking lot, as she unlocked the Honda and put her purchases on the front passenger seat, she began to feel like a sly operator, slipping off the grid with the ease of a senior CIA agent.

Which was when someone behind her said, "Is that you, Bibi? Bibi Blair?"

59
THE FIRST TO
RECOGNIZE HER TALENT

Bibi swung around to confront a woman who was vaguely familiar, but no name came to mind. Maybe thirty. Lots of tumbling blond hair. Face as smooth and unlined as raw chicken flesh with the pebbly skin stripped off. Pert nose, porn-star lips. Teeth white enough to blind. A projecting bosom on which a line of crows could perch.

"Hope you haven't gone too big-time literary to remember us little people, Gidget. It's not even been six years."

"Miss Hoffline," Bibi said, not because she could confirm the woman's identity from the visual clues, but because no one other than her eleventh-grade English teacher had ever called her Gidget.

"These days, it's Marissa Hoffline-Vorshack. Married right at the top two years ago. His name's Leopold. Real-estate development."

Bibi almost said, *If that's his name, why aren't you Marissa Hoffline-Development?* Miss

Hoffline, however, had been a world-class mistress of mean, capable of eviscerating you with such finesse that, if you were hurt by her sharp tongue, she could successfully argue that you had misunderstood either her intention or every word she'd said. Better not to get into a pissing contest with her. Instead, Bibi said, "You look . . . really good."

"Four years ago, I refreshed myself a little. Nice of you to notice."

Before she had refreshed herself, Miss Hoffline had been a thirty-five-year-old brunette of the mouse-brown variety with crooked teeth and the chest of a sixteen-year-old boy. This transformation involved industrial plastic surgery, at least a quart of Botox, and more than a little voodoo.

"Of course I don't teach anymore. Don't have to. That's my café-au-lait Bentley over there. But I always tell people," said Mrs. Hoffline-Vorshack, "I was the first to recognize your talent."

That was a crock and a half. She had focused more criticism on Bibi than she had on any of the other kids in the class, especially when the subject was her writing. Bibi had benefited from many good teachers in high school, but it was for one like this that kids had long ago invented spitballs.

As if Mrs. Hoffline-Vorshack saw a flash of resentment in her former student's eyes, she said, "I was always a little hard on you, dear, just a little, because you needed some prodding now and then to reach your full potential."

Bibi managed a smile that must have looked like that on a ventriloquist's dummy. "I appreciate that. Well, nice to have seen you again."

Leaning closer, so that her heroic bosom seemed about to topple her off balance, the woman said, "May I ask one question?"

Bibi wanted only to be gone from there and off the grid, which would probably happen quicker if she allowed the question. "Sure, of course," she said, expecting a nasty crack about the ancient Honda.

Instead, Mrs. Hoffline-Vorshack asked, "Has your novel made enemies for you? Why are you packing heat?"

For a moment, Bibi blanked on the word *heat,* but then she said, "A gun? But I'm not."

"Now, really, Gidget, my Leo gets threats, a man of his position, so he has a concealed-carry license. If you've got a trained eye, as I have, a very sharp eye, no tailoring is good enough to entirely conceal the telltale bulge."

There was no telltale bulge. The shoulder rig held the pistol at Bibi's side, in the roomiest part of her blazer.

"Well, sorry to say, your eye has misled you this time. I've no reason to carry a gun."

As Bibi started to turn away, the woman gripped her by one arm. With concern that was no more real than her bosom, the refreshed ex-teacher said, "Oh, damn, you don't have a concealed-carry permit, do you? Bibi, really, you can get in a lot of trouble, you really can. Carrying without a license, you could go to prison."

The parking lot was busy with shoppers going to and from the store, and Mrs. Hoffline-Vorshack had the volume, although not the graceful cadences, of an auctioneer. People were looking at them, curious, frowning.

With through-clenched-teeth intensity, Bibi said, "I have no gun. Now let go of me."

The woman let go of Bibi's arm, only to grab her left lapel and pull aside her blazer, revealing the holster and pistol. "You always were a bit of a rule-breaker, girl. Always. But being the first to recognize your talent, I don't want to see you ruin your career."

Bibi clawed Mrs. Hoffline-Vorshack's hand off her blazer. "Lady, what is *wrong* with you? Get away from me."

"If you don't have a concealed-carry permit, you should take that off right now, this very minute, and put it in the trunk."

A few passersby stopped to watch the altercation. They must have been people who never saw TV news. These days, in situations like this, if you didn't keep moving, you became part of the body count.

"I *have* a concealed-carry license," Bibi hissed, and she started around the Honda to the driver's door.

The former English teacher caught up with her between the headlights. "If you really, truly had one, then why didn't you say so already? Why didn't you?"

Turning a withering glare on her assailant, Bibi bit off each word of her reply. "Because. I. Don't. Want. Every. Idiot. To. Know."

Mrs. Hoffline-Vorshack's resistance to withering was equal to that of granite. "Don't you snap at me, young lady. If you have a license, show it, and I won't worry you'll ruin your life. Otherwise, I'll have to call your parents."

"I'm twenty-two years old, for God's sake."

"Not to me, you're not."

As Bibi reached the driver's door with the former teacher close behind, one of the onlookers stepped forward. Tall, muscular, with a weathered face and a walrus mustache, wearing a bandana around his head and a tank top unsuited to the cool morning, arms and shoulders and neck crawling with tattoos of reptiles and spiders, he looked as if he'd stepped out of a version of Ray Bradbury's *The Illustrated Man* written in an alternate universe where Bradbury had dropped acid while at the keyboard. "Excuse me, ladies. Maybe I can negotiate a little peace here."

Bibi seized the moment. "This woman insists she knows me, I've never seen her before in my life, she's a mental case."

Wounded by the accusation, Mrs. Hoffline-Vorshack turned to the hulking would-be arbitrator to defend herself against Bibi's slander, stepping away from the Honda and pointing to her car in the facing row of vehicles. "Do you see that Bentley over there, *my* Bentley? Mental cases do not drive café-au-lait Bentleys."

As the woman made her case to be judged sane, Bibi got into the Honda and started the engine. When she gave the car too much gas as she pulled out of her parking space, Mrs. Hoffline-Vorshack reeled back as if in danger of being run down, but the illustrated man did not flinch, as though he had no doubt that his pumped physique would prevail undamaged in a collision with a mere sedan.

Driving away from the big-box store and into the street, Bibi raised her voice as she had not done during the bizarre encounter: "What the blazing hell was *that* about?" The confrontation seemed to have been more than a chance interaction with a former teacher. She sensed in the incident a suggestion of design, a prefiguring of an event to come, some elusive meaning that she needed to pin down and examine.

60

THE PANTHER OF LOST TIME

A few blocks from the big-box store, Bibi took refuge in the parking lot of a strip mall. In addition to the line of shared-wall businesses, a freestanding building housed Donut Heaven, on the roof of which a golden halo revolved above a giant glazed doughnut.

Although the disposable phone promised "instant activation," she wasn't surprised that the call-back confirmation would take a while.

In the meantime, she read the instructions for the electronic map while brooding about the ludicrous encounter with Mrs. Hoffline-Vorshack, which continued to seem important and to be tied somehow to her current troubles. To imagine that the former teacher was part of the conspiracy against her, however, would be to step out of justifiable paranoia onto a steep path toward mania. If Hoffline-Vorshack, why not the unnamed arbitrator with the walrus mustache and the swarming tattoos? And if him, why not every customer of the nearby Donut Heaven? Everyone in every car passing in the street? *Everyone everywhere?*

"Better chill, Beebs," she warned herself.

When the map, with its GPS link, was up and running, she tried to locate 11 Moonrise Way, the address that had been spelled in Scrabble tiles on the table in Calida's home office. She didn't have the name of a town or city, but the device allowed her to search also by county. There was no Moonrise Way or Lane or Street or Avenue or Boulevard or Parkway anywhere in Orange County or in the surrounding nine counties. Without a city name, the search process proved tedious when compared to what she could have achieved with her laptop, but using her online account might allow the Wrong People to locate her as soon as she logged on.

When her disposable phone came into service, she considered calling her parents. They might be hungover from the previous night's celebration, though clearheaded enough. If they hadn't already tried to phone her, they would soon, and they would become alarmed as, one after another, their calls went to voice mail.

But if Terezin and his crew had the connections and capabilities of which he had boasted, they might be able to monitor Nancy's and Murphy's phones as readily as could Homeland Security. In that case, if Bibi called her parents, Terezin might capture the electronic signature of her disposable phone, thereby making it possible to track her again, putting her back on the grid. To remain invisible, she could phone only people that he would not expect her to call.

Among the county's more than three million souls, she was, for the moment, if not forever, alone.

Reluctantly she switched off the phone, put it in her purse, and took out the hardcover book that had belonged to Calida. Opening the volume, she thought she saw the inlaid-leather panther spring into motion, leaping toward the spine. Startled, she almost dropped the book, but when she closed the front cover, the panther remained as it had been, frozen in a pounce.

She turned the blank pages, hoping to glimpse again the rippling ghostly lines of script that had swum across the paper, schooling words too pale and swift to be read. But the phenomenon did not repeat, though she paged front to back, back to front, as the light dimmed to darkness and the darkness then faded into light. . . .

When she looked up from the book, Bibi thought more time had passed than just a minute or two. She felt as though she was rising from a kind of waking sleep that had held her for long hours, and in fact she yawned and blinked and worked some saliva into her dry mouth. But the sensation of having been in a trance, of sloughing off the grip of some hypnotic power, had to be a misapprehension, because she still felt full from breakfast and because she was not stiff and achy from having sat for a long period behind the wheel. According to her wristwatch, only a few minutes had passed.

Nevertheless, she closed the volume rather than gaze into it again. And when she returned it to her purse, she said, "Something's very wrong here."

61
AS I LAY DYING

This was one of those days when the fog mimicked the wave action of the sea but in slow motion, gradually receding in the weak warmth of morning light, though never pulling entirely off the coast, then surging inland after an hour or two, reaching not quite as far as previously, retreating once more before returning.

When Bibi drove back into Newport Beach, she had to turn on the headlights long before she reached the bridge to Balboa Peninsula. Once she was cruising on that long arm of land that bulwarked the sea and embraced the harbor, she set the windshield wipers on intermittent to wipe away the insistent condensation.

Kelsey Faulkner's address was in the commercial zone before the super-pricey real estate of Peninsula Point. A tourist destination in warmer months, this district varied between two and three blocks in width, oceanfront to harborfront. It was a fabled piece of ground that brought to mind Dick Dale and the Del-Tones, who created surfer music there in the 1950s, though its flatness inspired in nervous types occasional visions of the obliterating power of a tsunami.

Bibi parked in a metered lot and walked through sea-scented fog to the address, which was an unlikely location for the home base of a cult of homicidal lunatics. The shop, Silver Fantasies, offered handcrafted silver jewelry that ranged from inexpensive souvenirs such as leaping-porpoise pendants to exquisite necklaces and bracelets that sold for a few thousand dollars. It was open on an off-season weekday morning, which meant they enjoyed a large local clientele.

Bibi had often seen the place in passing, but having little interest in jewelry, she had never ventured inside. The cheaper items hung on brass racks. The better pieces were displayed in glass cases.

The thirty-something woman sitting at a corner worktable, polishing a bracelet, might have been cast forward in time from the late 1960s. In a long swishy cotton skirt, tie-dyed blouse, crocheted dog collar, and dangly silver peace-symbol earrings, she could have gotten on the stage with any band of that period and been taken for one of them as long as she held a tambourine.

She looked up from her work, smiled, and said, "Not the kind of day they're dreamin' about when they're California dreamin'."

"Better than a tsunami," Bibi replied, though she had never before been one of those nervous types. "Is Kelsey around?"

Pointing to a door at the rear of the shop, the woman said, "In his studio. Just go on back."

Although it was unlikely that she would be dismembered in the workroom of a jewelry shop, Bibi hesitated.

"It's okay," the woman said. "He's not smelting or anything, just designing some new pieces." She frowned. "You do know him?"

Bibi hesitated. "My dad knows him."

"Who's your dad?"

"Murphy Blair. He owns —"

"Sure, Murph. He's cool. Go on back."

Faulkner's studio was more industrial than she expected of an artist-slash-craftsman. Small but arranged for efficiency. Clean but smelling of metal polish and machine oil. Four small high windows at which the fog pressed its blank face.

About fifty, with a mane of white hair that reminded Bibi of Beethoven's, Kelsey Faulkner perched on a stool at a draftsman's table. He was sketching a necklace.

He looked up and smiled. "Now, here's a sudden light in a dreary day."

If the woman in the front room had prepared Bibi, she might still not have been ready for his face. Half of it was handsome. The other half was out of *Phantom of the Opera:* a gnarled mass of keloid scars and furrowed flesh, blister-red twisted through with greasy-looking white tissue. The scars distracted from — but didn't disguise — underlying problems with the structure of cheek and jaw, as if he had suffered a hard impact at speed. Most of his left ear was gone, and the remainder resembled a crust of fungus.

Although Bibi told him that he made lovely jewelry, and though she thought that she concealed her shock, Faulkner read her reaction correctly. He spoke a bit slowly, with precise diction, as though calculation must be required to avoid speaking with an impediment. "I'm sorry. Rita did not prepare you, did she?"

"The saleslady? I said you knew my father. She just assumed. . . ."

"Who is your father?"

"Murphy Blair."

"Nice man. So enthusiastic. He buys my jewelry for your mother."

"That's how you know him?"

"It has been many years since I chose to meet anyone new, other than those customers who insist on expressing their regards to the artisan." He indicated the sketch. "I have my work, my apartment upstairs, my books. That is enough. Sometimes too much."

Because the silversmith seemed to invite the question, Bibi asked, "What happened?"

After a hesitation, he cocked his head and regarded her with greater interest than before. "You are not like the others, are you?"

"What others?"

He studied her for a moment, and then said, "Any others."

"I'm just me. Like anyone."

"Different," he disagreed. "Yours is not just cheap curiosity."

Sensing that he was analyzing her and not yet finished, Bibi said nothing, concerned that pressing him would silence him.

"You do not pity me. Compassion, yes, I see your compassion. But no pity, none of the quiet disgust or contempt that comes with pity."

She waited.

Faulkner closed his eyes and, after a moment, nodded as if in response to some conversation with himself. When he opened his eyes, he said, "A young man clubbed me with a length of steel pipe. While I was unconscious, he raped my wife, my lovely Beth, and stabbed her twenty-three times. As I lay dying . . ." He corrected himself. "As she lay dying, he poured acid in her face. And then in mine. The burning acid, the fierce stinging, woke me as he was leaving. I lived. Beth did not."

Bibi would have settled into a chair if one

had been available. "Who was he?"

"Robert Warren Faulkner. Bobby. Our only child. Sixteen years old at the time."

"My God."

At that moment, the ruined face didn't trouble Bibi. The man's eyes were what she found distressing, yet she could not easily look away from them.

"I'm sorry," she said, and he looked away.

The central element of the sketch on the drawing board was a stylized rising bird, wings spread. It might have been a phoenix.

"Your face," Bibi said. "It could be made . . . much better."

"Yes. Surgery. Reconstruction. Some radiation and corticosteroid injections to prevent new scars from forming where the old ones were removed. But to what purpose? Beth will still be dead."

Bibi could think of no response, and if she found the words, she knew that she should not speak them.

"You see," the silversmith continued, "the boy was obsessed with Nazis, the war, the death camps."

"Auschwitz-Birkenau. Terezin," she said.

"Dachau, Treblinka, all of them. And because this animal Hitler was interested in the occult, Robert developed an interest as well. Beth became concerned, wanted to consult a therapist. I said, no, at that age, many boys are fascinated by horrors of one kind or another. It is part of growing up. Nazis. The walking dead. Vampires. One thing or another. He will outgrow it, I said. I had no clue what was happening in his head. Beth had a suspicion, intuition, but I had no clue. Until . . ."

Fog seeking blindly at the high windows. The soft rumble-roar of an airliner, fresh from John Wayne Airport and gaining altitude over the sea.

Out in the salesroom, Rita greeted a customer. Muffled voices.

Bibi said, "What happened to him?"

"They never found him. He took our money, some things of value. He had a plan. But I think he is dead."

"Why do you think so?"

"In all this time, he would have called to torment me. Toward the end, he had become arrogant, verbally abusive. He enjoyed my reaction to his insolence."

"How long ago did it happen?"

"Seventeen years."

"He'd be thirty-three now."

In the other room, conversation and soft laughter. Business as usual. Outside, the voice of the airliner fading toward Japan.

The silversmith said, "Why are you here, Miss Blair?"

She surveyed the studio. "Are you afraid he might come back?"

"No. His cruelty is such, he would rather I

live . . . and suffer."

She met his eyes. "But if he did come back? What then?"

From the shelf under the tilted drawing board, Kelsey Faulkner drew a pistol. Evidently, he kept it with him at all times.

Bibi wasn't convinced. "After all, he is your son."

"He was my son. I do not know what he became." He regarded the pistol with a solemn longing before returning it to the shelf. "It will never happen. Because I do not deserve the satisfaction."

Bibi didn't believe that her last question was germane, that silver was a meaningful link, but she needed to ask it nonetheless. With the tiles spelling ASHLEY BELL aligned in her mind's eye, she said, "Have you ever made bowls, Mr. Faulkner? Silver bowls?"

"Only jewelry. My talent is limited. I am no Georg Jensen." His smile was not truly a smile, for its mother was melancholy. "But you didn't answer my question. Why are you here, Miss Blair?"

"Good-bye, Mr. Faulkner. I hope you get that satisfaction."

62

A SMILE FROM THE PAST

In the parking lot, behind the wheel of the Honda, Bibi got her money's worth from the quarters that earlier she'd fed to the meter. She spent a few minutes studying the photo of Ashley Bell, though she didn't know why and didn't see anything in the face that she hadn't seen previously. No less than before, she felt a poignant kindredness and a compelling desire to give everything she had to the search. No, that was not quite right. She wasn't compelled, wasn't driven by some exterior force, not by any conventional motive that she could name. Rather, she was *impelled* to find the imprisoned girl, pressed forward by an urgent inner prompting, not by mere desire but by need, as though she had been born and had lived twenty-two years for one purpose, which was to spare Ashley Bell from whatever outrage her captors intended to perpetrate upon her.

She put aside the photograph, opened her laptop, and dared to go online for a brief monster hunt. She quickly found the story, a sensation at the time, when she had been only five and oblivious of what occurred beyond the sphere of her family. In those days, the Faulkners had lived farther down the coast, in Laguna Beach. Bibi already knew more than she cared to know about the savage details of Robert's attack on his parents. She wanted photographs of him, and on different sites she located seven, six of them apparently provided to the authorities by people other than his father.

Two snapshots showed him at ages too young to be useful for her purpose, and in the other five, he was between fourteen and sixteen. A handsome boy, even striking, he stared directly into the camera, solemn in every instance except one, when he was fourteen and smiling broadly, posed against a backdrop of palm trees bracketing an ocean view. Bibi resisted the temptation to read wickedness in the tilt of his smile or derangement in the sheen and squint of his eyes; he looked like any other boy and, instead of a future murderer, could as easily have been a saint in the making.

The two photos taken closest to the night of the crime — in the first, he was fifteen, in the other sixteen — revealed that Robert had changed. Undeniably, his posture was more aggressive, and there seemed to be a challenge in his attitude. Bibi was not imagining an arrogance in his expression, almost a sneer. He wore his hair shorter than before, especially on the sides. He parted it on the right, as always, but more severely, so that white scalp showed like a chalk line. Combed to the left across his brow, the hair spilled down his temple in a familiar way, and after a moment she saw that he had styled it after Hitler's haircut.

She had intended to send the best picture to her parents with a warning to be on the lookout for a dangerous man who resembled this young boy. But now, she realized, seventeen years would have changed Robert so much that a photo from his adolescence would be inadequate proof of his current appearance. Besides, Nancy and Murphy would want to know why he was dangerous, what threat he posed to her, what mess she had gotten into. If she answered their questions, they were more likely to be targeted than if she told them nothing.

Or were they?

On Balboa Boulevard, traffic cruising down-Peninsula toward the Wedge, one of the most famous and dangerous surfing spots on the planet, and traffic headed up-Peninsula roiled the insistent fog. White masses churned around the Honda, as if the world Bibi knew had dissolved, as if from the atomic soup of its diffusion, a new world was forming, one that would be hostile to her at every turn.

Robert Warren Faulkner, alias Birkenau Terezin, living under a more ordinary name as yet unknown, had threatened her mom and dad if she contacted them. He wanted to keep her isolated, the easier to deal with her when he found her. But she suspected that no matter what she did, Nancy and Murphy and Pogo and everyone she loved were already on Terezin's termination list. Like the genocidal maniac whom he so admired, Terezin would want a final solution, eliminating not just Bibi but also all the people who cared about her enough to ask questions and pursue justice after her death.

Paxton Thorpe could be no help to her in the current crisis, and she didn't for a moment fantasize about him riding to the rescue from some distant corner of the world. But she allowed herself to dwell on him for a few minutes because the beauty of the man — mind and heart and body — purged some of her anxiety, inflated her hope.

She started the car and pulled onto the street. She knew where she had to go next, but she didn't have any idea what she would do when she got there. Solange St. Croix lived in Laguna Beach, which Bibi had known for years. But in searching for photographs of Kelsey Faulkner's homicidal son, she had noticed that the professor's house and the scene of the crime shared the same address.

63
Sleeping on a Sea of Troubles

Deep in the floating city, Gibb had lain sleepless.

A Navy SEAL was trained to endure things that he once would have thought he could not survive. And if he could not sustain physically and mentally and emotionally through the worst shitstorms of war with his confidence intact, he needed to get out of spec ops and become a mall cop or a librarian, or whatever the hell. As a SEAL, you saw — and confronted — things no one should have to see, horrors that would leave most people in need of therapy for years, but you could not let what you saw make you cynical, diminish you, or in any way corrupt you. Once you bought into valor, it was your residence forever; you could neither sell it like a house nor remodel it into something less grand, and if the day came when you refused to live there anymore, you would also be unable to live any longer with yourself.

Nevertheless, SEALs were of course afraid

at times, and like everyone else, they had bad dreams. That first night after taking out Abdullah al-Ghazali and his crew, in a four-bunk cabin aboard ship, Pax Thorpe had muttered and exclaimed in his dreams. Having plunged rather than fallen into sleep, Perry and Danny had not been disturbed by their lead petty officer's brief and mostly quiet outbursts.

Gibb and Pax were in the lower bunks, a narrow aisle separating them. Although exhausted from the mission, Gibb had been for a while unable to sleep, and he had listened to Pax's peculiar outbursts, committing some of them to memory.

In the morning, over breakfast, he had said, "Pax, you sounded like you were at a Hitchcock triple feature last night. Who threw acid in whose face?"

Pax had gone pale as he looked up from his mess tray. "Damnedest dream. Crazy bits and pieces, none of it connected, but way vivid."

"Was it Hitler raped his mother," Gibb asked, "and whose fingers did he cut off? Man, when you give up spec ops, you should get a job writing for one of the crazier cable-TV shows."

64
A LITERARY LION'S DEN

In Laguna Beach, the murder house stood three stories tall on a steep street, inland of Coast Highway, where the residences faced either north or south, in both cases lacking ocean views but still expensive. There were enormous old trees, shallow front yards, and an eclectic mix of architectural styles, some poorly conceived. The house where Beth Faulkner had died was moderne, slabs of stucco and smooth teak decks piled like the layers of a wedding cake baked for a bloodless bride and groom as romantic as carrots.

At that hour of a weekday, Dr. Solange St. Croix would most likely be at the university, guarding the standards of contemporary American fiction and dispiriting young writers. Bibi parked across the street and watched the house for half an hour. No one appeared on any of the decks or in any of the rooms beyond the expansive windows.

The fog was somewhat thinner than it had been in Newport, though still thick enough to backdrop an urban version of *The Hound of the Baskervilles*. And of hounds there was no shortage, a parade of Lagunans walking a dog show's worth of breeds uphill and down. No one seemed to find it odd that a woman in a baseball cap and sunglasses should be slouching in a junker, conducting surveillance. Laguna prided itself on being an artist's colony that accepted all classes and cultures, not merely tolerating eccentrics but delighting in them.

After taking off the cap and sunglasses, Bibi proceeded boldly to St. Croix's front door. When no one responded to the bell, she moseyed to the back of the residence with the practiced nonchalance of an experienced housebreaker. The doors and windows were locked, though the rear door to the garage was secured by a flimsy lockset. Even if the house had an alarm, the garage was not likely to be on the system. She could have slipped the latch by sliding a credit card between door and jamb; but she had left her purse in the car.

When she considered returning to the Honda to get her Visa card, something snapped in Bibi. Not a big snap. Not like the thick trunk of her psychology splitting all the way through and toppling. But not the subtle crack of a twig, either. Her resentment at the disruption of her life, the anxiety and frustration and bewilderment arising from the frightening events of the past eighteen hours, had stressed her to the point that something had to give. Just one branch broke, one branch in the elaborate tree that was Bibi, and it was labeled CAUTION. To hell with her Visa card. She didn't need no stinkin' Visa card. She kicked the door. She didn't regret the noise. She *liked* the noise. She was accomplishing something at last. She kicked again. With the third kick, the latch gave. The dark garage welcomed her.

She found the light switch. No vehicles. She pulled shut the door behind her.

The interior door, between the garage and house, had a solid core and a serious deadbolt. She could kick it until she dropped of exhaustion, without effect. A credit card would be useless, too.

Gardening implements hung on a wall. Nearby stood a workbench with drawers flanking the knee space. She found a variety of tools tumbled in the drawers, including a screwdriver and hammer.

At the lowest of four door hinges, she inserted the blade of the screwdriver between the head and the shank of the pivot pin, and pried it half an inch out of the hinge barrel. She tapped the bottom of the screwdriver with the hammer until the pin came free. Soon all four were extracted, tossed aside, ringing across the concrete floor.

Each hinge barrel was formed by five

knuckles; two were part of the frame leaf, three were part of the center leaf. Without pins to hold the knuckles together, they separated slightly, but the door remained in place. "No quitters," she muttered. With the screwdriver, then with the claw hammer, she pried open a crack between door and jamb, big enough to hook her fingers through. She wrenched on the barrier until — scraping, screaking — the hinge knuckles parted and the door stuttered outward maybe two inches, arcing across the threshold. No alarm. Sweet. It was now held only by the deadbolt, which wouldn't swivel like a hinge. As she struggled, the wood began to crack around the screws that secured the mortise lock. The engaged bolt rattled against the striker plate. She grunted and cursed and put everything she had into the battle until, after more splintering of wood, the door came open just wide enough to allow her to squeeze through into the kitchen, where she stood listening to the house and wiping sweat off her brow with the sleeve of her jacket.

Sometimes Bibi wished she was Paxton. He would have used a packet of C-4 explosive to blow open the door and take out a portion of the wall with it. Neighbors were tolerant in Laguna. They probably wouldn't complain until the second or third explosion.

Filtered by the marine layer that swaddled the town, morning light floated through, rather than pierced, the floor-to-ceiling windows, leaving shadows in places, providing an adequate though mysterious somber radiance like that of a late-afternoon snowscape.

As she moved through the ground floor, one chamber opening to the next with minimal space given to hallways, she thought that the construction must be far better than the exterior architecture. The sounds of the busy world didn't intrude. Pale limestone floors, the sparest possible use of area carpets, no draperies whatsoever, marble fireplace surrounds, mirrors of remarkable depth, steel-and-leather furniture so acutely angled and forbidding that it seemed to have been designed by an insect consciousness: Every hard surface should have rung with brittle echoes of every noise that Bibi made, but she walked in silence, like a spirit, as if this were a temple buried for centuries under a hundred feet of desert sand.

There were moments when she felt as alone as she had ever been, but other moments when she paused to listen intently, more than half convinced that someone waited here for her, like a trapdoor spider anticipating her fatal step.

The ground floor clearly was intended for entertaining, for the cocktail parties and literary soirees that were legendary among Dr. St. Croix's fellow faculty members, guest lecturers, and students. Bibi had not lasted long enough in the writing program to have been invited here; yet room by room, detail by detail, everything upon which she turned her gaze seemed familiar. With uncanny accuracy, she could predict what waited around every corner, beyond every doorway.

In those cold and sparely furnished spaces, nothing explained the professor's role in recent events or confirmed that she was in some way connected to Terezin. If there was a study or home office where some clue was most likely to be found, it must be on the second floor.

Bibi climbed an open spiral staircase of glass and steel, past large windows where the fog pressed a legion of half-formed faces.

The second floor was alike to the first, with a glitz-free home theater, a lightly equipped gym, and finally the study that Bibi had hoped to find. A Spartan room in the vein of St. Croix's on-campus office. Two black-and-white abstract paintings. Bookshelves largely empty. A forbidding couch. A black Herman Miller office chair, the only comfortable-looking furniture in the house, stood behind a desk of brushed steel and gray-enameled panels.

All this, too, was disturbingly familiar.

Only the desk offered possibilities, though not many. The study lacked a computer. Not a single object stood on the desktop. There were four drawers, in which Bibi found nothing of interest.

In the southwest corner of the study, a single flight of stairs led to the third floor. For the first time, she had to switch on a light. At the top, she arrived at a black-lacquered door.

Bibi suspected that when there were guests in the house, this door would be locked, for it and the stairs that led to it felt like a fateful passage to a forbidden realm. The lock was not now engaged.

As she gripped the doorknob, she knew what she would surely find beyond, not the precise details but the essence: rooms that were in stark contrast to everything on the first two floors.

When she stepped across the threshold and, with a wall switch, turned on several artfully positioned stained-glass and blown-glass lamps, she passed from stark modernism to high Victorian. The door opened onto a parlor with hand-printed wallpaper in a colorful floral pattern. Delicate lace curtains overlaid with maroon-velvet tasseled-and-fringed draperies. Two étagères full of porcelain collectibles. Chesterfield sofa. Studded-leather armchair. A large circular side table, covered with fabric that itself was covered with a crocheted overlay, accommodated portrait busts and enameled ornaments and small framed drawings.

Bibi felt akin to the children who discovered Narnia, as though she'd passed into another world, but also as if she had returned to a place she'd visited before. The contrasting sumptuous fabrics and the extreme clutter were, even for the period, evidence less of a passion for Victoriana than of a troubling obsession.

Beyond the parlor, a master-bedroom suite offered more of the same. The centerpiece was a bed with an elaborate layered canopy, its four posts carved with twining vines and gilded flowers.

Bibi stood just inside the bedroom, both enchanted and filled with misgiving, wondering if anything of interest might be found in the nightstands. Before she could explore further, the black-lacquered door at the head of the stairs slammed shut.

65
SILENCE LIKE A CANCER GROWS

As Bibi turned toward the door between the bedroom and the parlor, the time seemed to have come for her to draw the Sig Sauer from her shoulder rig.

Pax had given her a few days of instruction at a shooting range, and in his company she had fired hundreds of rounds at paper targets in the form of human silhouettes. She had been concerned that in a crisis she would make a wrong decision, shoot when she should hold her fire, accidentally take down someone other than her target. Her defense had always been words, and if she shot off the wrong ones, an explanation and an apology had remedied her mistake. But apologies didn't heal a mortal chest wound.

When no one appeared in the portion of the parlor that Bibi could see through the doorway, when the silence became so attenuated that she began to feel she was being tested, perhaps mocked, she overcame her lingering inhibition and drew the pistol. She held it in her right hand, with the muzzle aimed at the ceiling.

She glanced at a window, wondering if beyond it lay one of the teak decks to which she could flee if necessary. Her journey through the house had disoriented her. She didn't know in what direction this window faced, and the fog that cloistered the coast prevented her from getting her bearings by the intensity and angle of sunlight.

Silence could be an effective strategy. It frayed the nerves and encouraged the imagination to invent one anxious-making scenario after another, until you mistook every smallest and most innocent sound for the start of the expected assault, and were at a fateful moment distracted from the true threat. With every step that Bibi had taken in this house, her apprehension had been whetted, until now it was razor-sharp.

In movies, the silence-tortured character asked, *Is someone there? Who's there? Hello? What do you want?* The answer to that last question would always be a variation of Terezin's response when Bibi, on the phone, had inquired of him what he wanted from her: *Only to kill you.* Therefore, silence should be met with silence — and with well-considered action.

She brought the pistol down into a two-hand grip, arms extended, as Pax had taught her. She cleared the open doorway fast, bedroom to parlor, staying low, sweeping the gun left to right, right to left.

No one crouched behind the Chesterfield or the armchair. No one sheltered behind the voluminous draperies.

Bibi stood alone, wondering if the door had been slammed by a draft. But the tight construction of the house disfavored drafts no less than it fostered silence. She did not believe in dramatically timed currents of air any more than she believed in coincidences.

Silence now lay deeper than any ordinary hush, as deep as though commanded by a sorcerer's spell. She could not hear her own breathing or the knocking of her heart, and therefore it was a weak odor, faded almost beyond detection, that alerted her. Not a perfume. More subtle than the most diluted and refined product of flowers or spices. It might have been the smell of clean hair rinsed free of the slightest trace of a shampoo's fragrance, or skin likewise scrubbed of all sweat and soap. Neither a pleasant nor an unpleasant scent, it was as disturbing as it was faint, suggesting a cold, implacable presence.

When Bibi turned, pistol still in a two-hand grip, Solange St. Croix halted only seven or eight feet away. The professor seemed to have resolved out of thin air, until Bibi saw beyond her the entrance to a bathroom with pedestal sink and claw-foot tub. In the interest of perfecting the Victorian décor, the door was integrated seamlessly into its surroundings, the lower portion stained and trimmed with molding to match the wainscoting, the upper section wallpapered.

The woman was dressed as always in a stylish but severe suit that would have served her well had she been a mortician. Graying hair pulled back tighter than ever and captured in a bun, skin paler than before, lips all but bloodless, she seemed to have been born of the fog that licked the lace-curtained windows.

Wary of the pistol but not intimidated, St. Croix came no closer to Bibi, but began slowly to circle her, as if waiting for an opening. Her intentions weren't obvious, because she carried no weapon, though it would not have been a surprise if a knife had appeared magically from tailoring that seemed too severe to conceal one.

In a mutual strategic silence, the professor circled 360 degrees and Bibi turned in place to follow her. Which of them was the moon and which the planet, it was hard to say. St. Croix chewed on her lower lip as if biting back words, and throughout her revolution, she met her former student's stare without looking away for an instant. Her blue eyes were two jewels of hatred.

As the professor began a second circling, bumping against the side table, rattling the art and curios upon it, she said, "And now another outrage. What are you doing here, Miss Blair? What did you come to steal? Or is it something other than theft that gets you off, something degenerate, something kinky?"

Instead of answering, Bibi said, "Why were you having breakfast with Chubb Coy?"

Squinting, eyes glittering through her lashes, St. Croix said, "So you still follow me, do you? After all these years?"

"The opposite is true, and you know it."

"The opposite of what is what?"

"You're the one who followed me. I was in the restaurant first."

"You're the same lying bitch you always were. A sick little lying bitch. But you're not half as clever as you think you are."

Although there was nothing cuddly about the woman, she had a feline quality, as intense and merciless as a cat on the hunt.

Bibi said, "What do you have to do with Terezin, with Bobby Faulkner?"

Still circling, perhaps calculating whether she could come in under the pistol, St. Croix said, "Is that someone I'm supposed to know in whatever fantasy or scheme you're cooking up?"

"Seventeen years ago, he killed his mother in this house and nearly killed his father."

The professor didn't dispute that statement. She didn't react to it at all. "Are you ready to admit what *you* have done, Miss Blair?"

"I broke in here to find something that might explain how you're involved with the murderer, Robert Faulkner, with Terezin."

St. Croix stopped circling. The image that she projected so forcefully to the world was one that she also cherished, which was why she made such an effort to suppress the evidence of her natural beauty, a little of which was always evident nonetheless. At this moment, however, her expression of contempt was so fierce that the last traces of loveliness were purged, and she was the very avatar of animosity, of pure detestation.

"I mean," she said, "what you did *then,* the rotten damn thing that got you thrown out of the university."

"I wasn't thrown out. I quit."

On the two previous occasions that she and the professor had a confrontation regarding Bibi's unknown offense, St. Croix hadn't been this over-the-top furious. But now she worked herself from rage to fury, too hot for the cool priestess of the written word.

"You quit. Yes, you quit. Because if you hadn't, I would have seen that you were thrown out on your ass."

Frustrated, of half a mind to shoot St. Croix in the foot to force her to stop being so enigmatic, Bibi said, "Okay, all right, so tell me what I did."

"You know damn well what you did." Her cold eyes were hot now, the gas-flame blue of the fire in a pet-cemetery cremator.

"Pretend I don't know. Tell me. Spit it out and humiliate me. If it's so bad, then make me feel like the shit you think I am."

A man said, "Enough of this."

Chubb Coy had opened the black-lacquered door and entered the third-floor suite. He wore a black suit, gray shirt, no tie. His pistol was fitted with a sound suppressor.

Bibi kept the P226 on the professor, who was nearer than the chief of hospital security (and whatever the hell else he might be).

Judging by her reaction, St. Croix was no less surprised by Coy's arrival than was Bibi. "What are you doing here? You have no right. This is my *home*. First this sneaky little bitch and now you? I won't tolerate —" She failed to finish the sentence before Coy shot her twice in the chest.

66
HE WHO WOULD RATHER
DIE THAN SHARE

For an instant, Bibi thought that Chubb Coy had meant to shoot her, but, as a consequence of being a poor marksman, had killed the professor instead. However, when he declared, "She would have been a better woman and teacher if someone had been there to shoot her every morning of her life," his intention was no longer in doubt.

Bibi had seen the terrible aftermath of murder but never the act committed. Whatever she might have imagined about such a moment, all that she had written or considered writing about a homicide, failed to capture the shock of it, the piercing and hollowing wound of being witness to a life ended prematurely, the immediate sense that a world ended and with it all the experiences of she whose world it had been. The horrible convulsive reflex of the body as each bullet impacted. The light of being at once extinguished in the eyes. A collapse so different from the fall of anyone with still a spark of life, the hard and undignified drop not of a person but of a thing. Solange St. Croix, no friend of Bibi's, nevertheless evoked in her a pang of grief, not all or even most of it for the professor, but for herself, too, and for everyone born into this world of death.

That she had any compassion at all for St. Croix was remarkable, considering that, when the woman fell, a knife slipped from her sleeve. A switchblade, judging by the operative button on the handle.

The suppressed sound of the two shots did not crash wall to wall, but was like quick words whispered in some incomprehensible language, absorbed without echo by the layered fabrics and the plush upholstery of the Victorian parlor. Even in that muffled moment, as Dr. St. Croix changed from person to remains, Chubb Coy lowered his weapon, thereby making it clear that he would not shoot Bibi, though he did not holster the gun.

"What the hell?" she said, letting the words out in a rush of pent-up breath. *"Why?"*

Coy said, "Such rage. The foolish woman lost control of herself. That babbling. Tongue so loose it might have fallen out of her mouth. I've got interests to protect."

"What interests? She was one of you. You had breakfast with her this morning."

Those blue-flecked steel-gray eyes, which previously were as sharp as scalpels, carving in search of lies to reveal them like tumors, were now blunt bulkheads keeping secret all thoughts that lay behind them. "You don't understand the situation, Miss Blair. There are many factions in this. Some factions may be allied with others now and then, but we aren't all on the same side. This is a high-stakes game, and in a high-stakes game, most people are out for themselves."

"What game?" Bibi demanded. "What's all this about? Where is Ashley Bell? What are they going to do to her?"

His round and amiable face produced an infuriatingly charming smile. "You don't need to know."

"I do. I *need* to know. People want to kill me."

"And they will," he assured her. "To keep the secret, they will kill you six ways at once."

"What secret?"

He only smiled.

When she aimed the pistol at him, he continued to smile — and put away his weapon. "You don't have what it takes to kill a man in cold blood."

"I do. I will."

He shook his head. "Cop intuition. Anyway, I'd rather die than share anything with you."

Bibi lowered the pistol. She said, "Ashley is just a child. Twelve? Thirteen? Why does she have to die?"

He shrugged. "Why does anyone? Some say we'll never know, that to the gods we're like the flies that boys kill on a summer day."

She hated him for his studied indifference. "What kind of bastard are you?"

That smile again. "Any kind you want me to be, Miss Blair."

When he started to turn away from her, she said, "Are you with him, with Terezin?"

His blunt eyes sharpened briefly as he turned to her once more. "That vicious fascist creep and his crypto-Nazi cult? Miss Blair, you almost make me want to kill you for that suggestion. I despise him."

"Well, then, the enemy of your enemy —"

"Is still my enemy. Accept the inevitable, girl. You're easy prey. As a boy, Terezin was a dog, and now he has gone back to the wild. He's a wolf now, like and yet unlike all other wolves, always running at the head of the pack. He dreams of turning the world backward, of a younger world, which is the world of the pack. They'll drag you down sooner than later. You think it's a cult, and it is, but it's bigger than you think. There are a lot of these cockroaches, and they have resources."

He walked out of the Victorian suite. She started after him, but then stopped, halted by a suspicion that at some point in the past few minutes, he had given her a clue that she had missed, had left for her the frayed end of a thread that, if she were to wind it on a spool, would unravel the mystery in which she found herself, revealing every warp and weft of this intricately woven conspiracy. She stood there in the company of the corpse, in the colorful riot of Victoriana, looking but perhaps not seeing, listening in memory to their conversation but perhaps not hearing.

67
A Little Time to Chill

If Chubb Coy had left a thread for her, a clue, Bibi could not find it in the third-floor parlor or remember their conversation vividly enough to tweeze out that frayed end. Baffled, exasperated with herself, she pocketed Dr. St. Croix's switchblade. She snatched up a decorative pillow from the sofa, unzipped the fringed cover, stripped it off, and slipped it over her right hand as if it were a glove. As she made her way down through the house, she tried to recall everything that she had touched, and she paused to wipe each item clean of any fingerprints she might have left.

If she was charged with the murder of Solange St. Croix, that would bring an end to her search for Ashley Bell as certainly as if Terezin murdered her. And if it happened that the arresting officer was one of the Wrong People, he might claim that she had resisted arrest, whether she had or not, justifying a bullet in the head.

She wondered what she would be like if she

got through this alive. Paranoia was now in her blood, like a viral infection, and there might not be a cure for it. She could envision herself in the grip of agoraphobia and social phobia, afraid of open spaces and of people, unable to leave her apartment, living behind a locked door and blinds closed tight.

"Screw that," she said as she crossed the living room.

In the kitchen, on the island, stood a large designer purse that had not been there when Bibi had first entered the house. It must be St. Croix's, left when the woman came through the ruined door from the garage. Whatever else might be said about the professor, no one could deny that she had guts, seeking out the intruder on her own, although she had most likely somehow known the identity of her quarry. Bibi took the purse and continued wiping away fingerprints into the garage, where the dead woman's Mercedes still ticked and pinged as the engine cooled.

There she paused to open St. Croix's handbag, in which she found, as expected, a smartphone. She used it to call her father's cell number, which wouldn't compromise her disposable model if the Wrong People were monitoring Murphy's phone traffic.

He answered on the second ring. "You got Murph."

"Hi, Daddy."

"Bibi! We've been trying to reach you all morning."

"I've been dodging calls."

"Dodging even your own parents? What's wrong?"

"Nothing's wrong. I'm fine."

"Don't flow me a load of feel-good."

"Relax, old man. It's just that I was dying two days ago, and I need a little me time to get a handle on that."

"Tell me! All morning, I'm one minute grinning like a dog and the next minute all verklempt."

Hearing the strong emotion in his voice, Bibi said, "Don't get verklempt on me, Dad."

"I just love you so much, honey."

"I love you, too. But, you know, I want to keep this quick. I'm going down the coast a little, find a cool place to hang out for a couple days."

"A little time to chill."

"Exactly. Maybe Carlsbad. Or La Jolla. I'll let you know when I have a motel. I'm sorry I didn't bring back Mom's BMW this morning."

"That's when we started to worry. But don't you worry, kiddo. We'll hustle over there and fetch it ourselves. Hey, last night, how was Calida?"

"Memorable," Bibi said. "We'll talk about it in a couple days, when I see you."

She almost asked about the silver bowl and

lettered tiles in his office, about the packet of needles and the white-cotton rag with the bloodstains. But she didn't know where that question would lead, and she *didn't want* to know. She wouldn't doubt her parents. Couldn't. In times as turbulent as these, but also in the seeming humdrum of daily life, which always proved to be more meaningful and consequential in retrospect, each of us needed to rely on people of constant character and truths that were immutable. She knew her parents' weaknesses, which were minor and easily forgiven, and she believed, based on long experience, that they were as reliable as anything in this world. If she ever discovered that they were not what they seemed, she would be devastated, and the word *heartbroken,* made trite by overuse, would have fresh and poignant meaning for her.

"Tell Mom I love her."

"She'll worry anyway. So will I."

"I'm walkin' the board, Dad."

"If you say so. Nobody walks it better."

"Okay, then. Just remember that. Bye."

She hung up and was wiping the phone clean when it rang. She took the call but didn't say anything.

Terezin evidently now maintained a round-the-clock monitored tap on Murphy's cell. He said, "Ah, there you are, lovely Bibi."

Hoping to unsettle the arrogant bastard just a little, she said, "Hello, Bobby."

"So the girl detective has made some progress. You must have visited my father. Once I'm done with you, perhaps I'll visit yours."

Crossing to the door that earlier she had kicked open, she said, "You're thirty-three, but you've never grown up. Your taunting is childish. Tedious."

"You want tedious, read your novel. I just did. It's a toss-up which needs burning the most — that book or its author. Anyway, day after tomorrow, I'll be thirty-four. I promise to be all grown up then. Too bad you can't come to the party. Ashley will be there. My guest of honor. It'll be the last chance you'll have to find her alive. It all begins again. The little Jewess's role is historic."

She thought he was trying to keep her talking, to get a GPS fix on the phone, but he terminated the call. Maybe he already knew where to find her.

Bibi wiped the phone clean once more and threw it across the garage.

68
A Man, a Dog, a Moment

Although it might be a sunny March day inland, the fog would not relent along the coast. As noon approached and the lowering element failed to lift, there was every reason to expect that it would remain throughout the afternoon.

In the Honda, Bibi tossed the professor's handbag and decorative pillow cover on the passenger seat. She fished her keys from a pocket of her blazer and started the engine.

The immediacy with which Terezin had traced and called back the professor's cell number alarmed Bibi. Maybe Homeland Security could do that trick. But how wired into the government security apparatus could this vicious mother-killer be? His quickness seemed more supernatural than techno-savvy.

She didn't think he could drop a couple of assassins into the neighborhood by drone or circus cannon as fast as he had placed the call. But she remembered what Chubb Coy had said: *There are a lot of these cockroaches, and they have resources.* She wanted out of there yesterday.

She drove uphill, under a canopy of tree limbs, and on the left-hand sidewalk, near the corner, she spotted a man walking a dog. A tall man in a hoodie. Walking a golden retriever. Bibi almost failed to see them in the fog, a ghostly pair, hardly more substantial than an apparition, and then they turned the corner, out of sight.

With the thick mist and the chill in the air, a hoodie made sense. Dozens of people would be wearing hoodies to walk their dogs in this weather. And a golden retriever wasn't unusual. This wasn't the guy from the hospital the night before last. Couldn't be. Ridiculous.

At the intersection, she didn't brake for the stop sign, wheeled left around the corner, and scanned the street. More trees. Parked cars and SUVs and light trucks. There, on the right-hand sidewalk, man and dog moved away through the earthbound clouds, less real now than they'd been when she had first glimpsed them. If this was the night visitor at the hospital, he couldn't be on the same side of the fence as Terezin. This man had wanted her to live, not die.

She raced forward, and from the right-hand curb, a pickup pulled into traffic. Bibi stamped on the brake pedal and blew the horn, and the Honda yelped and shuddered, and the other driver blew his horn longer than she had, a back-at-you statement. By the time that the pickup jockey reached the next intersection and turned downhill, she had lost track of the man with the dog.

Then she saw them half a block uphill, on the farther side of the street, passing through an opening in a low stone wall, into a park. By the time she drove up there and curbed the Honda in a no-parking zone, the duo had melted into the mist among the cascading branches of a grove of California pepper trees.

As parks went, this wasn't a sprawling affair, not a destination for tourists, but a modest neighborhood amenity, maybe ten acres that encompassed a walk through the pepper woods, a children's playground with spiral slide and a safety-first fun-free plastic-eyesore version of a jungle gym, as well as a big open grassy area where dogs could chase Frisbees and tennis balls. At the north end, the ground rolled gently into a canyon, and along that crest were positioned picnic tables and two small gazebos that offered a vista on sunnier days.

The man and dog were to be found in none of those places, and in fact she encountered no one else, either. Into the shifting curtains of mist, she called out, "Hello" and "You, sir, with the beautiful dog," but no one replied.

The canyon was deep, and the fog appeared to condense in its depths, so that she could not see the bottom or even a significant distance down the slope. The abyss was rugged, and the way eventually grew steep, a kingdom of snakes and bobcats and coyotes into which no sensible person would venture blindly.

In that eeriness of fog-bearded trees and deserted gazebos and abandoned playground equipment, Bibi began to feel that she was being watched. Not only watched, but also manipulated, drawn forward. She was alone, far from the Honda. Although she had the pistol in her shoulder rig, she no longer felt safe.

As she headed back toward the street, a chill like the tip of an icy finger traced her spine from the small of her back to the nape of her neck. She broke into a run, certain that someone or something must be on her heels. When she cleared the opening in the low stone wall and saw Pogo's aged Honda, she halted and pivoted, tensed for a confrontation. No one pursued her.

She'd always before been able to trust her intuition. Maybe that was another difference about this new reality, this world-gone-mad.

No sooner had this thought troubled her than she was given good reason to trust herself once more. Deep in the park, near the limits of visibility that the fog imposed, the man in the hoodie manifested out of the cold white blear, the leashed dog slightly ahead of him. They faded away and, after several seconds, returned to existence, strolling leisurely among the pepper trees.

The dog-walker had to have heard her seeking him. She almost called out again, but restrained the impulse. Even if this was the man at the hospital, she suddenly knew — without understanding from where this perception came — knew in mind and heart, in blood and bones, that by coming face-to-face with this man in the pepper woods, she would be destroyed. He might not be her enemy, but in some way he was nevertheless a threat to her. An existential dread overcame Bibi, so that she could not for a moment draw breath. Then she got into the car, shut the door, and drove away from there with no destination in mind, drove until she felt . . . not safe, but safer.

69
CASH, KEY, AND CONTACT

In rebellion against the claustrophobic fog, which had begun to cloud her thoughts almost as effectively as it shrouded the seaside communities, Bibi drove north to Newport Coast Drive and a couple of miles inland to a shopping center bathed in sunshine. She parked in a quiet corner of the lot, in the feathery shade of nonbearing olive trees, as far as possible from the busy Pavilions market.

If Chubb Coy and the dead professor had known what car Bibi was driving, they might have shared that information with others, and she might soon need new transportation. Lacking a GPS, the Honda could not be easily tracked wherever it went. Her enemies would have to be lucky to spot it in the hustle-bustle of Orange County's millions, but they seemed to have a lot of luck.

According to Coy, arrayed against her were not merely Terezin and his large cult; there were other "factions." She didn't know what to make of that information. Only a day ago, had anyone babbled about a secret occult-powered fascist conspiracy, Bibi would have regarded them as citizens of Cuckoo City. Now she was being asked to fold into that idea the existence of other conspirators with different goals; Chubb Coy was adamantly not a fascist. Could it really be true that, per Shakespeare, our world in all its complexity was a stage and all its people merely players, and *at the same time,* per H. P. Lovecraft, that below the main stage were unknown others on which different dramas played out, secretly affecting the lives of everyone upstairs?

She didn't want to believe that. Life was tenuous enough without having to worry about what trolls and molochs might be scheming in the basement. Yet it seemed that, to find Ashley Bell and to hope to survive the search, she needed to proceed as if this paranoid vision of the world was indisputable.

Indeed, as she watched people coming and going from Pavilions and the other stores, she quickly realized that she could adapt to this new "reality" more easily than her parents ever would. Their surrender to fate — *it'll be what it'll be* — encouraged no serious pondering of cause and effect; by laying everything at the doorstep of fate, you were reducing the intellect from the status of a world-changing tool to that of a toy with which to invent amusements that would soften the world's sharp edges. Bibi liked the sharp edges. They kept her alert. They made her think harder. They added interest to life.

By contrast, there wasn't much of interest in Dr. St. Croix's roomy handbag. Bibi hoped to find it crammed full of evidence of criminal acts and nefarious intentions, all of it pointing to the whereabouts of Ashley Bell. But aside from the usual junk, there were only three items of interest.

The first was an envelope containing five thousand dollars in hundred-dollar bills. Chances were, this was either money that the professor had been paid under the table or a payment she was prepared to make to someone else. In either case, it was more likely to be related to some dirty business than to a legal transaction.

Bibi considered the moral implications for five seconds and then took the money. It didn't feel like theft. It felt like wisdom. When she used her credit cards, she risked revealing her location. She had no way of knowing what cash she might need before she completed this task or died trying.

The second item was either a real wasp or a perfectly rendered little sculpture of one frozen in a lozenge of polished Lucite, its stinger curved in the strike position. Attached to the lozenge was a key chain holding a single electronic key. Not for a car. No company name or logo identified it. She had never seen one like it. The electronic key to St. Croix's Mercedes was by itself on a second ring, and yet another ring held several conventional keys.

The third thing of interest was a paper napkin bearing the red logo of a restaurant chain celebrated for its hamburgers but also for the fact that it served breakfast all day. On the napkin was the name Mrs. Halina Berg, a phone number, and an address in the Old Town district of Tustin. The handwriting was bold, arguably that of a man. In any case, the good professor hadn't written it; she was famous for the notes with which she decorated the manuscripts of students, all in precise printing of exquisite readability, some being brilliant and/or enigmatic writing advice, some withering criticism. Perhaps she ordered only water for her meal with Chubb Coy at Norm's because she'd already eaten breakfast elsewhere.

Halina Berg.

Calling ahead seemed like a bad idea. Like asking to be met with guns and handcuffs. Besides, if another housebreaking was required, leaving a name beforehand would be foolish.

70
COOKIES, TEA, AND DARK HISTORY

Although Bibi had driven through this neighborhood numerous times over the years, she didn't know it well. So she was surprised when, without consulting the numbers painted on the curb or those on the houses, she knew the Berg residence the moment that she saw it. A two-story rambling Spanish Colonial Revival house of considerable charm, it was set well back from the street, shaded by tall and majestic live oaks crowned to perfection.

An elderly woman was sweeping the stoop. She did not look up as Bibi drove by and parked half a block away.

When Bibi returned on foot, the woman broomed clean the last of the stoop tiles and greeted her visitor with a smile that a loving nana might bestow upon a cherished grandchild. Although the sweeper appeared to be in her eighties, time had performed one of its rare kindnesses with her face, allowing a suggestion of her early beauty to remain, while plumping and gently folding her features into a pleasing fullness, applying the techniques of soft sculpture instead of its usual hammer and chisel.

"Would you be Mrs. Berg?" Bibi asked. "Halina Berg?"

"I would be, and I am," the woman said, with the faint trace of an unspecifiable European accent echoing down the years of her voice.

The expression on the winsome face, the generous smile, and an intimation of quiet amusement in Mrs. Berg's brandy-colored eyes all conspired to suggest that she knew who Bibi was and why she had come to pay a visit. Yet she seemed to harbor no hostility whatsoever, no hint of malevolent intent or capacity. If that was a misreading of the woman, well, there was always the Sig Sauer P226.

When Bibi identified herself, Mrs. Berg nodded pleasantly, as if to agree, *Yes, that's right,* and when Bibi claimed that Dr. St. Croix had sent her, Mrs. Berg said, "Come in, come in, we'll have a nice sit-down with tea and cookies."

Bibi hesitated to follow the old woman across the threshold. But she could think of nowhere else to go. She had no other leads beyond this name and address. Anyway, if Hansel and Gretel had not risked being roasted for dinner by the wicked witch, they would not have found her trove of pearls and jewels.

The ground-floor hallway was lined floor-to-ceiling with books, and unlike the shelves in St. Croix's office, no empty space remained on any of these. Mrs. Berg led her past archways to a living room and a dining room, the open door to a study; each of those spaces was furnished to its purpose, though they served also as extensions of the through-house library, with more bookshelves than bare walls.

One section of kitchen cabinets, that with glass fronts, was filled with books, too, and none of them appeared to be cookbooks.

As she prepared a plate of homemade cookies and brewed the tea, Mrs. Berg explained that neither she nor her late husband — Max, who had died seven years earlier — had family, nor were they blessed with children of their own. "We had each other. That was miracle enough. And we had our mutual love of books. Through books we lived this life and thousands of others. Never a dull minute!"

Rather than repair to the parlor, they sat across the kitchen table from each other, as if they were longtime neighbors. The sugar cookies were rich with vanilla. The dark-brown tea, almost as black as coffee, might have been bitter if it hadn't come with a choice of either honey or peach syrup as sweetener.

"Delicious," Bibi declared. "Both the cookies and the tea. The tea is . . . formidable."

"Thank you, dear." Leaning forward with apparent curiosity, Halina Berg said, "Now tell me, who is this Dr. Solange St. Croix?"

Puzzled, Bibi said, "But I thought you knew her. When I said she sent me, you brought me right into your home."

Smiling, waving a hand as if to dismiss the misunderstanding, the old woman said, "Goodness gracious, I brought you in for tea because you're Bibi Blair."

A sense of familiarity with the house returned, and Bibi looked around the kitchen, wondering.

"I read your novel," said Halina Berg, with those four words resolving the mystery. "You're that rare thing — an author who looks even better in person than in her bookjacket photo."

Having published only the one novel, Bibi was not accustomed to being recognized as a writer. She explained that Dr. St. Croix was the founder of a renowned university writing program.

"How perfectly boring," said Mrs. Berg. "It's *you* I'm interested in, dear."

There followed a few minutes of considered and articulate praise for Bibi's writing that gratified and embarrassed her at the same time.

As if in recognition of the discomfort occasioned by her guest's modesty, Mrs. Berg said, "But we can talk more about that later, if you'll indulge me. One of the secondary characters in your book, the Holocaust survivor . . . I am intrigued by the insights you achieved with her, given your youth. But first, Dr. Solange St. Croix. I don't want to be mean, dear, but that's such a pretentious name. I wonder — is it the one she was born with? Ah, but that's neither here nor there. Why on earth did this woman I don't know send you to me?"

Bibi almost said, *I don't know,* which would have been awkward, but fortunately she said instead, "Research. Maybe she'd heard about your enormous book collection." That sounded peculiar if not totally lame. A comment Mrs. Berg had made a moment earlier, considered with her slight accent and her age, suddenly gave the old woman a possible historical context that inspired Bibi to say, "Research about the Holocaust."

Mrs. Berg nodded. "Many people know of my . . . background. Perhaps this Dr. St. Croix was aware, I survived both Terezin and Auschwitz."

71
AN OLD WOMAN WITH A JUNK-SHOP MEMORY

When she spoke of the ghetto at Theresienstadt, now Terezin, and of Auschwitz-
Birkenau, Halina Berg's appearance changed.
Her true years became evident in the plump
planes of her face, and amusement neither
gathered around her mouth nor dwelt in her
eyes as before. The music went out of her
voice. She spoke with neither anger nor sorrow, but with a steely resolve, as if she could
not speak of it at all if she allowed herself
stronger emotions.

In 1942, when Halina was eleven, the Nazis
forcibly transported tens of thousands of
Europe's most privileged and accomplished
Jews to the fortress town of Theresienstadt —
scholars and judges, writers, artists, scientists,
engineers, musicians — there to await trans-
feral to one of the death camps. Halina's
parents were musicians with the symphony,
he a bass clarinetist, she a violinist. Consequently, due to the courage and will to live of
its people, Theresienstadt had a rich cultural

life in spite of the oppression, the threat of death, and the continuous dying all around. Crowding was terrible, food scarce, sanitary conditions unspeakable, and communicable diseases rampant. Halina's mother died in a typhoid epidemic. Half starved, her father was transported to Auschwitz, where he was murdered with many thousands of others, but Halina was not sent with him. Mere weeks before Auschwitz was liberated by the Allies, she was taken there with other girls and boys, many of whom perished. Of fifteen thousand children who passed through Theresienstadt, no more than eleven hundred survived, perhaps fewer than two hundred.

"Humanity is capable of any atrocity," she said. "But when you understand the extent of this cruelty, the unprecedented viciousness, the immense scale of the horror, it seems beyond the power of mere people to conceive and execute. It seems demonic."

When the old woman fell silent, Bibi took it upon herself to bring the teapot to the table and refresh their cups. As she did so, she was overcome by a feeling of having performed this act before, not just the pouring of tea, but pouring from this same pot, in this very kitchen. The moment of déjà vu quickly passed. Because she didn't know what to make of it, she could only put it aside for consideration later.

By the time Bibi returned to her chair, she

thought she knew what Dr. St. Croix would have come here to ask. Perhaps she shared with the professor a need to know what supernatural power it was that the man called Terezin possessed.

"I've heard that Hitler was into the occult," Bibi said. "In all your reading, in your *experience,* have you found that to be true? Is there any book in your collection you could show me, that might —"

Raising one hand to indicate that there was no need to prowl the extensive shelves, Halina said, "I've been blessed or cursed — I'm not sure which — with an eidetic memory. Whatever I dump into my mind stays there, and I have perfect recall. That sounds neat and orderly, but it's definitely not. Everything is stuffed in there everywhichway. Sometimes I need a minute to sort through it. . . ."

Bibi waited, watching as the old woman sipped her second cup of tea.

At last Halina said, "Hitler was a bit of a pagan, but not entirely that. A vegetarian. He would not allow mice to be killed when they invaded his house in numbers. He believed that the fatherland, German land, had a mystical power that could be drawn upon by the volk, the people of pure German blood. He wasn't a Christian, could not be one, because of Christianity's roots in Judaism, so the layered occult system that grew from

Christianity — angels, demons, witches, séances, all of that and more — was of no interest to him. But the idea that there was mystical power in German earth and that the pure-blooded volk could draw upon it to become supermen . . . *that* is indisputably an occult concept."

Bibi said, "It didn't work out well for him."

"I'm not a big believer in most things occult," Halina said. "But I do believe the world is a more mysterious place than we often recognize — or care to admit. If there is some strange natural power in the earth under us, some magnetic current yet undiscovered, and if there are individuals who can tap it, then they're probably those men we say have charisma. Not silly movie stars and singers, not the cheap charisma of entertainers. I'm speaking now of those with great charisma, the power to infect enormous numbers of others with their ego-driven fantasies. Hitler. Stalin. Mao."

Although Bibi had added sweetener to her second cup, she wasn't enjoying the tea. She slid it aside.

Halina said, "The Hindu saint Ramakrishna said that when a man becomes a saint, followers swarm to him as wasps to honey. Because he had to become holy to achieve his charisma, a saint won't misuse that power, that control over others. But if a common man, a volk, with no saintly quality, with in fact an inflated ego, a narcissist, should tap into this magnetic current or whatever, he could draw legions to him . . . and lead the world to ruin."

Bibi was disappointed. "And that's the extent of his occult leanings? The mystical power of German land? You never read anything about him being interested in any kind of divination?"

"No."

"He was never intrigued by séances, mediums, ceromancy, halomancy, necromancy, that kind of thing?"

"Not to my knowledge. But I am not the world's primary expert on Adolf Hitler."

From her purse, Bibi withdrew the electronic key attached to the Lucite fob. Indicating the encased wasp, she said, "Something about this feels occult to me."

Halina Berg's eyes widened. She fisted her hands as if to prevent herself from reaching for — and touching — the exotic object. "A wasp in the posture of stinging," the old woman said, "was the official symbol they chose for themselves, just the unit of the Schutzstaffel garrisoned at Theresienstadt."

"Schutzstaffel? The SS?"

"Hitler's praetorian guard, shock troops, his supreme instrument of terror. The primary symbol of the SS was a death's head. But the unit running Theresienstadt likened itself to *Der Führer's Wespe,* his wasp, the

389

sting behind his policies and directives. The camp commandant had the image on his door."

Returning the key and the wasp to her purse, Bibi said, "I'm sorry if I've distressed you."

Halina opened her fisted hands and then closed them around her cooling cup of tea. "It's just a thing, a bug in plastic, it should not disturb me. It's only a coincidence anyway, a novelty key chain. It has nothing to do with Theresienstadt." She took a sip of her bitter tea. "The fools never seemed to realize they were comparing themselves to an *insect.*"

"Did the wasp have any occult meaning for them, for the SS unit that ran the ghetto?"

"No. Not that I was aware. Although . . ." She became thoughtful, staring into her tea as if to discern something in its darkness. "For a few months, there was one Gypsy in the ghetto. He'd been sent there by mistake. Jews and Gypsies were imprisoned separately, and always exterminated with groups of their own. The camp commandant should have sent the Gypsy elsewhere, but he delayed for two months, three, maybe longer. There were rumors that a small group of SS officers were intrigued by the Gypsy's readings . . . palms, castings of wax, maybe even a crystal ball. But I don't know if there was any truth to the gossip. The wasp symbol had been there before the Gypsy . . . and it was there after."

They remained at the table awhile longer, but they said no more about Hitler or about the occult, or about charisma, as if they both felt that they had drawn too close to some line they must not cross, as if to speak further of these things, just then, would be to invite malice upon them. They spoke of trivial matters. They did not return to the subject of Bibi's novel. When a decade faded from Halina's face, when the music came into her voice once more, and when she smiled as she had first smiled while standing on the front stoop, Bibi felt that the time had come to go, although she promised that she would return.

72
Questions Not Asked

That March afternoon, the westering sun cast off silver rather than golden rays, minting piles of coins from scattered altocumulus clouds that glimmered against a faded-blue sky. At street level, it was a bright but curiously dreary light that made the 55 freeway and then the 73 toll road seem like metaled causeways between nothing and nowhere, and all the racing vehicles like robots engaged in heartless tasks centuries after the abolition of humanity.

On the way to the bookstore in the Fashion Island shopping complex in Newport Beach, Bibi couldn't stop wondering why she had not asked Halina Berg two important questions. The first: *Have you ever heard of Robert Warren Faulkner?* The second: *Have you ever heard of Ashley Bell?* They were the two key figures in this drama, after all; the girl was in urgent need of being rescued, and the mother-murdering Bobby was intent on preventing her from being found. Bibi had assumed that Dr. St. Croix had wanted to speak with Mrs. Berg to explore the connection between Nazis and the occult, but that might not have been her intention. Whatever mysterious faction she aligned with, whatever her purpose in this madness, the professor might have been under the impression that the survivor of Theresienstadt and Auschwitz could tell her something related to Faulkner or Bell, or both. Even if Mrs. Berg claimed never to have heard of them, there would have been something to be gained by watching her reactions to the names.

Not that there had been any reason to believe that Halina's history might be different from the one that she had laid out in her cozy kitchen. She'd been credible. Even if she was not the Holocaust survivor that she claimed to be, she was a lover of books, therefore not likely to have anything in common with a man who said that he hated most books and bookish people. Besides, had she been aligned with Faulkner/Terezin, she would have let him know that the woman he wanted to kill was sitting at her kitchen table drinking tea.

If Bibi couldn't be sure that she had gotten from Halina Berg all the woman had to give, she was *convinced* that she had missed something during her encounter with Chubb Coy in the third-floor Victorian suite in St. Croix's house, and that it had to do less with what he'd revealed than with how he'd said it. There had been certain familiar statements and phrases, and now her memory began to serve her better than it had earlier, which was why she needed to visit a bookstore.

As she exited the toll road at Jamboree Boulevard, crawling west in heavy traffic, Bibi heard the start-up music that indicated her laptop had come alive. It was lying on the passenger seat. After searching for the photos of Bobby Faulkner, she had logged off and her computer had shut down. Now she flipped up the screen and found it bright, ready to go.

When the westbound lanes clogged, she used the touch pad to try to log off. The laptop remained on. She reached farther, to the power switch, clicked it, clicked it, but it didn't work.

Not good. In fact, very bad.

Ten minutes from Fashion Island in that stop-and-go traffic, she came to a halt when a traffic light yellowed to red, with ten or twelve vehicles in front of her. Directly ahead idled a landscaper's open-bed truck full of mowers, blowers, trimmers, rakes, and white tarps plump with grass clippings.

She didn't want to do what she knew she was going to do, what she believed she had to do. After she tried the power button twice again, without success, she closed the laptop, opened the car door, got out, and hurried forward to the open-bed truck. She flung the computer over the tailgate, darted back to the Honda, got behind the wheel, and pulled shut the door without looking at any of the people in the cars around her, who might have been interested in knowing what she'd just done and why. Let them wonder. It was California; you never knew what anyone might do next.

She had hoped the laptop would tumble in among the gardener's equipment, but it landed smack in the middle of one of the large marshmallow-looking tarps bulging with clippings. As if it were on display.

The traffic signal didn't change fast enough to suit her. She couldn't guess what might happen next, but she knew for sure that when the big boot came down, aimed at your neck, it was better to be on the move than sitting still.

Did the latest models of computers emit an identifying signal even when they were switched off? Could someone in authority reach out to that signal and activate your laptop? The newest model TVs included cameras that watched the viewer and micro-phones that could listen, to allow interactive entertainment. It was a negative-option component; you got it whether you wanted it or not, and you had to take active steps to cancel those features. Not that it necessarily disconnected when you were told it did. Who knew? If someone in authority could reach out and switch on your laptop, and if the laptop contained a transponder with an identifying number, then it was like a flashing neon sign announcing HERE SHE IS, COME AND GET HER!

The signal turned from red to green, and traffic began to move, but Bibi thought it would probably never again, for as long as she lived, move as fast as she wanted. The throng of vehicles, spaced like beads on a necklace, progressed as far as the next intersection, at the crown of a hill, before halting again. She was now six or eight places from the commanding light, and the landscaper's truck remained in front of her.

She heard the bass throbbing only a moment before the helicopter soared over the brow of the hill, immense in visual impact if not in fact, flying about sixty or seventy feet above the roadway, far below legal minimum altitude for the circumstances. It wasn't a standard two- or four-seat police chopper, and it wasn't a humongous military job, but rather a sleek blue-and-white corporate craft, what Pax would call a "medium twin," powered by two engines, with an eight- or nine-passenger capacity. High-set main and tail rotors. Advanced glass cockpit. Maybe eight or nine thousand pounds of machine and fuel, coming at her like a missile, framed in her windshield, seeming lower than it actually was. The engine noise and the air-slam of the rotary wing escalated instantly to a violent roar as the chopper passed overhead, then diminished as it swept downhill, above the lanes of waiting vehicles.

Red winked to green, and the steel-Fiberglas-rubber sludge began to move once more, across the brow of the hill. Bibi said *"Yes!"* and slapped the steering wheel when the landscaper's truck turned right, off the boulevard and away from her.

Crossing the intersection, she checked the rearview and side mirrors, didn't see the helicopter, but then heard it approaching from behind. The volume didn't grow as loud as it had before, because the craft turned north and gained a little altitude to clear some old trees. She glanced right and saw it disappear as if in pursuit of the landscaper.

As slow and inept as she had felt now and then during the past eighteen hours, she now felt quick and clever. Nevertheless, she warned herself, nothing in this game was ever easy. And she was right about that.

73
JUST BEFORE THE SWARM

The vast acreage of the parking lot was sometimes insufficient for the crowds drawn to Fashion Island, but this time Bibi had many choices. Near Neiman Marcus, she tucked Pogo's pride between a red Ferrari and a silver Maserati, accomplishing two things at once: by contrast calling attention to the Honda and thereby making it appear that its driver had no reason to want it to pass unnoticed; and at the same time giving the owners of the flanking vehicles a reality check, in the event they needed one.

She pulled her hair back in a ponytail and secured it with a rubber band that she carried in her purse for that purpose. After she put on the sunglasses, she wished that she had a more complex disguise. Like a burka. No one would profile and bother a woman in a burka, even if she was radioactive and ticking.

The photograph of Ashley Bell lay on the passenger seat. Rather than just turn it facedown, she rolled it loosely to make it fit in the glove compartment.

When she got out of the car, she couldn't see the helicopter, but she could hear it in the distance. She needed only a three-second listen to be certain that it was approaching. Glancing at her watch, she saw they had required barely five minutes to determine that their quarry was not aboard the landscaper's truck and that they had been bamboozled. Coming at once in this direction instead of buzzing off on a random route, they must be tracking another transponder signal in addition to the one emitted by the laptop.

St. Croix's purse. Nothing left in it had been of interest to Bibi, but perhaps it contained a transponder; maybe the professor had been a subject of interest to them, in which case anything she carried, including the purse itself, might have been switched out with a wired version.

Remarkable, how smoothly the butter of paranoia spread across the bread of life.

Bibi snatched St. Croix's purse out of the car, eager to be rid of it. At the nearest entrance to the open-air part of the mall, a FedEx driver transferred packages from the back of his truck to the equivalent of a laundry cart, for delivery to various stores. As Bibi passed, his attention was on the cargo in the vehicle. She shoved the handbag out of sight between the boxes in the cart, and she kept moving.

When the noise made by the helicopter abruptly spiked, she glanced back and saw it a couple hundred yards to the northeast, so low that it passed between two of the office towers and hotels that ringed the immense retail island at the heart of the complex. In the open, crossing Newport Center Drive toward the mall, the aircraft began to drift to port, to starboard, to port, as if the searchers aboard were trying to get a final fix on whatever signal they were tracking.

She could see no name or corporate logo on the fuselage, only a registration number on the engine cowling. Whoever they might be, either they were law-enforcement authorities exempt from air-traffic regulations or they were people of such wealth and influence that they felt immune from prosecution.

Having locked his truck, the FedEx driver pushed the cart toward Bibi, whistling a happy tune. Reaching into her purse, she wondered if she should get rid of the electronic key with the wasp encased in the Lucite fob. Even as small as it was, perhaps it, not the purse, emitted the signal that drew the helicopter toward her. Everything could be miniaturized these days. She was loath to throw it away unnecessarily. It meant something. A clue. A key. Eventually she might need it. The deliveryman rolled the cart past her, into the labyrinth of radiating shop-lined avenues where a few thousand people busied from store to store.

She kept the key, zippered her purse shut, and set off in a different direction from that taken by the FedEx guy. The chopper, racketing low over the mall, had a distinctly wasplike quality.

74
HERMIONE, HERMIONE, AND THE MEN IN BLACK

In addition to the department stores that were integrated into the acres of single-story shops, Fashion Island offered a three-story indoor mall, Atrium Court, where the large Barnes & Noble outlet was located. Brooding over a few things that Chubb Coy had said after shooting Dr. St. Croix, Bibi purchased three collections of stories by Flannery O'Connor, Thornton Wilder, and Jack London.

While searching for the London, she shared the aisle with two teenage girls. One was of Asian extraction, with thick, silky black hair and eyes as large as those of a child in a Keane painting; the other was a blonde, wearing eyeglasses with red-plastic frames; both were leggy, as physically awkward as they were attractive. She could not help but hear their conversation, which after a while took an ominous turn.

"What about this one?"

"The movie sucked."

"Movies usually suck."

"I like John Green."

"But his movie sucked."

"It wasn't his fault. Hollywood cooked it with crap."

"Here. What about Alice Hoffman?"

"I get off on Alice Hoffman."

"Everybody likes Alice Hoffman, except the robots-and-aliens digit-head losers."

"My sister's slaving through Herman Melville in college. She says it's like passing a kidney stone."

"She ever pass a kidney stone?"

"She *is* a kidney stone. So who do you think they are?"

"The men in black? Maybe the president's going shopping."

"These aren't cop guys. They're butthole spiders."

"So is something bad going down?"

"No. They're not shoot-and-shout-Allah types. What about Salinger?"

"Holden Caulfield is such a babbling depressive."

"He's not a depressive. He's a screwed-up child of privilege. Anyway, you're sometimes a depressive."

"I'm not sometimes a depressive. I'm sometimes a realist. So if they aren't going to kill everyone for God, what're they doing?"

"They're looking for somebody."

"Who?"

"Whoever. The one with the earring could be looking for me, and I truly wouldn't mind."

"Like that's going to happen. When he saw you undressing him with your eyes, he gave you this look like, *Go away, little girl. I've got someone to beat up.*"

Holding her three books, Bibi turned to the teenagers. "You want to know who they're looking for? They're looking for me."

They regarded her like two baby night owls surprised by a light.

"How many of them are there?" Bibi asked.

The blonde said, "For real, they're looking for you?"

"Or," Bibi said, "this is some brain-dead YouTube joke show, and I've got a camera up my nose. Can you help me? How many are there?"

"At least twenty," the brunette whispered, though there was no need to whisper. "They're everywhere."

"Way more than twenty," the blonde said. "They've all got these little phones in their ears. There's a freakin' swarm of them."

"Men in black — you mean like the movie, suits and sunglasses?"

"No," the brunette said, graduating from a whisper to a stage whisper, "they're all dressed different, but they're still the same. They have a look. You know, like they've all got somebody's boot up their ass."

"How's everyone reacting to them?"

"Everyone who?"

"The other shoppers, mall security, everyone."

The blonde shrugged. "We're maybe the only ones who noticed."

Her companion agreed. "We notice things. We're super-observant, because we're among the one percent, brainwise."

"We're super-observant," the blonde amended, "because basically we don't have a life of our own."

"We have a life, but it sucks like a movie."

The blonde said, "One thing we've noticed is these days people see all kinds of things they don't want to see, so they go blind."

"Selectively blind." The brunette had stopped whispering, but her huge dark eyes were bright with a spirit of adventure.

Bibi said, "You know where the term *butthole spiders* comes from?" They shook their heads. "In the days before indoor plumbing, outhouses had wooden seats with holes cut in them. Spiders loved to build their nests and breed down in all the crap."

"Gross," the brunette said.

"Gross but cool," her companion decided.

As a plan occurred to Bibi, she said, "What're your names?"

In a bit of practiced theater, the brunette pointed to the blonde and said, "She's Hermione," as simultaneously the blonde returned the gesture, saying, "She's Hermione."

"Two Hermiones?"

The brunette said, "Our mothers were fangirls of a certain age."

When Bibi still didn't get it, the blonde said, "They were über-impressionable high-school seniors with middle-school tastes when the Harry Potter books were all the rage. They still haven't gotten over them. Hermione Granger is Harry's friend."

"We've read the series, of course," the brunette Hermione said. "It's a daughterly obligation."

"It's a gun-to-the-head thing," blond Hermione said. "Read 'em or die. But they were okay."

"Listen," Bibi said, "I need help. After I buy these" — she put the three books on a browser's chair, unzipped her purse, reached into it — "I need you to walk with me to my car. They're looking for a woman alone." She handed five hundred dollars of Dr. St. Croix's money to one Hermione. "They won't look twice at a woman with two teenage daughters." She handed five hundred to the other Hermione, who squinted and chewed her lip as though she might try to negotiate a higher price, but then accepted the cash.

"You don't look old enough to be our mother."

"Then let's pretend I'm your sister — the one who *isn't* a kidney stone."

75
GIRLS, THUGS, AND THE REMADE WOMAN

Wearing her baseball cap and sunglasses, one Hermione on each side, Bibi came out of the ground floor of Atrium Court, into the open-air mall. Keeping a leisurely pace. Head up, not tucked down as if trying to hide something. Twenty feet ahead of them, holding a large paper cup of Starbucks coffee, stood a formidable man with a hands-free phone looped around one ear, trying to look like a patient husband killing time while he waited for a tardy wife.

The blond Hermione whispered, "Butthole spider," and then continued in the excited voice of a thirteen-year-old girl. "All I'm *saying* is a boy band should have *boys* in it, not old guys with hair growing out their ears."

The other Hermione was affronted on behalf of her idols. "It's a freakin' *reunion* tour, they can't be nineteen on a *reunion* tour."

"Jo," said the blond Hermione, for they had decided to use the name of the sister they most admired in *Little Women,* Josephine, as Bibi's fake-sister name. The Louisa May Alcott novel was a little corny, but it was beautiful, too, and you couldn't help but love it, and of course cry buckets, in fact rivers, Niagaras of tears; all that Bibi learned while in line with them at the cashier's station. "Jo, Jo, Josephine — do you see? — Meg here is getting old-lady hormones, panting after a bunch of geezers."

"They were cute then, and they're cute now," Bibi said as they walked by the thug with the Starbucks. "Anyway, they're only thirty."

"Well, I want *boys* in my boy bands, that's all. Hey, before we go, let's stop at that cool place, get some espresso and beignets."

The other Hermione said, "I totally adore beignets."

They were passing the large koi pond, where people gathered to watch the brilliantly colored torsional beauties glide through the water, delicate fins wimpling.

The blond Hermione said, "We *both* totally adore beignets and espresso. You do, too, Jo. I know you do."

A man with a hands-free phone sat on a bench beside the koi pond, watching not the fish but the people moving along the main promenade.

"If I stuff you with beignets not even three hours before dinner," Bibi said, "Mom will skin me alive."

"Oh, yes, your beastly mother, the human-skinning devil," said the brunette Hermione. "Jeez, when did you become a grown-up all of a sudden?"

"It happens to the best of us," Bibi assured her as they turned a corner, onto the last few hundred feet of promenade, toward Neiman Marcus and the parking lot where the Honda waited.

From behind her sunglasses, she scanned the crowd of shoppers and spotted other men like the first two, all dressed casually but each wearing a sport coat or another jacket that could conceal a shoulder rig and a weapon. The girls had been right. Some of the thugs were lean and sleek, with slicked-back hair like gigolos in silent movies, some were bulls with shaved heads, and others were former high-school football stars with clean-cut faces and styled hair, but something about them was so adamantly the same that she could have drawn a line from one to the other as easily as connecting the stars of well-known constellations. Maybe it was their alertness, their pent-up energy as apparent as that of wolves poised to pounce, or just an evil aura. A lot of people would laugh at the idea of an evil aura, because they didn't believe in evil, only in problematic psychologies, and if Bibi had once been one of those who would have laughed, she wasn't anymore. The girls were also right that these hatchet men were every-where.

"I want to get a pair of those new jeans," said blond Hermione, "the ones with the decorative stitching on the side seams and the hot words on the butt pockets."

Brunette Hermione said, "Like your mom is ever gonna let you wear them before you're thirty."

"I'm gonna wear them, all right. A guy has to read your pockets, he's looking at your butt, which is how it starts."

"How what starts? Getting hit on by a pervert?"

As if the swarm of trigger men wasn't a gauntlet hard enough to negotiate, Bibi spotted a serious complication forty or fifty feet ahead. Marissa Hoffline-Vorshack, former eleventh-grade English teacher, remade woman married to a multimillionaire, self-appointed enforcer of the concealed-carry laws, apparently spent the day going from one shopping experience to another, acquiring until the trunk of her café-au-lait Bentley couldn't hold another item. She stood at a display window, coveting whatever it offered, holding two shopping bags from upscale stores.

Bibi thought they might be able to pass behind the woman and away while she re-mained mesmerized by the merchandise. But the risk was too great. If Mrs. Hoffline-

Vorshack turned from the display window and came face-to-face with her former student, she would see through the sunglasses and the baseball cap. No disguise short of a gorilla suit would deceive the bitch.

"Wait," Bibi said, halting the girls. "You see that woman ahead, she's expensively but inappropriately dressed, the one with the two shopping bags? I know her. She's louder than a Mack truck. She'll blow my cover. I'm going to duck into this store and pretend to look at a dress. You stay out here, chatter with each other — you're doing great, by the way, really super-great — and when she's gone, come inside and tell me. But I mean really gone, off where we won't run into her."

"This so kicks it," brunette Hermione said with evident delight.

Blond Hermione agreed, "It kicks the crap out of it."

Her arrival signified by a five-note set of electronic chimes, Bibi pushed through the glass door into the store before which they had halted. Two well-dressed thirty-something female salesclerks were conferring at the back, though they probably were required to call themselves fashion consultants or style assistants, or something equally high-end and lowbrow. Bibi went to a rack of dresses on the left, turned away from the windows, and fingered the merchandise with apparent interest. She hoped this was one of those places where the style assistants were trained never to approach a newly arrived customer too quickly, lest it appear that the store needed to sell its wares rather than fight off an excess of customers.

One of the salesclerks had meandered a third of the way from the back, pausing here and there to adjust an item on one of the display tables, when the five notes of the chimes announced the entrance of another customer. If the clerk was a missile locked on to Bibi's cash potential, she had an instantaneous retargeting capability, because she declared with what sounded like genuine delight, "Mrs. Hoffline-Vorshack, what a lovely surprise," and moved toward the newcomer.

76

TWO DEAD GIRLS

At that moment in Fashion Island, Bibi might have been persuaded that her parents' surrender to fate was the wisest course in a world that seemed intent on doing to you what it would, violating its own declared rules of cause and effect. Encountering Mrs. Hoffline-Vorshack twice in one day, after not having seen her for almost six years, and just when Bibi had to wend through phalanxes of murderous men without drawing attention to herself . . . well, it almost made her throw up her hands, walk to the nearest bar, order a beer, and wait to see what happened next, a miraculous reprieve or sudden death.

The second salesclerk strode forward, greeting Mrs. Hoffline-Vorshack without giving the impression of eagerness, and took from her the burden of the two shopping bags, to "keep them safe during your visit with us," while the first clerk, having been stricken with amnesia as regarded Bibi, wanted to know if Mrs. Hoffline-Vorshack would enjoy coffee or perhaps an aperitif. Being a woman of social grace and propriety, the wife of the real-estate developer wondered if it might be too early to imbibe other than coffee. But when she was assured that it was always cocktail time somewhere in the world, she wondered if they had any of "that delicious champagne," and of course they did.

Throughout the royal entrance and the ceremonial greeting, Bibi kept her back turned to her former teacher, but she expected to be recognized at any moment. She had no confidence that the ponytail, the cap, and the sunglasses pulled halfway down her nose would shield her from discovery and another upbraiding. Then the only way to stop Mrs. Hoffline-Vorshack from following her outside and loudly accusing her of carrying a concealed weapon without a permit would be to shoot her, which was not a viable solution, though an appealing one.

The promise of good champagne proved to be like a hook in the lip. Following the salesclerks, Mrs. Hoffline-Vorshack was reeled toward the back of the shop, past tantalizing garments and jewelry in which, for the moment, she revealed no interest.

When Bibi realized that she had been spared, the reprieve felt nearly as miraculous as the remission of brain cancer. As she exited the store, the five-note chimes seemed like a supernatural warning that might be saying,

She-will-yet-find-you. Because Bibi did not believe in coincidences, she didn't need a translation of the chimes to know that her former teacher was not done with her and that this particular wheel-within-wheels, which had begun turning at the big-box store, had at least one more revolution to go.

Hermione and Hermione were abashed by their failure to warn Bibi that the loud-as-a-Mack-truck woman had been descending on her. She had seemed to be going *past* the shop. She had turned so suddenly for the door. She was a *bitch supreme,* the way she looked at them with contempt. Those knockers coming at you were terrifying, like a couple of *torpedoes.* And those *mean-little-piggy* eyes.

Bibi assured them that they had done all they could, and the three of them set out again for the end of the main promenade and the parking lot beyond Neiman Marcus, talking about whether tattoos were cool or creepy and whether it was better to be cool and stupid or uncool and smart.

Pogo's Honda still stood between the Ferrari and the Maserati. As far as Bibi could tell, no one was watching it. Evidently, Terezin's thugs didn't yet know what she was driving.

Nonetheless, she worried that it was reckless to have the girls accompany her all the way to the car, and possibly walk them into a violent confrontation. On the other hand, if the Wrong People were watching *them,* their sister act would be at once suspect if they parted at the car and the Hermiones returned to the mall.

She didn't much like herself when she asked them to ride with her out of the parking lot, as far as Newport Center Drive, which encircled the mall. But the threat to the girls, in this most public of places, seemed less real than Terezin's promise that Ashley Bell would die on his birthday, the day after tomorrow. Having passed the bag of books to the blonde, having fished the car key from her purse, Bibi slipped her right hand under her jacket, letting it rest upon the holstered pistol, as they approached the car.

No one rushed them as she keyed open the doors. People were walking to and from their vehicles or cruising in search of parking spaces, and everyone appeared to be without sinister intentions.

Hermione and Hermione were more taken with the ancient primer-gray Honda than they were with either the Ferrari or the Maserati, perhaps because it was an exotic vehicle in this province of luxury. Blond Hermione settled into the backseat. Brunette Hermione wanted to ride shotgun, still gripped by a spirit of adventure and hoping to milk another small thrill or two from the experience before it ended.

As Bibi backed out of the parking space, the blonde spoke from the backseat. "Instead of letting us out on Newport Center, can you take us down to Coast Highway, drop us off there?"

"Sure. Which side of the highway?"

"West. If you're going south, that is."

"I'm going wherever you need me to go."

When she had reversed fully into the aisle, no vehicle rammed them, no bullets shattered the windows.

"If you drop us off at the corner of PCH and Poppy," the blonde said, "we can walk from there to my house."

"Done deal."

They came to the end of the aisle, and no immense black SUV swerved in front of them to block their way.

They drove past a restaurant where one of the bulls with a shaved head and one of the silent-movie-gigolo types were standing together, talking. As the smooth lean one took the hands-free phone from his ear, the bull looked at the Honda but showed no alarm.

In the passenger seat, the brunette said, "What will they do if they catch you?"

"Kill me."

Only a few minutes earlier, the girls would have been excited by the revelation of such high stakes, but not now.

"What did you do?" the brunette asked.

"Nothing."

"Can that be true?"

"So far, yes. Listen, it's better you don't know anything more. I'm grateful for your help. I won't ever forget you."

The blonde had one more question. "Is there a way out for you?"

"There's always a way out," Bibi said. "Don't worry about me."

Having retreated earlier, fog was on the march again in this last hour of daylight, and no doubt it would surge a couple of miles inland, there to establish its tents for the night. Just before they reached Coast Highway, which at that point was a quarter to a half mile from the sea, a white wall rose before them, a towering slow-moving tsunami of mist through which headlights swam like golden koi.

Bibi turned south, and they rode in silence the rest of the way, until she parked on the right, just short of Poppy Avenue. The brunette opened her door and scrambled out. Then she turned, leaned back in, said, "Good luck, Jo," and dropped the five hundred dollars on the passenger seat.

"Hey, no, honey, you earned that," Bibi protested.

"You need it more," the girl said. "I'm not on the run."

The blonde took her friend's place and said, "Hang tough, Jo. Don't let the freakin' butthole spiders win." She tossed the other

418

five hundred onto the money that the brunette had given back, and she closed the door.

Awkward in a coltish way, not yet having grown into their grace, the girls walked south, leaning into each other, sharing thoughts. The color of their clothes and the details of their forms faded as they proceeded toward the source of the fog. Even after they turned onto Poppy Avenue, Bibi could see them, because the corner property was a parking lot that served the Five Crowns restaurant, with no structures intervening. Hermione and Hermione looked back and waved. They probably couldn't see her clearly, but Bibi returned their wave.

Considering how short a time she had known the Hermiones, she had developed a remarkable affection for them that now became even more poignant as they dwindled and eroded into the mist. Perhaps what so appealed to her was their combination of gameness and vulnerability, knowingness and innocence.

As the friends paled out of sight, Bibi thought, *There go two dead girls.*

That grim sentiment so surprised her that she sat up straighter behind the wheel, disquieted by the possibility that those five words were prophetic, that the girls weren't walking home, but instead were headed toward their imminent deaths. She started to open the driver's door into traffic, and a horn blared. The sound startled her out of superstition's grip, and she sat for a moment, letting her nerves unwind a little. She was no prophesier, no crystal-gazing Gypsy. She had no power to see with certainty five minutes into her own future, let alone into that of others.

She realized that the disturbing thought — *There go two dead girls* — was an expression of her sense of isolation, for now they were dead to *her,* never to be seen again, and once more she was alone in her flight and quest. In fact, an awful loneliness overcame her, more intense than any she had known before, an almost disabling *weight* of loneliness, pinning her, paralyzing her. In spite of being illegally parked, she thought that she might sit there until night fell, until dawn followed. She could not turn to anyone she loved, for fear they would become Terezin's targets. Paxton was different. Pax could deal with threats. *Pax, please come home, please.* To the authorities, her story would sound like the fevered rambling of a deranged mind, and she would be suspect number one in the murders of Solange St. Croix and Calida Butterfly. As the fog thickened around the Honda and the headlights of passing cars repeatedly washed over her, she was swamped by confusion, seeking solace in something perilously like self-pity.

Until she couldn't stand herself anymore. Which was after about ten minutes. Damn it, there were things she could do, answers she could seek. Many of them were locked inside herself. She knew their basic shape and, like a blind woman in a house half known, should be able to feel her way to a fuller understanding.

She waited for a break in traffic, pulled onto Coast Highway, and drove south as if her life depended on it.

77
THE COLLAR THAT RESTRAINS HER

In Laguna Beach, the atmosphere was apocalyptic, fog seething like the smoke from a world afire. The unseen sun was so exhausted that the last light of the day had neither force nor color, a bleak and eerie radiance that might have been intended not to illuminate but to penetrate the bones and print X-ray images of her skeleton on the sidewalk, fossil proof that humanity had once existed.

Every third store seemed to be a gallery. Fortunately, there were as many clothing stores as art merchants, and Bibi was able to buy a change of clothes. She purchased a soft-sided suitcase with wheels, and in a market she bought a junk-food dinner, among other items.

On her way back to the car, she passed the Bark Boutique, which sold toys and other gear for dogs. One of the items in the window was a leather collar that arrested her attention because it reminded her of Olaf's collar before he was Olaf, when he had come to her out of the rain, though his had been worn and cracked and caked with mud.

The memory that troubled her now, however, was not of the day the dog arrived, but of an incident that occurred three years after his death, when she was nineteen and moving out of her parents' bungalow into an apartment. By then, instead of a single carton of books stored in the back of her closet, there were four filled with overflow volumes from her shelves. She sat on the floor, sorting the contents, putting aside titles that had lost meaning for her. In the last box, she discovered that she'd packed the books so as to create, at the center, a hollow in which were several objects, including a chamois cloth wrapped around Olaf's old collar. She had forgotten that she'd kept it. If she once had a sentimental attachment to it, she felt none now. The loop of leather was cracked, filthy, mottled with long-dormant mold, the buckle bent and rusted. There was no reason to keep it. But again she did not throw it away. In fact . . . What had she done? Hadn't she gone to a business-supply store and bought a fire-resistant metal document box? Yes. Twenty inches square and ten inches deep, with a piano-hinge lid and a simple lock and a brass key, for the storage of grant deeds, wills, insurance polices, and the like. Hadn't she put the chamois-wrapped neckband in that box, as well as the other items she had found with it? Yes, but . . .

Now, at the display window in downtown Laguna, staring at a similar leather collar, Bibi could not recall what other items she had found in the secret hollow within the carton of books. And what had she done with the metal document box? Where was it now?

As the tires of passing vehicles swished and fizzled on the wet pavement, as fog laid a shine of dew on her face, as trees dripped, as great moths of vapor throbbed wings against the panes of the streetlamps, Bibi felt like a stranger to herself.

With her latest round of purchases, she returned to the Honda, which was parked near the east end of Forest Avenue. Minutes later, on Coast Highway, she began looking for a motel on the north side of town, someplace where no one would find her but where she might begin to find herself.

78
In Hiding from a Nonexistent Husband

The motel deserved neither a five- nor a four- nor perhaps even a three-star rating, but it looked clean and proudly kept and, most important from Bibi's perspective, anonymous. She parked on a side street two blocks away and walked, pulling the wheeled suitcase.

A lone woman manned the front desk in an office painted pale Caribbean blue and yellow. The counter was a free-form slab of koa, either genuine driftwood or sculpted to suggest a heroic history of shipwreck and travail, red and lustrous and with a watery depth.

These small motels were often owned by a couple, and the clerk was as gracious as if welcoming a guest into her home. The badge on her blouse identified her as Doris. She was pleased to accept cash, but their policy required a credit card and a driver's license for ID, which was probably in case the guest trashed the room.

"He didn't let me have credit cards," Bibi

said. "He cut up my driver's license." She surprised herself when her mouth trembled and her voice conveyed fear, bitterness, and anguish. She was no actress. Her true condition, anxiety and loneliness, provided the emotion with which she sold her story of spousal abuse. "I came in a cab partway and walked till I saw this place." Her vision blurred with tears. "He won't come here to make a scene. He doesn't know where I've gone."

Doris hesitated only a moment before making an exception to the rules. "Do you have family, dear? Someone to turn to?"

"My folks are in Arizona. My dad's coming for me tomorrow."

Wanting to avoid seeming either nosy or unconcerned, Doris said, "If he hit you, girl, then you should report him."

"He more than hit me." Bibi put one hand to her stomach, as if with the memory of a punch. "A lot more than hit."

She signed the register as Hazel Weatherfield, with no idea where she got that from. She said it was her maiden name.

Three rooms were available, all in a row, and she took Room 6, farthest from the street. It was simply furnished but cozy.

Sitting in one of the two chairs at a small round table, she ate a dinner of cashews, dried apricots, and aerosol cheese squirted on crackers, washed down with a Coke from a motel vending machine.

While she ate, she studied the photo of Ashley Bell, and heard in memory Terezin's voice, when she had spoken to him on St. Croix's phone: *Too bad you can't come to the party. Ashley will be there. My guest of honor. It'll be the last chance you'll have to find her alive. It all begins again. The little Jewess's role is historic.*

He fancied himself the heir of Hitler. Evidently, he had made it his mission, even if with one symbolic victim, to launch again the Final Solution to "the Jewish problem." The swarm of cultists — both airborne and ground troops — that had sought Bibi at the shopping mall suggested Terezin's intentions were ambitious. But whether he meant to kill one Jewish girl in celebration of his birthday or had also planned a terrorist atrocity that would result in many more deaths, either way Ashley Bell would die if Bibi couldn't soon find her.

If this had been a time of widespread sanity, a mere decade or two ago, Bibi might have found it hard to take Terezin seriously. But the world had gone mad in recent years. Anti-Semitism, that vampiric hatred that could never quite be staked through the heart and turned to dust, had infected not only the expected foreign capitals but also politics here in the States, and not just politics but academia and the entertainment industry as well. It was nearly epidemic among all elites, though fortunately not among average Americans, who so far and for the most part seemed immune to the fever. What could once have been dismissed as the unlikely plot of a bad movie must now be regarded as a real threat. Terezin had followers and a significant source of funding, all that was needed these days for him to join the myriad groups blasting away at the foundations of civilization.

And in addition, he had some kind of occult power. Bibi knew from personal experience that it was more than charisma drawn from a mystical magnetic current in the earth, as Halina Berg had proposed, though that might be part of it. She wished she had a better idea of what paranormal resources he possessed, a wish that turned her mind to the mysterious book of the panther and gazelle.

Finished with dinner, she took from her purse Calida's curious little book. She returned to the table with it.

Three times, she had glimpsed lines of cursive writing flowing swiftly across the creamy paper, pale gray and seen as if through water, so that she hadn't been able to read them. Now she riffled through two hundred or so blank pages, alert for the manifestation of the script. Just when she thought the phenomenon would not recur, she saw it, and then again, but still the words flowed at such speed and with such distortion that she could not track them — though this time she recognized the writing as her own.

She didn't understand how her handwriting could appear, even in this ghostly form, in a book to which she'd never put pen or pencil. But that was only one more ingredient in this stew of mysteries.

From her purse, she retrieved a pen and sat again with the book, wondering what might happen if she *did* write in it. She hesitated, but then began to inscribe lines from "The Evening of the Mind," a poem by Donald Justice that she particularly admired. As she started on the second line, the first disappeared from the page, vanished left to right, in the order that she had put down the words. By the time she finished the second line, it was the only one to be seen, and it flowed out of existence while she finished the third.

As when she'd paged through the book in the parking lot that served Donut Heaven, she had a sense of time passing in units much larger than seconds or minutes, and she felt . . . spellbound. She became aware of something flickering in her peripheral vision, and though turning her head required effort, she slowly brought her gaze around to the right. Apparently oblivious of Bibi's presence, a woman in a uniform, perhaps a maid, flitted about at an inhuman pace, as if in a film projected at high speed, and it wasn't a motel room anymore, it was someplace else.

Startled, Bibi dropped her pen, let go of the book — and found herself alone in the room, everything as it had been. The Barnes & Noble bag on the bed. Her wheeled suitcase beside the bathroom door. According to her watch, not more than a minute or two had passed.

Nothing she had written remained in the book. Where had those lines by Donald Justice gone?

79
PAXTON REFLECTING

Pax sat alone in the lounge, listening to the roar of engines as airplanes taxied and were airborne, but thinking about St. Angelus Meadows, the family horse ranch in Texas. His folks had on the one hand been disappointed when he chose not to go from high school into the family business; but they were proud to say their boy was a Navy SEAL. Of his three brothers, Logan, two years his junior, had also made it in the SEALs, while Emory and Chance had forgone military service, somewhat reluctantly, to work the ranch, get married, and have kids. Angelus was great for kids, a fine place to grow up with a deep attachment to the land and family that kept you balanced all your life. There was the river for swimming, the dogs always ready to play and chase, winters white and magical, summers hot and green, walking doves and quail up from the tall grass in the autumn hunt, and of course the horses, the beautiful and wise and joyous horses.

They raised Appaloosas, ideal working horses for their own ranch and for sale to others. Paso Finos for aficionados of that exquisite riding horse with its singular gait. Likewise Andalusians and Belgian Warmbloods, magnificent for dressage, show winners more often than not. And there were the quarter horses bred and raised and raced. You could spend a life with horses, day and night, and never become blasé about them, about the ever-charming colts in spring, about their intelligence, their capacity for affection, their beauty and grace.

Bibi was born a surfer, not a horsewoman. Pax loved to surf and especially with her, but the horseman could never be trained out of him. It was a question for which they had to puzzle their way to an answer. They had talked about it some, but he still had a few months left of his commitment to the teams, and neither of them had doubted for a moment that they would settle the issue to their mutual satisfaction — if given a chance. The coast or the high plains, or both, or neither. It wouldn't matter which, as long as they were together.

The door opened, and an aircrewman leaned in from the hallway. "Chief Petty Officer Thorpe? Your ride is ready."

Pax rose from the chair and hefted his big duffel bag, relieved to be in motion once more.

432

80
THE TRUTH SHE
DARES NOT FACE

After murdering Professor St. Croix in her Victorian hideaway, Chubb Coy had revealed the existence of factions in this bewildering conspiracy, but perhaps he'd meant to convey more than that to Bibi. Some of the things he'd said were not phrased as Chubb Coy would say them. Certain expressions were not characteristic of his speech. In fact, she had recognized three instances where he seemed to be making literary allusions, which was the last thing she would expect from him. By all evidence, he wasn't a bookish man. He seemed more likely to quote a sports star than to toss off a line from Shakespeare.

Bibi wondered if, in that Victorian parlor, Coy felt monitored, if in fact he knew that he would always and anywhere be overheard by some dangerous authority while in her presence. It was as though he knew that she herself — not her purse or her clothes, but her very body — was wired for transmission of everything she said and heard. That was a wildly paranoid and deeply unsettling thought. Absurd. Preposterous. But she couldn't think of another reason why he would speak to her in code, which was what she suspected he had done. His code consisted of veiled references that he must have prepared in advance to use the next time he encountered her, which happened to be on the third floor of St. Croix's house. References to works of literature that he seemed to think she would know.

Before opening the three volumes that she had bought at the bookstore in Fashion Island, she sat at the motel-room table with a pen and the small spiral-bound notebook that she carried in her purse. Searching her memory, she tried to recapture and write down, as best she could recall, the pertinent things Coy had said. Ten minutes later, they were before her on the page, in her neat script.

The first instance. After shooting Dr. St. Croix, he had said, *She would have been a better woman and teacher if someone had been there to shoot her every morning of her life.*

Bibi knew where that one could be found. She opened *The Complete Stories* by Flannery O'Connor and located one of the most terrifying short stories ever written: "A Good Man Is Hard to Find." She turned to the last page of the piece, after the merciless murderer had killed the last member of the family, and she read silently the applicable sentence: *"She would of been a good woman,"* The Misfit said, *"if it had been somebody there to shoot her every minute of her life."*

The similarity in phrasing and sentiment between what Coy said and the line from the story couldn't be accidental. He must have spoken those words with the intention of snaring Bibi's attention and by indirection transmitting to her some vital piece of information.

The second instance. When Bibi had asked why Ashley, a mere child of twelve or thirteen, had to die, Coy had said, *Why does anyone? Some say we'll never know, that to the gods we're like the flies that boys kill on a summer day.*

Thornton Wilder. The volume contained three of his short novels. She turned to *The Bridge of San Luis Rey,* a story concerning the five people who died in July of 1714, when the finest footbridge in all of Peru collapsed and dropped them into an abyss. Bibi scanned the last few pages, but eventually she found what she wanted much earlier in the story, at the end of the first chapter: *Some say that we shall never know and that to the gods we are like the flies that boys kill on a summer day. . . .*

Again, the similarity required intent.

The third instance. Bibi had asked if Coy

435

might be allied with Terezin, and he had replied adamantly that he despised the fascist creep. When she had suggested that the enemy of his enemy — meaning her — might be his friend, Coy rejected her and said, *Accept the inevitable, girl. You're easy prey. As a boy, Terezin was a dog, now he has gone back to the wild. He's a wolf now, like and yet unlike all other wolves, always running at the head of the pack. He dreams of turning the world backward, of a younger world, which is the world of the pack.*

Jack London. The lead story in the volume was "The Call of the Wild," which concerned a good dog named Buck, half St. Bernard and half Scottish shepherd. He was torn from a cozy life in California and sold into a kind of slavery as a sled dog in the Klondike, during the Alaska gold rush of 1897. Abused, he adapted to his new rough existence, came to understand the essential wolf in himself, and escaped to a better life in the wilds, where he paid back humanity for its cruelty.

In this case, part of Coy's allusion was to the plot of the story itself, the device of the dog reverting to its fierce inner wolf. The actual quotes from the text were smaller than in the first two instances, but in the final paragraph Bibi found this: *. . . he may be seen running at the head of the pack through the pale moonlight . . . as he sings a song of a* *younger world, which is the song of the pack.*

At first it seemed that these three references were unlikely code because they would be too hard to work into conversation. But then she realized that if Coy had for some time *intended* to kill Dr. St. Croix, he would have known how he could use the O'Connor quote. And since he could be sure Bibi would at some point speak of Ashley Bell and Terezin, the conversation could easily be manipulated to use the Wilder and London excerpts.

But what message did he hope to convey by this elaborate ruse, by this maddeningly indirect communication? If he secretly wished to help her, couldn't he have more easily slipped a note to her — or a twenty-page detailed report, for that matter? There could be no doubt that his references to the three authors were calculated, but did such an enigmatic form of communication suggest that he was clever and sincere — or that he was capricious and deranged? The longer she puzzled over the three allusions, the more they seemed to say only the obvious: that Coy was a nihilistic killer like The Misfit, that Terezin was a ruthless wolf with demented fantasies, that Ashley Bell's murder would be an act committed by an idiot, full of sound and fury, signifying nothing. A code was not devised to convey secretly what both the sender and receiver already knew.

Frustrated, all but crackling with nervous energy, Bibi got up to pace the room, and the moment that she became more physical, her mind went into motion, too, shifting from the issue of the literary allusions to the possibility that she carried within herself some device that broadcast everything she said and heard. To whom? Not Terezin, for if he had such an intimate connection with her, he would already have found and killed her.

How would a transmitter be implanted? Surgery? But she had no scars. Injection? Microminiaturization, nanotechnology . . . There were experts who insisted that, one day soon, incredibly complex machines made of surprisingly few molecules could travel the bloodstream, reporting telemetrically on the patient's health from an interior perspective, even removing plaque from arteries and performing other procedures on the microscopic level. If one day soon, why not now? If for medical purposes, why not for surveillance?

This was the road to madness. Kafka Land. She was suddenly afraid not because she believed that she had been injected with a tiny transmitter, but because for a minute she had seriously considered the possibility. Which was ridiculous. Lunatic.

She went into the bathroom and repeatedly splashed cold water in her face. She rubbed vigorously with the towel, as if needing to slough off some thick and clinging residue.

When she looked in the mirror, she knew the face but not its aspect, not the haunted quality, not the dread that paled the skin, not the foreboding that pinched the mouth.

"Go away," she said to the woman in the mirror. "I don't need you." She had no use for the weak Bibi who might have been. She needed to be the Bibi she had always been.

She returned to the bedroom and sat at the table and studied Coy's three allusions, comparing what he'd said to the sources he had not always precisely quoted. She considered them in the context of the ornate Victorian parlor in which he'd made them. She thought about the three stories, their plots and characters and themes and subtext. She brooded about the authors, recalling what she knew of their lives and interests beyond their writing.

A possibility occurred to Bibi, something that Coy might have been trying to say. If her mind had always been spinning when she was a girl, it had for years now been ceaselessly weaving, a tireless loom that issued an ever-changing fabric of impressions, sentiments, thoughts, ideas, concepts, theories. The possibility that occurred to her began as one frail thread, hardly noticed in the rush of thoughts and worries, but in seconds there were other threads feeding into the web, and with astonishing speed a pattern formed, a possibility so alarming that she erupted off her chair, knocking it over.

Doors in her mind, long closed, began to ease open, and once-forbidden rooms of memory welcomed her. She was all at once five years old and alone in her Mickey-lit bedroom with something evil, ten and hiding a dog collar, sixteen and struggling against a desire that could destroy her. Dizzy, weak in the knees, she stumbled to the second chair, grabbed the headrail with both hands to steady herself, closed her eyes, and in a voice stropped sharp with terror, she said, *"No, no, no."*

81

THE ULTIMATE TRAITOR

A thin acrid odor.

Bibi opened her eyes and looked around at the toilet and the shower and the white towels on the chrome rack, not sure whose bathroom this was, but then she remembered the motel. Pogo's car parked two blocks away. Hazel Weatherfield, the abused wife. Hazel's daddy coming from Arizona in the morning. Cashews and crackers and apricots and aerosol cheese.

She felt strange. Neither good nor bad. Neither relaxed nor tense. Neither afraid nor confident. There was an emptiness in her. A hollowness. A drained feeling. She thought she had lost something, though she couldn't recall what, so it must not have been important.

If there had been visible smoke, it had dissipated quickly, leaving only an unpleasant odor.

Hadn't she been leaning on a chair? Now she found herself leaning on the Corian countertop of the bathroom vanity. Curled in the sink were furry gray forms, like dead caterpillars. Ashes. The remnants of fully burned strips of something. Beside the sink lay a butane lighter. She recalled buying it in the market, in Laguna, where she had purchased the makings of her dinner, a toothbrush, toothpaste, and other items. Never having smoked, she didn't know why she needed a lighter. Well, obviously, to burn something.

She raised the stopper, turned on the faucet labeled COLD, and washed the ashes into the drain. The swirling water reminded her that she had been dizzy, but she was not dizzy now.

Indecision held her at the bathroom vanity. She was not confused or uneasy, just directionless. Then she returned to the bedroom.

One of the straight-backed chairs was overturned. As she set it right, she noticed three books on the little dining table. The spine of each volume had been broken, so that it lay open in a limp two-page spread. Excisions had been made, pieces of three pages sliced out with the switchblade that had slipped from Dr. St. Croix's sleeve when Chubb Coy had shot her.

Bibi's spiral-bound notebook also lay on the table. It was open to a blank page. Evidently, she had intended to write something.

Her mood had begun to change. She felt less detached. Coming into focus.

The books puzzled her. O'Connor, Wilder, London. She recalled buying them, but she didn't know why. She didn't have time to read, not with Terezin and his crew trying to find her and kill her.

Chubb Coy. The books had something to do with him.

Suddenly she knew what she had done. Captain's memory trick.

She loved the captain. He had helped a troubled little girl keep her sanity. But the help he had given had not resolved her problem (whatever it might be), had only taught her to suppress all knowledge of it. The thing of terror had not been vanquished. It still lived and waited. Waited for her to open the door and be consumed by it.

Trembling, shocked, she sat at the table, staring at the vandalized large-size paperbacks.

In the professor's house, Coy had said something peculiar, the importance of which Bibi had at first not understood. She could not recall what it had been. Of course she couldn't. She had burned it from memory in a childish ritual that worked less because of the six magic words Captain had taught her than *because she desperately needed it to work.* What Coy said must have had something to do with the three books; it had alarmed her, brought her into the presence of a truth so monumental that she had not been able to face it.

She used the switchblade to cut what remained of the three key pages from the books. She folded them and put them in the spiral-bound notebook and slipped it into her purse.

The room was warm, but Bibi felt carved from ice. One more name could be added to the list of the many people conspiring against her. She could not entirely trust herself.

■ ■ ■ ■ ■

5
OUT OF THE ASHES
OF MEMORY

■ ■ ■ ■ ■

82

RETURNING TO THE PLACE THAT SHE CALLED EVIL

With only her gun and her purse, Bibi left the security of her motel room, which was an imagined security anyway, as imaginary as every moment of seeming peace and safety in this new world that she inhabited. *Thank you, Calida Butterfly, or whatever the hell your name was.* Now every stronghold proved to be a place with paper walls, every hideaway a trap. Instead of a stout barrier, every door was an invitation to threats natural and supernatural. The lesson here was the opposite of what the old adage advised: You should always look a gift horse in the mouth. A gift horse or a gift masseuse. A relaxing massage, and then chardonnay and a silly-fun session of divination, and the next thing you know, you've attracted the attention of an incarnation of Hitler, and you've invited occult forces into your life, and you've been spared from cancer only so that some lunatic can stab you to death with a thousand pencils. She wanted to kick someone's ass, but there was no one she could find to kick, except maybe Murphy and Nancy for hiring Calida, but Bibi wasn't going to boot *them.* Honor thy father and mother, and all that. She left the motel in a mood of righteous indignation and exasperation too consuming to be sustained.

Although it was only 7:40, Laguna Beach appeared to have closed down for the night, the mist-shrouded hills sloping through silence to the sea, the traffic already midnight-light as the ocean sloughed off ever thicker masses of land-hugging clouds, a lone coyote howling out of a canyon as if lost and grieving for its vanished pack.

She drove Pogo's Honda north into the blinding murk, which seemed appropriate, given that her life had become a dismal swamp of puzzles and enigmas, that all the potential futures she'd foreseen for herself were now dissolved into a soup of possibilities she did not want to contemplate.

Although the swarm of cultists that had descended on Fashion Island surely didn't remain there hours later, Bibi went instead to another mall. She purchased new copies of the story collections by Flannery O'Connor, Thornton Wilder, and Jack London. She also bought a flashlight, batteries for it, and a Scrabble game.

From there, she traveled south once more, to Corona del Mar, where she cruised past the sweet bungalow in which she had lived for nineteen years, until she had moved to her apartment. A year later, Murphy and Nancy had sold the place to a couple, the Gillenhocks, who made their money in cattle-rustling and cockfighting. Well, the story was that they were successful investment bankers who were able to retire at fifty-three, but the one time Bibi met them, she felt that they were no more investment bankers than she was a concert pianist. The Gillenhocks had spent the past two years offering ever more money to the reluctant-to-move people who owned the property next door, until they acquired it as well, meanwhile working with an architect to design a residence that would, they no doubt hoped, leave their neighbors abashed and envious.

Only recently, the combined properties had been surrounded with a construction fence: chain-link with a green polyurethane overlay for privacy. Although the landscaping had been torn out and hauled away, the buildings had not yet been demolished.

She parked two blocks from the bungalow. She put batteries in the flashlight, which she would use only in the garage apartment. She left her purse under the seat and locked the car and walked streets that were familiar even in the obliterating fog.

The night was as still as a funeral parlor, the houses like mausoleums in the mist.

In addition to a large gate at the front, the

construction fence featured another off the wide alleyway, to which houses backed up from parallel streets. All the garage doors were here. At any moment, a car might turn in at one corner or the other, the driver remoting a door ahead of him, and even in the near white-out, she would be seen.

The privacy material was fixed on the exterior of the fencing, and she had to slash it with Dr. St. Croix's switchblade in order to be able to get toeholds in the chain-link. Unlike the rest of the fence, the gate had a top-rail that covered the cut-off twists of steel, eliminating the risk of puncturing her hands. She went up and over the gate, into the carport next to the garage.

In the brick-paved courtyard, something about the angles and the juxtaposed planes of the surrounding buildings magnified the vague exhalation of the sea into a somewhat less faint draft that set the fog in slow motion counterclockwise. Bibi felt as if she were being drawn upward even before she climbed the stairs to the apartment above the garage.

The apartment door wasn't locked. The place was empty. Nothing remained to be stolen. Vandals would be discouraged by the fact that the buildings were soon being torn down; no one cared what damage they might do.

She switched on the flashlight, partly hooding it with her hand, but confident that the pale glow wouldn't inspire curiosity in anyone outside. The apartment had been stripped of furniture when the house sold. The blue-and-gray speckled linoleum, dulled by dirt, littered with bits of paper and a few dead beetles, had split in places and curled back from the baseboard.

Bibi stood where she had stood on the morning that she found him dead, when she was ten years old. He'd been at his breakfast when it happened, a bowl of cereal and a plate of toast on the table before him, his newspaper folded open to the opinion pages. He must have gotten to his feet before he'd fallen and hit his head on the corner of the table. He'd been lying on his left side. A lake of blood had gushed from nose or mouth, or both. Blood colored his staring eyes as well, and his lashes were jeweled with scarlet tears.

She'd thought someone killed him. Even so, she had not run in fright. She had been too devastated to have a capacity for fear; she had room only for grief. She'd said aloud, *Grandpa, no. Oh, no, no. I still need you, Grandpa.*

That had been the only time she ever called him Grandpa. For the first couple of weeks after he moved in above the garage, she didn't know that he was her mother's father. By then he was forever Captain to Bibi. He preferred it that way, too, because he felt that Bibi's mother would be rubbed raw by hearing the G-word all the time. Nancy didn't call him Dad. To her, he was Gunther, his first name. He said that Nancy had it right, that he had never been a good enough father to deserve to be called Dad. But as far as Bibi was concerned, he had become a perfect grandfather.

There had been no hostility between Nancy and the captain, just a distance that couldn't be bridged, a staining sorrow neither knew how to wash away. There was even affection sometimes, moments when you could glimpse how things might have been between them.

The coroner declared the cause of death was an aneurysm, a rare type, that burst with force. The captain didn't know he had it. He'd bled out so fast, there was no hope.

Nancy had wept, surprised by the intensity of her grief.

The weeks after Captain's death had been hard for all of them, hardest for Bibi. When the golden retriever came to her out of the rain, a friend when she most needed one, she called him Olaf, because that was Captain's middle name. Gunther Olaf Ericson, United States Marine Corps, retired.

She had warned the dog to stay away from the apartment because evil dwelt there. But nothing wicked had roamed those rooms when the captain lived in them. Because of him, it was a fine place. The evil came only in the weeks after he passed away.

Now, twelve years after those bad days, she had returned to learn if that evil might still linger. Or if not the abomination itself, something that would help her to recall what had happened in the attic. As she had written in her little spiral-bound notebook, that incident was one of three lost memories that were somehow the roots of her current crisis.

Call this shock therapy.

Or desperation.

She had not brought the butane lighter. On the walk between the motel and the Honda, she had dropped it in a public trash can. She hadn't purchased another lighter at the mall. If she achieved some breakthrough, the recovery of a crucial memory, she would not be able easily to employ the captain's memory trick and erase the newfound knowledge before putting it to use.

Following the flashlight, she went from the kitchen into the empty living room, darkness reclaiming the apartment behind her, darkness to either side of her, darkness retreating ahead, but only where the cold white LED beam forced it to relent.

She'd been aware of an unpleasant smell in the kitchen; but it lacked strength. By the time that she reached the bedroom, the odor intensified. A stink nurtured by two years of abandonment. Mold thriving in the walls. Mouse piss.

In the bedroom closet, she reached to the

dangling pull-cord with her left hand and drew down the folding ladder.

83
WHAT DO YOU NEED MOST?

Bibi did not switch on the attic lights. The electricity had probably been disconnected in preparation for the demolition crew. Even if power was available, she preferred not to ascend into the glare of the gable-to-gable string of bare light bulbs that she had been grateful for twelve years earlier. She had been scared on that previous adventure but also driven by a not unpleasant expectation; and she wanted to recapture as much of that mix of feelings as she could, the better to jar her memory. As an adult, she didn't scare as easily as she had back in the day. A greater measure of darkness might juice the fear factor.

When she reached the top of the ladder and stepped into the attic, the flashlight silvered the fog drifting through one of the screened vents just under the eaves, a slowly churning mass, almost pulsing, like the ectoplasm summoned from another world during a séance. She recalled the long fingers of fog questing through the same opening on that Sunday morning twelve years earlier.

The central aisle flanked by rows of shelving was as before, although everything once stored there had long ago been removed. The shelves were backed with sheets of Masonite, preventing her from seeing into the side aisles until she arrived at the head of each.

On that far-away Sunday, maybe there had been a presence in the next to the last aisle on her left, though Bibi did not expect to encounter it now. She hoped only that, standing where she had stood then, teasing herself into a similar frame of mind, she might recall a useful fragment that had survived the flames of the captain's memory trick.

The flashlight flensed away the darkness to the left, and no figure loomed there. She probed the side aisle to her right. It was likewise deserted.

A final pair of side aisles were unexplored, but logic insisted that she needed to remain in the precise spot where she had stood on that previous occasion. She faced to the left, trying to summon a recollection of whoever or whatever had moved from shadow into light.

She listened to settling noises in the old structure, of which there were many, breathed in the rankness of mold and rodent droppings, shivered not from fear but from the chill of the night, and waited, waited.

Although uneasy, even apprehensive, she wasn't fearful to the degree she had been as a young girl. She doubted that she could recapture that anxious mood to a sufficient extent in the current environment. So she switched off the flashlight, plunging the attic into perfect darkness.

That was better.

Her apprehension acquired a sharper edge. The settling noises seemed to become more numerous and were certainly more intimate than they'd been before. Some might have been caused not by the shifting of inanimate materials, but instead by mice or rats, or by songless night birds roosting in the rafters. Without vision, she had a keener sense of smell. The odors were not more pleasant, but richer, with greater nuance. She thought that she heard someone breathing nearby, a quick and shallow respiration, but when she held her breath, she realized that she had been listening to herself.

The recollection came with no flash-and-dazzle, no trumpets of revelation, only two voices, hers as a child and the captain's. The conversation that she recalled had occurred long before his death, not here in the attic, outside in a place where the black limbs of a tree cradled orange fire but were not set ablaze.

"Holy shit," Captain says.

"Yeah."

"Sorry, Bibi. Bad language."

"It's okay."

"I mean, look at me," Captain says, "I'm still shaking."

"Me, too."

"Good God, you kept this all to yourself for so long."

"Like eight months. I had to keep it myself. Till you."

"But I've been here six months."

"I had to be sure, would you be okay to tell."

"Sonofabitch. Sorry, Bibi. But *sonofabitch*! This is nuts."

"I'm not crazy."

"No. Of course you're not, sweetheart. You're the furthest thing from crazy. That isn't what I mean."

They are sitting in the chairs on the small balcony outside his apartment. The sun is orange, but still more than an hour from the sea, blazing through the branches of the ancient front-yard ficus that towers over the bungalow, beaming fire and spilling shadows into the courtyard.

Captain says, "So you decided right from the start, you can't ever tell your mom and dad."

"Not ever, never."

"Why?"

"I don't know so much why," Bibi says. "I just know I can't because . . . of the way they are. Yeah, they're real nice and real smart, and all. . . ."

"They're good people," Captain agrees.

"I love them lots."

"You better damn well love them, missy. They deserve it."

"Yes, sir. I know. I do."

"You never stop loving them."

"No, sir. I won't."

"They brought you into the world because they wanted you. And they sure love you to pieces."

"But if they knew," Bibi says, "they'd get it all wrong."

"Almost anyone would, not just them."

"They wouldn't mean to."

"No, they wouldn't."

"But if they get it all wrong, what happens to me? To them and me and everything?"

"That's something to worry about, all right." He holds his hands up and stares at them. They are still trembling. He looks at Bibi. "How old are you for real?"

"Same as yesterday. Six and a half."

"You are and you aren't."

"You know what I mean about Mommy and Daddy, how they are?"

Captain is quiet, but he's thinking so hard and fast that Bibi wouldn't be surprised if suddenly she heard his mind spinning. Then he says, "Yeah, I do. I know what you mean. But I'm not sure I can put it into words any better than you can."

"So is it wrong not to tell them?"

"I can't believe you kept it to yourself, almost eight months since it happened. Afraid and never showing it."

"But is it wrong not to tell them?"

"No. It's not wrong or right. It's what's best for you . . . for everyone."

The silent sun slides limb by limb through the tree, and the mosaic of light and shadow on the courtyard floor slowly changes.

Captain says, "Tell me, what do you need most?"

"You mean . . . like what?"

"What do you most want to do about all this?"

"I wish none of it ever happened. I don't want to be scared so bad."

Captain says, "So you need to forget what happened, why it happened, how it happened?"

"But I can't. I can't ever forget."

He held out one of his big hands, and she put her tiny hand in it, and they sat like that for a while, holding hands from chair to chair, as he seemed to think about the situation, and then he said, "Maybe there is. Maybe there is a way to forget."

Bibi snapped from memory into the present, from the orange light of a westering sun into the pitch-black attic, when someone behind her put a hand on her right shoulder.

Startled, she simultaneously switched on the flashlight and fumbled it, dropped it. The beam rolled on the particleboard floor, sweeping a bright arc across the center aisle.

She ducked away from the hand on her shoulder, reached down, grabbed the flashlight, rose, pivoted, and slashed empty air with the beam. No one.

The last two side aisles — one to the left, one to the right — still had not been explored. If someone had actually put a hand on her, he might have retreated into one of those spaces.

Valiant girls were never conquered by their fear. Valiant girls understood that if everyone backed away from confrontation with evil, this world would be a prison from pole to pole, ruled with cruelty and brutality by the worst of humanity, no corner left for freedom. Every retreat, every appeasement, was one step down a staircase to Hell on Earth.

She drew the pistol. A one-hand grip was never good, but she needed her left for the flashlight. Forward then, swivel to the left, to the right. If someone had touched her, he wasn't in either of the last two aisles, and there was nowhere else that he could have gone.

84
WHILE WAITING FOR
AN ESKIMO PIE

Like a community of ghosts, fog escorted her down the apartment stairs and across the courtyard to the bungalow. She had come here to visit the two places where the lost memories of her youth might still be found, the second being her former bedroom. Because the house had been stripped of everything having value — from used appliances to antique fixtures — and because demolition would soon occur, the back door was unlocked.

She entered a house that had once been warm and welcoming, that had resonated with conversation and laughter and music, where her dad and mom had sometimes pushed aside the kitchen table to dance in the middle of the floor, where Olaf had been the family fur child for six happy years. None of those memories had been purged from Bibi, and she expected, after an absence of only three years, to be bathed in nostalgia when she crossed the threshold, to see at every turn the best moments of a blessed childhood and adolescence.

Instead, the air hung cold and damp and thick with a fungous scent. The flashlight revealed dirt and damage everywhere it probed: a ceiling discolored and sagging from an unchecked roof leak, holes in the plaster through which ribs of lath were revealed, a largely decomposed rat with eyeless sockets and tight grin of pointed teeth, empty hamburger containers and soda cans and candy wrappers perhaps discarded by the salvage workers in the first phase of demolition. But the disrepair and debris did not alone transform the familiar into the alien. Beneath the chill in the air and the bleakness of ruination lay another coldness, a frigid emptiness that had nothing to do with the want of furniture or the lack of central heating, that resulted from the absence of the human spirit.

By the time Bibi reached her bedroom, she understood as never before that *home* wasn't a place but rather a place in the heart. In this troubled world, everything was transient except what we could carry with us in our minds and hearts. Every home ceased to be a home sooner or later, but not with its demolition. It survived destruction as long as just one person who had loved it still lived. Home was the story of what happened there, not the story of where it happened.

In the barren bedroom, where the plaster

was now cracked and pocked and scaling, where the once lustrous wood floor was scarred and dull and splintered, Bibi felt the deepest chill of all. With only the inadequate brush and palette of the flashlight beam, she could not paint a picture of how the room had been. All the joy of the books that she had read here, all the glamor of distant rock-'n'-roll radio stations to which she had listened late into the night, marveling at differences in local cultures expressed in the style and patter of the DJs: None of that helped her to recall what a nurturing haven this had been. Instead, she saw it now as a somber and lonely space, where she had begun to lose a part of herself, where fear had driven her to sequester from recollection things of enormous importance.

She had come here with the hope that something she saw would free the imprisoned truth of what had happened in this room seventeen years earlier. What intruder had terrorized her, crawling in the dim glow of the Mickey Mouse night-light, and ultimately into her bed and under the covers?

The memory she regained, however, was of another conversation with the captain. It had taken place in the kitchen, a day or so after their tête-à-tête on the balcony above the courtyard. Murphy and Nancy were out for the evening at a concert. Captain cooked for Bibi and himself: his favorite recipe for chili-cheese dogs, with oven-baked fries bought at a supermarket from the special freezer section known only to currently serving and retired members of the Marine Corps. After they had finished eating at the kitchen table, as they were waiting to see if they could free up enough stomach room for an Eskimo Pie each, the captain raised the subject of forgetting.

Captain says, "I was taught a memory trick by this Gypsy in the Ukraine, after it wasn't a part of the Soviet Union anymore. Is that right? Come to think of it, I might have learned it from this hundred-year-old shaman in Vietnam. Wherever and whoever, it's a good trick and I've used it to forget terrible things I saw and couldn't live with."

"What things?"

"Things you see in war that will destroy you if you can't stop thinking about them."

"Tell me one."

"If I hadn't played the memory trick on myself, if I could remember those things, I still wouldn't tell you."

"Yeah, but I told you about what happened to me. I showed you how it happened and everything."

"And I almost wish you hadn't, missy."

Having eaten their hotdogs by the light of six candles in small red-glass votives, they sit now in that warm flickering glow, the captain nursing a second beer and Bibi pretending that her

465

Coke with a lime slice is a grown-up drink that might give her a hangover.

She says, "I like tricks. There's this magician, he comes in Pet the Cat sometimes. I saw him make cards just disappear in front of my nose."

"Making bad memories disappear is a thousand times harder. It's true magic. I bet that magician fella brought the cards back —"

"Yeah, he did. Like poof!"

"— but once you burn memories with this trick of mine, they won't ever come back. Are you still sure forgetting is best?"

"I'm sure," Bibi says. "I don't want to be afraid all the time. Aren't you sure, Captain?"

"Sometimes . . ." He falls quiet. Then he begins again. "Sometimes, I start thinking around the edges of one of the holes. One of the memory holes. Thinking around the edges, trying to pull the burnt threads together. I try to fill it in. The hole. I get obsessed with filling it in. Sometimes what I fill it in with is maybe even worse than what was there in the first place."

Bibi doesn't know how to respond to that. The captain seems almost to be talking to himself, so maybe she doesn't need to say anything.

In sunlight or in shadow, the captain is a striking figure, so tall and strong, with his mane of white hair and weather-beaten face and eyes that are full of sorrow even when he laughs. In candlelight, he is yet more compelling, like someone in movies, the man you must go to when everything goes wrong, the one the hero

466

seeks out when he's at rope's end and needs guidance.

After considering her question through the remainder of his beer and after getting a third from the refrigerator, he says, "Yes, I do think it's for the best, though God help me if I'm wrong. You know what hypnotism is, missy?"

"Sure. The guy swings a watch on a chain, like in front of your eyes, and makes you cluck like a chicken."

"It isn't just for stage shows. It can be used to break someone of smoking cigarettes or to overcome, say, a fear of flying. And for other good, healing purposes. For the memory trick to be useful, the voodooist had to hypnotize me first."

"Why?"

"While I was under hypnosis, he implanted the unshakeable belief that the memory trick would work. Later, because I believed that it worked, it did work. You understand?"

She squinches her face. "Maybe not."

"Well, that's the beauty of it. You don't have to understand it for it to work."

"Maybe I don't understand that, either." Bibi sips her lime-slice Coca-Cola and tries to give Captain the same serious look he gives her, so that he'll know she isn't being a baby, that she's thought about this and wants it for good reasons, though she can't imagine one reason that would be bad to want it. "Help me. Please. You've got to, Captain. Help me like the Gypsy

467

voodoo helped you."

For a while, the captain says nothing. He is full of silences this evening, not his usual self. He doesn't look at Bibi but at his can of beer, at the candles, at his left hand and the two stumps where his little finger and ring finger should be.

Finally he picks up one of the red-glass votives. Although he holds it by the thick bottom, it must still be hot, but he doesn't seem to mind the heat. He looks at Bibi, and there is something in his eyes that she couldn't in a million years put a name to, but it makes her terribly sad, though not just sad, it makes her afraid for the captain.

He tells her to push aside the glass of Coca-Cola and to put her hands in her lap, palms up, and relax. Everything is going to be all right, he says. She has nothing to worry about, nothing she needs to fear. He is going to make everything right. She must listen to his voice, which has become softer and lower, listen to his voice and watch the candle flame pulsing in the red-glass cup, watch the flame, watch it without turning her head, follow it just with her eyes, the flame, and listen to his voice. He begins to move the votive back and forth before her eyes, back and forth in slow, smooth, shallow arcs, like a pendulum. . . .

When she returns, she has no awareness of having been gone. She thinks nothing has happened, but he says that the hypnosis part is over. Now they are ready to play the memory trick. He provides her with an index card and a pen. Together they decide on the words. She must forget not only what crawled across her room that night eight months earlier, but also why and how it had gotten there. When the petition is airtight, when it leaves no loose end that might unravel, Captain retrieves a pair of tongs from a kitchen drawer and presents them to her for the burning.

She is convinced that the memory trick will work, that it is magic of the highest order and will make her life normal again, that the ugly scary memories will vanish like the magician's deck of cards and, unlike the deck, will never return.

She grips the index card with the tongs.

From his chair across the table, Captain picks up one of the votives and holds it out to her.

The quivering flame stands as high as the rim of the glass.

Bibi turns the tongs so that one corner of the index card points into the votive, cleaves the flame, and is ignited.

In the jaws of the tongs, the burning object might be a cocoon, for from it arises a bright butterfly of fire that flexes its wings across the white cardstock, which peels away in gray ribbons. The butterfly appears about to leap free, to shake loose the remnants of the white chamber of resurrection that its larval form had woven for it and soar into luminous flight, but instead it collapses into a midge of flame.

Captain tells Bibi to open the tongs, so that the fragment of card trapped between its jaws will be consumed.

Bibi obeys, and the burning scrap falls to the red-Formica top of the dinette table, the same cool chrome table that one day will be in her first apartment, the table at which ten lettered tiles will years later spell the name ASHLEY BELL.

The final twist of combustible paper has its bright moment, and in two seconds dwindles into ashes.

The captain sweeps the ashes off the Formica, carries them to the trash compactor, and blows them off his hands, into the trash.

When he returns, he stands watching his young granddaughter for a moment before he asks, "What are you afraid of, Bibi?"

"Afraid of? I don't know. Well, there's this old dog, two blocks over, it's not friendly. And I sure don't like wasps at all."

"Have you ever been alone at night in your bedroom and been afraid that something else was there with you?"

She frowns. "How could something be with me when I'm alone?"

Instead of answering her, he says, "I guess the night-light makes you feel safe."

"Stupid silly Mickey Mouse," she says, and makes a face that no one could mistake for anything other than exasperation. "I'm not a baby anymore. They shouldn't treat me like a baby. I'm not a baby anymore, and I'm never gonna be a baby again — that's how it works."

"You've not even once been glad to have Mickey there?"

"Nope. I'd break him, you know, by accident, if that wouldn't be wrong. I might do it anyway." She notices the tongs still in her right hand. She sniffs the air. Her eyes widen. "We just did it, didn't we?"

"Did what?"

"The voodoo Gypsy memory trick."

"Yes, we did. How do you feel?"

"I'm okay. I feel good. Wow, that was cool, huh?"

"Do you have any idea what memories you burned?"

She tries to think, but then she shakes her head. "Nothing. I guess I didn't need them. What did I forget?"

At the refrigerator, he opens the freezer compartment. "Are you ready for that Eskimo Pie?"

The memory is so vivid that when it wanes and leaves Bibi once more in a house prepared for demolition, she can for a moment smell the lingering scent of the burned index card.

For sixteen years, she had neither recalled the incident in her bedroom nor dreamed of it, until the previous night, when she'd fallen asleep in the armchair in her father's office, above Pet the Cat. The architecture of forgetfulness was at last collapsing, but not quickly

471

enough. She still could not recall the nature of the thing that had stalked her in this room, neither the how nor the why of it, only that the incident had occurred.

Although of low wattage, the glow from Mickey Mouse had been more diffuse than the brighter but narrow beam of the flashlight, which revealed less of the room than had the cartoon guardian. As Bibi probed here and there, she realized that she had gotten all she could — and less than she hoped — from this trespass.

She thought of something she had learned about the captain during a conversation with her mother, a month after his death. *Psychological warfare, interrogation-resistance techniques . . .*

Nancy had been estranged from her father for both justifiable and petty reasons. During his four-plus years in the apartment above the garage, the valley between them had been bridged; Nancy's real father-inflicted wounds had healed, and she had come to recognize those that were imaginary. After his death, she had been struck hard by grief, and over the weeks following his burial, she had talked about him at greater length and in more depth than ever before.

He had remained a combat soldier and officer far past the age when other men needed to switch to desk work. A stint as a trainer of recruits did not give him satisfaction. For the last decade of his career, he'd become an intelligence officer, in part supervising the gathering and analysis of information about the nation's enemies, but primarily committed to development of defenses against psychological warfare and to formulating interrogation-resistance techniques that soldiers, when captured and held as prisoners of war, could employ to deny crucial information to the enemy.

That detail hadn't seemed relevant when Bibi was ten and first heard it from her mother. Of the thousands of things, both important and trivial, Nancy told her about her grandfather, that was one of the least interesting. But now she realized that one way to resist interrogation would be to have a memory trick, a way of forgetting those facts the enemy might most need to know.

Surely the other presence in the vacant bungalow must have made small noises as he worked his way toward her. She must have been too lost in memories to separate the telltale sounds of a stalker from the ticks and creaks of an old house easing toward the ruin that was wanted of it.

Her flashlight was a beacon that made of her an easy target, and it revealed her attacker only in the penultimate moment, when abruptly he abandoned stealth and rushed her from the doorway.

85
THE LIBRARY OF BABEL

In the instant before impact, the ice-white flashlight beam stuttered across his looming face. Broad and blunt, cleft-chinned and beetle-browed, it was a countenance familiar to victims through thousands of years, seen on marauders and plunderers, on those who tortured with hot irons and exquisitely sharp skewers, on those who lynched and beheaded and those who wielded the clubs in the gulags.

He crashed into her with devastating force, he the bull and she the china shop, so that she thought something essential inside her broke on that first contact. As he collided with her, he seized her and lifted her, his momentum barely diminished, and carried her with furious intent, slamming her into a wall. Pain flashed down her spine and through her hips, around her ribs, up her spine and across her shoulders and down her arms, her breath bursting from her with such violence that with it went the ability to inhale.

The flashlight had flown from her hand and now lay in a far corner of the room, washing the juncture of two walls. The backflow of light was too dim for Bibi to make out the details of the face immediately before her, only the shape of the skull, like the head of some demented and hornless minotaur in a nightmare. That terrible moment was only prelude to worse.

As she gaped in shock and in a failed attempt to draw breath, his mouth found hers, and he thrust his tongue between her lips in a loathsome imitation of a kiss, his breath hot and spittle foaming. She wanted to bite his tongue all the way through, bite it off, but she couldn't get her breath or work her jaws, the impact having paralyzed her. Pinned, arms useless, she wasn't able to reach for the pistol in her shoulder rig. Pressing obscenely against her, the attacker realized that she was armed, eased up on her just enough to thrust a hand under her blazer, tore the Sig Sauer from the holster, and threw it across the room. He yanked the T-shirt out of her jeans and got his hands under it and groped her breasts, as she at last inhaled, drawing into her mouth his exhalation scented with onions and bacon grease.

With breath came muscle control, coordination, and fierce determination. She raised her right foot to plant the sole and heel flat against the crumbling plaster, tensed calf and thigh. Although jammed between wall and beast, she managed to drive her knee between his legs. The shot was not the ball-crusher she hoped, but it made him grunt and relent just enough so that she could shove him back a half step and slip past him.

He swung one hand and swatted her alongside the head. The blow rang through her skull, and though she didn't see stars, concentric rings of darkness welled through her eyes and made a vortex of the room. She staggered, stumbled, dropped to one knee. He booted her in the backside, and she sprawled facedown, terrified but also mortified by her near helplessness when contesting with brute strength and savage purpose. He dropped to his knees and roughly rolled her onto her back, knocking aside her flailing fists to seize her by the throat and apply just enough force to make her understand that he could choke her to death one-handed if he wished.

She could see his face again, shadowed but complete enough to reveal his demonic and implacable intention, a deeply perverse desire unmistakable in his green eyes. Hulking, bull-strong, as broad-faced as a steer, he seemed at the same time reptilian, as if he gave out from every pore the poisonous smell of the venom in which his brain was steeped. Clutching her throat, his face a pale moon of madness floating above her, he said, "I can screw you and then kill you or kill you first.

But if you make me kill you first and I can't have the fun of doing you alive, then I'll kill you so slow and nasty, you'll think it's taking half a lifetime." When she gagged out a curse, he pulled back his left fist, big as a sledgehammer, aimed it at her face, and said, "You want to say that again, bitch?" One punch would shatter her nose and the orbit of one eye, and a second would split her lips, break out teeth, fracture her jaw, after which no surgeon in the world would be able to put her back the way she had been, supposing that she survived. For this monster, sex and violence were one and the same desire, and either would be as satisfying as the other. When she hesitated, he pulled the fist back farther and worked her tender throat with the steel fingers of his right hand, and he repeated his question: "You want to say that again? You want to curse me, you stupid skank?" She wheezed out, "No." He asked if she'd take the quick kill or the slow, and she said, "Quick," meaning that she would endure rape in return for the minimal mercy of which he might be capable. "Terezin," he said, "put a guard on places you might go, and I lucked out. He doesn't want you. He just wants you dead. But I get my fun first, like he'll get his birthday fun with that little bitch."

He let go of her throat but backhanded her across the face, a hard slap meant to confirm his dominance, to knock out of her any last trace of rebellion, to leave her stunned long enough for him to straddle her. One knee to either side of Bibi, still not having fallen upon her, he unbuckled his belt as she looked up at him with a pretense of weakness and resignation. When she crossed her arms over her breasts, he laughed at that expression of maidenly modesty, and his laugh was a low wet sound that reminded her of his tongue in her mouth, nauseating her anew. Busy with the zipper of his pants, eager to expose himself, he didn't notice that her right hand was under her blazer, didn't realize that she was probing an interior pocket. The handle of Dr. St. Croix's switchblade came smooth and cool into Bibi's hand, the nub of the release under her thumb. She drew the knife from beneath her coat, and the blade sprang out for use, seven inches long and razor-sharp and as pointed as a rapier.

As his jeans slid down his hips, his left hand pulled at his underpants, and his right was already deep inside the pouch of the garment, fondling what he sought to free. His eyes, heavy-lidded with insane desire, widened only when her hand thrust forward. He saw the wicked knife an instant before he felt it. His shirt split as if it were paper, and his flesh proved no more resistant than butter. The blade went in to the hilt. His left hand closed over hers, as if to extract the switchblade in such a way as to minimize further damage, but Bibi twisted it before yanking it out of him, cross-cutting the original wound. And thrust it again, past his grasping, ineffectual hand. And tore it free. She heaved up, rocked him. He fell not upon her, but to her right, and she scrambled away from him.

In the heat of it, under the hammer and seemingly helpless, Bibi had remained cool, had done what needed to be done, as best she could do it. But now fright rode her back and whipped her, and her spinning mind spun out at once a dozen ways that she could still end up dead here in her old bedroom.

He would have a gun. He hadn't thought he needed it. Pride in his brute strength and the pleasure of physically overwhelming her had ironically made him vulnerable. But the gun would be under his coat — was he wearing a coat? — or in an ankle holster. And right now he was surely fumbling for it.

She recovered the flashlight, swept the floor with it, saw her pistol. It was at the farther end of the room. Near the closet door. She would have to circle the would-be rapist to get to it.

He struggled to sit up, a bear of a man, his neck so thick and corded that it would have foiled a hangman's noose. No coat on this chilly night. Or he'd left it in another room before creeping up on her. Jeans and a bloody Hawaiian shirt. Arms sculpted by thousands of hours in a gym.

Quick but wary, hobbling, wincing with pain from the beating she had taken, Bibi circled him. She recovered the pistol, inexpressibly grateful that Pax had insisted she have it and learn to use it.

The barbarian was sitting up now, trying to reach behind himself and under his Hawaiian shirt, no doubt seeking a holstered weapon belted in the small of his back. The effort strained his damaged guts, and he strove to bite off a grudging squeal of pain each time he found that he couldn't twist his torso even slightly to reach what he sought. His face glistened with sweat, his eyes with hate.

Bibi wanted to be gone from there, but she had to see this through to the end. She put the flashlight on the floor, aimed at the bastard, and she stood over him, just out of his reach. In spite of her two-hand grip, the pistol jumped up and down on target, as though it had a will of its own. Even in his agony, the barbarian took note of the twitching gun, and Bibi saw him take note of it. Any sign of weakness invited violence. She steadied herself. "You make a wrong move, and I'll shoot you dead."

He seemed to have given up the idea of reaching the gun at his back. His face cleared of hatred and rage and pain. He sat there like a giant infant, legs splayed, hands palms-up in his lap, as though bewildered that his misbehavior had resulted in these consequences.

He didn't look at her when he spoke, and there was no strong emotion in his voice. "You'll never get out of this alive."

If Bibi might have answered him, the blood bubbling on his lips suggested there was no point to either argument or interrogation.

"It's the Library of Babel," he said, spitting blood with the strain of forming words. "An infinite number of rooms. No way out."

He fell backward from his sitting position, and his skull rapped the floor. But he felt nothing, for he was dead, and bewilderment, too, was gone from his face, with nothing to replace it.

86
TO BREAK HER SPIRIT

Bibi wanted to be gone from the bungalow, but not with the urgency that she had desired escape only moments earlier.

First, sickened by the need to do so, she went through the dead man's pockets and found nothing. She rolled him onto his side with the intention of extracting his wallet from a hip pocket, but he carried no wallet.

She sat on the floor, with her back against a wall. She tasted blood each time she licked the throbbing corner of her mouth, and she chose not to count all the places where she ached. Now she waited for calm to settle upon her, and not just calm but also a sense of being fully and rightfully acquitted.

That Bibi had killed in self-defense should not have brought her to despondency and certainly not to despair, and in fact it did not. To kill wasn't the same as to murder, because killing was done to protect oneself or those who were innocent — or, in war, to deny the aggressor the fruits of his onslaught and to preserve the kind of civilization that valued life and freedom above ideology, above even peace and justice, two words easily and routinely perverted by most authoritarians. The ability to recognize this was why the work of Solzhenitsyn meant so much more to her than the novels of Tolstoy, and always would.

In this case, Bibi had killed to save herself and to have the chance to find and save a girl named Ashley Bell. Horrified by the necessity of killing, she nevertheless sat there without serious doubt about her actions.

She kept the flashlight trained on the dead man and delayed her departure for no reason other than to consider his reference to the Library of Babel. He didn't seem to be the kind of man who would, by his nature, make such an allusion.

That library was a literary conceit with which several writers had played over the years, though it was most widely known because of a short work of fiction by Jorge Luis Borges, "The Library of Babel."

Imagine an infinite number of rooms, stacked atop one another, in which are stored not only all the books ever written but also all the books that ever will be, each of them in every dialect of every language known to mankind and of every language yet to be learned or formed in days to come. In addition, there is a book of the life of everyone who has ever lived or will live, and an infinite number of other volumes of all genres and purposes that could be imagined. There are books that make no sense and books that seem to make sense but perhaps do not. And the sheer quantity ensures that no one can read a sufficient percentage of it to arrive at an explanation of the library, life, or anything else.

Bibi found it to be a depressing story, if the author would even have wished that it be called a story, a kind of nihilism that would deny its nihilism.

As his dying words, the would-be rapist had said, *You'll never get out of this alive. It's the Library of Babel. An infinite number of rooms. No way out.* He could have had only one intention: to break her spirit, which was the desire of his boss, Terezin.

If such a learned reference was out of character for this thug, he must have been told to memorize those lines. And if he memorized them, he had intended to speak them to her face after he raped her and just before he slit her throat, to be sure that in the end she was robbed of all hope. When it happened that the death of the night would be his, not hers, he still performed according to his program.

If sentinels had been stationed at other places where she might have gone, as the brute claimed, all of them must have memorized the same lines about the Library of Babel. Terezin's search for her was evidently even a bigger operation than she'd imagined. His obsession with her suggested that she posed a serious threat to him.

Bibi tried to think if she had left fingerprints on anything. The knob on the back door. She'd wipe it when she left. She would take the pistol and the switchblade with her. The filthy floor and the scaling plaster walls weren't surfaces from which a police-lab technician could lift anything useful. Her prints on the dead man's skin? Possible? Yes, but not likely. She sure wasn't going to wipe him down, no way.

Besides, she would have left a few hairs. A few drops of blood. If the police technicians were as omniscient and brilliant as those on the CSI television shows, she was doomed. But of course the TV version was more fantasy than reality.

Although there was no one to hear, she refused to groan when she got to her feet. Not just to the dead man but also to Terezin and all the rest of them, she said, "Go to Hell."

87

NO DRAGONS, NO SKULLS, NO HEARTS

Seaside, from high white cliffs, the fog came down in slow avalanches, burying the peninsula and the harbor beyond it and the shore beyond the harbor. Each traffic light stood like a cyclops, peering through the mist in red rage or green jealousy or cowardice. For all that was revealed of them, the passing vehicles might have been lantern-eyed beasts that had journeyed out of one mythology or another into Newport.

Accustomed to parking a couple of blocks from her destination, the better to keep Pogo's Honda a secret from those who would track her if they could, Bibi left the car on Via Lido. She walked west to the corner and a few blocks south on the boulevard. She'd never before visited the place toward which she was headed, had just noticed it in passing. Terezin's people could not be expecting her to show up there. She was cautious, anyway.

On the mainland, a far-away siren grew

nearer as perhaps an ambulance made its way toward Hoag Hospital. The periodic bleat of the foghorn at the distant mouth of the harbor. The muffled music of a live band performing in a club.

She encountered a dozen or more pedestrians. They emerged from the murk as if born in that moment, sometimes with a dog on a leash. The canines were always grinning, elated by the cool wet night, the people not so much. Although it was a King Charles spaniel, the first dog reminded her of the morning pursuit through the park in Laguna. After that she half expected to be confronted by someone in a hoodie with a golden retriever, but she saw neither.

The electric-blue neon was at first a meaningless scrawl in the mist, floating like a balloon animal representing a species unknown on Earth. As she approached, the blue resolved into glowing glass script that spelled the words *body art*.

The tattoo parlor aimed to be a bit more upscale than most, although not to an extent that bled away its air of counterculture and rebellion. Striking images hung in the window — a winged horse, a leering death's head, Rocket Raccoon, a busty Vampira, a serpent with jeweled scales, a heart twisted around with brambles and pierced by thorns — implying that the artist-in-residence could make of your skin a first-rate gallery of pop art.

The spacious front room had a glossy Santos mahogany floor and walls papered with dozens of imaginative designs. Of the four chairs provided for customers, two were occupied by bearded men in their thirties who seemed to style themselves after the band ZZ Top. Their arms were sleeved with interwoven images. A younger man perched in a kind of barber's chair with tilt-back capability, where hand and arm decorations could be outlined and colored while interested parties observed. In the back, past a bead curtain, there would be rooms with padded tables for those who needed to lie down to present their backs and chests and more intimate areas of anatomy to the needle master.

Bibi was accustomed to men's interest, but the three in the tattoo parlor paid more complete and solemn attention to her than usual. They were talking animatedly when she opened the door, but fell into silence as she closed it behind her, as if a celebrity or a goddess had arrived. She knew it wasn't beauty that hushed them as much as it was what the beast had done to beauty: her scraped left ear caked with blood, the bruise along her jaw, the half clotted and half weeping cut at the swollen corner of her mouth.

To the twenty-something guy in the barber's chair, she said, "How long a wait till I can get a tattoo?"

Climbing off his perch, he said, "No wait at all. Kevin here, and Charlie, they just stopped by to bullshit."

Charlie, whose hair and beard were prematurely white, nodded at Bibi and said, "Ma'am."

Kevin wore a black cowboy hat, which he lifted off his head and put back again. "Pleasure."

"I'm Josh," the tattooist said. When Bibi didn't offer a name, he continued, "I can do anything you want, anything on the walls here or in one of these albums of customer photos."

"No dragons, no skulls, no hearts," Bibi said. "Nothing but four words on my wrist, all where a sleeve will hide them."

Josh produced a notepad and pencil. Bibi printed the four words, one per line, just as she wanted them.

After holding up the pad so Kevin and Charlie could read what she'd printed, Josh said, "I got a book of scripts here —"

"Block letters," she interrupted. "Simple and black."

"I can garnish the words with bats or birds or —"

"Just the words."

Disappointed, he said, "Don't seem worth doing — just letters."

"It's worth it to me," Bibi assured him.

"What's the price?"

He named one, and she accepted.

When Bibi got into the chair, Josh said, "You'll have to take off the jacket."

Because she was carrying the pistol in the shoulder rig, she said, "That's not how we're going to do it." She pulled the jacket sleeve up to her elbow and with it the long sleeve of her T-shirt. She pointed to a spot about two inches above the most prominent wrist bone. "Start there, centered on the arm, and please keep the lines tight."

As he set out his instruments, Josh said, "You want a couple of aspirin or Tylenol?"

"Will it hurt much?"

"Oh, well, what I meant is — aspirin because of what happened to your face there. But this'll sting a mite."

"Thanks, but I'll do without."

Charlie glanced at Kevin, and Kevin nodded solemnly, and Charlie shook his head, and they both looked sad.

"You don't seem spittin' angry," Josh said, "which maybe you should be. Sorry for sayin'."

"I'm not angry," she said. "Anger doesn't solve anything. I'm just damn-all determined."

"Determined what?" Charlie wondered.

"Determined nothing like it's going to happen to me again."

Silence ruled until Josh had completed

three letters, and then Kevin said, "Hope you don't mind my sayin', miss, but a woman like you doesn't need to put up with that kind of crap."

"With *any* kind of crap," Charlie elaborated.

"That's nice of you," she said. "But I didn't put up with it."

"Glad to hear it," Charlie said.

After a while, Kevin gave her another opening to share her story. "I got a feelin' I'd hate to see the other guy."

"You would," she agreed.

"Hope to hell he's nursin' a broken nose or somethin'."

"He's dead," Bibi said.

They were all quiet then, until Josh finished.

The flesh was slightly inflamed and swollen around the four words, one per line, but they were neat and readable. Josh wrapped a few layers of gauze around his work, taped it in place, and gave her a small tube of antibiotic ointment to guard against infection.

"Treat it like a wound for two or three weeks. Don't wash it. When it itches — slap, don't scratch."

When Bibi paid for the tattoo, he said, "It didn't fulfill the artist in me, but it was nice doin' business with you, Ashley."

"That's not my name," she corrected. Under the bandage was a promise scored into her right arm: ASHLEY BELL WILL LIVE.

■ ■ ■ ■

6

THE GIRL WHO WAS
AND WASN'T THERE

■ ■ ■ ■

88
THE BEST WESTERN
THAT WASN'T

Tattooed and renewed, Bibi returned to the Honda, where she had parked it on Via Lido. She sat watching the street and its businesses melt away in the thick tides of mist, partially re-form, and melt away again, over and over, as if some celestial power had ordered the end of the world but kept having second thoughts.

When she worked out what she would say, she used the disposable cell phone to call her mother.

"Bibi? We thought you'd call long before this. Did you get a motel? Where are you staying?"

"I drove all the way to San Diego, Mom. Then I played tourist for a while, it's a cool town, and then I found a nice little place for dinner." She didn't lie, not about anything important, and she particularly didn't lie to her parents; however, to her own ear, she sounded as though she was becoming at least a good apprentice liar. Although keeping

Murphy and Nancy ignorant about her situation was necessary in order to keep them off Terezin's execution list, Bibi didn't feel justified and wanted to get through the deception as fast as possible. "Anyway, I have a room at the Best Western. It's clean and quiet, and I'm going to sleep like a stone."

"Which Best Western?" Nancy asked.

"The Best Western Best Western. You know, the chain."

"But there must be several of them in San Diego."

"Well, I don't know, it just says Best Western on the building."

"There must be another part to the name. Best Western Downtown, Best Western Old Town, Best Western Harbor, something like that."

"I don't think so."

"Look for an ad card on your nightstand or a brochure in the drawer. It'll have the full name. Go look."

"Okay. Wait a sec." Bibi clamped the palm of her hand over the phone and counted to twenty while she watched the less than thrilling spectacle of the fog. "Okay. There's both an ad card and a brochure, but they just say Best Western. Anyway, it doesn't matter, I'm happy and well fed and sleepy, and I'm only staying one night. Tomorrow I might drive back up to La Jolla, stay there a day or two."

She expected her mother to demand that

she go to a window and describe the part of the city immediately around the hotel, but Nancy said, "You're not going to surf at La Jolla Shores, are you?"

"No. I'm not surfing anywhere. Too chilly for me."

"Your dad says there's a storm in the South Pacific, supposed to be some smokin' behemoths rolling in from Baja to La Jolla Shores. You *did* just get out of the hospital, remember."

"I don't even have my board with me, Mom. I'm going to spend the day shopping for things I don't need, indulging myself. Listen, there's something I wanted to ask. About the captain. About Grandpa."

"I know you still think of him often."

"I do," Bibi agreed. "But this is a research thing, for the novel I'm writing. Did he ever talk much about when he was an intelligence officer? About the interrogation-resistance techniques his team developed?"

"That was all classified stuff, sweetie."

"But he talked about it a little."

"Very little."

"Did he ever say anything about memory suppression?"

"Which is what?"

"Making people forget things. Wiping an entire experience out of your mind, so you don't remember it ever happened."

"That sounds more science-fictiony than

anything your grandpa would have been working on."

"The research I've done so far tells me it's possible. But if it's possible, I'm wondering how it could be undone."

"This is for the book you've been working on? It sounds awful science-fictiony."

"It's not really. Not at all. Anyway, I'm wiped out. I need to grab a nightcap from the honor bar and hit the sheets."

"If you need downtime to put the whole brain thing behind you, then you should damn well make it total downtime, honey. Forget your work for a few days."

"You're right, Mom. I will. Okay. Gotta crash. I love you. Tell Dad I love him. Tell him I'm not going to paddle out into any smokin' behemoths in La Jolla Shores."

After declarations of love bounced back and forth a few more times, Bibi terminated the call and switched off the phone.

She piloted the Pogomobile off the peninsula, onto Pacific Coast Highway, and motored slowly through a phantom sea of fog, heading to her motel in Laguna, trying to convince herself that she was not a natural-born liar. As a troubled child, she had withheld things from her parents, all the secrets that she had revealed to Captain, but she was pretty sure she hadn't told them bald-faced lies. Some people thought that novels were a kind of lie, because the stories and the characters were made up, but fiction could be a search engine with which you could find elusive truths and peel them layer by layer, especially those truths that writers of nonfiction rarely if ever considered, either because they did not believe such truths existed or because they did not want them to exist. By the time that she reached Corona del Mar, she decided she was a liar, but not a mean or vindictive one.

En route, she stopped at a supermarket and bought extra-strength Tylenol. And aspirin. And Motrin. A big tube of unscented analgesic cream. No matter how much she overmedicated, she wouldn't blow out her liver in one night. Valiant girls should be able to take a lot of physical punishment without complaint, but they weren't invincible. She didn't like admitting that she hurt and that she was getting stiff from the knockabout she had endured, but self-delusion wasn't necessary to remain resolute. Gauze, tape, iodine. A family-size bag of Reese's peanut-butter cups. However she might die, she wasn't at much risk of dropping dead from either diabetes or arteriosclerosis.

She bought a pint of vodka, too. Her motel didn't have an honor bar like the well-stocked one that she had imagined for the Best Western that wasn't.

In Laguna, she parked two blocks from the motel. Carrying the electronic map that she'd purchased earlier in the day, the Scrabble game, the bookstore bag containing fresh copies of the three story collections, and the items from the supermarket, she returned to her room, stopping only to get a bottle of Coca-Cola from the vending machine.

Although she wasn't much of a drinker, she looked forward to a couple of shots of vodka with her Coke, to fortify her for what might lie ahead. On the other hand, she suspected that in the next hour or so, she had a good chance of locating Ashley Bell, in which case she would need to be clearheaded and ready to roll.

89
MASTER OF HER FATE, CAPTAIN OF HER SOUL

Bibi took off her blazer, mixed Coke and vodka in a motel glass, popped a pair of Tylenol, and sat at the small table to compare the text in the new copies of O'Connor, Wilder, and London to the pages from which earlier she had cut out lines with the switchblade. She repeatedly read the words that she excised and burned and forgot, but studying them did not bring enlightenment. If these lines or part of these lines, or variations of them, were what Chubb Coy had said to her in Dr. St. Croix's third-floor Victorian retreat, they no longer triggered a revelation, perhaps because she had forgotten in what context he said them, or simply because the captain's memory trick could not be that easily undone.

Putting the books aside, she turned to the lettered tiles from the Scrabble game that she had purchased. She didn't possess a silver bowl, didn't need one. She had no desire to engage in divination. Now and then over the years, she'd heard people warn that playing with a Ouija board could be dangerous, that when you posed questions to it and received answers, the responses didn't come from the board, but from some spirit realm, from an entity that was not necessarily benign. And even if that entity didn't boldly deceive and mislead with its answers, you had opened a door to it by initiating contact, after which it might not remain content to stay with the dead or the damned or with whomever it currently hung out. For other reasons — surfing, books, boys — Bibi had never been interested in Ouija boards. She had not given much credence to the notion of malevolent entities crouched in some Otherwhere, waiting for unsuspecting and ignorant humans to open a mystical gate for them. But if there might be any truth to such beliefs, Scrabblemancy would be no less dangerous than seeking answers from the Ouija. Besides, she wasn't going to thrust a needle through the meat of her thumb, especially considering that she suspected the answer to Ashley's whereabouts had already been conjured by Calida Butterfly in the hour before she'd been murdered.

Someone knocked softly on the motel-room door. Three quick faint raps.

What fresh hell is this? She drew the pistol and got to her feet and waited.

When the knock was not repeated, she went to the door and peered through the fisheye lens into a self-distorted world herewith further distorted. In the fall of light from the exterior lamp directly above the door, neither Death nor anyone else stood at her threshold in the atmospheric fog. She kept one eye to the lens, in case her elusive visitor returned to knock again. A minute passed, and then another, and her patience wasn't rewarded.

She considered going to one or both of the windows and easing aside the blackout draperies. Not a good idea. If she revealed her position, she would be an easy target.

Call the front desk? Report a prowler? Doris might still be on duty. Sympathetic Doris would believe her. *No. Don't put anyone else at risk.*

There seemed to be nothing better that she could do than return to the table. The knocking had been feather-soft, almost an idea of a sound. Maybe she imagined it.

She arranged twenty-seven Scrabble tiles in two lines, one above the other, just as they had been on the round table in Calida's home office. The first line was ASHLEY BELL. The second offered an address: ELEVEN MOONRISE WAY.

According to the electronic map, that address did not exist in Orange County or anywhere else in Southern California.

The previous night, in Bibi's kitchen, when they sought to learn why she had been spared from cancer, Calida hadn't been able to find the correct message in the first eleven letters. She had arranged the tiles to read A FATE SO EVIL, then EAST EVIL OAF, and VIA LEAST FOE. Bibi had discerned the true message: TO SAVE A LIFE.

Likewise, in the second group of letters, Calida found SALLY BHEEL and SHELLY ABLE, but neither name felt right. Bibi spelled ASHLEY BELL, which subsequent events had proved to be the correct name.

Most likely, in the seventeen letters of this address, Calida hadn't arrived at the pertinent combination. For some reason, logical or supernatural, Bibi — and Bibi alone — might be required to puzzle out the true location where Ashley could be found.

Of the many synonyms for the word *street,* only two could be formed from that combination of letters. Not AVENUE, not BOULEVARD, not HIGHWAY or PLACE or CIRCLE or DRIVE or anything other than WAY and LANE.

She tried using LANE. But working with the remaining thirteen tiles, she couldn't form a credible word or two without leaving unused letters. Evidently, LANE was wrong, and WAY was correct.

A finger tapping lightly on a windowpane. *Tum-tum-tum-tum-tum.* As quiet as the previous knocking. Repeated. *Tum-tum-tum-tum-tum.* The window to the right of the door.

Her table stood to the left of the door. At a distance of twelve or fifteen feet from the farther of the two windows, Bibi couldn't be certain that the cause of the noise was what it seemed to be. Maybe just a large moth bumping against the glass. But could a moth be so busy in the mist, which would quickly saturate its fragile wings and weigh it down?

To one side of the Scrabble tiles, the pistol lay ready. She put a hand on it. Although she had never fired it at anyone, she knew now that she could do the deed. She had stabbed a man to death with a knife, after all, which was a more disturbing — because more intimate — method of killing. Intellectually, she'd long known the difference between killing and murder. Now she understood it emotionally, and her sensitivity to the abomination of violence and the necessity for mercy would not dangerously restrain her if the moment came when killing was justified.

She waited for the furtive tapping at the window to come again. Nothing.

The door featured a deadbolt in the mortise lock, a second and independent deadbolt above that first assembly, and a stainless-steel security chain.

By comparison, the windows could be easily breached.

When nothing further occurred, Bibi sipped the vodka-spiked Coca-Cola. *Pax, whatever mess you've been sent to clean up, you damn well better stay alive. I need you here, big guy,*

I need you.

Now that she had rejected lane and settled on WAY, the remaining fourteen letters could not be formed into a single sensible word. Nor two words that were likely to be a street name.

She decided that the number, ELEVEN, might also be correct and that only MOON-RISE must be wrong. Calida had found the word because it was obvious, and perhaps she had stuck with it because it appealed to her exotic nature.

The abbreviations for south and north — *So.* and *No.* — had to be considered. Bibi started with the former and began making a list in her spiral-bound notebook: *So. Remino, So. Mirone, So. Inmore, So. Emorin.* . . . If the street bore somebody's surname and had been meant to honor a local family or a valued person, there would be perhaps a score of possibilities.

Tum-tum-tum-tum-tum. At the nearer window. Two feet from where she sat. The heavy blackout draperies prevented anyone from knowing her precise location.

After straining from the soup of letters as many possibilities as she could for the south and north lists, she quickly made another — and shorter — list using all eight letters in MOONRISE but without specifying a direction. She switched on the electronic map and began inputting the addresses, starting with the shortest list.

Tum-tum-tum-tum-tum. Tum-tum-tum-tum-tum. The sound came from both windows simultaneously. So feeble. If not moths, imagination. No reason to react until glass broke.

11 Omni Rose Way.

NOT FOUND.

11 Rose Omni Way.

NOT FOUND.

Tum-tum-tum-tum-tum. Then more insistent though still quiet. *Tumtumtum, tumtumtum, tumtumtum.*

11 Rose Mino Way.

NOT FOUND.

11 Simeroon Way.

NOT FOUND.

11 Morisoen Way.

NOT FOUND.

A scratching noise at the door. Like a dog standing on its hind legs and digging at the wood with its forepaws. Whatever it might be, if she opened the door, it would not be a dog.

11 Sonomire Way.

On the screen of the electronic map appeared a cartographic spread of Orange County. A blinking red indicator drew her attention to Sonomire Way in the southeast quadrant, in unincorporated land under the county's jurisdiction rather than that of any city. She summoned a full-screen view of the quadrant, and then of the fourth of the quadrant in which the street was located.

Sonomire Way was one in a grid of sixteen three-lane streets named this Way and that Way. The distance between streets and the lack of alleys resulted in blocks too large to serve as residential neighborhoods. She assumed it must be a business or industrial park, although no legend on the screen identified it by name.

When the scratching at the door ceased, someone insistently tried the doorknob, rattling it back and forth. There was no chance that this was an imagined noise or the work of a fog-loving moth, because she could see the light purling along the curve of the knob as it turned back and forth.

The knocking, the tapping at the window, the scratching, and now the testing of the lock didn't seem to be the actions of someone who seriously wanted to get at Bibi right away. The entire performance felt like an attempt to distract her from finding a new word in MOONRISE, from the electronic map and the search for Sonomire Way.

The doorknob stopped turning. No one knocked or scratched.

As she switched off and unplugged the map, Bibi thought about the moment earlier in the evening when she had turned traitor against herself. Because of that self-betrayal, she had not purchased another butane lighter.

If she became aware of tearing a sheet of paper into small pieces, with the intention of flushing it down the toilet, she would hope to be able to turn away from that intention, puzzle together the fragments, and read what she had meant to commit to a memory hole. That she had been a reluctant — even un-aware — treasonist did not mean she had reformed or was ineffectual.

If *she* had been the one trying to distract herself from the search for Sonomire Way, however, the noises at the door and the windows should have been imaginary; yet she was certain she'd heard them. And she definitely saw the doorknob turning back and forth. If the sounds and the testing of the lock were real and if also she was the perpe-trator of those distractions, then she must possess some paranormal power that she used unconsciously, like the living equivalent of a poltergeist.

The prospect of having such a power didn't please her. If that was part of what she'd long hidden from herself by using Captain's memory trick, she would prefer that the knowledge remained scattered ashes. If she managed to save Ashley Bell, all she wanted thereafter was to return to the tracks of a normal existence, to the life that cancer — and this obsession with the threatened girl — had derailed. Ordinary daily life, which so many people thought had no flash or filigree, was to Bibi at all times extraordinary; so much magic and wonder were at work in the world, so much mystery in its depths, that she didn't want — and couldn't cope with — any more than what it offered to anyone who was willing to *see.*

After shrugging into her blazer, she carried the electronic map in her left hand, the pistol in her right, and paused to put an eye to the peephole. If the scratcher at the door waited for her, it was not immediately in view. The two-block walk to the Honda through fog and threat, as well as the events to come on Sonomire Way, promised to be a daunting test of her daring and courage. But whatever happened, even if this proved to be a test to destruction, the night ahead had two virtues: first, the much desired end of this ordeal was coming fast; second, she doubted that it would be dull.

She opened the door.

90
THE FIRST SHOCK OF THREE

The door was closed, and Pax knocked on it, and Nancy opened it. She flung her arms around him and hugged him with something like ferocity, as if doubting — and confirming — his solidity. Then Murphy joined them, and he was a hugger, too. They stood in a three-way embrace for a minute before Paxton's future in-laws, trembling and trying to suppress small wordless expressions of anguish, ushered him to the hospital bed as if to casketed remains standing ready for a ceremony in a church. Bibi, indomitable Bibi, lay insensate, comatose, dressed in pajamas, hooked to heart and brain-wave monitors, wearing an electro cap with its many electrode contacts across her scalp, catheterized, being hydrated and nourished by an intravenous drip.

A nurse with a milk-chocolate face as lovely and ethereal as that of a Raphael Madonna, hair pulled tight and braided at the back, was preparing to change the bag of fluid on the

IV rack. The name PETRONELLA crowded the width of her uniform badge. She smiled as Pax appeared bedside, and although he wore civilian clothes, she said, "You can't be anyone on Earth but this sweet girl's Navy man."

Kindled by those words and by the sight of Bibi in such dire circumstances, Paxton found himself at a pivot point, inevitably transformed by an insight into himself and into the meaning of his life, and more than an insight, a revelation. From a Texas horse ranch to the special operation that had resulted in the death of Abdullah al-Ghazali, Pax had been born to be a Navy SEAL, as surely as the quarrel of a crossbow, fired by a master archer, would whistle from bowstring to the center circle of a target. For him, as for every SEAL, two commitments were sacred above all others: one to the members of his team, one to his country. Family, God, community, and freedom were sacred as well, but it was the warrior way that all else he loved must shine in the shadow of his duty to those with whom he fought and to the country for which he put his life at risk. You were first a soldier or you weren't a soldier at all. You expressed your love of family primarily by putting yourself in the line of fire for them, by dying for them if that's what proved to be required. But as he stood bedside, gazing down upon Bibi in a coma, acutely aware that she was vulnerable and possibly lost to him, his love for her intensified like the fission of nuclei in the generations of a chain reaction. Such a profound tenderness overcame him, he knew that now and forever, in whatever cause he might be asked to give his life, he would in fact be giving it for her, and that although he would die for her, he would rather live for her, whether that meant an end to his Navy career or not.

In Pax's mind, clear as speech, he heard Bibi say, *Peter Piper picked a peck of pickled peppers — perfectly pronounced, Petronella.* If he had not been looking at her, he might have thought that she had indeed spoken, so clear and resonate were those words. But her lips didn't move, and her brow remained smooth. Her eyelashes didn't flutter, although in spite of her untroubled brow, her eyes moved ceaselessly beneath the lids: the rapid eye movements of a dreamer deep in dreams . . . *perfectly pronounced, Petronella.* Nothing like an auditory hallucination had happened to Pax before, and he found it more disturbing than he might have expected.

When his gaze rose from Bibi to Petronella, where she stood by the IV apparatus on the farther side of the hospital bed, Pax must have appeared to be unsettled by something more than his fiancée's condition, because the nurse regarded him with concern. She cocked her head and asked, "Are you okay?"

He was manifestly not okay. Being shot at wasn't as bad as this. There had been hard moments in tight places, with the world crumbling underfoot, when he had imagined his demise, when he would have preferred death to some of the immediate alternatives. But if Bibi perished, Pax would suffer death by proxy, and having died, he'd nonetheless be required to live in a world for which he no longer had a heart, one of the living dead. He loved her, yes, and he had asked her to marry him, yes, but until now, until here, he had not understood how completely the very threads of her were woven through him.

"Are you okay?"

Before Pax could think what to say to the nurse, Nancy spoke from the foot of the bed, her voice wrung by emotion. "I brought Bibi here last Tuesday. The worst day of my life. Dr. Chandra gave her the diagnosis Wednesday. It was such a very busy day, a terrible day. We wanted . . . We wanted to have dinner here that evening, like a defiance dinner. . . ."

"Just the three of us," Murphy continued, when Nancy could not. "Only primo takeout, like cheeseburgers with jalapeños and chili-cheese dogs and every damn thing you're not supposed to eat, like what Nancy said, in defiance. But Bibi said we were tired and she was tired. She just wanted to eat a little something and use her laptop to research this

514

damn brain cancer, she wanted to know all about it and fight it with everything she had."

Red-eyed, cheeks riveted, mouth soft with grief, Nancy said, "That's the last we ever talked to her."

"It won't be the last," Murphy said. "Our girl will come out of this." He put a hand on his wife's shoulder. "She has to."

Nancy said, "Sometime Wednesday night, she went into a coma. They say coma never happens with this disease, at least maybe not until the final stage, not until the very end. But it happened with her."

None of this was news to Pax. He'd spoken with Nancy and Murphy by phone a few times since the blackout had been lifted Friday morning and the news about Abdullah al-Ghazali had broken. But they seemed to need to go over it again, and because Pax was rocked by the sight of Bibi as pale and still as a corpse on a catafalque, he was glad they wanted to hold forth, giving him time to gather himself.

He had needed almost two and a half days to learn what had happened to Bibi, to get an emergency leave, and to fly first by military craft and then by a civilian airline halfway around the world, at last to come to the hospital by cab rather than delay long enough to arrange a rental car. This was 1:00 Sunday afternoon, the sky blue and clear beyond the window. She had been in a coma almost four days.

As Petronella finished changing the IV bag, she said, "I was on duty Wednesday evening. She wasn't a complainer, so when she said she had a bad headache, I gave her the maximum allowable meds. Headaches, sometimes bad ones, come with this kind of cancer. That was shortly before seven o'clock. It's been a strange case ever since."

Looking up from Bibi, Pax said, "Strange? Strange how?"

"Strange everywhichway," said Petronella. "First, they can't find a cause. The glioma web isn't so large that it's putting enough pressure on the brain to induce a coma. Brain imaging doesn't show any intracerebral hemorrhage. No hypoxia, no significant impairment of blood flow to any part of the brain. Liver or kidney failure would intoxicate the brain with poisons. But her liver and kidneys — they're chugging right along. And it's a profound coma. I mean, this girl is deep under, yet" — she gestured toward the five-wave readout on the illuminated screen of the electroencephalograph — "just look at her brain waves."

Paxton looked, but he didn't know what to make of what he saw.

"I'll give it to you in a few bites," the nurse said, "but it's a whole lot more complex than this. The doctor should explain it to you — if he can. Your girl is exhibiting the wave patterns of someone who's asleep and someone who's awake *at the same time.* And they're nothing like the wave patterns of anyone in a coma. She seems to be way under, in that deep place where she isn't even dreaming — but look at her eyes. That's REM sleep, dream sleep."

Murphy sought reassurance anywhere he could get it. "I think it's hopeful, how weird it is."

"I don't see how it's hopeful," Nancy disagreed. "I'm scared."

Reaching across the raised bedrail, Pax took Bibi's right hand in his. It was warm but as limp as if it were boneless.

"After I gave her the medicine for the headache," Petronella revealed, "the last thing I said to her was, 'I'll keep checking on you.' And I did. I thought she was just sleeping."

As with the Peter Piper tongue-twister, Pax heard Bibi's clear voice saying, *Quick now, here, now . . . At the still point . . . Neither from nor towards . . . Where past and future are gathered.*

He knew those weren't her words, that she was quoting someone. Although he felt that he should recognize the source, he did not.

On first hearing her voice, he'd thought it must be an auditory hallucination. This time he knew it was nothing as simple as that, nothing for which he could fault either his hearing or imagination. But if he knew what it wasn't, he didn't yet understand what it was.

On the farther side of the bed, where Petronella had seconds earlier recalled the last thing she'd said to Bibi, the nurse turned her attention from Pax to her patient — and did something between a shocked recoil and a comic double take. It was one of those moments that sometimes caused Bibi to wonder aloud whether human reactions were these days what they had always been or if more than a century of movies had influenced our response to every stimulus, so that in the instant between the experience and our processing of it, we were unconsciously reminded of Cary Grant and Katharine Hepburn, Bradley Cooper and Jennifer Lawrence, of how they had reacted in similar situations in films, tailoring our performances to resemble theirs, our natural human responses distorted.

Eyes wide, raising one hand to her breast, stunned by something that focused her intently on the left side of Bibi's face, Petronella said, "What the blue blazes is *this*?"

On Bibi's right, Pax could not see what was happening, but from the foot of the bed, Nancy saw, and Murphy saw, and they cried out.

91

THE SECOND SHOCK OF THREE

Paxton released Bibi's limp hand and circled the hospital bed in time to see the abrasions finish spreading across the helix and antihelix and lobe of her left ear, tiny beads of blood forming in the wake of the injury, which seemed to have no cause, appearing as magically as stigmata. The crimson drops swelled from the damaged tissue and, with impossible acceleration, thickened into the gooey coagulum of first-stage healing. As that occurred, with it came a bruise originating at her left temple, at first the watered red of a cheap vino on the darker end of the blush-wine spectrum, seeping through the flesh along her jaw line. Nancy said, "Ohgod, ohgod," and shuddered with dread, no doubt thinking the same thing that had alarmed Pax: that this bruise and worse wounds would develop across Bibi's face until before them would lie a woman afflicted with some bizarre disease, the effects of which mimicked a brutal beating. As the bruise reached her chin and spread no farther, as it darkened to burgundy and then to plum, and as the sticky clots of blood began to dry into a crust on her ear, a small cut bloomed crimson at the left corner of her mouth, and the flesh swelled slightly. This new wound would have bled down her chin if it had not, as the injuries before it, progressed in mere seconds from fresh laceration to first-stage healing. With that, the stigmata ceased forming, and the injuries stabilized. At least for the moment.

Paralyzed by the spectacle of Bibi's transformation but then stung into action when the changes stopped, Petronella snatched up the call button that was looped by its cord around the bed railing, and she connected with the fourth-floor nursing station. With an authority born of years of patient crises successfully resolved, she told the responding nurse that she needed to see the shift supervisor urgently in Room 456. "We've got a situation here."

"What just happened to my girl?" Nancy demanded of the nurse with uncharacteristic and unwarranted accusation. Reason had been frightened out of her, and anger rather than unreason had replaced it. "What the hell happened to her poor sweet face?"

Murphy put an arm around her and, in a voice pressed thin by anxiety, said, "Easy, honey, easy, she doesn't know what happened." When Nancy tried to throw off his arm, he held her tighter. "Nobody could know what that was. That was fully crazy. But Bibi's going to be all right."

"Look at her, look at what's happening to her. She's not all right, damn it."

"No, but she's going to be. She'll walk the board as good as anyone, better than you and me, like always."

Nancy held fast to her anger, bristled with it, and it seemed that her short shaggy hair responded to some electrical charge in the air. If her eyes did not actually flash, they appeared to flash, and the muscles bulged along her clenched jaws. But it was useless anger in that it had no target, human or otherwise, and was in fact less real than it was a desperate defense against the despair that a surrender to fate encouraged.

Regarding the traveling lines of light spiking left to right across Bibi's cardiac monitor, Petronella said aloud but mostly to herself, "Her heart rate never changed. Or her blood pressure."

Pax stood immobilized and bewildered by what he had witnessed, which was not good. Whether ambushed or leading a planned assault, he was always quick to respond to events, not the least reluctant to change strategy and tactics. Considered action was always better than considered inaction, but you had to have something to consider, hard facts and a set of circumstances that allowed commonsense analysis. He knew that the face of this beloved woman bore the marks of a beating, not evidence of disease. Having tracked down some of the worst psychopaths who had made the news in the past several years, trailing in the wake of evil, Pax had seen enough women and men after they had been beaten to extract information from them, to teach them to fear the new boss, and just for the pleasure of violence. He knew what he was looking at, and he yearned — with an adolescent passion for vengeance and with a grown man's loathing of cruelty — to find and kill whoever had done this to Bibi. One big problem. Anyone not present for the flowering of the stigmata might think him insane if he gave voice to the thought, but the perpetrator seemed to be a ghost that attacked her in some realm to which Pax had no access, an Elsewhere that she at the moment occupied in addition to this world of her birth.

The shift supervisor, Julia, fortyish and pumped, with the glow and stride of a fitness fanatic, bustled into the room, received a report from Petronella, and regarded Pax with evident suspicion, no doubt because of his size but also because of the thunderstorm of an expression that had occupied his face since he had watched Bibi bleed and bruise. Any doubt that Julia might have had about Petronella's incredible story evaporated when she took a closer look at Bibi's injuries and saw that they were not fresh. She had been in the room less than an hour earlier, to reset the cardiac monitor when an alarm sounded for no good reason, which happened from time to time; and on that visit, Bibi's face had been unmarked.

No less mystified than the rest of them, Julia nevertheless had the priorities of a good manager in this age of endless litigation. She wanted everyone to remain where they were until she could get the chief of hospital security to film interviews with them in situ. Nancy's misplaced anger flared, but Murphy quickly soothed her, and Julia promised to return in ten minutes.

In the absence of the shift supervisor, the conversation did not become as animated as Pax expected. The four of them had been witness to an extraordinary event, and although they had seen precisely the same thing from the same angle, the normal human tendency in the face of the unknown was to rehash the experience until the life had been talked out of it, until they had spun off into a confabulation about such tenuously related subjects as UFOs, Bigfoot, and poltergeists. Perhaps they were constrained by the fact that Bibi's life, already being stolen from her by brain cancer, suddenly appeared to be in even more immediate jeopardy from an enemy unknown and, for the moment, seemingly unknowable.

What little they said to one another was less speculation than words of comfort, and their attention was less on one another than on the dear girl in the bed, to whom some other injury might at any moment be inflicted by a phantom presence.

Keeping her promise to the minute, Julia returned with the chief of hospital security, a former homicide detective who had retired in his early fifties to begin a second and less risky career. He was a white-haired long-faced large-boned figure with a natural dignity that might have made him seem less like a cop than like a judge, if judges these days had still been as reliably dignified as they had once been. His name was Edgar Alwine. He introduced himself to Nancy and Murphy and Pax, repeating his name and title to each, as if they could hear him only when addressed directly eye to eye. His handshake was firm, his manner warm, and Pax liked the guy.

Alwine asked Nancy and Murphy for permission to record close-ups of their daughter's facial injuries, assuring them that the images would remain part of her file, not to be distributed beyond a limited number of the medical staff. He'd hardly begun to operate the camera, however, when he exclaimed at something, and everyone crowded around the bed to witness another inexplicable blackening of Bibi's body, captured this time on film as it occurred.

92
THE THIRD SHOCK OF THREE

This time Bibi's face did not serve as the canvas, and the medium of disfigurement wasn't bruising and abrasion. Her arms lay at length above the top sheet and thin blanket. The right sleeve of her pajamas was rucked up halfway to her elbow. On her bared forearm, about two inches above her wrist bones, neatly formed black letters began to appear one at a time, as if her skin were parchment on which an invisible penman were printing his brand, to lay claim to her, body and soul. Although the words included no curse or demonic name, the crisp black letters appeared one after the other with such implacable intent that they could be regarded only as an ominous sign, no matter what their ultimate meaning might prove to be.

Murphy cringed from this inexplicable imprinting as if the message were being carved into his daughter's flesh with a knife, turning away repeatedly only to look back again each time, saying "This is wrong,

wrong, this is wrong."

Against fear, anger was an inadequate defense, and Nancy could no longer sustain it. At the foot of the bed again, she stood aghast, robbed of the power to move or speak, transfixed by the manifesting letters, as if they would spell out both her daughter's doom and her own.

Pax hoped to hear Bibi's voice in his mind's ear as before, even if it might be as enigmatic as on the two previous occasions. But as the first two lines on her forearm completed a name, and as a third line began to form, he heard nothing except expressions of amazement from the two nurses. And from Edgar Alwine, an observation: "It's a tattoo, isn't it? A very simple tattoo, perhaps poorly removed by laser and now resurfacing. Is that possible?"

"Bibi didn't have any tattoos," Nancy said.

Nancy's *didn't* rather than *doesn't* suggested an unconscious resignation, a despondency if not despair, that chilled Pax. When he spoke, his intention was as much to correct the verb tense, regarding Bibi, as to clarify her position on tattoos. "She isn't against them. She admires them when they're really beautiful. But she doesn't have any desire for one. She says a tattoo is a means of satisfying one emotional need or another, but she satisfies hers in other ways."

While the chief of hospital security filmed,

527

while the two nurses watched with the puzzled gravity of those whose fundamental certainties were proving uncertain, while Nancy stood benumbed by horror and helplessness, while Murphy bit on the knuckle of one fisted hand — the fist an expression of his desire to confront his daughter's unknown tormentor, the biting of the knuckle emblematic of the confused child within the man — while the floodgates of the setting sun poured forth torrents of scarlet light that washed against the window, the fourth and final line welled into view on Bibi's forearm, one black letter at a time, and the message — or the promise or the challenge, or whatever it might be — was complete: ASHLEY BELL WILL LIVE.

"Who is Ashley Bell?" asked Edgar Alwine.

No one in the room had heard of her.

"Where is Bibi, who is this name on her arm, how is any of this happening? Why? I don't understand," Nancy said.

Such misery informed the woman's voice that her husband, usually quick to console and reassure her, evidently felt inadequate to the task. He turned to Pax with an expression familiar to any team leader in combat; he wanted guidance, and if not guidance, then confirmation of his own instincts, and if not confirmation, then reassurance.

But here Pax felt a lack of competence that he had never felt in battle. He did not know what to say to Murphy. He did not know what to do. He felt awkward. Awkward and useless and stupid, and he hated feeling all those things. That might be who he was at this moment, in this unprecedented situation, but it was not who he had been until now and, by God, would not be who he would be going forward. Since his earliest memories of his family and the horse ranch, there had been a rhythm to his life with which he had always been in step, no matter what changes in tempo might occur. The rhythm was still there. It was always there. The rhythm was a thing outside himself, not of his creation, and all he needed to do was hear it again.

Nancy went around to Bibi's right side and took her hand. But she seemed either to be repelled by the limpness of that hand or, more likely, not repelled but dispirited by it, by the lifelessness that it implied. Perhaps the four simple and yet mysterious words, from which she could not take her eyes, suggested to her a previously unconsidered system to the world requiring that she follow a path of thought she found disturbing or daunting, for it seemed to Paxton that Nancy's distress was of a complex character, that it was not solely grief prompted by the calamity that had befallen her daughter. Whatever other fears and worries might be troubling her, she turned from the bed and went to the window and stood staring out into the vast sky, where gulls rowed through an ocean of air or caught waves of wind and surfed without need to consider an approaching shore.

Edgar Alwine had yet to film anyone's statement regarding the inexplicable appearance of the injuries to Bibi's face. Just as he was about to start with Petronella, the door opened, and a youngish physician in a white lab coat entered, having been informed of the extraordinary stigmata but not yet of the four-word tattoo. He went directly to the patient and was equally astonished and concerned by what he saw. He brought himself up to speed by listening attentively as Petronella told her story to Alwine's camera. The evident depth and sincerity of the doctor's concern disposed Pax to like the man even before they were introduced.

As they shook hands, Dr. Sanjay Chandra said, "When I told Bibi that she had one year to live, she gave me this look, such a look, I don't think I could have broken eye contact if I tried, and she said, 'Really just one year? We'll see.' *We'll see!* I've been so impressed with her, I've allowed myself the unallowable, to think that, well, maybe she'll gain another year or two, even be the first to beat this thing, maybe do the impossible. But now this coma and these . . . these phenomena. I've no idea what to make of this. I'll need extensive consultation with colleagues, other oncologists, neurologists, I don't even know who yet."

He rounded the bed to Bibi's left side, to the EEG workstation that stood on a trolley cart. As he used the keyboard and pointed to things of interest that he called forth on the monitor, he spoke of the five brain waves — gamma, beta, alpha, theta, delta — of their frequency ranges, their amplitude, their purpose in optimal mental functioning. At times there were twenty wave-tracking read-outs on the screen at once, not five, but they represented the feeds from the many electrodes in the electro cap that Bibi wore. The system was also capable of 3-D brain mapping from four perspectives, and Dr. Chandra brought some of those images onto the screen, not maps of Bibi's brain in the moment, but selected studies from the past few days, about which he had particular comments. There were as well a feature called coherence analysis and another called power-spectra displays.

Pax understood more of it than he might have if anyone but Dr. Chandra had explained it, though most of the information passed as far over his head as a 747 at cruising altitude.

He came away with the essence of the situation, however, and that was enough to confirm what he suspected. Something unprecedented was happening, something as consequential as it was strange. It might be a historic development in the annals of medicine, but perhaps historic also in a broader sense.

Each of the five brain waves was indicative of a specific brain function, and there was an ideal level that represented superior performance. Gamma waves were associated with learning, cognition, perception, information processing, and the binding of all senses into a coherent order. Too little gamma activity signified learning disabilities and depression. Too much was linked to anxiety and stress. Optimal beta waves ensured good memory and problem solving. Ideal alpha waves were present when you were relaxed but with good focus, not daydreaming. Model theta waves meant your creativity, emotional connection, and intuition were all humming at their peak. Optimal delta-wave patterns were present when your immune system and natural-healing capacity were fully engaged, and also indicated deep restful sleep.

"When you're awake," Dr. Chandra said, "the five brain waves are ever-present, but only one is dominant at any one time, depending on what state of consciousness you're in."

Murphy and Nancy must have heard this before. But she turned her back to the window to listen, and Murphy moved close to Pax, giving his full attention to the physician, as did the two nurses.

Edgar Alwine filmed Dr. Chandra, perhaps

not so much as part of his litigation-prevention file, but because he, too, sensed that in this moment, in this room, history might be made.

Calling onto the screen a simpler display than twenty feeds, revealing the five wave patterns of Bibi's brain in real time, Sanjay Chandra said, "But there is not at any moment a dominant wave in her brain. Right now, each of these patterns is optimal, ideal. There is no precedent for this. It has never been observed before. Until her. And it's been this way since we first hooked her up to the EEG Thursday morning, three and a half days ago."

"Could it be a malfunctioning machine?" Paxton asked.

"No. That's what we thought. But this is the second EEG we've used. It's reporting the same activity as the first."

"What does it mean?" Alwine asked, prodding the doctor for the purpose of the video.

Chandra regarded the screen in silence for a moment, marveling at the five dancing wave lines. "It means that since falling into the coma, she's not really been in a coma at all, not as we understand a coma. She's been in multiple states of consciousness simultaneously, while the rest of us are always in one. She's at the same time deep asleep and functioning at a high cognitive level. She's learning and *ferociously* processing information and rapidly searching her memory and problem solving and being enormously creative, maintaining a vigorous emotional connection — while also deep asleep and dreaming."

Into Paxton's mind just then came the beloved voice, clearer than it had been on the previous two occasions, the voice that he had hoped to hear again. Although she spoke only ten words, they were of such importance and had such a powerful impact that, stunned, he gripped the footrail of the bed to steady himself; and had there been a chair nearby, he would have collapsed into it.

93
HEART TO HEART IN A DESPERATE HOUR

Bibi stepped out of Room 6 into post-midnight Laguna Beach. If something had earlier rapped-tapped-scratched the windows and door to get her attention, it was either gone now or watching her from a secluded lair in the white eclipse of fog. Carrying the electronic map in her left hand, the pistol in her right, she walked through dense clouds that all but required radar navigation, the city quieted as if by a plague that had left no animal or insect life in its wake. In the canyons, the coyotes had chosen hunger over a blind hunt and had gone to bed. In their roosts, the birds stood wrapped in silent wings. Only the streetlamps, by their regimented placement, could be known for what they were. All other lights — of homes or businesses, or churches with pastors holding irrational expectations of late-hour converts — were blurred and hazy and forlorn, robbed of defining shapes, their distance impossible to judge, some of them encircled by faint coronas or multiple coronas, but others like sinkholes of light only slight degrees away from going as black as dead stars.

Anything could have happened in that murk. Anything could have taken her if she was wanted. But she arrived intact at Pogo's Honda.

After she put the portable GPS, the pistol, and her purse on the passenger seat and settled behind the wheel and locked the doors, she considered calling Pax. Had he phoned her in the past twenty-four hours, he would have gotten either voice mail or Terezin, since she had abandoned her phone with her Ford Explorer. But of course he had not reached out to her, because he was on a mission, under orders to run silent. And if she called him, she would only be disappointed by the failure to connect.

Except for the fog, she would not have bothered to switch on the GPS. She had memorized the route to 11 Sonomire Way, where she would find the imprisoned Ashley Bell — if Calida's last act of divination had indeed produced hidden knowledge before she'd been relieved of her life and her fingers. In these occluding clouds, however, a guiding voice that precisely counted off the distance to every turn would be a great assistance.

She started the engine and switched on the headlights, which tunneled all of twelve or fourteen feet into the fallen sky, but before she drove away from the curb, she was overcome by the desire, the need, to speak to Pax as though he could hear her, half a world away, without a phone. This was the romantic nonsense of a child or a teenage girl, but she was both those things in addition to being an adult, for she remained all that she had ever been.

She closed her eyes and took a few deep breaths and thought that she would express her love and longing for him. But when she spoke, she surprised herself by saying, "Pax, I need you. I am not dreaming. Find me."

No one else heard Bibi, but she came through loud and clear to Paxton. *Pax, I need you. I am not dreaming. Find me.*

If, since entering the hospital room, he had not twice before heard her voice, he might have thought he imagined this or might have wasted time trying to explain it away. The previous two incidents — the tongue-twister involving Petronella's name, and the stuff about still point where past and future were gathered — had prepared him to accept the reality of the phenomenon and to remain alert to every word that might come and to the nuances of what she said.

Unlike the former transmissions — or whatever they were — this one was directed to him by name. Comatose, apparently unaware of everyone around her, Bibi must in fact know that he had arrived. He'd read of coma patients who, on recovering, reported hearing every word spoken while they'd been apparently insensible. If anyone in such an isolate condition would remain firmly anchored to the wakeful realm above the waterline of sleep, it would be his Bibi, who so loved the world and all its wonders.

Furthermore, she'd spoken to him the moment Dr. Chandra had said that she was in multiple stages of consciousness simultaneously while also deep asleep and dreaming. She must have heard the physician. And she had specifically said that she was not dreaming, in spite of what could be read in the brain waves, in spite of the rapid eye movement, which always signified that a sleeper lay deep in dreams.

Edgar Alwine had begun to film Nurse Julia, and those in the room, all but Pax, were fixated upon her account of the inexplicable emergence of the four-word tattoo.

Find me. Bibi had said, *Find me.* She was lying in bed, there before his eyes, and didn't need finding. Pax could have attributed her request to delirium or merely to the confusion that plagued the mind when it was lost in the false world of a coma, whatever that might be like. But she had sounded so like herself, so to-the-point and assertive, not panicked or bewildered, calm and determined to be heard. He didn't know how she could reach out to him in this way or why she couldn't convey the nature of her plight and her needs in a more detailed and helpful manner, but the restrictions under which she had to function were no excuse for him either to shrug off her request or to wait for further communications that might never come.

But if Bibi, in whatever deep and strange place she currently inhabited, wasn't bewildered, Pax certainly was, and he didn't know what he could do to help her.

The amorphous fog writhing in the headlight beams as if intent on finding a suitable form to wear henceforth, the low rumble-purr of the car engine like an expression of animal pleasure at the prospect of the journey ahead, the first thin exhalations of welcome heat from the floor and dashboard vents, the witchy light from the instrument panel reflected in her eyes as she met her own otherwise dark gaze in the rearview mirror . . . Every detail of the moment suddenly seemed to be a portent of an approaching event, fraught with hidden meaning and ripe for divination by crystal ball or tea leaves, or Scrabble tiles.

Bibi sat behind the wheel, considering what she had said aloud to Pax, and wondering why she'd said it. Although he was half a world away, the fact that she'd spoken to him wasn't strange to her, only *what* she had said.

Why say that she wasn't dreaming, when of course she wasn't, being wide awake? Why ask him to find her when she wasn't lost? She understood the needing-him part. She always needed him. And in the current madness, just having him at her side would smooth some of the craziness out of the night.

She was reminded of the key thing she had learned since she'd left her apartment and gone on the run: that she kept secrets from herself, pieces of her life that had been lost to Captain's memory trick. Because she had recovered parts of those memories, she knew now that they hadn't been rendered into ashes and blown away forever. They were barreled and stored and awaited discovery. Maybe the answer to why she'd said what she'd said to Paxton would become clear to her when she found that memory barrel, hammered a hole at the bottom, drained it, and learned, to the last drop, what was in it. Meanwhile, she couldn't understand herself or fully trust herself, which was frustrating but not as frustrating as being dead of cancer.

"So get on with it, Beebs," she said. She wasn't the only girl in trouble. Ashley Bell would be murdered — and suffer who knew what horrors and indignities before the lethal blow — perhaps as soon as twenty-four hours from now. When she pulled away from the curb and drove slowly south on Pacific Coast Highway, the GPS began to offer directions, like a little spirit guide in a box.

Pax was accustomed to knowing what to do and doing it. Navy SEAL training was an intellectual, physical, and emotional ordeal, a test to near destruction, being torn down so as to be built better, an education Harvard couldn't match, a cultivation of honor and valor and integrity and ethics that could survive even the crucible of war, at the same time creating a sense of brotherhood that would survive a lifetime without corrosion. The intent of spec-ops schooling was to make you confident but never arrogant, bold but never reckless, prudent but never shy of reasoned risk, sagacious rather than shrewd, determined rather than willful, and in every sense — intellectual, physical, emotional — strong enough to kick ass. You became a SEAL to be able to do whatever was necessary, and to be unable to do was to die a little.

He was dying a little as he watched Edgar Alwine film Murphy's statement and watched Bibi lying immobile in her bed. She was beset by cancer, by coma, but there was something else going on, damn it, something that excited the medical experts as much as it baffled them, something that Pax thought might be the salvation of his girl. But he was reluctant to let his natural optimism inflate itself, as it was wont to do, because this world offered more false hopes than real.

Just then the answer to his question — what to do? — opened the door and walked into the room. Pogo. His name was Averell Beaumont Stanhope III, but everyone called him Pogo, in part because he would not answer to anything else. He had long been Bibi's best pal, closer to her than any girlfriend. She didn't know where the nickname came from; he had been Pogo as long as she'd known him. Pax respected the kid and found him good company, but he didn't yet know him well. He knew only that with most people Pogo played dumb but wasn't, that he truly didn't care about money, that he pretended to be lazy but was not, that in spite of movie-star good looks, he was so lacking in vanity that he had need of a mirror only when he shaved.

Pogo shook Pax's hand, but only en route to the hospital bed, where he stood, looking down at Bibi, tears forming in his eyes the moment that he saw her. When Edgar Alwine began filming Nancy's statement, Pogo learned what had everyone agitated. Pax saw the kid brighten as the paranormal nature of these recent events inspired hope, but then a measure of sobriety tempered his expression, as if he instinctively perceived the danger of unrestrained optimism, following in his own way the very progression of Pax's attitude.

When he could draw Pogo aside, Pax said quietly, "There may be some things we can do to help her, but not here."

"What things?"

"My guess is, I'll figure that out as we go."

"You'll figure it out — but it's real?"

"No bullshit. You heard Nancy say what happened. There's more they don't know about."

"But you do."

"That's right."

Although Bibi had said that Pogo was more realist than dreamer, the kid proved not to be one of the legion of knee-jerk skeptics who worked to make the world a more bitter place by doubting the motives and wisdom of anyone not a clone of them. He was at once game: "What do you need me to do?"

"Do you have a car?"

"Yeah. I call it a car," Pogo said, wiping his eyes with his fingertips, drying his fingers on his jeans, "but a lot of people have other names for it. A thirty-year-old Honda, primer for paint, but still sweet in its quiet way. Do I drive?"

"Why wouldn't you drive? It's your car."

Pogo smiled. "Man, this could be totally sacred — on the road for Bibi with the Incredible Hulk riding shotgun."

■ ■ ■ ■

7

TWO GIRLS NEEDING TO BE FOUND

■ ■ ■ ■

94
THE GIRL WE ONLY THINK WE KNOW

Pax tossed his duffel bag into the back of the Honda, hulked into the front passenger seat, and pulled the door shut as Pogo turned the key in the ignition, which settled the issue of whether the car was the junker that it appeared to be. It was not.

"You worked on the engine."

"Now and then."

"Maybe it's a Humvee in disguise."

"If this baby were a Transformer," Pogo said, "about the most it would change into is a 1968 Dodge Charger."

"As good as it gets. The 440 Magnum?"

"You've got an ear for gear." Pogo drove out of the parking lot and turned right into the street.

Pax said, "You had to make some space to fit it. But the body looks factory normal."

Pogo grinned. "Wouldn't be fun if it looked like what it was."

They were going to Bibi's apartment. It seemed the most logical place to start. Nancy had given them her key, assuming only that Pax was staying there, not that he had another purpose as well.

"You sometimes think," Pogo asked, "the Bibi we know isn't the full Bibi?"

"She is exactly what she says she is. That's part of her beauty. No deception. No masks. But I know what you mean. She's at the same time a mystery."

"She's way deep," Pogo said. "She's got these currents running through her, they come up from some abyss, so deep that if you tried to scuba down there, you'd be crushed, you know, by the weight of all the ocean above."

Pax nodded. "Sometimes it's like she doesn't know about herself what you just said."

Braking to a stop at a red traffic light, Pogo spoke without glancing at Pax, though they were both wearing sunglasses and were therefore somewhat armored against the revelation of sentimentality. "I don't know if I'll ever love anybody as much as Beebs. She's a sister to me, sister and brother and best friend, she's the whole package. It means so much, man, I wouldn't ever try for anything else, and spoil the way it is."

"I know. You don't have to say it. She feels the same."

"Well, I just wanted it clear between us. Made me so damn happy when I first met you and you were what she said you were."

"She deserves me, huh?"

"She deserves better, but you're worth settling for."

Pax laughed, and the traffic light changed, and he said, "You ever considered being a SEAL? I think maybe you'd make it."

"I was born a seal, lowercase. Made for the ocean, but not the Navy. I'm not a dude with ambition."

"I know," Pax said. "Aspiration is your thing, not ambition. Skill rather than money. Honor rather than fame."

"Bro, you have me confused with another Pogo."

"Don't think so. I know what's under the hood. I have an ear for gear."

They were silent for a block or so. Although the day was mild, the hard March sunlight laid a wintry glaze on window glass and white stucco walls, and even painted glistening icy-looking edges on the stiff green blades of the fan palms.

"You really think we can help her?" Pogo asked.

"I can't stand to think anything else."

"But brain cancer, a coma. Woof. A lot of bad news."

"Cancer, yeah. But it's not a coma. The brain waves prove that much. Not a coma."

"Then what is it?"

Pax had been thinking about that since the

third time Bibi's voice had come to him. "We see her lying in the bed, and we think that's her, that's Bibi, but maybe it's not. Not all of her, anyway."

Pulling into the parking lot behind Bibi's apartment complex, Pogo said, "Tell me you aren't gassing off on some evil-twin trip."

"When you're asleep and dreaming, you're in a sense dead to the real world, you're living in the dream. Bibi's not dreaming, but —"

"According to the brain waves, she's dreaming."

"The EEG also says she's awake, which isn't exactly the case, either. Anyway, *she* said she's not dreaming."

"Said? Said when?"

As Pogo slotted the Honda between younger vehicles of higher pedigrees, Pax sighed. "Okay. Here goes." He recounted the three times that Bibi had spoken inside his head. "On one level, she's aware of what's going on in the hospital room . . . but right now it's not where she's living."

"Yeah? So where *is* she living?"

"Damn if I know."

"Living somewhere without her body."

"I'm not saying it makes sense."

"I thought that's exactly what you were saying."

"I'm saying, whether it makes sense or not, it's what seems to be true. And she wants me

550

— us — to find her."

Pogo switched off the engine. Blond, tanned, eyes as dark and clear as sapphires, he looked in profile less like a standard-issue California surf rat than like a ship's captain in the making. There was about him an aura of competence and responsibility that could be discerned also in the lines of his face, though a decade or two might pass before subtle evidence in the bone became obvious to everyone. Whatever he might make of himself, however, he would always be of the sea; just looking at him, you could almost hear waves breaking on the shore. After pondering, Pogo said, "I don't know if I believe in telepathy."

"Don't know I do, either," Pax admitted. "One thing I *do* know — wherever she is, even if it is a dream, what happens to her there affects her here. The bruises, the abrasions, the tattoo."

"This is mondo weird."

"I have a hunch, when we figure it out, it won't be weird at all. When we've got all the pieces, it'll make perfect sense."

"Totally clever, how you got me to jump into this at the hospital, before you let me know what a kelphead mission it is."

"You'd have jumped in with both feet anyway. What's a kelphead?"

"A fool. Bad surfer. Hardly ever on his board, mostly wiped out with his head in the kelp. I was one before she taught me the right moves. 'Find me,' huh? How does that work?"

Removing his sunglasses, Pax said, "Seems logical to start here at the apartment."

Pogo took off his shades. "What if we suck at this Sherlock stuff?"

"We won't."

As Pax opened his door, Pogo said, "What happens to her there affects her here?"

Pax turned his head and met Pogo's eyes. He knew what question would come next, because anyone who truly loved her could not leave it unasked.

The kid said, "Then what if . . . what if she dies there?"

"She won't," Pax said, and got out of the car.

95
A FAMILIAR HOUSE
NEVER SEEN BEFORE

The voice of a stern but caring woman, who might have been a nurse or an elementary-school teacher before recording directions for a GPS system, encouraged Bibi through fog and darkness. She drove south along the coast to Laguna Canyon Road, then inland along that twisty route, which had its dangerous stretches even in the best of weather.

She indulged no superstition regarding the world after midnight, didn't believe that she had entered the witching hour when broom-stick riders filled the sky, but she had a sense of impending occult menace on this particu-lar night, as on no other. Justified paranoia plucked the harpstrings of her nerves until she half expected that, behind the cataracts of fog, the world was being rearranged like a vast stage undergoing set changes. Balancing that irrational fear was an intuitive feeling that Pax must be coming home to her, that in fact he was already nearby. From time to time, she glanced to her right, with the peculiar expectation that he rode in the passenger seat, but of course he was never there.

As the canyon road wound among the folded foothills, the fog that slowly tumbled like great masses of dripping white laundry gradually gave way to sheer curtains and then to isolated tattered scraps. By the time she passed under the first freeway and turned off the canyon road onto a state route, no shred of mist remained, and a while later, after she passed under the last of the county's freeways, she came to lonely territory, low hills and arid meadows of scraggly grass, bleak in the moon-chilled night.

Her virtual companion, whose succinct guidance had thus far been flawless, spoke for the first time out of character, as should not have been possible. The voice sounded like that of a young girl. "In two hundred yards, you will want to stop at a house on the left."

The highway topped a low rise and turned to the right as it descended, and ahead stood the promised house, soft light in its curtained windows. Two things about the three-story residence caused Bibi to take her foot off the accelerator and let the car coast down the gentle slope. First, it seemed to belong not merely in another state than California but on another continent, not here in open country but on a city street, with other houses crowded against it. Although lacking porch or portico, with no grand steps leading up to the front door, the house looked stately, its brick walls enhanced with limestone quoins at the corners and limestone surrounds at each window. Four chimneys pierced the steeply pitched roof, which might have been of slate. In addition to the strangeness of such a house in such a place, a feeling of familiarity caused Bibi to bring the coasting car almost to a stop. She had never traveled this highway before, had never seen this house. She could not recall having seen one very like it anywhere else, and yet moment by moment it seemed more familiar to her, until she was gripped by full-blown déjà vu.

As she eased past the place, a sudden memory flashed into her mind's eye: Ashley Bell in a white dress with pale-blue lace collar, standing at a third-floor window, gazing out from this very house. She could recall nothing else, neither the occasion nor the date, but the memory was so clear and so poignant that she knew it must be real. The feeling of kindredness between Bibi and this girl, which had overcome her upon first seeing the photograph in Calida's office, the sense of an equivalence between them, a sisterhood, rose in her once more, even more intense than previously. *Ashley Bell in a white dress with pale-blue collar, standing at a third-floor window . . .* If Bibi had known this child, then here was *another* incidence of self-deception, another part of her life edited out and burned away with the use of Captain's memory trick.

She didn't dare swing the Honda into the dirt driveway and approach the house boldly. There were countless foolish ways to die, but she hoped to avoid the egregiously stupid ones. She accelerated, drove over another low rise, out of sight of the residence, and parked on the shoulder of the highway. She sat contemplating her next move, trying to decide whether it might be egregiously stupid or just stupid. But in the end, there was nothing else she could do other than investigate the house.

The young girl's voice that had issued from the GPS might have been that of Ashley Bell. Who else could it have been? There was no other child in this affair. After an absence of some hours, the supernatural forces that Calida had let into Bibi's life seemed to have returned.

96
THE BOX OF
ORDINARY THINGS

Bibi's apartment was tastefully furnished in mid-century modern with Art Deco accents, simple and clean and welcoming and, in these circumstances, mysterious. Paxton dropped his duffel bag inside the front door. He stood with Pogo, surveying the living room, the dining area, the open kitchen beyond, listening warily, as though something unknown and unpleasant might materialize at any moment.

"What're we looking for?" Pogo asked.

"Anything that doesn't seem like our girl."

"That's kind of vague, don't you think?"

"It's as clear as could be. If someone laid out three hats and said one of them was Bibi's, you'd know which it was — wouldn't you?"

"She doesn't like hats."

"Exactly. If you see a hat, it's suspicious."

"So a hat is just like a metaphor for anything unBibi."

"We'll know it when we see it."

"We will, huh?"

"If we're expecting to see it, yes. People go through life failing to see all sorts of amazing things because they aren't expecting to see them."

"Do *all* Navy SEALs have a tendency to go mystical?"

"War," Pax said, "either dulls the mind to despair or sharpens it toward intuitive truths."

"Who said that?"

"I did. Let's split up the rooms."

"I'll take her study," Pogo said. "You take the bedroom. I wouldn't feel right, looking through her lady things."

Pax didn't feel right looking through them, either, although not entirely for the same reason that Pogo would have found the task disconcerting. When he was eleven, a week after the sudden death of Sally May Colter — his much loved maternal grandmother — his mom had taken him to Sally's house to pack the woman's clothes in boxes to donate to a thrift shop. They also sorted through Sally's books and jewelry and bibelots, deciding which items should be given to which friends and relatives as remembrances of her. That would have been a grim day, if his mom hadn't told him numerous stories about Sally that he hadn't known and that had kept her fresh in memory all these years. Going through the drawers in Bibi's nightstands, highboy, and dresser, he repeatedly felt as if he were conducting a preliminary assessment to determine what would need to be disposed of upon her death.

In the walk-in closet, standing on a three-step stool, he found the metal lockbox on the highest shelf. It was about twenty inches square, ten inches deep.

He could not imagine anything more un-Bibi than this. She was practical, and the box was not. Fire-resistant but not fireproof, it would buckle in a vigorous blaze, and the lip of the lid would sneer open, inhaling flames. Portable, it was no obstacle to a burglar, but instead invited attention. And what was the point of having a lockbox for which you taped the key to the lid, as she had done?

Having finished searching the study, Pogo was looking through the kitchen cabinets when Pax entered and put his discovery on the dinette table. Against the red Formica, the metal box with its baked-on black finish looked ominous, as if they might be wise to call in a bomb-disposal specialist to deal with it.

"Something?" Pogo asked.

"Maybe."

They sat at the table. Pax used the key. The piano hinge was a little stiff, but the lid opened all the way. Most of the contents lay under a rumpled chamois cloth, which held within its loose folds a worn and cracked and dirt-crusted dog collar.

Lifting that item with one finger, Pax said,

"Have you seen this before?"

"No."

"Why would she keep such a thing?"

Pogo took the collar, and as he examined it, dirt crumbled between his fingers. "Jasper," he said, reading the name that had been neatly scored into the leather.

"Did she once have a dog named Jasper?"

"Kinda, sort of." Frowning, Pogo pointed to another object in the document box, a spiral-bound notebook. "It's full of stories about a dog named Jasper."

The notebook measured perhaps six by nine inches and was almost an inch thick, containing well in excess of two hundred lined pages. On the cover, the name and logo of the stationery company had been painted over, creating a pale-beige background for a beautifully designed and rendered pen-and-ink Art Deco drawing of a leaping panther and a leaping gazelle, each on its hind legs and bounding away from the other.

"I drew that for her," he said, "I drew special covers for most of her diaries and notebooks. She loved Art Deco even then."

"I didn't know you had such talent."

Pogo shrugged.

"How old were you when you did this?"

"She was . . . ten when she wrote the Jasper stories, so I'd have been eight."

"You had this technique at eight? Hell, you're a prodigy."

"I'm no Norman Rockwell. Drawing ability shows up early, that's all. A sense of form. Perspective. People go to art school not to learn it, just to refine it. I could have. But there's lots of things I could have done. Could-do only matters if it's also want-to-do."

Everyone, Pax believed, was more than she or he appeared to be, and one of the saddest things about the human condition was that most people never realized what talents, capacities, and depth they possessed. That Pogo had taken a full measure of himself must be one reason that Bibi so loved him.

"Why a panther and gazelle?"

"It's just a cool design. If there was another reason, I don't remember."

Pax fanned through the pages of neat handwriting, much like Bibi's cursive script twelve years later, but with girlish flourishes that she no longer employed. Sometimes she dotted an *i* with a tiny circle, sometimes not, apparently preferring the circle when the word was particularly colorful, and she always dotted *j*'s with asterisks.

"She wrote the first draft of each story in a tablet," Pogo said. "Edited it a couple times. Then copied it into the notebook."

Short stories filled two-thirds of the volume. On the first blank page following them, Pax discovered two lines of verse that he recognized as coming from one of Bibi's favorite poems, "The Evening of the Mind" by Donald Justice: *Now comes the evening of the mind / Here are the fireflies twitching in the blood.*

The stories had been written in blue ink. These lines of verse were in black. The blue had faded with time. The black remained dark and appeared freshly inscribed. Not a single *i* had been capped with a circle instead of a dot; and there were none of the other flourishes to be found in the handwriting of the ten-year-old Bibi.

Still puzzling over the leather collar, Pogo said, "She told me Olaf was wearing a worn-out, muddy collar when he showed up in that rainstorm. But she never told me there was a name on it."

"Jasper. The name of the dog in these stories. Maybe she knew someone who had a dog named Jasper and this was his collar."

Pogo shook his head. "The dog in the stories is her invention. Entirely. And it was smaller than Olaf. A black-and-gray mongrel, not a golden retriever. This collar would've been too big for Jasper."

Pogo turning the leather strap. The buckle softly clinking. Bits of dirt flaking through his fingers and onto the table.

He said, "What're the odds that she'd write all those stories about an abandoned dog named Jasper, and one day an abandoned dog named Jasper would show up at her front door?"

"The best in Vegas couldn't figure those odds," Pax said. "Maybe what you're wondering is . . . could it have been a coincidence?"

Looking up from the collar, Pogo said, "You think it could be?"

"Bibi doesn't believe in coincidences."

"Yeah. I know. But could it be?"

"I don't believe in them, either."

Putting down the collar, with the name revealed — JASPER — Pogo said, "Then what the hell? Why did she never tell us?"

Pax didn't know what to make of this development. He was pretty sure, however, that although the shared name seemed like a small if freaky detail, Jasper the fictional mongrel and Jasper the golden retriever who became Olaf were of considerable importance. Intuition, the knowledge that comes before all reasoning and teaching, raised the hairs on the nape of his neck and lowered the temperature of his spine.

Instead of answering Pogo's question, he said, "Let's see what else is in this box," as he picked up a small Ziploc plastic bag of the kind that people often used to hold the day's vitamin pills or prescription medications. It contained a withered scrap of scalp with an attached lock of hair, the lower third of which was matted and crusted with what must have been dried blood.

97

WHERE SHADOWS LIVE
THEIR SHADOW LIVES

Armed and anxious, Bibi argued silently with herself about the necessity and the wisdom of venturing uninvited to a house as strange as the one that stood like a massive gravestone in a desolate plot of the Mojave Desert. She approached the residence overland rather than along the county highway, through sand and loose shale and parched vegetation, all vaguely phosphorescent under the moon, which deceived as much as it illuminated. She was noisier than she would have liked, especially as she had imagined herself whidding through the arid landscape with the grace of a coyote. At least the night was chilly enough that she didn't have to worry about rattlesnakes, though she thought that scorpions might be scuttling through the darkness.

The house faced north, and she arrived at the east wall, along which she made her way, cautiously looking in the lighted windows, which were curtained only with sheers. The rooms were furnished, but quiet and without occupants.

As at the front, the house at its south side lacked a porch. Only a six-foot-square pad of bricks presented the back door, which had been broken down as if with a battering ram that had torn it off its hinges. The breached door lay cracked and splintered on the limestone floor of a hallway lit by frosted-glass sconces. The evidence of violence should have turned her away. She went inside.

She had never seen the house before, and yet it felt familiar. She had a fragment memory of Ashley Bell standing in a front window, in this place. The voice issuing from the electronic map, telling her that she would want to stop here, had been that of a young girl, perhaps that of Ashley. Bibi could not retreat. Impossible. She had been spared from cancer TO SAVE A LIFE, and only she stood between Death and a girl of twelve or thirteen.

The fallen door rocked underfoot, an unavoidable clatter, though she got quickly off it. No one called out or came to see who might be responsible for the noise. The residence stood in silence.

Upon entering the house, Bibi had also entered a peculiar state of simultaneous knowing and not knowing. It wasn't quite déjà vu, the illusion of having experienced something before that in fact one was encountering for the first time; she not only recognized things as she encountered them, but also had continuous presentiments of what lay ahead. A laundry room to the right of the hall. Yes. A walk-in pantry to the left. Yes. And ahead, yes, the kitchen. But though she could predict what room came next, she could not recall having been there before.

The kitchen was rather primitive by twenty-first-century standards. No microwave. No dishwasher. The gas range and undersized refrigerator — bearing the name Electrolux on its door — were many decades old, and yet looked new or at least well maintained.

In the other rooms, the furniture was oversized but sleek and modern, Art Deco pieces of Amboina wood, others of polished black lacquer, all of it expensive in its day and far more expensive now, having become über-collectible. Here and there, a chair or a desk had been overturned; but most things were as they should be. The glass in a break-front had been smashed but not the contents that the cabinet displayed. The destruction wasn't systematic, instead almost casual, as though whoever did it had come here on a more important task than vandalism and had committed this damage only in passing.

As Bibi returned from the drawing room to the front hall, she glimpsed swift movement to her left, a dark and darting form. Tall, thin, stoop-shouldered. She pivoted toward it, pistol in a two-hand grip, but no one was there. If the presence had been real, surely it would have made some sound — swift footsteps, a creaking of mahogany floorboards, a ragged inhalation — but the uncanny silence was not disturbed. Besides, the figure seemed to have moved with inhuman speed, crossing the hallway from room to room in a fraction of a second.

The window from the fragment of memory, in which she had seen Ashley standing in a white dress with pale-blue lace collar, was on the third floor. She climbed stairs to a landing, and then another flight. As she neared the second floor, an inky form, so swift and fluid that Bibi had only the impression — not the conviction — that it was human, appeared above her and plunged past her. Although the figure did not brush against her, a coldness prickled across her in its passing, and she almost lost her balance. She fell against the railing, remained upright, and turned to look down, in time to see a shadow disappear off the landing, onto the first flight of stairs.

She couldn't know if it might be the same spirit — if *spirit* was the word for it — that she had seen in the ground-floor hall, but she sensed that it was not flinging itself through the house in a rage, that it was instead a spirit in extreme torment, sustained here by anguish, vigorous with the energized despair called desperation.

When she got to the second floor, she found a dead man lying faceup on the carpet runner. He appeared to have been beaten to death with truncheons wielded by a man or men for whom physical violence was an intoxicant. His clothes were a blood-soaked shroud, his face and skull a cratered terrain from which she had to look at once away.

His crime had been resistance. He had dared to protect his own. She didn't know how she knew this, but she knew.

If Ashley Bell was still here, perhaps she would be on the third floor, in the room with the window seen in the fragment of memory.

Heart racing, feeling as might a deep-sea diver in a pressurized suit struggling toward the surface countless fathoms overhead, Bibi went up more stairs. The pistol was strangely heavy, and her wrists ached with the weight of it.

98
A LITTLE TROVE OF TRAUMAS

Sitting in Bibi's kitchen, Paxton repeatedly thought that they needed candlelight, that he should put half a dozen or more votives on the table, though it was only 2:15 in the afternoon, with sunlight strong at the windows, and though the occasion certainly didn't call for a romantic atmosphere. And several times he detected the rich fragrance of roses, although there were no roses in the apartment, nor any air freshener, as far as he could see, that might explain the phantom scent. These odd sensations felt akin to those moments in the hospital room when Bibi's voice had come to him.

The perfume of roses wafted over him again when he stared in puzzlement at the tiny plastic bag that contained a desiccated scrap of human scalp from which sprouted a lock of thick white hair matted, around the roots, with dry rust-red blood.

"Well, if we're looking for unBibi," he said, "this seems about as un as it gets."

"In a way, yeah, and in a way, no," Pogo said. "The day of her grandfather's funeral —"

"Captain, you mean?"

"Yeah. Everyone came from the cemetery to the bungalow for the usual get-together. You know — food, booze, memories. Like seventy or eighty people. It was a crowd, it got noisy. I realized Beebs wasn't there anymore. She was torn up. She loved the guy. I figured if she'd go anywhere, she'd go to the ocean. So I walked down to Inspiration Point, and there she was, sitting on a bench. She didn't see me until I sat beside her — and she was holding that little plastic bag in both hands."

Pax said, "This is the captain's hair?"

"Yeah. Seems when the aneurysm broke, he must've shot to his feet before he fell. He was a tall guy. On the way down, he hit the edge of the table hard, right at the sharp corner. Left behind that piece of skin and the hair stuck to it. Bibi took it after she found him, kept it."

"Why would she do that? Seems too macabre for her."

"She didn't say why, and I didn't ask. We've always been totally open with each other about most things, you know, but there's always been this need-to-know clause, too, and neither of us ever violates it. She made me promise not to tell anyone, and I didn't

— until you. Anyway, I was just eight, she was ten, she was teaching me to move from a bellyboard to a shortboard, and she was a goddess to me. She still is. Always will be. You expect a goddess to have secrets, it's part of their mystery, and you don't want to learn their secrets, because if you learn them, you die."

Pax considered the contents of the plastic bag for a moment, but then put it aside to examine the remaining four items in the metal box.

99

THE GIRL WHO LOVED HORSES

In the third-floor hallway, beyond the topmost of the stairs, a dead woman lay as further testament to the savagery of those who had invaded the house. Perhaps the corpse on the second floor had been her husband, and she had stood here as a last defense against the invaders, because not far from her lay, of all things, a pitchfork that would have no purpose in this elegant and stylishly furnished residence. The tines of that rustic weapon were not wet with blood, so Bibi could only assume that this poor woman, who lacked the effective defense of a gun, had no chance to wound the murderers of her husband. She didn't want to examine the corpse, but she felt obliged to have a quick look at it, as if she owned a portion of the responsibility for what had happened here and must answer for it, though of course she was not accountable for what Terezin and his followers might do to anyone. They would do the same — or worse — to her if they got the chance. The woman had been shot more than once. In stomach, chest, and face. Bibi looked away, less in horror than in pity, as if to conduct even one more second in autopsy would somehow make her complicit in the murder.

She didn't think that she would find a third dead body, but she proceeded along the hallway in dread of precisely such a discovery. If Ashley had hidden in her room, they would have found her and taken her away. According to Terezin himself, he wanted the girl for his upcoming birthday. Most likely, on that day, she would be raped in imaginative ways, later tortured, and then murdered in a ceremonial manner, as in his madness he set out to launch once more the Final Solution of what Hitler called "the Jewish problem." But if the cultists, Terezin's followers, had *not* taken the girl from the house, if she had resisted, as her father on the second floor and her mother on the third had resisted, their intention of taking her alive might have been foiled.

When she came to the room on the left, at the end of the hall, where the door stood half open, Bibi knew what else she would find in addition to either a dead girl or no girl at all: horses. Pistol in her right hand, aimed at the floor, no longer concerned that any of the fascist murderers remained in the house, Bibi crossed the threshold.

Her premonition was fulfilled: paintings of

horses, bronzes of horses, porcelains of horses, books about horses. This house was one more thing that Bibi had forgotten, apparently by using Captain's memory trick. She had been here before, but she didn't know when or for what purpose. Hour by hour, she found more memories that had been burned, fragments of which survived in ashen form: this house, this room, the fact that Ashley Bell loved horses, might ride them as well as admire them. She thought, *I must know Ashley, I must at least have met her once!* Why else would this residence be familiar to her? How else could she have known about the horse motif in this bedroom?

The doors of a tall built-in armoire stood open. The clothes that had hung within it had been taken out and thrown on the floor.

She approached it with trepidation, although she did not raise the pistol. The secret panel in the back of the armoire, which Bibi had somehow known would be there, had been slid aside. The closet-size space thus revealed was unoccupied. If the girl had hidden there, Terezin and his men had found her.

100 THE CLOCK, THE WATCH, AND THE OVENS

Suddenly Paxton felt that they were running out of time. The sensation came out of nowhere, for no apparent cause, an impression of a brink looming, a void beyond. He became certain that Bibi was receding from him, captured by someone sinister and being carried away at high speed, in what direction and to what destination he couldn't know. Which made no sense. She was comatose in the hospital. Nobody could abduct her from a secure medical facility. And if her condition had changed, Nancy or Murphy would have been on the phone to him.

The fourth item in the black metal box was a small recorder. It contained a microcassette, but they couldn't listen to it because the batteries were dead.

While Pogo searched pantry shelves and kitchen drawers for spare batteries, Pax examined the fifth item, a twice-folded sheet of lined yellow paper on which were written a number of quotations and the attributions of their sources. The handwriting wasn't Bibi's, neither her precise adult script nor the decorative girlhood variant. The strong, slanted cursive seemed to suggest that a man had composed the list. The cheap paper was deteriorating at the corners, foxed by time and skin oil; and it had been opened and closed so many times that, at some point, the folds had been reinforced with Scotch tape.

Pax began reading the quotations aloud for Pogo's benefit. " 'This world is but canvas to our imaginations.' That's from something by Henry David Thoreau."

Pogo said, "The Walden Pond guy."

"So you paid attention in school, after all."

"No matter how much you try to keep that stuff out of your head, some of it gets in."

"The next one's also from Thoreau. 'If one advances confidently in the direction of his dreams, and endeavors to live the life which he has imagined, he will meet with a success unexpected in common hours.' "

Having found a package of Duracell AAA batteries, Pogo brought two of them to the table. "Was Thoreau the Walden Pond guy *and* the power-of-positive-thinking guy?"

"No. That was Norman Vincent Peale. This next one's by someone named Anatole France. 'To know is nothing at all; to imagine is everything.' "

"Maybe I'm seeing a theme," Pogo said as

he removed the dead batteries from the recorder.

"Me, too. Imaginations, imagined, imagine. Here's one from Joseph Conrad."

Pogo said, "The *Heart of Darkness* guy."

"Kid, you are such a fraud." Pax cleared his throat and then read, " 'Only in men's imagination does every truth find an effective and undeniable existence. Imagination, not invention, is the supreme master of art as of life.' "

"That's heavy, dude."

The sense of time running out, of some catastrophe looming over Bibi, grew stronger. Pax glanced from his watch to the wall clock, where the second hand swept smoothly around the face but where the minute hand *twitched* from 2:19 to 2:20, clicked like a trigger.

"Here's another one. Kenneth Grahame wrote —"

Pogo interrupted. "He's the *Wind in the Willows* guy. Mr. Toad, Mole, Badger, Ratty, the Piper at the Gates of Dawn, and all that."

"So he wrote, 'As a rule, indeed, grown-up people are fairly correct on matters of fact; it is in the higher gift of imagination that they are so sadly to seek.' You know who Wallace Stevens was?"

"A poet guy. New batteries don't help. The recorder is biffed."

"Biffed?"

"Biffed, totally thrashed, broke, whatever. But I know someone who can fix it."

"So this Wallace Stevens poet guy wrote, 'In the world of words, the imagination is one of the forces of nature.' There's one more. You might have heard of him. Shakespeare. 'And as imagination bodies forth / The forms of things unknown, the poet's pen / Turns them to shapes and gives to airy nothing / A local habitation and a name.' "

Pogo considered Shakespeare, and then shook his head. "It'll give me a migraine. What do you figure the list means?"

"Whatever it means, I think her grandfather wrote it."

"Captain. Yeah. And I think she's the one who opened it and read it so often, she wore out the creases."

Pax glanced from his wristwatch to the digital time readout on the microwave, to the digital readout on the conventional oven, to the window, where the afternoon light had not begun to wane to any appreciable degree. Nevertheless, within him, a clock spring of worry wound tighter, tighter.

"You got a dance to go to?" Pogo asked.

"Bibi's talking to me again," Pax decided.

"What's she saying?"

"It's not words this time. It's a feeling. That time's running out. That someone bad is coming after her, and fast."

Pogo looked grim. "The brain cancer."

"Not some*thing* bad — some*one.*"

"Nancy and Murph are with her, one or the other, usually both, and not just them."

"It's not something that'll happen in the hospital. It's going to happen . . . wherever else she is."

Pogo said, "I know we're in the Twilight Zone. I accept that. But it still sounds nuts when you say things like that."

Pax took the sixth item from the document box, a children's picture book with a story told in short sentences and simple words. *Cookie's Big Adventure.*

"That's been in print forever," Pogo said. "It was Nancy's favorite when she was little. She gave me a copy when I was five."

"Didn't Bibi like it?"

"Yeah, I guess. When she was little. Personally, I didn't think it was such deathless literature."

"If she liked it," Pax said, "why isn't it on a shelf in the living room or in her office?"

"Beats me." As Pax leafed through *Cookie's Big Adventure,* Pogo took the final item from the lockbox. "The saint bitch."

"The who?"

Brandishing a few pages of typescript that were held together with a paper clip, Pogo said, "This is the piece Beebs wrote for the professor who made her bail out of the writing program." He affected a snooty voice to pronounce her name: "Dr. Solange St. Croix."

"In this case," Pax said, "snarky doesn't work when your name is Averell Beaumont Stanhope the Third."

"Point taken. You ever read this?"

"She told me about it, but I never saw it."

Pogo passed the four pages to him. "Read it. Maybe you'll see what pissed off the great professor. Neither of us can figure it."

Glancing from watch to clock to ovens, Pax said, "Maybe I should read it in the car, while we're going wherever you're getting the cassette recorder fixed."

"It's in the box with this other stuff, maybe it has something to do with what's happening. Read it now."

Relenting, Pax read the pages aloud, interrupting himself with laughter a few times, although the amusing lines were never mean. "Totally Bibi."

"Vivid," Pogo agreed.

"But I don't see why it made the professor go ballistic."

"Okay, then. Maybe that's our best first lead."

"How so?"

"Why don't we visit Saint Bitch and ask her what made her blow like Vesuvius? I know where she lives."

Pax no longer consulted the wall clock or the wristwatch, or the LED readouts on the ovens, because behind his face rather than upon it, unseen but sensed, a sweep hand swept away the seconds. He was as acutely aware of the passage of time as he'd been in certain moments of battle, felt time flowing as sand might feel as it slid through the pinched waist of an hourglass. They had found a trove of curious objects, but they had deduced little from them. Considered action was always better than considered inaction, even if talking to a college professor about her response to a student's writing, five years earlier, didn't seem to be enough action to amount to a damn.

"Okay," he said, getting up from the table. "Let's go see the professor."

"You do the interrogation," Pogo said.

"It's not an interrogation. Just a chat."

"The way she treated Beebs, I wouldn't mind waterboarding her."

"I never waterboarded anyone. Never used thumbscrews, electric shocks to the genitals, bamboo shoots under fingernails, never played loud disco music at anyone to break him — none of that Hollywood stuff. Psychology and a good shit detector are mostly all you need."

Pax folded the sheet of handwritten quotations about imagination and paper-clipped it to the four pages of Bibi's writing that had so incensed Dr. St. Croix. He tucked them into the panther-and-gazelle notebook that contained the stories about Jasper the dog. He didn't see any reason to take the dog collar or the children's book, or the little plastic bag with the lock of Captain's hair, and Pogo had the tape recorder that needed to be repaired.

"Hang in there, Beebs," he said, and Pogo asked if he thought she could hear him, and he said, "No. But it's not the first time I've talked to her out loud when she wasn't there to hear."

101

Devious and Numerous

While Bibi made her way down through the house from which Ashley had been kidnapped, sidling around the gruesome corpses, two spirits of different sizes darted initially at the periphery of her vision, as quick and elusive as bats, although the size of people. They were as silent as before, and again she sensed that they flung themselves through the house in a state of torment, not fury. They moved even faster than before, in a frenzy. With sudden unpredictable lunges, they began exploding from the periphery into her immediate presence, startling her even after she came to expect these assaults on her nerve. She began to think that they wanted something from her and that it was something she could not — must not — give. Repeatedly, with growing boldness, these featureless figures brushed her in passing. Because they lacked substance, she could not feel the pressure or texture of their touch, but each time a chill shattered through her, a chill that didn't arise from within, as earlier, but burst through her in distinct shards, like a shrapnel of ice, so that in spite of the absence of pain, she half expected to see bloodstains spreading through her clothes.

Overcome — in truth, *slammed* — by an urgent need to be out of the house, alarmed but not terrified, rising to the challenge of the alarm rather than fleeing in response to it, she holstered the pistol to free both hands. As she descended the stairs from the second floor and crossed the foyer to the front door, she swung her arms at the spirits when they leaped upon her, as if to warn them to stay clear. Because they were as weightless as shadows, she was powerless to throw them off or backhand them aside. She felt foolish, clumsy, but she was convinced that if she didn't mount a resistance, they would become more aggressive and perhaps gain the power to pose a real threat.

She erupted from the front door, across a simple brick stoop, and into the yard, an expanse of sandy earth and stones and clumps of pale weedy grass that had perhaps never been green, all dimly illumined and heavily shadowed by the moon. As she had hoped, the spirits did not follow her out of the house, remained tethered to its rooms, in which they had lived and died and lived again in grief.

Bibi ran and stumbled and almost fell more

than once before she reached the graveled shoulder of the state route, where she turned to look back at the house. The residence still appeared to be misplaced in space and time. She gasped for breath, waiting for the place to sink as Poe's House of Usher had sunk. But there was no black and lurid tarn here, as there had been in the story, no muck into which the structure could be submerged.

With no need to return overland, she followed the pavement to the east, where Pogo's Honda was parked alongside the road. As she walked, she thought of the spirits in the house, about what they might have wanted from her.

Of the several wants that came to mind, there was one she knew must be true the moment that it occurred to her: They wanted to delay her, hinder, hamper. Which meant they had not been, as she'd thought, the spirits of Ashley's dead parents, the shot woman and the beaten man. She had been spared from brain cancer in order TO SAVE A LIFE, Ashley's life; but there were forces, both human and supernatural, that wanted Ashley dead.

If the girl was murdered, perhaps Bibi's cancer would return, for she would have failed to earn its remission.

The walk back to the Honda seemed longer than it should have been, and she began to worry that she had already passed the place where she had parked it, that the car had been stolen, leaving her with no choice but to continue on foot to Sonomire Way.

Delay. Hamper. Hinder. The ink-black bat-quick spirits in the house had not been the only entities that had sought to impede her since all of this had begun. When she had been at the small table in the motel room, making new street names from the lettered tiles that spelled MOONRISE, something had knocked on the door, had scratched at the door, had tapped at the windows, distracting and delaying her word search before at last she found SONOMIRE WAY. The fog! The first night, the hampering fog billowed in from the sea, slithered inland, and the following day, it retreated only to repeatedly return, until with sunset and this second night, it thickened into a blinding mass that had slowed her significantly. Now it seemed to her that the fog had been unnaturally dense and persistent, that it had been settled upon her not by Nature but by whatever power Terezin could command to oppose her actions and retard her progress.

Still no Honda.

She began to run.

Maybe the greater rush of blood from her laboring heart shifted gears of thought in her brain, because as she sought the car, a new and disturbing possibility demanded consideration. Maybe her enemies were not as devious and numerous as they seemed to be. She could have imagined the knocking-tapping-scratching at the motel, for when she had opened the door and ventured outside, there had been no threat.

If the inky spirits had not been real, they had been hallucinations, which represented a level of self-deception suggesting derangement. After all, she had earlier turned traitor against herself, cutting the lines from the books by O'Connor and Wilder and London, burning them in the motel-bathroom sink, to prevent herself from confirming some suspicion she'd had about Chubb Coy.

Of course she could not be her *only* enemy. For one thing, she couldn't imagine a massive fog bank into existence. The fog had to have been conjured by Nature or by Terezin using his occult power.

Didn't it?

Did it?

She stopped in the middle of the highway. Heart knocking in its cage of ribs. As if it would slip free and beat away into the night and leave her defeated, dead upon the blacktop. An immense, terrible, vaguely discerned secret — secret or lost memory — swelled darkly at the back of her mind. Bibi could sense its presence, its awesome size, and she knew that its revelation would be devastating. She stood waiting on the road. Waiting. The black sky and its moon, its planets, its infinite array of stars began to weigh on her, and a weakness came upon her, so that she thought her knees would fail. An eerie electronic whine, what she imagined tinnitus sounded like to those afflicted with it, rose from ear to ear, and she thought, *It's just the inner workings of the damn brain monitor,* but had no idea what she meant by that, nor what she intended when she reached to her head to pull off the confining electro cap and found, of course, just the baseball cap. Her vision blurred. Or was it the world around her that blurred, that began to lose coherence, began to diffuse?

She closed her eyes.

In that instant, she knew what must be happening to her, and she rallied in anger and self-disgust. Fate. She was giving in to the illusion that fate dictated the possibilities of her life. Whatever will be will be. *Que sera, sera.* Screw that. She loved her parents, but she was not them. Fate did not rule her. She was the master of her fate, the captain of her soul. She would not quit. SURRENDER was not a word that could be made from the lettered tiles of her name. She had come this far, and she would not quit.

The trillions of stars weighed less heavily upon her, and the dark matter that constituted most of the universe lifted from her shoulders. And if the piercing whine had been the cry of planets rotating around their liquid cores or something ordinary, in either case it stopped. She opened her eyes, walked eastward, and the night that had begun to blur now clarified. When she topped a low rise, the Honda waited on the descending slope, where she had parked it.

Before she opened the driver's door, she looked to the north, across the highway, where the raw land rose slightly, appearing softer in the night than it would in daylight, folding upward like gray blankets under which lay an army of sleepers. Whether a sound had alerted Bibi or her attention had been drawn by supernatural means, near the limit of vision she saw the tall figure in the hoodie, and then the dog, both faintly silvered by the moonwash.

Her initial impulse was to cross the road, call out, and hurry toward the pair, here where no fog could shroud them and foil her. But then she realized that they were alike to the fog, and to the ink-black spirits in the house, serving the same purpose as whatever had knocked-tapped-scratched at the motel-room door and windows. They were here to distract and delay her. That had been their purpose from the beginning. They had not healed her. By whatever singularity of her immune system or act of providence she had been made well, the cancer must have been cast out before the man and dog appeared in her hospital room. Whether they were flesh-

and-blood or occult entities haunting her, she would learn nothing from them even if she managed to catch up with them and snared the tall man by a hoodie sleeve.

However ardently Bibi hoped to save Ashley Bell, no matter with what persistence she tracked the girl, there was someone — Terezin, but perhaps someone for whom Terezin was merely a front man — who was equally determined to thwart her. As she watched the ghostly man and dog walking at a distance precisely calculated to minimize their visibility and maximize their other-worldly quality, Bibi wondered if the murder of Ashley was not her enemy's ultimate goal, if possibly the girl was only a lure with which they were drawing their most-desired victim, Bibi, to a place of no escape.

She turned away from man and dog, got into the car, and started the engine.

102
THE WICKED WITCH LETS HER HAIR DOWN

Stucco for bread, teak decks for meat, garnished with stainless-steel-and-glass railings: Dr. St. Croix's house was stacked like what in another era would have been called a Dagwood sandwich, named for the hapless Dagwood Bumstead, a cartoon character once much loved by readers of newspaper funny pages but now largely forgotten. Paxton knew Dagwood from the *Blondie* comic strip, because his grandmother Sally May Colter had enjoyed it almost as much as her all-time favorite comic, *L'il Abner*. Books had been published, collecting many years of both strips, and Grandma had owned them all.

At the front door, Pax said, "Remember, honey works better than vinegar."

"You've seen the photo in that magazine Bibi has? Yeah? Looks to me like the famous professor *thrives* on vinegar."

"Maybe she's not even home," Pax said, and he rang the bell.

He almost didn't recognize the woman who

opened the door. Gone was the tailored, expensive, but drab suit. She wore an *ao dai,* a flowing silk tunic-and-pants ensemble, white with irregularly placed peacock-blue and ultramarine-blue and saffron-yellow flowers, classic Vietnamese apparel, a garment as feminine as any in the entire world of women's fashions. Her hair was usually drawn back into a bun that looked as dense as stone, that gave her the severe appearance of a nineteenth-century pioneer woman who had been hardened by decades spent in a contest with the heat and cold and wind and Indians and innumerable hardships of the prairie; however, on this Sunday afternoon, she had let down her graying hair, which revealed itself as less gray than silver-blond, lustrous and thick, as silken as the *ao dai.* Her skin, always flawless in photographs and public-television appearances, was flawless now, but appeared more like flesh and less like quartz. Her eyes, which Bibi had once described as the blue of the chemical gel in a refreezable ice pack, were precisely that color, but there was nothing icy about her stare. Clearly, the professor had once been a head-turning boy-stunning all-American babe; at fifty-something, she still was, when she wasn't being her public image.

"Dr. St. Croix —" Pax began.

Before he or Pogo could say another word, Solange St. Croix saw the ink on Pax's right bicep, said, "I don't believe it," and with one finger pushed up the T-shirt sleeve that half concealed his only tattoo. It was the official SEAL emblem: an eagle in an overwatch position on a trident that was also the cross of an anchor, with a flintlock pistol in the foreground, rendered in shades of gold with black detailing. "Are you a fraud, young man?" she asked.

"Excuse me, ma'am?"

"No, you're not," she decided. "You're the real damn thing, an honest-to-God Navy SEAL. I've only met one before, and everything I wrote about him is locked away where no one can see it, where it'll remain until I'm old enough to want everyone to see it."

Letting the T-shirt sleeve slide half over the tattoo once more, the professor looked at Pogo and smiled, and Pogo blushed, which Pax had never seen him do before.

To Pax, with girlish enthusiasm, she said, "I could use a jolt of the exotic. Tell me you're here in an official capacity, on a mission of grave importance, you're military intelligence conducting an investigation on which the fate of the nation depends."

"Not the fate of the nation, ma'am. But it *is* a matter of life and death," Pax said.

He didn't confirm or deny that he was with one branch or another of military intelligence, allowing her to infer that, with academic perspicacity, she had known the truth of him at first sight. Judging by her manner and the delighted surprise in her eyes, Pax thought that this Sunday had been of a grayer cast than she had hoped, as perhaps had been some number of days before it, and that she would insist upon the risk of believing he was what she imagined, welcoming them into her house. More than anything at this moment, perhaps she needed color in her life, while Pax and Pogo offered all the hues of a box of forty-eight crayons.

"Ma'am, I'm Chief Petty Officer Paxton Thorpe, and this is Averell Beaumont Stanhope the Third."

"Of the Boston Stanhopes?" the professor asked.

"No, ma'am," Pogo replied, lest there be no Boston Stanhopes and her question a trap. "Of the Virginia Stanhopes." Which was a lie, but a reasonably smooth one.

Pax said, "If you can spare us fifteen minutes, we'd be most grateful, but we can meet with you tomorrow, in your office at the university, if you prefer."

He still half expected her to ask for proof that he was with one intelligence service or another, whereupon he would be able to produce only his military ID, which would not identify him as what he was now pretending to be. But she stepped back from the door and welcomed them inside and led them through dramatic but sterile rooms of starkly modern décor, her *ao dai* both loose and yet clinging to her as she seemed almost to float through the shadowy spaces with the grace of a brightly painted koi in half-lit waters. She was barefoot, and her feet were small for a woman of about five foot eight, like the well-formed feet of a child destined for ballet.

"I have to stir the soup," she said, and brought them into a spacious kitchen with a maple floor finished in a gray wash, matching cabinets, black-granite countertops, and stainless-steel appliances. The soup-in-the-making stood on the cooktop, blue flames caressing the bottom of the large pot. "Potato leek," she said. Pax smelled potatoes and leeks and tarragon and an abundance of butter. Padded stools were lined up along one side of the large center island, and St. Croix suggested they sit there.

On the island stood a bottle of eighteen-year-old Macallan Scotch, a container of half-and-half kept cool in a bowl of ice, and a Baccarat-crystal on-the-rocks glass containing those three ingredients. Whether Dr. St. Croix began drinking by 3:10 on the average Sunday or whether this indulgence was an exception, she evidently felt no need whatsoever to justify herself. After she finished stirring the soup and set the lid askew on the pot, she produced two more Baccarat glasses. With the certitude of someone who had always done what she wanted and encountered no objections, the professor neither asked if they would join her in a cocktail nor inquired if they would like something different. Standing across the island from them, as she spoke of her love of cooking and built the drinks, Pax realized that declining the Scotch would be taken as a gross insult and that in spite of her girlish delight in their visit and her hospitality, she could turn on them in an instant.

Pogo watched her through squinted eyes, as if he suspected that she might be concocting poison, but he appeared to have reached the same conclusion as Pax.

As St. Croix pushed their drinks across the black granite to them, she said, "So . . . you called it a matter of life and death."

Concerned about dropping Bibi's name without preparation, Pax injected the equivalent of Scotch and cream into the absurd military-intelligence fantasy. "Life and death, yes, and although it sounds melodramatic, it's also a matter of national security."

"A little melodrama is good now and then," the professor said. "If life were nothing but Raymond Carver stories, we'd all go mad."

Pax knew who Raymond Carver was, but he thought it more in character if he looked puzzled for a moment before continuing. "Anyway, we're here to ask you about a person of interest to us —"

"A suspect," she interrupted, seeming to

take this as seriously as some people took the con men who phoned and, posing as IRS agents, induced them to wire money to foreign bank accounts.

"A suspect, more or less," Pax said. "But we're not able to share the details of her activities with you. For security reasons."

"A woman? I know a genuine security threat? How stimulating!"

"Yes, ma'am, a former student. Bibi Blair."

The Sunday softness in her face hardened into school-day stone. "That syphilitic little whore."

103
VALIANT GIRLS
DO NOT GO MAD

Paranoia of a reasonable potency was an essential survival tool. But intense and universal paranoia of the everyone-I-know-is-an-evil-space-alien variety was the mantra of a loser. The landscape promoted disorientation. Small clusters of buildings punctuated the barren vastness, but at that hour all were dark, seemingly long abandoned. In the black land, a glow only far to the north. Square miles of yellow and cold-blue scintillation. But not a light that confirmed civilization. An unearthly fungal phosphorescence. Hot plains of radioactive glass. As Bibi drove through the ever stranger and more hostile night, as it seemed that she had driven out of California into a place with no name and no exit, she felt herself traveling a narrow line between sanity and derangement, her balance precarious.

In spite of the antibiotic ointment that the tattoo artist had applied, under the layers of enwrapping gauze, the four words on her right wrist burned as if something worse than inflammation must be at work. Bacteria eating through the flesh. Or a toxic chemical imparted with the ink. The eighteen letters stung. Itched. She had been told not to scratch. She'd left the analgesic cream and fresh bandages at the motel. Nothing with which to change the dressing. No time to change it, anyway. She wondered if the increasing irritation of the eighteen small wounds might arise from an *intentionally* imparted infection. But since she had chosen the parlor at random, worrying that the tattooist might be in league with Terezin was as flaky as the evil-space-alien theory.

When for a few minutes she encountered no traffic moving in either direction, she wondered if roadblocks had been set up behind and ahead of her, and she waited to turn a bend or top a rise and find an execution squad of Wrong People. On the other hand, when a vehicle appeared in the oncoming lane, she tensed in expectation that the windshield of the Honda might dissolve in a rain of gunfire. Every motorist closing in behind her might be a tail, and when she cut her speed to let him pass, he always lingered alongside her — or she thought he did — to look her over with malevolent intent.

She was still fifteen or twenty minutes from Sonomire Way when a disturbing sound rose above the rubber-on-road hum and the drone of the engine. The flapping-flopping noise was like the struggling of a freshly caught fish in a sportsman's creel, and at first she thought that it must be a tire shedding tread. In that case, she would have felt such a problem translated to the steering wheel, a strong pull toward the deterioration, but she didn't.

A subsequent silence didn't reassure Bibi, and after less than a minute, the noise came again, this time perhaps from under the car. Something that had slipped loose must be slapping the pavement. But the Honda continued to purr along, and no warning lights appeared on the instrument panel.

The third time she heard the sound, she realized that the source was within the vehicle. On the backseat. Or on the floor behind the front passenger seat.

Then she understood what it must be.

The previous night, asleep in the armchair in her father's office, above Pet the Cat, she had dreamed the truth of what had happened in her bedroom when she was not quite six years old. The truth that she had hidden from herself by using Captain's memory trick of fire and forgetfulness. Not the whole truth, but part of it. In the dream, she had not revealed to herself the source and nature of the threat. Only that something malicious had come for her. Had come for her and crawled her room. Had gotten under the covers with her.

And here it was again.

After a silence in which the thing perhaps nursed its desire and considered its options, the slick and torsional sound rose again, as if this must be some slippery denizen of murky water and swamp mud, out of its element but hardly deterred, determined to make its way through this unfamiliar environment, toward what it wanted, needed. Toward her. To Bibi, it sounded as though the thing was trying to get purchase on the back of the front passenger seat, or to squirm up the transmission hump and onto the console between the seats, which should have been an easy bit of terrain to conquer.

On a straight stretch of highway, Bibi turned her head to look back and down, over the console. The pearly luminosity of instrument-panel gauges did not reach as far as the rear compartment of the car, where shadows pooled and moonlight rushing past the windows revealed nothing. If something coiled or quivered on the back floor, yearning to climb, and if it was watching her, its eyes did not shine in the gloom.

Starboard tires stuttered on the stony shoulder of the roadway. Bibi looked forward, pulled the wheel to the left, and brought the Honda onto the pavement again, just seconds short of a plunge off a low embankment.

Whether it was a sign of madness or common sense — or repressed knowledge guiding her without her understanding — Bibi told herself that if only she refused to hear the creature, refused to grant it existence, imagined it gone now and forever, she would be rid of it. Had that strategy worked for her when she had been a terrified child? She could not remember.

After a minute and the better part of another, the theory seemed to be confirmed, but then a new sound arose from the back of the car, what might have been a voice or an attempt at a voice. Low and wet, a gutteronasal clutch of syllables that formed no words but expressed nonetheless a craving, a coveting, a ferocious need, and such bitter and implacable rancor that mere hatred paled before it.

104
Boozer, Baker, Starmaker

After calling Bibi a syphilitic little whore, Dr. St. Croix took such pleasure in the idea of her former student being in trouble with agencies dedicated to national security that the hardness went out of her face and the Sunday softness returned, though her smile was akin to a vindictive sneer and would have been regarded with disquiet had she been in a roomful of church folk.

"I knew that deceitful bitch would step into deep shit one day. I hope it's deep enough for her to drown in it. She thinks she's more cunning than she is, and she took me for a sap who could be easily intimidated. Imagine a seventeen-year-old neophyte daring to attempt to manipulate a woman as experienced and connected and respected as I am. The little fool."

Paxton had a moment radically out of character for a Navy SEAL, a Bette Davis moment in which he wanted to throw his drink in the professor's face and say something so cutting that she would need the rest of the year to rebuild her ego. But that was not an effective technique of interrogation. Loyal Pogo was not as good as he should have been at concealing his rage, and before the professor might glance at the kid and read his revulsion, Pax smiled at him and winked and raised his own glass as if in a toast, though by the gesture he meant to say that taking a drink would be better than throwing a punch.

"I will do anything I can," St. Croix said, "*anything,* to help you convict Ms. Blair of whatever she's done. I don't need to know anything that's classified about the case, if only I can hope that she'll get something between life in prison and the death penalty."

She favored Pax with a seductive smile, and he said, "You have every reason to hope, ma'am, but you understand that I can't share even the smallest details of the pending indictment."

The professor brightened further, spread her arms so that the sleeves of her colorful tunic flared like butterfly wings. "What a lovely word — *indictment.* That's all I need to hear. I am in such a superlative mood, you cannot know, you cannot possibly know. I was about to start forming tarts when you rang the doorbell, so might I get on with that while you ask your questions, Chief Petty Officer?"

Pax could not quite compute the words *forming tarts,* but he said that, yes, of course she could continue with what she had been doing if it didn't interfere with his inquiry.

As the professor went to one of the two Sub-Zero refrigerators, Pax tried the Scotch with half-and-half. He was surprised to find the whisky had not curdled the cream, but even more surprised that Dr. St. Croix hadn't curdled it.

To medicate his outrage, Pogo had consumed most of his drink in one long swallow.

Barefoot and blithe, Solange St. Croix returned to the island with a bowl, over which was draped a dish towel. She whipped off the cloth to reveal a large ball of risen pastry dough. "I love to bake. I *adore* it." From cabinets she retrieved a baking sheet and twelve white-ceramic tart cups, which she also brought to the island.

She refreshed her drink and offered to refresh theirs. When Pogo accepted a second round, St. Croix smiled at him the way a fox smiled at a tender rabbit. Bartending finished, the fastidious baker washed her hands at the sink. She moved always as though she assumed she was being watched with erotic interest.

When she returned to the island and began pressing buttery pastry dough into the tart cups, she twinkled her blue eyes at Pax and said, "Now, what is it you want to know about

605

Ms. Bibi Blair? Were her parents drunk, doped up, or just tacky when they gave her such a frivolous name? Never mind. Sorry. You're the one who needs to ask questions."

Pax wondered at her quick and unqualified acceptance that they were something they had never claimed to be, that she deduced from a SEAL tattoo and little else that they had some law-enforcement role and an official mission. Perhaps the days were long gone when college professors built their courses with respect for logic and reason, and likewise conducted their lives with that same respect.

"Well," Pax began, "as you might imagine, we're most interested in why Ms. Blair was thrown out of the university writing program."

Raising her eyebrows, St. Croix said, "Nowhere is it written that she was ejected for any reason. The story is that she resigned of her own volition, perhaps because she found the coursework too difficult or the atmosphere of academic excellence not to her taste. Who can know but her?"

Pax smiled, shook his head. "Give us some credit for exhaustive backgrounding, Doctor. We know from various sources that there must have been something more to it. And we suspect that whatever she did to get herself forced out, back then, is an example of the behavior that makes her of such great interest to us now."

"Exactly," Pogo said, apparently concerned that he might seem superfluous and therefore suspicious.

St. Croix's attention was less on Pax and Pogo than on forming tarts. "I gave a writing assignment. The students were to choose someone they knew but whose residence they had never visited. The person could be another student, a university staff member, or one of their instructors. This was to be a test of their powers of observation and psychological insight, as well as their sense of characterization and their *imagination.* Each student was asked to create a richly detailed, vividly described, coherent, credible living environment for that person, whether it might be a dorm room or an apartment or a house. Ms. Blair chose me for her subject."

"Were you bothered by that?"

"Not at all. I'd put myself forward as an acceptable subject. I expected any student who chose me to have some fun with it. I am not thin-skinned. When Ms. Blair turned in her piece, I wasn't surprised that she described the first two floors of this house with accuracy. There had been lovely parties here, quite wonderful occasions, when faculty members and students of previous classes had gathered in a unique atmosphere both celebratory and intellectual. No, I wasn't surprised, but I *was* disappointed that she'd clearly sought out some of those people and grilled them about the layout of the house, the décor, the smallest of personal touches. This was supposed to be a *creative* exercise, not reportorial. Her descriptions were splendid, her writing unusually colorful and nuanced for a girl her age, but it was nonetheless something of a cheat to do what she'd done. Then, as I continued reading, much to my shock, I discovered that it was more than cheating, it was a crime."

St. Croix focused so intently on forming the tart shells that when she fell silent, Pax realized she must be using the task at hand to direct her energy away from the anger that, when expressed, made her look years older and hard and unappealing.

"Crime?" he asked. "What crime?"

Finishing the fifth cup, the professor said, "Burglary. Well, to be scrupulously fair, no, not burglary. She didn't steal anything, as far as I could tell. They call it housebreaking. She came into my house uninvited, when I wasn't here, and she roamed every corner of it, all the way through the third floor, which is not and never has been open to most of my guests. It was a monstrous violation of my privacy. My third floor is sacrosanct."

Pax knew that Bibi wasn't capable of such a thing, but of course he didn't leap to her defense. He only glanced warningly at Pogo.

After sipping her drink, St. Croix met

Paxton's eyes. "Why are you called a chief petty officer? There's nothing petty about you, so far as I can see."

"Oh, it's just the Navy's quaint way of differentiating between commissioned and noncommissioned officers. So we don't forget our place in the scheme of things."

"So we don't get uppity," Pogo said, proving that he had no talent for either deception or interrogation.

Pax expected that his answer to St. Croix's question might make her wonder if such a minor officer would likely be dispatched on an official mission in the civilian sphere, but then he realized from her half smile and the directness of her gaze that the woman hoped to let him know the door was open for a more personal conversation and anything to which it might lead.

He asked, "How did Ms. Blair force entry? Break a window, bust a lock?"

"No evidence of how," said the professor. "Which is what made it so unsettling. Clearly, she obtained a key. I was mystified as to how she could have done that. But I changed all the locks."

"You're certain she had a key?"

After taking another sip of her drink, St. Croix returned her attention to the pastry dough and the tart cups, making no further eye contact as she continued. "I am a strong and complex woman, Chief Petty Officer. I contain multitudes, as the poet said. I would have to be complex, with considerable depths, to have achieved my level of success and renown in the viciously competitive worlds of academia and literature, where the only sport more popular than logrolling is character assassination."

She fell silent once more, and Pax knew better than to press her.

After she finished forming the sixth tart shell and started on the seventh, St. Croix said, "Image is everything in the worlds I inhabit. I guard my image as fiercely as other people might guard their families, their fortunes, their sacred honor — if they believe there is such a thing. I am the founder of the most successful writing program in any university in the country. I am known to have an unerring eye for genius and the ability to nurture it. Certain of my former students have been invited to join the American Academy of Arts and Letters. Three have won the PEN/Faulkner Award for fiction, two have won the National Book Award, and two have won Pulitzers. The lesser awards are too numerous to recount. I am a starmaker. For someone in my position, an image of Spartan dedication to the written word at the expense even of my personal life, a reputation for cool indifference to everything but excellence in literature, makes me a laudable eccentric and an icon. My eminence would not be materially affected even if I publicly acknowledged that a few of the most renowned graduates of my program are pretentious fools of little talent. But with a woman as complex as I am, there are aspects of my personality that wouldn't be regarded as compatible with my public image and would in fact diminish it greatly. Therefore, I keep those interests strictly private and indulge them only beyond the view of those who would be offended by them."

Pogo sat goggle-eyed, as if his imagination were afire with images of her forbidden pursuits, as if he had forgotten that one of the controversial aspects of her personality that she felt the need to conceal was nothing more than an enchantment with Victoriana, the style and literature and perhaps the values of that age.

"Ms. Blair," the professor continued, "wrote her little document of extortion as if imagining that I were a woman of more facets than a well-cut diamond. She wrote of my third floor as if she found its secrets charming and my unadvertised interests proof of the depth of my spirit and intellect. But of course that was butt-kissing meant to disguise her attempted blackmail. She was demanding my praise, my mentoring, my endorsement of her talent, my power to make her a star in return for her silence."

Pax dared to say, "What if she was never in

your house? What if she only accurately imagined your . . . private interests?"

Looking up from the tart shell, St. Croix regarded him with the pity of the intellectually anointed for those doomed by genes or by circumstance to ignorance. "No one has an imagination of such power, of such intuitive genius, to know with accuracy what occupies a place in which she's never set foot. Her rich description of my third floor was as reportorial as what she wrote about the first two, not fiction but sleazy journalism, ninety-five percent on the mark. Hell, ninety-eight! The little bitch *was there.* She must have taken notes. That is a part of my life that I treasure to the extent that I rarely share it. The bed I sleep in most nights is on the third floor, not in my bedroom on the second. Only a trusted few have ever shared it with me, and none of them would have risked his relationship with me to conspire with that brazen, grasping little slut."

Without being consciously aware of what she was doing, the professor had formed the seventh tart and then had torn it apart as if she were rending her former student's throat. She threw down the mangled dough in disgust, wiped her hands on the dish towel, and resorted to her glass of Scotch and cream. If her equilibrium wasn't restored by the drink, at least she realized that in her ranting she had not given them a clue as to the nature of the secret enthusiasm she indulged on the third floor. She couldn't know that they had read Bibi's writing assignment, so she could only suppose that they were imagining every perversion from bondage with violent flagellation to animal sacrifice. Their wonderment appeared to amuse the professor, for her face let go of the anger that stiffened it, grew soft with coquettish intent. She licked a milky smear from her lips and said, "If you would like to verify my accusations against Ms. Blair, I'll let you read a copy of her piece and then take you up to the third floor to see for yourselves."

105
THE PASSENGER

Spitting out wordless expressions of malevolent determination, the unseen creature seemed to have squirmed under the front passenger seat, trying to negotiate the adjustment tracks and the substructure, intent upon making its way into the forward footwell, from which it might more easily spring upon her.

Unwilling to abandon the car to proceed on foot through this strange and hostile night, Bibi pulled the pistol from under her blazer and drove with only her left hand, which required her to let the Honda's speed drop.

If not cast back in time to that fearful night before her sixth birthday, she was at least cast back in spirit. There is no adult terror equivalent to what an innocent child experiences when first confronted with the truth that evil is not merely a figment of fairy tales, that it walks the world in countless forms, and that what it seeks most aggressively is the destruction of the innocent. With such an experience, childhood ends, regardless of the age at which that awful discovery is made. Bibi tasted again the metallic flavor of the first knowledge of evil, felt the childhood terror thrumming in her veins, her heart slamming as if it would either break the breastbone that armored it or hammer itself apart. The sense of helplessness that she had endured on that long-ago night was intolerable now, a condition to which she would not — *would not!* — allow herself to be subjected, not after all these years of striving to put behind her the primal — forgotten — horrors of her youth in favor of the ordinary fears and threats of a normal life.

"No," she said, "hell, no, no, this cannot happen, will not happen, *is not happening.*"

Even though the writhing, twitching, wretchedly graceless thing had been real in the bungalow bedroom, it was not real here. She had killed it that night, whatever it had been, killed it by a means that she could not remember. Seventeen years later, it could not return to torment her. It was of another place and time, it could not possibly materialize like a ghost to haunt her now. The thing thrashing under the passenger seat, calling to her in phlegmy knotted syllables with less meaning than the cries of any animal, was only another variation of the thing that had knocked on the motel door, tapped on the motel window, a *distraction* like the fog and the spirits in the house from which the girl had been kidnapped, like the man in the hoodie and the golden retriever that had tried to lure her away from the search for Ashley Bell.

Like Chubb Coy. The chief of hospital security. What did he have to do with any of this except to serve as a distraction, to thwart her by misdirection? He showed up at Norm's, at breakfast with St. Croix, later popped into the professor's Victorian retreat to kill her when she might have been about to make an important revelation, alluding to Flannery O'Connor and Thornton Wilder and Jack London, with whose work he was no more likely to be familiar than he was likely to be a master of particle physics.

Suddenly a truth about Chubb Coy circled Bibi, circled like a night bird gliding the darkness with a keen eye on its prey, the same truth from which she had recoiled earlier, the truth that she had burned with the memory trick. She drove with her left hand, the pistol clutched in her right, weaving along the lonely highway, her heart seeming to jump-jump-jump rather than merely beat, frenzied convulsions in her chest, and she thought, *He didn't quote those books because he wanted to, he quoted them because I made him do it.* That was not the truth that she rendered ashes in the motel sink, but it was somehow a funhouse-mirror reflection of that truth.

She didn't understand how she could make Chubb Coy do anything. That made no sense. She kept replaying the curious thought, trying to understand it, but instead of gaining clarity with repetition, it lost coherence — until she abruptly realized that the thing under the passenger seat, the unwanted passenger, had been silent for some time.

106

A Father's Intuition

Room 456. Sunday afternoon, 3:29. Blue sky beyond the window. Sun westering but not yet declining in a red swoon. On the EKG screen, the girl's heart rate spiking, the sound switched off but the trace line pumping, pumping faster. On the EEG, five brain wave indicators all tracking optimal patterns simultaneously, as every neurologist knew was not possible.

Nancy sat near the window, holding a newspaper that she hadn't requested but that she had accepted from a well-meaning young candy striper, seeming to read it but never turning from the front page to the second.

Perched on another chair with his smartphone, Murph checked the surf conditions in Australia. Byron Bay and Narrabeen and Torquay and Point Danger. Then on to Bali: wave height at Kuta Reef, Nusa Dua, Padang Padang. Mainland Mexico at Mazatlán and San Blas. Todos Santos in Baja California, and Scorpion Bay. Durban in South Africa, and Cape St. Francis. He wouldn't be surfing any of them today, probably never. He kept checking anyway. Pipeline and Sunset and Waimea on the north shore of Oahu. Honolulu Bay and Maalaea on Maui. He felt that he was losing his grip on sanity, sliding slowly into a defensive kind of madness.

Between Hawaii and Uruguay, he looked up from the phone and saw the EKG, where the heart trace was jumping above and below the midline, systolic and diastolic as they should be, not irregular, but faster than he had seen them track before.

In the bed, hair frizzed out around the grotesque electro cap, Bibi lay in silence, as she had lain for days. But then abruptly she groaned in distress.

Nancy dropped the newspaper and got to her feet. She reached the bed just as Bibi said, "No, hell, no, no . . ."

Waves and tides and far places forgotten, Murph scrambled bedside, the girl between him and Nancy.

Her sweet face squinched and her closed eyes closed tighter. ". . . cannot happen, will not happen, *is not happening.*"

Leaning over the bedrail, putting a hand on Bibi's shoulder, Nancy said, "Sweetie, do you hear me? Bibi, it's okay. We're here, honey. Daddy and me, both here."

"Not happening, not happening," Bibi insisted. She turned her head from side to side, as though afflicted. Denying, resisting.

Murph reached for the call button looped to the bedrail, but he hesitated to push it.

There was a father-daughter connection that had always been a mystery to him, a knowing without knowing how, knowing when she was safe and when she was not. She could be at the Wedge in wicked water, riding mountains, big quakers three times her height, with the very real danger of being swept into the stacked rocks of the breakwater at the harbor's mouth, where surfers had been killed, but he knew that he didn't need to worry. Another time, she might have been with a friend or two, riding bicycles nowhere more dangerous than on the paved "board-walk" that served the long peninsula or in the lightly traveled streets south of Balboa's lower pier; and he phoned her to suggest that she come home or stop by Pet the Cat to keep him company for a while. She'd always heard the vague note of worry in his voice, and she had always done as he asked, and nothing had ever happened to her. But he believed that something might have happened if he hadn't phoned her and changed the pattern of her day. It wasn't as powerful as clairvoyance, this connection, but it was stronger than a hunch.

When Bibi groaned again and rolled her head upon the pillow, Nancy moved her hand from the girl's shoulder to her bruised face.

"Honey, can you hear me? Will you wake up for your mom? Can you wake up and smile for Daddy and me?"

In that way of knowing without knowing how, Murph understood that, as irrational as it seemed, Bibi was safe in the coma, or at least safer than she would be if she woke. The injuries to her face and the tattoo, as mysterious as stigmata, argued against what he felt, but the feeling remained undiminished. In fact he sensed that the coma was her only hope, that somehow in the coma she had a chance to . . . to what? Somehow defeat the cancer? The gliomatosis cerebri that no one had ever survived? Was that truly a possibility or only a father's desperate wish? He watched her eyes twitching rapidly beneath the pale lids, looked at the five brain waves describing their optimal patterns, a phenomenon never before witnessed, and he thought about who Bibi was, the unique girl she had always been, and his desperate wish seemed like a rational hope.

Bibi repeated, *"Is not happening."*

Putting a hand to her daughter's brow, which was half covered by the electro cap, Nancy again urged her to wake, to return to them.

"No!" Murph whispered, but with such force that he startled his wife. "No, no, no, baby. Let her sleep. She needs to sleep."

Nancy regarded him as if he were the king

621

of kooks, a spleet, a geek-a-mo. "This isn't sleep, Murph. This is a damn hateful cancer coma."

Indicating the brain-wave readout, he said, "It isn't a coma. It's . . . something."

Nancy looked from him to the precious girl, to him again, and whatever she saw in his face, his eyes, gave her pause.

A blush suffused Murph's brow, his cheeks, a heat not quite like anything he had felt before. Fine beads of perspiration prickled his face, a sweat of awe, if there could be such a thing. His face must be glazed and shining; and he knew that his eyes were. Staring at his daughter, reassuring his wife, he said, "She's walking the board."

107
By the Skin of Their Teeth

In the Honda, across the street and twenty yards uphill from Solange St. Croix's house, Pogo sat behind the steering wheel, and Pax sat shotgun. Scattered through a rich currency of shadows, gold coins of sunlight shimmered on the windshield.

"Holy moly, Batman," Pogo said. "What would have happened to us if we'd gone up with her to the third floor?"

"I think my SEAL training would have been enough to get me out alive. I'm told you can punch pretty hard with your right."

"Half-and-half with Scotch. Did her mother start her on that in the crib?"

Surveying the large sheets of heavily tinted window glass in the stacked slabs of the house, wondering if he and Pogo were watched in turn by the woman and if, catlike, she were licking cream from her lips, Pax said, "There's something about her that's almost likable. In fact, I feel sorry for her."

Pogo wasn't convinced. "How does that work?"

"She pretends she's made the life she wanted, but on some level, she knows she got it wrong. She wanted artistic influence, and she got raw power instead. She wanted a literary life, but she got a life of writers' conferences and symposiums and committees pressing for fiction to sell the approved social issues of the moment. Cocktail parties where networking takes the place of wit. Being targeted by envy blogs. She fancied herself a free spirit, Holly Golightly, but with a Jane Austen brain. But there's no room at all for free spirits in modern academia, with its speech codes and humorless moralizing. So she makes two lives for herself, or three for all we know, or four, and in the end there's no satisfaction in being multiple Solange St. Croixs instead of one."

Pogo stared at him.

After a moment, Pax said, "What?"

"I thought you just blew up things."

"I've blown up a lot of things." Pax looked at his wristwatch, at the dashboard clock, and felt again that time was running out. "We better get moving."

Starting the engine, Pogo said, "Well, all I know is, she pushed Beebs out of the writing program and humiliated her in a supermarket that time. And she called her some pretty rank names."

As they drove downhill toward Coast Highway and the commercial heart of Laguna Beach, Pax said, "Okay, position check. For some reason, we don't know why, Captain gives Bibi a list of quotations celebrating imagination."

"Yeah. And she reads it so often, she just about wears out the paper."

"So then Captain dies. Bibi's ten, she's brokenhearted, deep in mourning. She writes stories about an abandoned dog named Jasper."

"Hundreds of pages of stories."

"And one day a dog named Jasper shows up out of the blue."

"Yeah. But she hides his collar with his name on it."

"You're sure she never told you about it."

"Never did," Pogo confirmed, and he turned north on Coast Highway.

"Then she's seventeen," Pax said, "and she writes about St. Croix's house —"

"It's a stupid lie that Beebs got a key and went in there."

"Of course. But just by observing St. Croix, by considering the professor's psychology, and by applying her imagination, she got it uncannily right. How's that possible?"

"Well, because she's Beebs."

"I'm not Watson, and you're for sure not Sherlock." Pax checked his G-Shock watch again. "Can you make a little speed?"

As usual, Laguna traffic came to a choke point at Forest Avenue. Pogo said, "I've souped up this crate, but it doesn't teleport."

Pax said, "Sorry. It's just I think we don't have much time to work this out, we've got to move."

"Move. Okay. But where are we going?"

Pax took a deep breath and blew it out. "I don't know."

108

THE ENDURING CHILL

Bibi parked alongside the highway, certain of being alone in the car. Relatively certain. For the moment.

She needed to get to Sonomire Way and find Ashley Bell, but she also needed to regain control of herself. She had been plunging from one untenable situation to another, crisis to crisis, letting events knock her from here to there to anywhere, as if she were a pinball. Events could overwhelm anyone. Nobody could stand tall and unmoved in a tsunami. But she could fight the undertow. Keep her head above water until the tumult subsided, and then swim.

Worse, she had allowed herself to be manipulated. She had taken far too long to recognize that, by one ruse and then another, she was being distracted from her quest. She had invested too much energy and emotion — *and time!* — fearing and worrying about responding to things that were no real threat to her. Tapping at a window. Scratching at a door. Hoodie Guy and his dog. The tattoo was a different kind of distraction. Why had she gotten the tattoo? ASHLEY BELL WILL LIVE. She didn't need flamboyant displays of dauntless intentions, which wasn't her nature, quiet perseverance being more her style, didn't need rah-rah and you-go-girl cheerleading. The tattoo was a challenge, but to whom, to what, if not to fate? *And she didn't believe in fate.* She was the master of her fate by virtue of free will. In her life, she *was* fate.

Earlier, she had killed the engine. Now she started the car again, but didn't switch on the headlights.

She was living in both the present and the past, at least in the sense that occurrences in the past — forgotten, half remembered — shaped events now. She knew how to cope with the present, how the world of now worked and how to make her way through it to her best advantage. But she was lousy with the past. When moments of potential revelation arose, she needed to seize them and peel away the thick skin of all those yesterdays, to see what fruit waited within.

As well, she was living in two worlds. She'd been living in two since Calida Butterfly began to seek hidden knowledge at the table in the kitchen. The first world was that of cause and effect, reason and design, where truth was discovered by intuition and observation. The second world was far wilder, a place where the supernatural no longer remained behind a veil, to be recognized or not, but frequently burst into view. Within the past hour, Bibi had begun to understand that her past, through the year that she was ten, had been lived in the second and wilder world.

From her purse she extracted the beautiful leather-bound book that had belonged to Calida but in which she had seen faint gray lines of her handwriting fluidly flowing and vanishing across the pages. She realized only now that it had been the cursive script of her childhood, much like what she produced these days, though with flourishes she no longer used. Somehow the book was a link between present and past, also between the two worlds in which she now lived.

She turned on the overhead light and opened the magical volume and searched through its blank leaves of creamy paper, but she did not see the ghostly script this time. The lines of the Donald Justice poem, which she had inscribed on a page and which had vanished, had not reappeared. They had not been written with disappearing ink. An ordinary pen. So the lines had gone somewhere. Like email, they had gone from one screen to another, one book to another.

To regain control of herself, to become again the Bibi Blair that she had been when all of this chaos started, she needed to knit together past and present, as well as the two worlds in which she lived. She did not know how the book could do that or *if* it could do that, but intuition suggested that nothing else at hand could serve that purpose. What good did it do to have a magical book if you did not in some way use it?

Bibi rummaged through her purse and found the pen. Although she sensed the petty god of time, in all three of its incarnations — past, present, future — washing away from her, and though near the center of her value system was the admonition to work and achieve — to *do* for the sake of doing — she put out of her mind the urgency of her quest for the girl. She gave considerable thought to what she should write rather than at once inking words onto the page.

As she began each new line, the previous line disappeared from the paper. When she was finished, she watched the last few words fade from view. Although it appeared as if she had done nothing, a sense of accomplishment welled in her and with it a fragile hope.

She put away the pen and the book, and she shook two capsules from the bottle of Tylenol. Her abraded ear and bruised face ached. The tattoo on her forearm stung in every vertical and horizontal line of its eighteen block letters. In the bottle that she had brought from the motel, enough warm

Coke remained to wash down the pain reliever.

She turned off the interior light, switched on the headlights, and drove back onto the highway.

Within seconds, the stern but caring voice of the woman that issued from the GPS began once more to give directions to Sonomire Way, a journey now of less than ten minutes.

To say that the fog returned would be to misrepresent both its origins and the quality of its locomotion. The mist did not drift in from the west, not from the sea that had birthed the previous clouds, but from the forbidding east, out of the Mojave Desert, where no source of water existed that could have generated such obliterating white masses. The fog came not on little cat feet, per Carl Sandburg, but in a racing flood so dense and swift that Bibi steeled herself for the impact, as if it would have the power of a wall of water, which it did not. From one instant to the next, the road before her and the landscape around her disappeared, and the headlights were hardly of more use to her than would be the memory of the sun to a coal miner trapped by a cave-in.

As she followed the instructions of the GPS, Bibi realized that the woman she had been, the woman she wished to be again, was not the woman she should have been, because she had never integrated within herself some key experiences of her childhood. She had, with the aid of Captain's memory trick, repressed information that would have had a profound effect upon the shaping of her character, of her intellect and emotion and will. To be formed even in part by half truths was to be ill-formed. With this realization, a different kind of chill shivered through her, a peculiar chill like none that she had ever known before. If in the hours ahead she learned the truth of her past, a change would descend upon her, would be *forced* upon her by new knowledge, and whether or not she saved Ashley Bell, she would never again be the Bibi Blair who had set out on this quest.

8
BIBI TO BELL

109

THE EIGHT-FINGERED WAITRESS AND THE POSSIBILITY OF DEATH

With nowhere else to go, with no leads to be followed at the moment, they went to Pogo's favorite restaurant. The three large sharks hanging from the ceiling were said to have been alive once, not made of plastic or papier-mâché, preserved by a taxidermist, their skin as glossy as if they were still wet from the sea, swimming one after the other in search of a good meal. Some claimed that an engraved medallion and ruby ring belonging to the legendary and mysteriously vanished surfer, Tommy Cordovan, had been found in the gut of the largest shark, but that was about as credible as another claim that in the same stomach had been found bones DNA-matched to the missing aviator Amelia Earhart. The walls were decorated with colorful custom surfboards and photographs of local surf celebrities dating all the way back to the 1930s, guys and — more and more as the years went by — girls who were largely unknown to the world outside of the Southern California community of devoted board-heads, but who were admired and regarded with affection and sometimes revered as demigods by members of the local beach tribe.

People came there for the food, which was good, but as much for the atmosphere, which was saturated with the romance of California as it had once been and, sadly, would likely never be again. Pax had not eaten breakfast, and both he and Pogo had missed lunch. They sat in a corner booth, in the welcome quiet before the dinner rush.

The waitress who brought menus was in synch with the intensity of the décor, if not with its theme. A well-tanned Amazon with a blond pageboy haircut, she stood nearly six feet tall, a fortyish looker who was a version of Nicole Kidman writ large. Her eyes appeared to be blue or green or maybe blue-gray depending on the angle at which she regarded you. Uniforms weren't required of the wait staff, and this woman — her badge identified her as KANANI, which was Hawaiian for *a beauty* — was dressed in white slacks and a white blouse accessorized with a red-silk sash worn as a belt and a red-and-gold silk scarf at her throat. Elaborate dangling gold earrings. Flashy bracelets. Eight diamond finger rings. She might have worn ten rings, except that she had only eight fingers. Ironically, on each hand, she was missing the ring finger, which was next to the pinkie.

Kanani smiled and seemed pleasant enough, but there was a remote quality to her, a sense that she held the truest part of herself in reserve, letting the world make of her what it would, which likely had little to do with who she really was.

After she had taken their orders for beer and had gone, Pogo said, "Beebs is fascinated with Kanani. I figure she'll put her in a book someday."

"What happened to the fingers?"

"Nobody knows. Someone asked her once — and wished he hadn't. I wasn't here when it happened, so I don't know if he was a smart-ass about it or just asking the question was enough to set her off, but Kanani decked him, knocked him out cold."

"And wasn't fired?"

"She's a good waitress. Besides, Wayland Zuckerman — he's the owner — is either head-over-heels in love with her or terrified of her. Nobody can quite figure out which."

When Kanani brought two bottles of Corona, two glasses, and napkins, she proved as dexterous as any ten-fingered waitress and more so than many.

Pax and Pogo ordered fish tacos plus a plate of enchiladas suizas with black beans and rice to be split between them.

"Where'd you get the Pogo moniker?" Pax asked.

"Don't have a clue."

"You really don't know — or the nickname is nobody's business, just like Kanani's missing fingers?"

"I never punched out anyone who asked me. I've been called Pogo as long as I can remember, and no one's ever taken credit for pinning it on me."

"There was a cartoon character way back, in the funny pages."

"Yeah, but I don't think that's where it came from. Everyone in my family's too serious to read the funny pages, and anyway that was before their time."

Kanani brought their food, and they ate with enthusiasm for a while before Pogo said, "I don't feel right, scarfing up tacos and beer, while Beebs needs us to be doing something."

"Except there's nothing to do right now. You want to call the AV god and see if he's got the tape recorder working?"

"At least that's something," Pogo said, and put down a taco to pick up his smartphone.

Earlier, on the way to see Dr. St. Croix in Laguna Beach, they stopped at the house of a guy named Ganesh Patel, a surfer whose passion for designing audio-video systems flowered into a business that he hadn't really wanted, that eventually he had sold for enough money to spend his life beachside. He'd explained that microcassette recorders of that type were long out of style, largely replaced by digital systems with greater storage capacity, but that he could fix their example of pathetic Neanderthal technology because he could fix anything.

Ganesh answered the call. For a minute or so, Pogo listened, saying only, "Uh-huh, okay, uh-huh, mmmm, cool, uh-huh, uh-huh. Latronic, dude," before he terminated the call.

Having been around the Blair family long enough to pick up some surfer lingo, Pax knew that *latronic* meant *later on* or *see you later.*

"He's taken it apart, he's got it spread out on his workbench," Pogo said, "and now he just needs to find the kink and put it back together right. Man, when he talks about this stuff, you'd think it was some hot chick he had laid out on that workbench."

"Everyone to his thing. Don't get me talking about the Carl Gustav recoilless rifle."

"Is that something that blows things up?"

"Beautifully," Pax confirmed.

They were nearly finished eating and thinking about a second beer when Pogo said, "You really think it's a possibility?"

"What is?"

"That wherever Beebs is, I mean besides the hospital, something could happen and she could die there and die here, too."

"She's got brain cancer, Pogo. Whether or not something really bad happens to her out there in the Twilight Zone, she could die from the glioma."

"Yeah. I guess. I mean, yeah, I know." He looked around at the yellowing photographs of the long-dead surfers, up at the sharks in their motionless but perpetual hunt, as if those familiar sights were new to him, as if the restaurant had become as strange as the surreal angles and metamorphic flow of a dreamscape. "But then . . . what's going to happen to us if she dies?"

After a silence, Pax said, "I don't want to think about it."

"Neither do I."

"Then we won't."

Finished eating, each of them ordered a second beer.

Pax had brought with him the spiral-bound panther-and-gazelle notebook. Now he opened it on the table to skim through some of the Jasper stories, looking for he knew not what, for anything that might be a clue that would help them fulfill Bibi's request: *Find me.*

They were stories written by a ten-year-old girl, but a damn smart ten-year-old. They had flair. They were compelling.

Nevertheless, Pax found himself repeatedly turning past the last tale of Jasper, to the first two blank pages that followed. On the left-hand page were the two lines from one of Bibi's favorite poems: *Now comes the evening of the mind / Here are the fireflies twitching in the blood.* He dunked a finger in his beer and wiped it across *Now comes the evening.* The black ink smeared readily.

"She didn't write this when she was ten. She wrote it recently. I'd guess within the last month, but maybe not nearly that long ago."

Squeezing a slice of lime over the lip of his beer bottle, Pogo said, "What do you think — does it mean something?"

"It has to."

"What does it mean?"

As Pax was about to admit that he didn't know, words began to appear as if by magic on the right-hand page, in the familiar elegant cursive script. Before all of this with Bibi, he had a few times over his twenty-eight years tasted the spice of the uncanny, but suddenly it was a staple of his diet. Its effects — a chill, a spidery capering sensation along the nape of the neck, a not unpleasant swelling of the heart — were as reliable as the oral heat and pop-sweat that attended the consumption of a habanero pepper.

Pogo, too, saw the words appearing, and Pax turned the notebook so that both of them could read the message as it formed.

The first line declared, *I am a Valiant girl.*

110
THE GIRL IN NEED
OF DISCIPLINE

On the electronic map, the grid of sixteen streets, eight east-west and eight north-south, was given no overarching name. But when the GPS announced that a right turn would bring Bibi to Sonomire Way, a monument sign resolved out of the dense fog, a monolith that might have been erected by godlike extraterrestrials to humble and inspire ape-stupid humanity to make something better of itself during the millennia to come. The slab stood about fourteen feet high and seven wide, polished black granite inlaid with a matte-finish stainless-steel band surrounding embedded Lucite letters that were a luminous blue now at four o'clock in the morning. The letters were smaller than might have been expected in those ninety-eight square feet of granite, as if the slab was a shout to get your attention and the words were a whisper, a name to be spoken only in a respectful hush: SONOMIRE TECHNOLOGY PARK.

Cruising slowly, cautiously along the four-lane street, Bibi had an impression of vast properties. Enormous low-rise buildings, four and five stories, yet of a scale incomprehensible, were revealed only by landscape lamps, which were in fact security lamps in elegant disguise, floods of pale light frozen in mid swash, and by scattered ranks of windows where people or robots labored in spite of the hour. The architecture was unintelligible in the fog and perhaps troubling even in clear daylight, inhuman and somehow militaristic, so that the structures were moored like massive battleships in the sea of mist, no, like starship fleets preparing to venture forth to extinguish not merely cities but entire planets.

"Eleven Sonomire Way, one hundred yards ahead, on the left," said the GPS.

Bibi pulled at once to the curb, killed the headlights and the engine. She turned off the electronic map and sat in darkness, as the fog invented the many caissons of a ghost army and rolled them slowly through the night. She kept thinking of the bludgeoned man and the gunshot woman in the house from which Ashley Bell had been kidnapped, their broken bloody bodies. Every injury that she had sustained earlier, in the battle with the brute in the Corona del Mar bungalow, seemed to ache more than ever. She needed to gather her courage; the one good thing about doing so was that, given how little courage she still had, she didn't waste much time in the gathering of it.

She got out of the Honda. The chunk and rattle of the closing door winnowed through the fog, the former traveling not very far, the latter perhaps attracting attention if anyone waited alertly for her arrival. The night pressed white around her, clammy, chilly. Fog in her ears. In her throat. Her lungs heavy with inhaled mist, she found the sidewalk and proceeded on foot.

Apparently not every property in Sonomire Technology Park had built out, for Number 11 was surrounded by a construction fence with a wide double gate, half of which stood open. A metal sign wired to the closed half of the gate declared THE FUTURE SITE OF TEREZIN, INC. The announced completion date lay less than fourteen months away; therefore, lost in the fog must be considerable construction, perhaps finished wings of a central structure or entire completed buildings.

The only light on the property glowed in the windows of one of two large double-wide construction-office trailers. She approached with caution across the unevenly compacted and littered earth, peered in a window, and saw a room containing six or eight office chairs surrounding what appeared to be a dining-table-size scale model of the project. It was a sprawling complex of scalloped and sweeping buildings that seemed about to be airborne, situated among plazas shaded by groves of phoenix palms, enlivened by numerous fountains as well as by a body of water large enough to be called a lake.

Beyond another window lay a room containing two large drawing tables adjustable to various heights and angles, along with support furniture. Architect's elevations and construction schedules were pinned to the corkboard walls.

She continued past a dark window to another where light leaked around a drawn blind and painted feathers on the fog. Muffled voices in that room tantalized her, but she couldn't make out what they were saying. Construction crews began early in the day, though not before dawn. Whoever conspired here might be discussing serious issues more pertinent to Bibi than the cost of concrete and the expected delivery date of the next truckload of steel beams.

She proceeded to the rear of the double-wide, where another window proved to be covered by a pleated shade. She continued around the corner, hoping that the office extended the width of the trailer and that it might offer a last pane of glass over which no shade had been drawn.

In the impossible Mojave fog, two parked vehicles were almost fully concealed in mist as thick as mattress batting, one of them an entirely possible Cadillac Escalade, but the other an improbable sedan. Visibility remained so poor that Bibi had almost passed the big car before she recognized the Bentley ornament on the hood. She stepped close to confirm that the paint, when seen in better light, was pale enough to be café au lait.

When two worlds collided without catastrophe and occupied the same space, a world of cause and effect and an unpredictable world where supernatural wild cards could be thrown onto the table at any time, it seemed inevitable that former teacher and remade woman Marissa Hoffline-Vorshack should be there regardless of the hour. According to the ever-changing rules of this game, of all the real-estate developers in California, the one in charge of the Terezin project could have been no other than the shopaholic's husband.

The most urgent questions now seemed to be where the grandly inflated breasts and the woman behind them were at this moment and whether Bibi could avoid the crazy bitch. Both were answered when the headlamps of the Bentley flared, dazzling Bibi, and the driver's door opened.

She who had been first to recognize the young writer's talent exited the sedan, limned by the interior light that flowed out after her and by the backwash of headlamps. As the woman approached, Bibi saw that she was dressed inappropriately for the hour and the place: stiletto heels, black toreador pants held up with a jeweled belt, a blouse that revealed enough cleavage in which to conceal a litter of kittens, and a white leather jacket with black detailing.

The former teacher, a subtle and calculating mistress of mean in the classroom, favored Bibi with an expression that was familiar from days of old, in spite of the extensive makeover of the woman's features. A smug power-trip smirk. Colored with the inexplicable resentment of someone who, though you never offended her, believed that you were owed revenge. The woman felt now, as always, justified in doling out a real injury for an imagined one, pleased to rain upon her target a storm of petty reprisals.

Except that this time they might not be petty.

"I would ask you what the hell you think you're doing here," said Hoffline-Vorshack. "But I don't care, and you would only lie, anyway. Like you lied about having a pistol and about possessing a concealed-carry license. You're still the little rebel and liar you always were."

The fog seemed to part for Hoffline-Vorshack, to vacate a space that she could occupy, as if she and the mist were two magnetic substances whose poles repelled.

"Stop right there," Bibi said. "No closer."

The woman stopped, but only after taking two more steps and forcing Bibi to back away from her. "Will you ever grow up, Gidget?"

"Don't call me that."

"Why? Because it strikes a nerve? Frivolous little Gidget, all about surfing and beach-blanket parties and looking cute in a bikini, an even more empty-headed and ridiculous version of your perpetually adolescent parents."

"You don't know anything about my parents, you don't know who they are."

"They came to parent-teacher meetings, didn't they? I knew them at first glance for what they were. And I've always known you're a girl in need of discipline."

Bibi didn't think anyone in the trailer could hear them, but she drew the pistol from her shoulder rig, just the same.

The former teacher's smile was a mezzaluna of contempt, no less sharp than the crescent-shaped kitchen knife of which it reminded Bibi. "You're gonna get yourself killed, you stupid girl, running around in the night, playing Nancy Drew. Or worse than killed. We can take you down and break you down so completely, no one could ever put you together again. And we will."

111
LIKE A MESSAGE IN BOTTLE

The wired sharks in a dead swim overhead. Decades of surfers, fit and tanned, standing tall with their shortboards and longboards, smiling on the walls. And on the table, on the notebook page, five words: *I am a Valiant girl.*

"This is wild," Pogo said. "But I know what that means."

"Me, too."

"Of course you, too. Those books."

"Those books," Pax agreed, his mouth gone dry, his heart finding a new rhythm.

The next two lines read, *When I saw her yesterday, why didn't I ask Halina Berg if she'd heard of Robert Warren Faulkner — is he a known neo-Nazi?*

"Either name mean anything to you?" Pogo asked.

"Halina Berg is vaguely familiar, but not the other."

"How could she see this Halina Berg yesterday? She's four days in a coma."

"She couldn't have."

The fourth line began to appear, flowed swiftly, and, with the concluding question mark, read, *Why didn't I ask Halina Berg about Ashley Bell?*

"The name in her tattoo," Pogo said.

For a minute or so, they both watched the notebook, waiting impatiently for a fifth line of script to appear, but then Pogo resorted to his smartphone.

Kanani returned to ask if they wanted anything more, and Pax said they didn't, and she left the check.

While Pax busied himself with calculating the tip and paying the tab, Pogo said, "It's not as bad as John Smith or Heather anything, but there are enough Ashley Bells spread around the country to waste more time than we have."

"Try Robert Warren Faulkner."

"Already on it."

Nothing more appeared on the open pages of the notebook. Pax was reluctant to leaf farther back in the volume, in search of more deeply buried messages, lest he disturb whatever connection allowed this communication from Bibi in her coma or from whatever Otherwhere she also inhabited. It was as if his girl, adrift on the sea of an alien world, had put a message in a bottle and tossed it overboard, and somehow it had surfaced on the shores of *this* world.

He picked up his Corona. Put it down

without taking a sip. His fingers were wet with condensation from the bottle. He blotted them on his jeans. He realized that he had grown nervous. He was rarely nervous. Cautious, concerned, alarmed, even afraid, yes, but seldom nervous. He tipped his head back and gazed up at the sharks. He knew how to deal with sharks. It was part of his training. He knew how to deal with the loss of men he fought with, brothers and friends, every one of them. He didn't know how to deal well with loss outside the context of war.

Pogo said, "There's a bunch of Robert Faulkners, but in a quick search, none of them with that middle name."

"Halina Berg."

Pogo came back to him quickly on that one. "It's a pen name. She wrote one book under it. Her first novel. Something called *Out of the Mouth of the Dragon*."

"Whose pen name?"

The smartphone was the planet in Pogo's hand, which billions of advertising dollars and the wisdom of uncountable pundits had assured him was tech magic, the only true magic. But when he looked up, his eyes seemed to see — and his face to reflect — the wonder of a witness to otherworldly mystery that, luminous and melodic, had just entered the comparatively dim and discordant world of high-tech.

"Halina Berg was a pen name for Toba

Ringelbaum."

As a girl, Toba had escaped the Jewish ghetto of Theresienstadt, where her mother died in a typhoid epidemic. Later, she survived as well the Auschwitz death camp, where her father perished. Decades after marrying Max Klein and emigrating to the U.S., she'd written a series of young-adult novels about a school for girls, Valiant Academy, where the multitalented headmistress was an adventurer and master of martial arts who not only educated her charges, but also led them on thrilling missions against villains who represented one face or another of the hydra-headed evil that was totalitarianism.

Pax knew all that because he knew Toba Ringelbaum. He had met her twice in Bibi's company. Pogo knew the old woman even better, having visited her often with Bibi.

Bibi had found the Valiant Girl series when she was ten and had read and reread the novels through her teens.

In the notebook, her handwriting seemed almost to glow: *When I saw her yesterday, why didn't I ask Halina Berg if she'd heard of Robert Warren Faulkner — is he a known neo-Nazi?*

That question gave rise to another one in Paxton's mind: Why would she refer to her friend and mentor Toba Ringelbaum by the writer's pen name?

"I'll call Toba," said Pogo, "if you want to go there."

"Oh, I want to go there, all right," Pax said. "But come on. Let's roll. I'll call her from the car."

112
TEACHER OF THE YEAR AWARD

In the headlight-silvered fog, which slowly but deliberately spiraled like galaxies in formation, Mrs. Hoffline-Vorshack stood within a pocket of clear air, as in one school of religious painting a saint always stood — or levitated — within a shining nimbus. Judging by all the available evidence, the former English teacher was no more saintlike than a worm, and in fact the worm had the moral advantage of not knowing the difference between right and wrong.

The "we" in her threat —

We can take you down and break you down so completely, no one could ever put you together again. And we will.

— put her in Terezin's neo-Nazi cult and eliminated any chance that the selection of her husband as the builder of Terezin, Inc.'s new headquarters had been a coincidence.

"Where's the girl?" Bibi asked. "Where are they holding her?"

"As if I'd tell you."

"Tell me."

"As if you need me to tell you."

"Does that mean something?"

"You know."

"Don't riddle me."

"Don't *make* me a riddle."

Bibi raised the pistol in her right hand.

"Gidget breaks bad," said Hoffline-Vorshack.

"By God, I will," Bibi said. "I'll shoot you."

She didn't know whether or not she meant the threat. Earlier she had stabbed the brute who beat her and tried to rape her, stabbed him to death, but that had been in desperation. And he'd been a stranger. It would be harder to kill someone she knew, even someone like this awful woman. Familiarity bred contempt, but it also bred civility, even if a reluctant civility.

Hoffline-Vorshack's face was a nest of snaky emotions — venomous contempt, hatred, arrogance. She ventured no closer, although her posture was belligerent. "You want to know something, you silly little goob, you ignorant spleet?" Never before had the former teacher used surfer lingo. "You've got this all wrong. You aren't putting it together right. If I was still teaching school and you were still in my class, I'd give you a D on this, and that would be a generous grade."

Bibi took the pistol in a two-hand grip. "Where is Ashley Bell?"

"You think you understand Bobby Faulkner, the mother killer? You think you've got his psychology down pat, you have a handle on his Terezin ID and the cult he's building? Gidget, you don't know shit. You're pathetic. It's not a cult. It never was a cult, not anything as clichéd as a cult." Bibi's hair frizzed in the fog, but in the bubble of clear air that Hoffline-Vorshack occupied, her tumbling blond tresses looked worthy of a shampoo commercial. "Look around you, *BeeeBeee*" — she made the name sound positively cartoonish — "look around and maybe you'll notice your cult has morphed into some kind of giant conglomerate that's building an über-expensive headquarters in the campus style. Maybe you'll realize there must be thousands of people involved in this operation, tens of thousands, *hundreds of thousands.* Does that make any sense for a crackpot Nazi cult? We're not crackpots, Gidget."

"But you are fascists."

"Everyone's a fascist these days, sweetie. The word has no power to sting anymore. The country has embraced all the fascist dictators we once shunned. Kissed and made up. It's respectable now. It's the true and preferred way."

Bibi raised the pistol, aiming it not at the woman's chest any longer, but at her face, from a distance of six or seven feet. From

Hoffline-Vorshack's perspective, the muzzle must look like a black hole with planet-rending gravity. "Where are they holding the girl? I'm not going to ask again."

"Good. You're not going to ask again. I'm tired of listening to you ask."

All of her life, Bibi had kept a governor on her anger, had consciously negotiated between the gracious, complaisant aspect of her nature and the darker part of herself that sometimes wanted to strike out, strike back. Her tendency to arbitrate herself into a courteous reaction, or at least one of quiet anger, was motivated not by a noble inclination, but by fear that she would lose control of herself. She suspected that, should she lose control, she had the capacity to do great damage out of proportion to the offense she had suffered, though no evidence, either internal or external, existed to support that suspicion.

"Where is Ashley?" she demanded.

A bark of laughter escaped Hoffline-Vorshack. "You just asked again. You said you wouldn't ask again, and you just did. Listen, Gidget, you don't need that little Jewess. You never have needed her. Don't you know a red herring when you see one, when you have actually dragged it across the trail yourself?"

Bibi was building toward rage. She loathed this woman. Marissa Hoffline had been a bad teacher. She would never in a thousand years have won any organization's teacher-of-the-year award. And now she was doing an equally bad job of being a wealthy wife, utterly without gratitude for the grace that had befallen her, transformed by money into an ogre of privilege and self-satisfaction. And she wouldn't stop talking. If she kept talking, she was going to spoil everything. If she kept talking, talking, talking, she was going to say something that Bibi didn't want to hear.

"You don't need the little Jewess, Gidget. Just do what you need to do. Confront the terrible truth, accept what you need to accept about yourself, *know* yourself, and then do the deed that needs to be done." Hoffline-Vorshack's face was such a portrait of self-righteous satisfaction that Bibi wanted to hit her. Hard. Again and again. Shut her up. Kill her. But it would be murder, not killing. There was a difference.

The anger that Bibi had long dreaded to express, swollen now to rage, was a consequence of repressed fear. She understood that much at last. Captain's memory trick didn't in fact burn away traumatic experiences. It flushed them down a deep memory hole, where they — and the fear associated with them — festered in the dark. For seventeen years, the fear had been at a low boil, until it became a thick and bitter reduction of fear, became enduring terror, became a suppressed anxiety laced with helpless foreboding.

"Know yourself, Gidget," Hoffline-

Vorshack repeated.

"Shut up."

"Learn your secrets."

"Shut up, shut up, shut up!"

The former teacher said, "You know I'm right, Gidget. He asked you what you needed most, and you said to forget. But what you needed most back then wasn't to forget. And it's not what you need now."

113
WHAT WORDS CANNOT DESCRIBE

The Spanish Colonial Revival house with its many charms. The hallways and rooms fortified with books. The kitchen table around which more conversations had been held than meals had been eaten. Toba's gentle and winsome face, her generous smile, her unfailing kindness. This was a pleasing place, comforting to mind and heart, but at this moment, Pax had neither the capacity to be comforted nor the time to allow the house and the singular old woman to work their magic.

Their hostess offered tea or coffee, both of which she brewed after Pax had called to ask if they might pay a visit, but he and Pogo declined. When Toba heard about Bibi's brain cancer and her collapse into coma four days earlier, she poured her full mug of tea into the kitchen sink, replaced it with coffee, and spiked the coffee with both Baileys Irish Cream and bourbon. She did all that before she could speak a word in response to the news, and when she was able to talk, there

was a tremor in her voice that wasn't characteristic. "I rarely drink, but there are times
when even drinking too much is not enough."

The rest of what they had to tell her regarding the strangeness of Bibi's condition — the
unprecedented brain waves, the injuries to
her face that appeared without apparent
cause (though for the moment they said
nothing of the tattoo) — didn't lift Toba's
spirits, but did engage her imagination and
energize her. They told her about Jasper and
Olaf and the long-hidden dog collar, about
the reason that Dr. St. Croix had driven Bibi
out of the university writing program.

Although Pax had brought the notebook
decorated with Pogo's drawing, they didn't at
once mention the lines that had appeared on
its pages as though written by a ghost. This
wasn't an interrogation, Toba being on their
side, on Bibi's side, but certain techniques of
an interrogator were of use in an informal
interview and even in casual conversation.
Whether you were talking to an enemy com-
batant or to a friend, information drawn out
in stages — in layers — tended to be more
detailed, included more useful revelations.
Not because the subject was purposefully
withholding information. Simply, the human
brain did not always know everything it knew,
needed time for one thought to tease out
another, to untie the many little knots in

memory and recover an experience to its fullest.

When they implied that Bibi had spoken the words *I am a Valiant girl* in her coma, Toba sprang up from her kitchen chair as if sixty years had fallen from her flesh and bones. "She loved those books. She was so industrious about finding my unlisted phone number, amazingly determined for a girl of just fourteen. She called and apologized for calling, for snooping out the number. Come, now, you two, come along, let me show you. Well, Pogo has seen it, but you haven't, Paxton. My study, where I wrote, where I write."

As they followed her along the ground-floor hall and its shelves of precisely ordered books lovingly maintained dust-free, up the open stairs to the second floor, and to her office, Toba said, "You see, the Valiant series earned a comfortable living, but they were never bestsellers. I received some mail from readers, of course, but I was not besieged by little girls knocking on my door. I was flattered by the trouble Bibi had gone to. And charmed by our few minutes on the phone. So I said she could visit with her mother if she wished. A half hour. And bring five or six books to be signed. I'd never done a formal book signing. It seemed overreaching to me, too proud by half. Who was I, after all, but Toba Ringelbaum, who should have been dead a dozen times? I wasn't Mr. Saul Bellow, though I might have wished to write so well! I found the girl enchanting, far too solemn for her age and yet delighting in every smallest thing, a knowledge sponge in search of something that I think always eluded her, still eludes her, whatever it might be."

That her office was book-lined came as no surprise. The large ultramodern U-shaped desk wasn't the heavy-footed European antique that Pax expected. The latest model computer with a screen that seemed the size of a billboard as well as printers and a scanner and a tech geek's array of the latest electronic gadgets proved that she remained in the game to an extent that Pax had not realized, and he was embarrassed now to have thought her largely retired in spite of her claim to be still producing.

Pogo said, "This is like a starship control station, Toba-Wan Kenobi. I've always known the Force was with you. Are you a dedicated social networker?"

"Not much, dear. I have better ways to waste my time. Besides, I find social networking too antisocial for the most part. But I think it's wise to keep an eye on it."

At a section of shelves devoted to the display of her novels, she had arranged the American editions of the Valiant books in the order of publication. There were forty-six of them.

"She calls me her inspiration and her mentor," Toba said, "and I might be vain enough to admit to the first, but not the second. How could I mentor a girl who, by the time she was seventeen and out of high school, was already a better writer than I am or ever could be?"

"Maybe you mentored her in other ways," Pax said. "The values the girls learned at Valiant Academy. A lot of people these days might find those corny or certainly out of date. But Bibi says the code of the Valiant girls is a brilliant expansion and application of natural law."

Toba was clearly pleased to hear this, but then she must have thought of Bibi abed in a hospital, lost in a coma, for she raised her mug and took a long draught of the spiked coffee. "If there was one thing she might have found in the Valiant girls that she didn't already have or didn't have in the fullest at fourteen, it was the wonderful concept of free will. She kept coming back to that in our conversations. That we are free to shape our own lives, that we can overcome. That there is a terrible danger in denying the existence of free will. The danger of deciding that we are meat machines, that all is meaningless and that we have no responsibility for what happens because of what we do."

Pogo said, "Should I tell her about the tattoo?"

Pax nodded.

The concept of four injected words appearing without the aid of ink or tattooist did not startle Toba Ringelbaum or require her to stretch her belief system to any degree whatsoever. She had made no secret of the fact that during her time in Theresienstadt and then when she had been freed from Auschwitz within hours of her scheduled execution, she'd had several experiences beyond explanation, when for a moment logic and the laws of nature were suspended in such a way that she was spared when she should not have been. Some would label these events coincidence, which is a tool of fate, but others would call them miracles, which have no need of fate. She had never spoken of the specifics of those experiences, not even to her husband, Max, because they were sacred to her and because she understood that the infelicities of language would diminish them. The ineffable would not be ineffable if it could be described.

When Pogo finished, Pax opened the panther-and-gazelle notebook to the page on which lines of Bibi's cursive script had appeared, and Toba listened without further need of spiked coffee as he explained how they had materialized and read them with her. Whether this was less or more astonishing than her indescribable experiences as a girl in the ghetto and in the death camp, he could not tell; however, he could see that they were of the same wondrous fabric, for she smiled and set her mug aside on the desk and said, "It's not hopeless, then."

"Why," Pax wondered, "would she refer to you by your pen name — Halina Berg?"

"I don't know," Toba said. "It's peculiar, isn't it?"

"Who is Robert Warren Faulkner?"

"Never heard of him."

"More important," Pogo said, "who is Ashley Bell?"

114
THE AWFUL WOMAN AND THE TERRIBLE BLOW

The fog that Bibi drew into her lungs seemed for a moment to fill her head, as well. Marissa Hoffline-Vorshack had spoken about events of which she could know nothing. *He asked you what you needed most, and you said to forget. But what you needed most back then wasn't to forget. And it's not what you need now.* She had never known the captain. He had died years before this awful woman had come into Bibi's life.

Dressed expensively for a cheap nightclub, dressed for a production number in an old Elvis Presley film, with spike heels and toreador pants and all that cleavage and the black-and-white leather jacket, standing in a bubble of clarity in the white murk, backlit by the Bentley, Miss Hoffline reinvented was *demanding* to be seen, to be considered and understood.

Bibi thought she heard something behind her, someone closing on her, revealed by the crunch of gravel. She pivoted, sweeping the night with the gun, but she found no one. Lights in the construction-office trailer, behind the window shades. Voices inside, less than half heard, unintelligible, perhaps not speaking English. Like voices from Beyond drawn to a séance and issuing from a scrim of ectoplasm floating in the air.

"They haven't heard us," said Mrs. Hoffline-Vorshack.

Bibi swung toward her former teacher, expecting to be assaulted in the turn, but the woman had not moved. Her look of triumph seemed to imply that she didn't need to attack Bibi physically, that she could destroy her with words.

"They haven't heard us and won't," Hoffline-Vorshack said. "Unless you want them to. You can always want them to."

Bibi still felt fogbound, mentally as well as physically, and even rage could not burn off the mists. Of all the ways she might have expected their confrontation to develop after Hoffline-Vorshack emerged from the car, this was not one of them. At no other point in the past two days had she felt so confused, with so little control over events.

"What do you want, Gidget?" Hoffline-Vorshack asked with a note of exasperation. "Huh? What do you really want?"

"Ashley Bell, damn it. Where are you keeping her?"

"Her location — that's just the next turn in

the narrative. *What you want* — now, that's a bigger issue. Character motivation. If you're driven to save the girl, if that's your motivation, you first need to learn the full truth about yourself. If instead you're afraid of that truth, if you're the coward I think you are, then your motivation is to remain ignorant of it, and you'll never save anyone."

"Why are you going on like this? What is this bullshit? We're not in a classroom."

"Aren't we?" There was such conviction in her voice and such challenge in her eyes that it seemed as if walls might form around the two of them, and rows of schoolroom desks appear. "What do you want me to be, Gidget?"

"Want you to be?"

"As you know, I'll be whatever you want."

The fog was everywhere, deep and opaque, everywhere except around Hoffline-Vorshack, but she was speaking fog, a machine of obfuscation.

"All you've ever been," Bibi said, "since my junior year, is an impediment. People don't change in a minute."

"So you want me to be an impediment, prevent you from getting to Ashley, prevent you from facing the truth?"

Surrealism had been woven through the past two days, but now its thread count seemed to be increasing rapidly.

"You'll be what you are." Bibi didn't want

this conversation. She wanted to end this encounter.

In spite of spike heels and skintight pants and breasts that were the opposite of aerodynamic, Hoffline-Vorshack moved fast, grabbing for the Sig Sauer with one hand, tearing at Bibi's blood-crusted ear with the other, missing with the first, scoring with the second. Bibi's cry of pain was silent, bitten off, choked down. As the teacher issued a zombie hiss through bared teeth, Bibi used the P226, but not as a firearm, as a bludgeon, brought the barrel down hard into her assailant's forehead, which produced a cruel but discreet sound. Hoffline-Vorshack dropped, sprawled facedown, head turned to her left, lighted and shadowed by the Bentley's headlamps, in a strangely graceful pose, as if this were a macabre fashion ad in which the model was pretending to be the victim of a crime. She might have been unconscious or on her way out, but she regarded her former student with one gimlet eye that would have killed if the extreme voltage of hatred in it could have been emitted in the form of an electric current. Maybe Bibi should have waited to see if the eye closed and the woman remained still, but the anger she had always been able to control now controlled her instead. She reversed her grip on the pistol, held it by the barrel, and brought the butt down on the side of Hoffline-Vorshack's head, not with full force, though still a terrible blow, hard enough that the fierce eye disappeared behind a fluttering but then stilled eyelid.

The violence equally thrilled and shamed Bibi, made her feel empowered though not exalted. If shame had not been part of it, she would have struck another blow, and another, until she'd seen the skull cave and the blond hair darken with blood. But she retained control of herself, cranked shut the vent that would have released her fear-spawned rage in volcanic gouts.

The voices in the construction trailer continued their muffled conversation. Urgently scheming or merely garrulous, plotting the destruction of a city with a nuke or playing poker — it was impossible to tell which.

If one of them was Vorshack, lucky husband, perhaps the other was Robert Warren Faulkner, alias Terezin. In which case she could surprise him, walk in and shoot him dead, deny him his birthday celebration and save the life of Ashley Bell. But would the leader of such a cult — such an *enterprise* — go anywhere without a couple of bodyguards? Unlikely. She couldn't know how many others might be in the trailer, stationed in rooms or a hallway into which she couldn't see from outside.

She thought it better to explore the acreage under development rather than force an ill-conceived confrontation, just as it was better not to dwell on the strangeness of her encounter with Marissa Hoffline-Vorshack and the bizarre way that it had ended.

What is your motivation?

To save Ashley Bell.

Is it really?

Yes. Ashley Bell. Save her or die trying.

The fog enfolded her.

115
TOBA'S LIFE OF FACT AND FICTION

The old woman appeared not to suffer from arthritis, for she moved quickly and without complaint, and there were no thickened and distorted bones in her fingers, no swollen knuckles. She wore no eyeglasses, and Pax doubted that she had resorted to contacts. There was about her a general air of good health, as though she had suffered so much anguish and terror by the age of eleven that, when she'd been borne out of Auschwitz, the exchequer angel that tracked the debts owed by every soul had excused her from paying any serious price for living well into her eighties.

She stepped past the collection of Valiant Girl novels in various languages, to other shelves where she kept the young-adult titles she had written outside that series. From the tightly packed volumes, she extracted the only book she'd written using the nom de plume Halina Berg. It was also her first published work under any name: *Out of the*

Mouth of the Dragon. The jacket art depicted a stylized dragon with human skulls for eyes, but the image was poorly conceived and perhaps quickly executed, unappealing. Although the words A NOVEL, under the title, provided buyer guidance, the work might have been in any of several genres.

"It sold poorly. A disaster. The package didn't say 'buy me,' " Toba noted, "but in truth I didn't have the skill to pull off the story I wanted to tell. It was meant to be a little journey through Hell that would nevertheless be inspiring. The story of a young girl who survived Dachau, overcame the trauma, and built a meaningful life in America."

"Your life," Pogo said.

"Actually, no, dear. But it is fact-based fiction. It spins off from a true story about someone I met in this country after the war. Her name was Arline Blum, but of course I changed it for the novel."

Scanning the front jacket flap, Pax said, "So the heroine's name is Ashley Bell."

"Easier on the American ear," Toba explained.

Pogo was as straightforward as the white line on a highway and as easy to read as a roadside sign. His puzzlement was obvious. "The tattoo on Bibi's arm — ASHLEY BELL WILL LIVE. She did live, but her name was Arline Blum."

"Is the woman still alive?" Pax asked.

"Sadly, no," Toba said. "She died four years ago."

"And Ashley Bell isn't really a person," Pogo said, "she's a character in a novel. So why the tattoo?"

"After that first visit with her mother," Toba said, "when she found out I'd written one novel as Halina Berg, Bibi insisted she had to read it. I told her the book was out of print, and for very good reason. My talent couldn't make good use of that kind of material. I found my métier in jolly adventure fiction for girls. But she charmed a copy out of me."

"Not just adventure fiction for girls," Pax said, because there was an eleven-book series about a Valiant Academy for boys, which he had read when still living on the ranch with his family, long before the idea of becoming a SEAL had taken root in him. "It helped Bibi and me click on the first date — we'd both read Toba Ringelbaum."

"Yes, she told me, and I was tickled. But the boy books didn't sell as well as the series for girls, I'm afraid. Otherwise, I would have written many more." The graceful folds of her well-aged face conspired in an expression of sheer delight, and her brandy-colored eyes brightened. "I found it so very exhilarating to climb into the young male mind, to imagine boys being boys and kicking butt with rollicking good cheer."

"Your girls kick butt, too," Pax said. "That's

675

a big reason Bibi loves those stories."

"Back to my question," Pogo said. "Why the tattoo? Where is Bibi? What is she dreaming? Or not dreaming — but doing? How is Ashley Bell a part of it?"

"Toba?" Pax said as he returned *Out of the Mouth of the Dragon* to her. "Any ideas?"

"There is one thing. One more strange thing." After the old woman shelved that book, she took down another nearby volume. "I didn't have many extras of the American edition, so I gave this one to Bibi, the British version."

Instead of a dragon, the cover featured the face of a beautiful young girl of perhaps twelve or thirteen. Pale-blond hair. Complexion as smooth as bisque porcelain. Remarkable violet eyes. The wide-set eyes, which shone with intelligence, the direct and limpid stare, the planes and curves of the face, and the faint suggestion of defiance in the set of the mouth seemed to reveal an appealing personality, as if in this case appearance and reality were the same.

"When Arline Blum read the manuscript of the novel inspired by her life," Toba explained, "the dear woman liked it more than she should have, considering I didn't do the greatest justice to it. She was always a lovely, generous person. Anyway, the British publisher wanted to have the face of Ashley Bell on the cover, instead of that horrid dragon.

They meant to have an illustrator paint it. I'd seen this photo of Arline when she was a girl, and I thought it perfect. She was agreeable to letting it be used. It was in black-and-white, of course, but the artist used it for reference, and painted the cover in the photorealistic style. I'm sure this is the only reason the British edition sold so much better than the American."

"She's kind of . . . mesmerizing," Pogo said. "Did she grow up to be this beautiful?"

"Yes, indeed. And her heart was more beautiful than her face. Like I said, four years she's been gone. I will always miss her."

As striking as it was, the portrait on the book jacket could not be considered strange.

Pax said, "Toba, we were wondering how — but also why — Bibi might have gotten that tattoo, why Ashley Bell is a part of this. And you said there was 'one more strange thing.' "

"In the novel," Toba said, "Ashley Bell survives Dachau, just as did Arline Blum, and comes to America, as did Arline, and by the early 1970s becomes a successful and highly regarded surgeon, as did Arline. My fiction was too beholden to fact. Modeled on Arline, Ashley Bell in the novel is a surgical oncologist specializing in brain cancer."

116

REALITY AND THE REALTOR

In the west, the sun settled toward the sea, and there were just enough clouds of varied textures to ensure, a quarter of an hour from now, the day would come to its end with a burning sky. As if melting, shadows elongated in the golden light, which would soon be red.

At the window in Room 456, Nancy looked down at the hospital parking lot and didn't like what she saw, didn't like it at all, and turned away. The rows of parked cars reminded her of caskets lined up the way that she had seen them on the news when men killed in war were sent home by the plane-load.

Murph had gone downstairs to the cafeteria to get sandwiches and pasta salads for dinner, which they would eat together in this room. Neither of them wanted to leave until visiting hours were over, and perhaps not even then.

While Murph was getting their dinner, Nancy had decided to bail out of the real-estate business, depending on what happened next. She loved selling houses, helping people who needed new homes, and she was good at it, better at being a Realtor than Murph was at selling surfboards, and he was pretty darned good. But if something happened to Bibi — not just the undefined *something,* face it, if she died — every property in the world would be, to Nancy, haunted. Every house she showed to every prospective buyer would have been a house where Bibi might have lived one day and raised a family with Pax. Every bare lot, waiting for an architect to finish the house design, would be a gravesite waiting for a headstone. Wrung like a rag in the hands of anxiety, that is what she told herself as she paced the room.

Although it sounded as if she might be making a bargain with fate, she wasn't promising to give up her career if only Bibi were allowed to live. There was no point in such dickering. That kind of sentimental gesture made you feel a little better if you were feeling like crap, gave you a sense of control when in fact you had none, but it was meaningless. What would happen would happen. Fate was a bitch; she made no bargains. What Nancy was really saying to herself, by planning to give up real-estate sales, was that losing her daughter so young would surely drain the meaning from her work, her life. But you had to face reality even when reality sucked.

She was standing at the foot of the bed, watching the comatose girl, when dried blood and fresh blood *flew* from Bibi's damaged ear, spattered across the pillowcase, the sheets. As though an invisible presence had clawed open the crusted abrasions, blood dribbled from them again.

117

THE TIDES OF NIGHT

For a hundred feet or so, Bibi made her way through a white-out worthy of an arctic blizzard, a white-out without wind or polar cold, but nonetheless disorienting and fearsome. When the lights of the construction-trailer windows were hardly brighter than the phantom phosphorescence on a just-switched-off TV screen, she took her flashlight from an inside jacket pocket and dared to switch it on.

If they had roaming security guards, she might be seen, but she could not worry about that. Intuition told her, the threats she faced from this point would not be as mundane as rent-a-cops. Since Pogo had brought the Honda to Pet the Cat, since she had set out on this quest, she had gone much farther than the miles on the odometer would attest. She felt as if she had traveled to an unknown country on an undiscovered continent, to the brink of a nameless abyss. There was the known world and the supernatural world that shadowed it, and the veil that had been deteriorating between them now began to dissolve entirely.

Or maybe it was another veil rotting by the moment, a veil between her life as she believed it to have been and her life as it truly had been, between what she was and what she could be. The abyss on the brink of which she stood was the truth.

Her body ached from the beating she had taken at the hands of the man she had killed, and her ear felt as if it were afire. She had left the Tylenol in the car. Didn't matter. The pain would not incapacitate her. It focused her instead, sharpened her senses.

The thick fog resisted the power of light, and the flashlight beam proved a feeble tool. The fog did not only pool and eddy and creep, but also clung to surfaces in a way not foglike. Within the general murk, thicker shrouds grew like moss on tool-storage sheds, on pallets of concrete blocks and stacked crates of cobblestones. It draped backhoes and forklifts and other equipment like sheets thrown over furniture in a house closed for the season.

She became aware of — or imagined — low swift shapes paralleling her in the cloaking mist. They were pale-gray and featureless, as low as dogs or bobcats, but they were neither of those animals, slinkier than dogs and larger than bobcats, larger also than coyotes, wolfish and elusive. She saw no eye shine, and if they were more than shadows of a threat conjured by her mind, they were as silent as spirits.

The property would feel huge in broad daylight; but at night and in this murk, it seemed to be even more immense, a county unto itself. Bibi more sensed than saw the swooping forms of completed and half-finished buildings akin to those in the scale model in the construction trailer. Twice she came upon enormous cranes balanced by massive counterweights, their girdered booms vanishing high into the mist, like fossilized upright carcasses from the Jurassic period.

She moved at a turtle's pace, and the farther east she went toward the back of the property, the more finished the project seemed to be, as if they had begun construction there and worked westward. At times the compacted earth gave way to cobblestone paths, to plazas paved with limestone inlaid with patterns in quartzite and granite, glimpsed through the turbid shifting mist. She circled the raised base of a fountain with a currently dry pool that must have been fifty feet in diameter, from the center of which rose what might have been, had the fog relented, a school of bronze dolphins leaping together, perhaps to spout water when the pool was filled and the pumps were started.

Bibi began to feel as if she had lost her way

in an amorphous maze that foiled her by continually altering the route that would allow it to be successfully navigated, but then she saw lights ahead. They were faint at first, and curious, two measured series of large spheres, the first row perhaps fifteen feet above the ground, the second row about fifteen feet above the first. As they grew slowly brighter, she suspected that they weren't floating spheres, but were instead windows formed like portholes, each six or seven feet in diameter. Her suspicion was confirmed when she drew close enough to make out the muntins that radiated from the center of each window and held the pie-shaped panes in place.

Although she could at first perceive the structure's shape only by inference from the size and placement of the portholes, it had the feeling of a gargantuan vessel. She approached it with a shiver of wonder, as perhaps anyone in 1912 would have, from dockside, looked up with awe at the towering *Titanic.* Even within a few yards of the place, when she determined that it was not a vessel but a building, she could not discern more than a fraction of its details, though she sensed that it was longer than a football field, domed like an airplane hangar, and without windows on the ground floor. Walking alongside the structure, sliding a hand over the curved wall, she decided that it was skinned in metal, and she felt large, regularly placed exterior ribs forged of steel.

By the time she reached one end of the building and found a flat wall, the wolfish stalkers, real or imagined, attended her in greater numbers, as though they had been trained especially to protect this special edifice to which Bibi now sought an entrance. They were shadows of shadows. Surely immaterial. Except, now she heard subtle panting and the tick-click of claws on paving stones. She had the pistol in hand, wet with condensed fog and perhaps with Hoffline-Vorshack's blood, but she had little faith that it would prove effective against the shadow horde — or even against one of them.

A fuzzy reflection of the flashlight flared in a matte-finished steel door, about five feet wide and eight tall, rounded at the top and protected by an overhanging cowl, medieval in spite of the material from which it had been crafted. There was no door handle or anything like a conventional keyhole, nor a slot into which she might insert a key card. The only possible lock release was a large oval hole in the wide steel frame encircling the door.

Bibi stood defeated for a moment but then remembered. From a pocket of her blazer, she withdrew the electronic key attached by a chain to the Lucite fob in which a dead wasp took wing forever.

118
HE CAN FIX ANYTHING.
ALMOST.

The house in Cameo Highlands was to music what Toba Ringelbaum's house was to books. Ganesh Patel, surf legend and audio-video god, had designed, manufactured, and sold a lot of through-house music systems; but in his own home, he had a standalone system in every room. The issues were volume, clarity, and ideal reverberation, and he was always making improvements to his equipment set-ups.

When Pax and Pogo stopped by to get the repaired tape recorder, the living room boomed with music Pax had never heard before. It was Hawaiian sway and steel guitar, it was rockin' piano, it was tied together by backup harmony worthy of Motown, and the lead singer sounded like Elton John if Elton had been born in Nashville and grown up listening to Johnny Cash. But it was good. Their host turned the music down just far enough that they didn't have to shout to hear one another.

"*This* little puppy," Ganesh said, presenting the cassette recorder on the palm of his hand, "was sweet for its time. Plus it made you feel as sly and cool as a spy, how you could conceal it, a microphone that pulled from across the room. Even if you interviewed someone openly, with this puppy on the table, it felt *clandestine.*"

"Could we turn the music down a little more?" Pogo asked.

Ganesh smiled and shook his head. "Not really."

He was thin and dark and intense, perhaps as intense as his paternal grandfather, who as a New Delhi street performer had tamed cobras with the usual flute, but also sometimes with just his hands, caressing them into a stupor at the risk of a lethal bite. Grandpa might or might not have been a snake charmer. He might or might not have stroked and tickled cobras into a trance with his bare hands. There were those who said that Ganesh had been born and raised in Boston, into a family that had run restaurants for three generations, and that the closest he had gotten to India was watching Bollywood musicals in his twelve-seat home theater. With his thick black hair and lean good looks and large, expressive eyes, Ganesh had all the success with women that he could handle, but he was not above tapping his cultural heritage — real and imagined — when he felt that the new beauty who attracted him would respond to an extra layer of exotic personal history. No one, not even the women, took offense at or disapproved of Ganesh's biographical elaborations, because he was unfailingly ebullient and entertaining and likable.

"This old dude on the tape," he said, "was he Bibi's uncle or something?"

"Her grandfather," Pax said. "Nancy's dad."

"Wow. More like Grandpa Munster than Grandpa Walton. Was he an alky or a serious mushroom-eater, or what?"

"He was a retired Marine," Pax said. "Never met him. He died before I showed up. But Bibi loved him. The music is really loud."

"Isn't it great? You can't help moving to it," Ganesh said, jiving in place. "You didn't say not to listen to the tape, so I listened."

"That's all right," Pogo said.

"I thought if it was a little damaged, I could do a transfer and clean up the sound. But it was clear. Clear and crazy. The old dude was flyin' on something, man, higher than Jet Blue could ever take him. He totally creeped me out. I had to put on this music to stop the centipedes crawling through my blood. He must've creeped out Bibi, too. Although it doesn't seem to have screwed her up any. How is our radiant Kaha Huna, by the way?"

Kaha Huna was the mythological Hawaiian goddess of surfing, sand, and sun. Ganesh wasn't being jokey or ironic when he referred to Bibi as a surfing deity.

Pax and Pogo had agreed not to broadcast Bibi's condition in the beach community. Perhaps in acknowledgment of the dread they would not otherwise discuss, they felt superstitiously that the more surfers who knew about her brain cancer and coma, the sooner she would die.

"She's good," Pax said, and Pogo said, "She's cool."

Bobbing his head in agreement but also to the music, Ganesh said, "She's sacy, she's stylin'. For a while I was in love with her from a distance. Maybe I still am. But I always knew I wasn't good enough for her. Are *you* good enough for her, Pax?"

"I'm gonna try to be."

"You better be."

"Thanks for this," Pax said, indicating the tape recorder in his hand. "Appreciate it."

"De nada," Ganesh said. "It was fun taking it apart and putting it back together. Just a knack. I can fix anything." He tapped the recorder. "Except I couldn't have fixed Grandpa Marine. That old dude was a serious head case."

In the Honda once more, putting the key in the ignition but letting the engine rest, Pogo said, "Grandpa Munster?"

"That's just Ganesh being Ganesh."

"I don't think so."

689

"We'll know in a minute." Pax switched on the tape recorder.

They had a good view of the sunset from Cameo Highlands. A magical Maxfield Parrish blue for the base color of the sky. Clouds on fire, orange and scarlet, blazing from San Clemente in the south to Long Beach in the north. The sun balanced on the sea, a fat round bead of blood.

119
THE MAN WHO DIDN'T BELONG THERE

The electronic key fit the oval hole, the wasp in the Lucite glowed like a lamp filament, and the pneumatic steel door whisked open. Because the chamber beyond the threshold had a high positive pressure, a gust of sanitized air blew across Bibi and chased the fog off her shoulders and back. As she stepped inside, none of the wolfish, shadowy stalkers lunged at her, which made her wonder if their purpose was to guard this building or rather to herd her into it if she failed to enter of her own will. Behind her, the door slid shut with a *whoosh*.

She stood in what might have been a reception hall, one designed to intimidate or inspire awe. It was about eighty feet wide, sixty deep, forty high, illuminated by adjustable pot lights recessed in the ceiling, most of which were directed straight down. Every surface was finished in panels of white quartz, which lacked the veining of marble and therefore presented a gleaming and uniform surface with depth. The only decoration appeared in the wall opposite the door: an inlaid twenty-foot-diameter disc of some blood-red stone, perhaps carnelian, which itself was inlaid with two parallel, highly stylized lightning bolts in black granite.

Bibi recognized the lightning as being a version of the double-*S* logo that had appeared on the front-page of *Das Schwarze Korps — The Black Guard* — the official newspaper of the Schutzstaffel, Hitler's chief instrument of terror. The colors of the Nazi flag were boldly represented in this enormous room, although reversed. Instead of red for the field, there was white; instead of a white circle, red; instead of a black swastika, the black double-*S* motif. Whatever use might be intended for this building, Terezin had made only a minimal effort to disguise his inspiration. Perhaps that was because, here in the tumultuous second decade of the new century, frightening numbers of people were either easy to deceive or wished ardently to submit to any belief system, no matter how delusional, that reassured them and justified their hatreds.

Bibi had fallen into a peculiar state of mind. She was afraid but not of this building or anything in it. Not of Terezin, if he were waiting for her in some other room. She was afraid of herself, of some potential in herself that she had long denied but that she might be unable to deny any longer.

She did not fear the bottled and stoppered anger that popped and spilled when she bludgeoned her former teacher with the pistol. Her rage and capacity for violent action were righteous rather than savage. Envy of others and hatred of others because of their race or creed or class were the source of the storms that sometimes destroyed entire civilizations, but they were not the source of her anger. If she raged, it was against barbarism and cruelty, against willful ignorance and arrogance, against the demonizing of one's opposition and the brutalizing of the innocent. She could control even that potent anger born from seventeen years of repressing fundamental knowledge of herself, which had left her with the fear of some act she had committed — and might still commit — but with no knowledge of what the act had been.

Besides rage, however, there was some other potential that she possessed, forgotten but not lost. It was coming back to her. In some way, the quest that she'd been on for two days was as much a search for that repressed truth as it was for Ashley Bell.

The immense white-red-black chamber was unfurnished except for what might have been a reception desk, a great block of midnight-black granite, so high that anyone manning it during an event would have to remain standing. As this object held the greatest interest,

693

she moved toward it. When Bibi had closed to within a few yards of the desk, Chubb Coy rose to his feet behind it. He held a Taser.

She had researched Tasers for her novel. There was the thrust-and-click stun gun with no more range than the length of your arm, and there was the kind that fired two small probes trailing fifteen-foot wires. Coy was armed with the latter. He said, "Damn it all, woman, I don't belong here." Propelled by nitrogen gas, the wire whispered toward Bibi and the probes pierced her T-shirt. The shock mapped her peripheral nervous system and disrupted its messaging along both sensory and motor nerves. Racked by pain, without control of her limbs, she crumpled to the white-quartz floor, stuttering a curse that her tongue could not complete.

120
THE HARD WAY

Bibi couldn't sharply focus on Chubb Coy. She twitched in her private world of pain and motor-nerve confusion, like some broken-back beetle in denial of its fractured shell. But she realized what he must be doing, understood him well enough to know that he was coming around from behind the desk, not done with the Taser, tossing aside the used cartridge, clicking another one into place. She had known him only a short while, but she knew his capacity for malice. She knew him well. Her expectation was at once fulfilled as indigo light bloomed behind her eyes and an alien current razored along radiant neural pathways, chattering her teeth, making her hands flop like the hands of a marionette operated by a drunk puppeteer.

Coy circled as Bibi crabbed on the quartz, leaning toward her and raising his voice. "Do you understand that I don't belong here? Do you get what I'm telling you? Are you going to stubbornly persist with this thread, the

Chubb Coy thread? Is the hard way the only way you can fumble yourself to enlightenment?"

Her eyes were full of tears, squeezed out of her by pain. Before her, the white quartz shimmered as if melting, as if it might have been composed of condensed and petrified fog that was about to return to vapor. Aside from Coy's shoes as he paced around and around her, the only dark object in view, approximately ten feet away, must be her pistol.

If she could get to the gun, she could use it. Pax had taught her how to use it. She was ready to use it now. No more hesitations. Use it not merely to intimidate. Not as a bludgeon. Pull the trigger. Empty the magazine. Kill the bastard.

"So I'm a retired police detective enjoying a second career as head of hospital security. That's logical. Sets me up as being maybe more skilled, more dangerous than your average rent-a-cop. Not bad. Not terribly clever, but credible."

He continued to circle her as she painstakingly dragged herself, shuddering and uncoordinated, inch by inch across a floor shimmering like a frozen sea under the pot lights. At times, the plain of quartz seemed to tilt precariously, so that she feared sliding at increasing velocity until she pitched across some brink, into a melt-smoothed vent flume that would spin her down — she was already dizzy — down into deep and deeper ice caverns.

"From the get-go," Coy said, "my job was to establish the air of conspiracy and paranoia that would thicken and become complicated event by event. But that's about all I was given to do. Except, of course, to be a distraction, to pop up when perhaps your thinking leads you toward the thing you find unthinkable."

The Sig Sauer lay inches away, frozen to the tilted ice field and thus resistant to the gravity that would have sent it spinning away from her. She reached for it with her right hand, which was coming under her control again.

Coy had clicked a third cartridge into the Taser, and he fired it into her back. The probes, which could bite through an inch of clothing, pierced her blazer and T-shirt with no difficulty, serpent fangs injecting a current similar to that of the human body. Techno mavens called it neuromuscular incapacitation, a solemn laboratory term for a total physical freak-out, the baffled brain no longer able to discern the difference between the body's natural signals and the storm of meaningless static, but the effect was more visceral and more emotional than the dry term suggested. With each shock, Bibi was thrown into a cold rushing river of sensation at the same time that she was robbed of any ability to control her reaction to it, and she wondered if with the fourth cartridge or the fifth, she would soil her pants and have the last shreds of dignity stripped from her.

Coy kicked the pistol away from Bibi's spasming fingers. The weapon spun beyond her blurred and salt-stung vision.

"Are you listening to me, woman?" Coy asked, booming at her as if he were a lowercase god of the elements, speaking in the language of thunder, and she were a groveling penitent. "Think about my name. Chubb is as frivolous as Bibi, don't you think? Yeah, sure, I'm being used to distract you, but part of me, just like part of you, wants you to find the truth, to be freed by the truth."

There was a metallic taste in Bibi's mouth, not the familiar coppery flavor of blood — she hadn't bitten her tongue — but more like sucking on rusted iron, and a bitter lump rose in her throat, either vomit or self-pity. Her flesh stiffened even as her bones seemed to have been reduced to jelly, quivering like aspic on a plate.

"I am restricted — *you* have restricted me — to only indirect means of breaking through the stubborn and resistant Bibi, to reach the other Bibi that wants to remember the full truth. And so I try to make you understand what I really am by speaking out of character. *Are you listening to me, Gidget?*"

She thought that she said yes.

"What did you say?"

"Yes."

"Yes, what?"

"I'm listening, yes." She heard the susurrant syllables hissing from her lips and across the quartz. "Yes."

He said, "I tried to make you understand by speaking out of character. Chubb Coy, former homicide detective, not known to have significant interest in the classics of American literature. Jack London, Thornton Wilder, Flannery O'Connor — they all just happen to be among *your* admired pantheon. *Are you listening, Gidget?*"

"Yes," she whispered.

"Listening isn't the same as *hearing,*" he declared, and with the cruel authority of a stone-temple god armed with modern technology, he slammed her with a fourth Taser cartridge.

She didn't black out. She didn't soil her pants, either. But she didn't feel like searching for the lost gun or like doing anything other than lying on the bright griddle of quartz, melting like a pat of butter.

His voice remained stern, but softer than before. "I try to alert you to what I am. You sabotage me, sabotage yourself with the memory trick."

She was looking at his shoes inches from her face. They were Gucci loafers. They should not be Gucci loafers. Too expensive for him. Too effete.

He walked a few circuits around her, saying nothing.

His socks were right. Not fancy designer socks with elaborate patterns. Plain black. A blend of man-made fabrics with just a little cotton. He could have bought them at Walmart, good working-cop socks.

He said, "Would you really rather die than learn the truth of what you are?"

"No."

"What did you say?"

"No. I don't want to die."

"Say it like you mean it."

"I. Don't. Want. To. Die."

After a silence, with pity that had an edge of contempt, he said, "Then prove it by dealing with me."

She was lying prostrate, head turned to the right. The injured left side of her face pressed against the stone floor. Her bleeding ear began to burn and throb again as the chaotic effect of the latest Tasering wore off and coherent messaging returned to her nervous system.

"Proving yourself to yourself doesn't mean you'll survive," Coy said. "You could still easily end up dead. Or insane. But dealing with me is a start. Deal with me."

Lying in the reception hall of a building in which a new world of fascist fury was being designed, she thought about what needed to be done. Editing. Revision.

From behind her came a rustle, a couple of soft thumps. As if some length of drapery had slipped off a rod, though the room had no draperies.

She waited. She listened. She heard nothing more.

When with an effort Bibi sat up and turned her head, she saw Chubb Coy's discarded shoes and clothing, a puddle of fabric in the jumble of which his shoulder holster and pistol and Taser could be seen. He seemed to have disrobed and disarmed and walked off naked, though she had heard no door open or close.

Earlier, in the motel, studying the London, O'Connor, and Wilder quotations, she had begun to realize not only that Chubb Coy had spoken out of character, but also that he *was* a character. One of her creation. The quest for Ashley Bell would have collapsed right there if she had not cut the words from the books and burned them in the bathroom sink, using the memory trick to preserve this world, which was now too fully formed to easily dissolve.

To an observer, she might have appeared defeated as she crawled on her hands and knees to the tall black-granite desk and sat on the floor with her back against its polished-slab front. She had lost her baseball cap. Her hair tumbled in disarray. If her battered face was as pale as her hands, pale almost to ash-gray, she must have looked at once weak and wild.

She was not weak, however, and wild only to the extent that she did not know what jungles waited within her or what powers, native to them, she would soon discover. She was not defeated. But she was in the cold grip of fright.

121
THE CAPTAIN REGRETS

Pax and Pogo stood with Bibi's parents, arrayed around her bed, watching her shudder and twitch under the bedclothes, as her exposed hands, palsied and plucking, seemed to flick something offensive from her fingertips, as though washing through the room were currents of stinging power that only she could feel.

The bizarre display alarmed Nancy to tears, but Murphy withheld the nurse-call button from her. Although no less distressed than his wife, he remained in the thrall of father's intuition, convinced that his daughter was for the moment not in danger, but instead that in essence, in mind and soul, she occupied a mysterious place more real than dreams and safer than the depths of coma.

The shaking and erratic movements subsided, and then faded away completely. She lay quiet and composed. The cardiac monitor, which had recorded a mild increase in her heartbeat, now reported an equally mild decrease. As during the episode, the five brain waves continued pumping at optimal strength and in optimal patterns.

Having heard the contents of the microcassette, Pax and Pogo had more reason than Murphy to believe that his hope was rational. They also had good reason to fear there was a mortal threat to Bibi that came from within herself, that perhaps no other human being had ever faced.

They recounted the salient points of their day. The lockbox and the items in it other than the tape, including the dog collar bearing the name JASPER. The visit to Dr. St. Croix. The reason Bibi had been forced out of the writing program. The panther-and-gazelle notebook, the lines of Bibi's handwriting that appeared before their eyes. The visit to Toba Ringelbaum. The identity of Ashley Bell: a fictional character based on fact, survivor of Dachau, brain-cancer specialist.

Nancy and Murphy were electrified by those discoveries and more than a little mystified, full of questions and keen for answers.

"We don't have all the answers," Pogo said. "But what's on the tape — it comes at you like a fully macking behemoth. Beebs is all we thought she was, but a whole lot more."

Before playing the tape for them, Pax wanted to know about the captain, Gunther Olaf Ericson. Nancy had been estranged from him for much of her life and had only found

a way to let him back into her heart after he had become so important to Bibi. What was it that had come between Nancy and her father, back in the day?

From what little Pax had said upon arrival in Room 456, Nancy was aware that the tape contained an explosive revelation that might forever change her understanding of both her father and her daughter. As she strove to condense a significant portion of her past into a montage of moments, she held fast to one of Bibi's limp hands. Her stare fixed sometimes on the floor, sometimes on the night pressing at the window, and sometimes on Bibi's face, but it darted often to the small tape recorder, which Pax kept in his hand as if it was too precious to put down and risk that it might be knocked to the floor, broken.

Gunther had been a good man, Nancy said. Basically good. He wanted to do the right thing. The problem lay in his priorities. He was perhaps a man who should never have married or, having married, should not have had children, yet he'd had two daughters, Nancy and Edith. A warrior at heart, and for the right reasons — love of country and family — he signed up for one tour of duty after another, making of the Marine Corps not solely a career but also a full life of such intensity that his domestic life as husband and father became pale to him, became like the episodes of a bland television program that he watched from time to time when war and cold war would allow. He loved his wife and his daughters, but he lacked the language of the heart in which that love might be properly expressed. He was fluent in the language of honor and integrity and sacrifice, able to understand men who risked their lives for their country, who would die to protect a comrade in arms. But he couldn't relate as easily to a wife who loved the small things of life, the quiet details in which it was said that you could discern the meaning of existence. Or to the daughters whose temperament was more like their mother's. Anyway, as children, they possessed no awareness of the dangerous nature of the world or of the sacrifices required to keep America safe, to spare them from the horrors and deprivations that so many people in other countries endured as the given nature of existence.

When Nancy's mother died in an accident, Gunther was away at war and didn't get home in time for the funeral. If he understood what his grief-stricken children needed from him, he didn't know how to give it. He seemed to be shaken if not devastated by his loss, but also bewildered, as though he had thought that all risk of death arose from the violence an enemy nation could wreak on his homeland, as if for him such threats as car accidents and house fires and cancer were abstractions, likely only as the consequences of enemy attack. He genuinely believed that a woman's touch was required to raise two girls, and as he didn't intend to remarry — "No one could ever replace your mom" — the woman he had in mind was his dead wife's sister, who did indeed welcome Nancy and Edith into her home.

"I never felt I really knew him," Nancy said, "until he came to live in the apartment over the garage. The way he was with Bibi . . . well, he found the father in himself, once war no longer needed him." Her attention returned once more to the tape recorder in Pax's hand. "You said he left that tape for Bibi. You're sure it's all right for us to listen?"

"It's not only all right," Pax said. "It's essential."

Pogo agreed. "But if a nurse or anyone walks in, we switch it off. It's too big, too radical, too freakin' wild to let it go beyond the four of us."

"If it *ever* goes beyond us — that's not ours to decide. That's Bibi's call," Pax said.

He put the tape recorder on the bed as Nancy and Murphy moved closer. He pressed PLAY. From the small speaker came a tinny but nonetheless impressive version of Captain's voice.

"My sweet girl, dear Bibi, this is my apology if it turns out one is needed. I have had a few years now to think about what I did, and I am less sure than I once was that it was the right

thing. *I am at times eaten by regret. I'm talking about the frightening event that I helped you to forget, but also about the memory trick itself, which you might have forgotten not because you were made to forget it, too, but because children naturally forget so much from their early years. . . ."*

122

BIBI ON THE BRINK

In spite of its brightness, the crypto-fascist atmosphere of the cavernous reception hall so oppressed Bibi that it called to mind a passage of music from Disney's *Fantasia* — "Night on Bald Mountain" by Moussorgsky. Recovering from four Taserings, she sat on the floor, her back against the black-granite desk, half seriously wondering if, when the lights went out, trolls would caper in the dark and ogres rise through the quartz floor from a world below, having ascended to devour the unwary.

She was über-wary. She was alert to the unfathomed dangers of being Bibi Blair. She had edited Chubb Coy out of existence. His clothes and other gear had lingered behind, but they had faded away when she looked steadily at them, as if her stare could function as an eraser. She thought she must be going mad. What *seemed* to have happened *couldn't* have happened. She couldn't eliminate someone by imagining him gone. Since shortly after leaving the hospital two days earlier, since she had allowed Calida Butterfly to seek hidden knowledge on her behalf, Bibi had been aware of supernatural forces at work in the world. But perhaps they had not been supernatural at all. Couldn't they as easily have been the delusions of a deranged mind? If Chubb Coy was so little real as to be vanquished with a mere wish, wasn't it possible that Calida, too, and Hoffline-Vorshack and the tattoo artist and the motel clerk and the nameless thugs and Robert Warren Faulkner — alias Terezin — were likewise no more than phantoms caused by a disorder of the stomach, by an undigested bit of beef, a blot of mustard, a crumb of cheese . . . ? Surely she could eliminate them by imagining them gone — *if* she had imagined them into existence in the first place. Derangement would not necessarily be apparent to the deranged.

Except . . .

Except that her struggle to stay free and alive during the past forty-eight hours, her arduous quest, and the search for Ashley Bell had been real enough, excruciatingly actual, verifiable by the myriad pains in her muscles and joints. By the hot throbbing ache in her torn and half-crushed ear. By the alternately recurring and receding pain in her jaw, a paroxysm that flared into higher waves when she clenched her teeth or touched her bruised face. If she couldn't edit away her pain, then the people who had inflicted it — and the person whom they served, their mother-killing cult leader — had to have been real, as well. *Didn't* they?

If Robert Warren Faulkner was a figment of her imagination, so was Terezin, and so was Terezin, Inc. If such a corporation did not exist, the building in which she sat did not exist, either, other than in her fevered imagination. Studying the acre of white quartz dazzling all around her, she tried to edit the structure out of existence, strove to revise recent events backward to the moment when she parked the Honda along Sonomire Way, before she ventured onto the property and encountered Marissa Hoffline-Vorshack. But the reception hall and the building that contained it did not dissolve.

Bibi wasn't certain if the seeming permanence of the building confirmed its reality or if, in her stubborn insistence on the reality of Terezin, Inc., she resisted editing the place out of the narrative. Regarding the rules of its delusions, a deranged mind was not likely to be consistent.

Adding to her confusion, further testing her sanity, she heard Captain speaking to her. The voice flowed into the reception hall as if from a public-address system, but it must be entirely in her head, remembered or imagined.

"My sweet girl, dear Bibi, this is my apology if it turns out one is needed. I have had a few years . . ."

She couldn't listen to this. Captain was dead. He had been dead for more than twelve years. In the months after his aneurysm, she had wanted him back. She had desperately wanted him to be alive again. She had been wrong to want such a thing. If she was unconsciously calling him back, his return would be no more right now than it would have been then.

". . . talking about the frightening event that I helped you to forget, but also . . ."

She refused to listen. By listening, she would begin wanting him back. She could not want him back. Dared not. Long ago, hadn't she learned why not? Hadn't she?

She struggled to her feet, leaning for a moment against the black-granite desk. Then she set off across the white quartz toward a distant dark object that could be nothing other than her pistol.

The captain seemed to think she might have forgotten about the memory trick. He began to tell her how it was done.

She reached the pistol and picked it up and turned in a circle, surveying the enormous room, wondering what to do now. Who would come after her next?

The captain kept talking. She could see his face clearly in her mind's eye. His smile. How much better things would be if Captain were alive. *No.*

Room 456. Five ideal wave conditions on the EEG. Bibi walking the board somewhere. The four witnesses around the bed. The girl not sleeping, not awake, yet also both of those things, lying in the bed, existing as well in a mysterious Elsewhere.

From the tape recorder, the captain spoke first about the memory trick, but not about why he'd used it. Nancy's face hardened perhaps with some of the resentment that had embittered her in the days when, as a child herself, she had felt abandoned by him. "What is he saying . . . that he *brainwashed* her?"

"It may have been a mistake," Pax said, "but he had a reason that seemed good to him. Listen."

He knew that the next revelation would incense both Nancy and Murphy, but the greater shock would come when the captain revealed what it was that he helped the girl to forget.

"The memory trick worked so well not because I got it from a Gypsy or a hundred-year-old shaman, or from any place magical, like I made it sound. It worked because it was developed by a lot of smart people in the intelligence community, a defense against interrogation by the

enemy. Once you were hypnotized and made to believe that the memory trick worked, it would work the rest of your life, whenever you needed to wipe something from your memory."

Murphy's tan had acquired a gray cast. "He *hypnotized* her?"

"Listen," Pax said.

"This next part is a little tough for me, Bibi. It sounds worse than it is. But I knew it wouldn't harm you in any way. See, sweetie, the hypnotism works so well to support the memory trick because the hypnotism itself is supported by a drug that puts the subject — in this case, you — in a state highly receptive to hypnotic suggestion. The night I taught you the memory trick, your mom and dad were out for the evening at a concert. We had dinner in their kitchen. Chili-cheese dogs and oven-baked fries. After dinner and before we had Eskimo Pies, I taught you the memory trick. The drug I mentioned was in your Coca-Cola."

Such outrage fired Nancy's face, Pax thought she might grab the recorder and throw it. He shielded it with one hand. *"Just listen."*

". . . your mom and dad were out for the evening at a concert . . ."

The voice wouldn't stop. Bibi couldn't keep it out because it came from within her. The longer that she listened, the warmer the voice

714

sounded, the more clearly she remembered Captain, how he had protected her. She had felt safe with Captain living above the garage and looking down on the bungalow, where her bedroom window faced the courtyard, Captain up there keeping a watch over her.

Bibi found herself behind the black-granite desk without quite knowing how she'd gotten there. Two tall stools would allow security men or receptionists to work at the desk. She occupied neither stool. Somehow she had retreated into the kneehole. Like a child seeking a refuge. A hiding place.

The captain said, *"I don't know what I might have done. I mean, how having a big hole in your memory might affect you over time. Too late I realized maybe there might be some . . . disruption of a child's psychological development. Using the memory trick when you're a grown man, that's different, your personality is formed. But what if . . . God help me, I hope nothing happens. Anyway, I don't see how you could have lived and had a normal life with that memory . . . more than memory . . . with that knowledge of what had happened, of what you could do."*

Bibi realized that the moment was approaching when she would learn the central truth of the half-recovered memory, the identity of the intruder — the *thing* — in her bedroom when she was five years old. She tried to shrink farther back into the kneehole as dread overcame her, a double dread born of the fact that it was Captain making this revelation. If her imagination were inspired to a bright and terrible creativity, maybe both he and the bedroom thing would be conjured here tonight, to prowl the reception hall for the one hiding place that it provided. And what the hell did *that* mean? Conjured? She was no witch.

"Six months after I came to live in the apartment, eight months after your terrifying experience, you finally trusted me enough to tell me about it. You felt you couldn't tell your mom and dad, that they wouldn't . . . well, wouldn't understand. Whether that was right or wrong . . . it seemed that forgetting was for the best. And there I was with a way to make forgetting possible. A coincidence? I've never believed in them. And knowing the kind of girl you are, how fast you're growing up — I mean, in mind and heart, so wise for one so young — I suspect eventually you also won't believe in coincidences. Anyway, you told me your colorful, very wild and dark story, and stupidly, in the way that unimaginative adults can be stupid when they've long lost their sense of wonder, I tried to dismiss it as just a bad dream. So you proved it to me. No experience in war ever so terrified me as what happened there in my apartment kitchen. The purpose of this tape, which I will tell you when I give it to you, is to serve as . . . I don't know . . . as some kind of restoration of the way things might have been, as some kind of therapy for you if it turns out I was foolish, even reckless, to help you forget what you had done, what you could do, if I was a damn fool to teach you the memory trick."

In the recess under the desk, Bibi wept for the captain, that he had suffered regret and worried about having harmed her, when in fact his coming to live above the garage had been a great blessing. This freshening of grief to no extent displaced her fear. She felt sorrow and terror in equal measure. And though she told herself that Valiant girls did not hide from anything, that they stood up and in the open, facing threats forthrightly, she remained in the shadowed kneehole, sitting with her knees drawn up to her chest, arms wrapped around her legs, and let out a thin sound of distress when, from out of the past, Captain's voice came to her with revelations.

123

A MOMENT IN HER LIFE
WITH BOOKS

Bibi loved the book as much as her mother had promised that she would, as much as her mother, too, had loved it when she was a little girl. *Cookie's Big Adventure.* Words and pictures. Bibi had graduated to books with more words a year earlier, and recently had been able to read them all by herself, without her mother narrating. She took pride in her ability to read at a level beyond her years.

Cookie, who was a gingerbread cookie in the shape of a man, with chocolate-drop eyes and a white-icing smile, was the best character in any book that she had yet to read. He was funny and cute and eager for adventure. Cookie came to life after being baked, while cooling on the baker's tray, though *why* was a mystery; the author didn't say. Cookie wasn't brittle, didn't break apart easily, as you might think he would. He was supple, strong, and quick. He remained gingerbread through and through, but there was magic in him, like in Frosty the Snowman.

When Cookie left the bakery and found

himself in a busy city, he was so happy to explore and discover and learn. He had scary moments, when a truck almost ran over him, almost smashed him to pieces, and when a hungry dog chased him. But for the most part, his adventures were exciting in a good way, and hilarious.

In the week since her mother had given her the book, Bibi must have read it a thousand times, maybe two thousand, she didn't count. Cookie sort of became her best friend. She didn't easily make friends her age. The kids in preschool were mostly boring. Aunt Edith and a few other relatives thought Bibi was *different.* She'd overheard them saying so to her mother. She didn't know what they meant, how she was different, and she didn't really care. If anyone had asked her, Bibi would have said that those same relatives seemed strange to her, and she could no more explain why they were strange than they seemed to be able to explain why they found her different. Then into her life came the amazing Cookie, who was different, too, with a brave heart and a daring spirit, much as Bibi wished herself to be. Cookie and Bibi, best friends forever.

Between readings of the book, Bibi some-times made up stories of her own about Cookie, his further adventures. She couldn't draw well. She didn't attempt to sketch his exploits. But she could see them vividly in her mind, in color, full of lively action, like waking dreams.

On this evening, after being put to bed and kissed goodnight, Bibi sat up again to read *Cookie's Big Adventure* several times, by the soft light of her bedside lamp, while the muffled voices and music of the TV came to her from the living room. Maybe she dozed off, the book hugged to her chest, because when she scooched up from the pile of pillows into which she had slid, the house was quiet. Her parents had gone to sleep.

She sat for a while, looking at her favorite picture of Cookie and talking to him as if he were indeed her friend and capable of listening, caring. She told him that she wished he would come to life for her, the way that he had come to life in the wonderful story, and she really did wish it, want it, need it. She could so clearly see him rising from the page of the book as he had risen from the baker's tray before setting out into the city.

When the incident began, it was pure Disney. But not for long. Cookie didn't at once spring from the book and stand before her, tada, arms spread, sparkling with sugar or fairy dust. He didn't speak to her in a cartoon voice. No, at first he turned his head slightly in the illustration, as if to assess Bibi more directly. She wasn't even sure it happened, that sly turn of his head. Then Cookie winked, and Bibi's eyes widened. Cookie's smile curved into a lopsided grin. Bibi's mouth formed an *O* of amazement; she let out the word "Oh," and gasped it back in. This wasn't an interactive book. The illustrations weren't holograms that changed depending on the angle at which they were viewed. Suddenly Cookie turned three-dimensional, while the rest of the illustration remained as it had been, and he began trying to extract himself from the two-dimensional image, which was when it wasn't quite so much a Disney moment anymore.

Bibi flung the book off the bed, to the floor, where it landed spine-up, standing like a tent, its fanned pages thrashing as the gingerbread man struggled to be born from them. She knelt on the mattress to watch, wondering but also fearing a little, perversely delighted but somewhat alarmed, transfixed by the sight of the book when it began to clatter this way and that across the floor, as if it were the A-frame shell of a large exotic bug.

Cookie was kind and funny and wouldn't harm even the hungry dog that had wanted to eat him. Nothing bad ever happened to the children in the books that Bibi read; those kids went on great adventures with talking animals, with elves and fairies, with favorite toys come to life and silly creatures from other planets, but nothing harmed them. When Cookie was finished pulling himself from the book, he would be like Winnie-the-

Pooh, and she would be like Christopher Robin, and they would be the best of friends. Most likely. But . . . But there was something about Cookie's lopsided smile that disturbed her. He had winked at her with one glossy chocolate eye, and that had been okay. The wink had seemed friendly, like sharing a little joke. But the smile made her think maybe they wouldn't be best friends forever.

The book fell over, flopped open on the floor. The gingerbread man rose from the pages, which beat around him like furious wings. He crawled out of the book, dark and strange and not much like the happy-go-lucky Cookie. He . . . No, *it*. It was not well formed, a lumpy and distorted figure, which staggered to its stumpy feet with effort. Not thin like a cookie but inches thick, six or eight inches tall. Twitching, jerking, graceless. It seemed to be tormented, white lips opening wide in what might have been a silent scream, rolling its misshapen head side to side, pulling at its flesh with mittenlike hands.

Flesh. Even from a distance of eight or ten feet, Bibi could see that this thing was not made of gingerbread. In the book, Cookie was made of gingerbread dough, rolled and shaped and baked. Of course that was silly. Even though she loved the story, Bibi had known that part was totally silly. That's why magic was needed, a little Frosty the Snowman magic, to make Cookie supple, strong, and quick. Bibi didn't know any magic. When she wished Cookie alive, she thought of him — if she thought at all about this part of his manifestation — as some kind of gingerbread animal, but what she got was all animal. Or it was less than an animal, elemental and primitive, as if a rotting mass of plant and animal tissue in a swamp had been lightning-struck and thereby animated with something less than life itself.

Still silently screaming, the thing picked up the book, which was bigger than itself, and flung it at Bibi. The whirling volume missed her but clattered against the bedside lamp, switching it off and knocking the shade askew.

Bibi would have fled if the minikin that she had wished into existence hadn't been standing between her and the door. The only illumination came from the Mickey Mouse night-light her parents had recently installed, which until now she had found embarrassing, which she had plotted to dispose of one way or another. She was a child, yes, but not a baby in need of a night-light. She was years past being a baby. As the thing on the floor hitched out of the Mickey glow, disappearing in the shadows, Bibi didn't want to scream for help, like a baby. Maybe she couldn't have cried out even if she'd wanted to, because her hard-knocking heart seemed to have risen into her throat, so that she couldn't easily swallow, and when she tried to say *Go away* to the minikin, no sound escaped her except a thin and tremulous wheeze.

Besides, if her mom and dad came running, maybe they wouldn't be able to see the thing. In stories, kids were often able to see elves and fairies and all kinds of creatures that grown-ups couldn't see because grown-ups didn't believe in them. Then she would seem like a big baby, and they would never stop treating her like one. Worse, the thing from the book, the terrible not-Cookie, might hurt them. It was small, evidently toothless, but it was strong for its size, considering how it flung the book. If they were hurt, the fault would lie with Bibi. They would say it wasn't her fault, "It'll be what it'll be," but she knew the truth was that it would be because she had made it be.

Kneeling on the bed, she listened to the thing creeping around the room. Judging by the way it thumped and scraped and squished, she decided it was even slower and clumsier than it had first appeared to be. There was no magic in it. Maybe it was blind. It seemed unable to scream or speak, so possibly it couldn't hear, either. Or smell. If the only thing it could do was fumble along the baseboard, it could only find her by chance. If it wanted to find her at all. Maybe it didn't have a brain. Maybe it wasn't able to want anything, just a stupid lump of twitching stuff.

Although her heart raced as fast as ever and seemed to pinball off her ribs even as it jumped into her throat, Bibi told herself that if she had wished the creature to come out of the book, she could wish it away just as easily. In fact that was what she had to do. Dispatching it was her duty. Her responsibility.

She slid under the covers once more, half sitting up against the pile of pillows, and she thought hard about the not-Cookie, picturing it crawling back to the book on the floor, slithering in among the pages, melting away into the illustration from which it had arisen. For almost an hour, there were silences periodically broken by new spasms from the creature. She was dry-mouthed and dizzy with wishing, with *imagining.* When eventually the horrid thing fell into a longer silence, she assumed that she had at last succeeded. She lay stone-still, listening. Second by second, minute by minute, she became more encouraged, though if her heart thumped not quite so fast as before, it beat harder.

Yet again the quiet ended. The thing scrabbled along a nearby wall. The lamp cord rattled against the back of the nightstand. If not by any of the usual five senses, the grisly little beast seemed to be finding its way to her by a sixth. She expected it to ascend to the top of the nightstand, two feet from her face. Then it moved under the bed and became quiet once more.

She had been wrong about it being brainless. It could think, all right. Think and know and want and seek. In the silence of the room, the only sound was within Bibi, the frantic pump in her breast, which beat her into a strange submission, into a kind of paralysis. But she could almost hear, too, the creature scheming in the darkness under the box spring.

She would never know how it progressed from beneath the bed and under the covers without her hearing it or sensing its movement. When it touched her bare foot, she threw aside the blanket and the top sheet, her scream no more than a dry whistle in her throat.

So it came to this. The confrontation of creator and created. In the dim light of the five-watt Mickey lamp, Bibi bending forward, seizing the thing with both hands, peeling it off her ankle. Cold but not slimy. Throbbing irregularly. Torsional. Difficult to hold. Her heart booming, quaking her entire body, breath fast and shallow and ragged, she wished it away, wished so hard that a headache split her skull, her ears popped as though from a change in air pressure, and a capillary burst in her nose, unraveling a thread of blood out of her left nostril. Yet the would-be best friend escaped her grip, twisting and flopping up her chest, toward her head. They were face-to-face when she seized it again, and the chocolate-drop eyes were not gentle or kind or chocolate, but wet holes in which pooled some thick, oily substance that she thought must be all the hatred in the world boiled down to just two spoonfuls. Openmouthed, the thing bent its flat face closer, closer, as if to suck out her breath of life. Migraine sawing through her skull, a blood haze tinting her vision, Bibi dug her fingers into the creature's yielding flesh and did not wish it away anymore, but *commanded* it to be gone, this abomination that she had imagined into existence. To emphasize her authority, she punctuated her command by spitting upon the thing. It relented, and as it stopped struggling and diminished in her hands, she heard the pages of the book thrashing somewhere in the gloom, as the thing that was not Cookie nevertheless returned to Cookie's world. When Bibi's hands were empty, the book gave out one last rustle, and a hush fell upon the room.

When she could find the strength to reach toward the nightstand lamp, she switched it on. The light was glorious. She wished morning would come to the window hours ahead of schedule. Just then, there could not be too much light. She leaned back against the pillows and the headboard. Blood trickled from one nostril, tears from both eyes. She thought she would throw up. She didn't. She thought her heart would never stop sledgehammering, but it returned slowly to a more gentle beat. For a long time she sat in a kind of catatonia, not because she couldn't move or speak, but because she didn't want to move or speak, wondering — worrying about — what new thing might be called into the world by a thoughtless gesture or one wrong word.

In time she slept.

Morning came.

She woke. She showered. She ate breakfast.

She was quieter than usual, which her parents noted, but her mind was racing as always, bobbin and spindle and flyer working at high speed, spinning wooly thoughts into taut threads, into ideas and speculations. Before her sixth birthday, her life had changed dramatically, irrevocably, and there was nothing to be done other than to accept what she was now. And be cautious. Never again wish into the world something that was not natural to it. Stories were good. They made life better, happier. But stories should remain between the covers of a book.

124

THE CAPTAIN AND HIS ALBATROSS

Pax stood watching numbers roll up on the tape counter and the twin hubs turning as tape moved through the guide rollers. He didn't listen as closely to the captain's words as did Murphy and Nancy, for he'd heard them in the car with Pogo and would never forget them. As the magnetized strip of acetate spooled from reel to reel, paying out the past, he felt it pulling him toward the future. He wondered, with a reverent awe but also with some apprehension, what the years ahead with Bibi would be like, this remarkable woman, if she survived to share her life with him.

During Captain's account, Room 456 seemed to emerge from the building in which it had been located, like a bubble from a bubble-blower's loop, becoming a world unto itself, afloat, so that if one were to open the door, no hospital corridor would wait beyond, but instead an intolerable nothingness. His voice grew as mesmerizing as the drug that he'd put in young Bibi's Coca-Cola. In spite of the outlandish nature of the story he told, none in his audience of four expressed disbelief, because they knew now of other instances when Bibi's imagination had shaped her life for better (Jasper, who was renamed Olaf) or worse (the writing assignment for Dr. Solange St. Croix). At one point, Nancy needed a chair, and Murphy brought one bedside for her. Throughout, the girl lay apparently insensate to this world, living in a different one of her vivid imagining.

After recalling for Bibi the incident in her bedroom, which he had helped her to forget, the captain recounted how she had brought the creature out of the storybook again, this time in the kitchen of his apartment above the garage, to prove the truth of her claim. That experience had been terrifying for both of them, though less so for Bibi, because she had once vanquished the thing and knew that she had power over it.

Speaking now from the cassette recorder as from the grave, the captain said, *"Bibi, considering that you lived with that secret for eight months before you shared it with me, and considering that you were haunted by what had happened and were fearful of what you might unwittingly conjure up next, I still think the best solution was the memory trick. There are no coincidences. I came into your life with the knowledge necessary to heal you, protect you, and I believe that I was meant to do just that."*

Getting up from her chair, as if her father stood in the room to be confronted, Nancy said, "Drugs, hypnosis, *brainwashing?*" But then she seemed to resign herself to the situation as it was and sat once more, still weak-kneed, as the captain continued.

"You have such a powerful imagination, so colorful and detailed and . . . deep. In time I saw it was a gift. An extraordinary gift. I think you're born to tell stories, Bibi. That's a wonderful thing. I've read more truth in fiction than in nonfiction, partly because fiction can deal with the numinous, and nonfiction rarely does. The human heart and spirit. The unknown. The unknowable. Storytelling can heal broken hearts and damaged minds. As a writer, Bibi, you could be a doctor of the soul. I began to worry that, with the memory trick, I stole from you part of your precious gift, denied you the chance to control it and to become all that you might be. So I began collecting quotations from famous writers, their thoughts about the great value of imagination. A foolish exercise? God, I hope not. Over the years, as I'm sure you remember, we talked a lot about those quotations, and in my fumbling way, I tried to make sure that you would develop your gift, that the knowledge lost to you regarding the full extent of your talent, the knowledge burned away with the memory

731

trick, would not prevent you from becoming all that you could be."

125

IN A WORLD OF
HER OWN MAKING

". . . in my fumbling way, I tried to make sure you would develop your gift, that the knowledge lost to you regarding the full extent of your talent . . . would not prevent you from becoming all that you could be."

Bibi had crawled out of the kneehole. She stood in the reception hall, a small figure in the vastness of white quartz, staring up at the circle of red stone and the two stylized lightning bolts centered in it.

Over the years, she had been troubled by a repetitive nightmare in which two robed and hooded figures, tall and shambling, deformed in limbs and spines, had carried a corpse wrapped in a shroud. Under a Cheshire moon, they brought the dead man through the brick-paved courtyard behind the bungalow, as she watched them from a window, terrified by their intent. They were, of course, returning Captain to the apartment above the garage, where he had died.

How strange the mind is, she thought now.

How it shrouds from itself some of its darker capacities.

In the dream, one of the transporters of the dead became aware of her and turned its hooded head toward her bedroom window. Just then the night always brightened, and she could see the countenance of Death for a moment before he turned away. That glimpse frightened her to such an extent, she did not — could not, would not — carry the image with her when she woke. But now she remembered: Within the hood had been not a stripped-bare skull, not a rotting countenance acrawl with worms and beetles, but only her face, pale and set in a look of grim determination. Hooded Death hadn't brought the captain home from the grave. Ten-year-old Bibi, his loving granddaughter — *she* wanted so badly to resurrect him. Dreaming, she'd intuited the formidable power of her imagination, of which she'd no recollection when awake, the knowledge having been burned away.

For all his doubts, Captain had been right to use the memory trick. In spite of the hideous experience with the gingerbread man, she would not have been able to resist the compulsion to bring the captain back. In fact, she understood now that in the weeks following his death, while visiting his apartment, she had unwittingly brought him out of the grave more than once, in the condition of an animated corpse, had brought him back and sent him away without any conscious awareness of what she was doing. The footsteps in other rooms. The wet blood dripping off his bedroom doorknob. The ominous presence in the apartment attic, which stepped out of shadow into light. Those had been brief, half-realized resurrections. Had she been aware that she could effect his return with her imagination, she would have brought him back in full, and the horror of what she'd done would have destroyed her.

When the golden retriever, Olaf, had died six years after her grandfather's passing, the memory trick must have begun to fail. Captain had been wrong to believe that traumatic experiences were burned away forever. They were instead flushed into a deep memory hole, there to fester until some stressful circumstance drew them toward the surface. Bibi had wanted to witness the dog's cremation, to be sure that he had been reduced to ashes, and she had not kept a twist of his fur, as she had kept the lock of hair and scrap of scalp from the captain's body. Whether consciously or unconsciously, she had been afraid that she would bring him back, imagine him with her again. Inevitably, he would have been a strange and menacing version of the dog she had loved. In spite of Olaf being only an urn full of ashes, she had yearned for reanimation. After spending three days locked in her room alone, struggling against the reckless love that would have led to resurrection, she had in desperation used the memory trick once more.

As Pax switched off the recorder and picked it up from the bed, Bibi opened her eyes.

He breathed her name, but she did not look directly at him.

Her gaze traveled right to left, left to right, alighting on no one, taking in everyone and everything — or nothing. She closed her eyes and remained unresponsive.

When Bibi turned from the red circle and the black bolts of lightning, the immense white reception hall and another white room had for a moment been integrated. Ten feet away stood a hospital bed, an array of associated monitors, an IV drip. Nancy, Murphy, Pogo, and beautiful Paxton were gathered around the bed, their attention focused on the patient, who was Bibi herself.

She understood at once what this vision meant, that it was not in fact a vision in the paranormal sense, that it was the truth of her condition, a revelation made by herself to herself, inspired by the captain speaking from beyond the grave. She was not surprised that she existed in two worlds simultaneously, and in two conditions. In the deepest recesses of mind and heart, she had known all along, but she had required this second narrative in order to rescue herself in the first. She had needed to break the hold of the memory trick, discover again the extraordinary power of her imagination, and use it to restore herself to health.

The one medicine that had always relieved her pain and healed her sorrow had been stories, reading them and writing them. She knew no other effective therapy.

The hospital vignette faded into the other world, other life.

A fleeting image rose in memory: herself at six, with Captain in the bungalow kitchen, holding an index card in steel tongs, the white cardstock suddenly on fire, a butterfly of flame flexing its wings, butterflies bright and beautiful in the captain's eyes. . . .

If the past could ever truly be past, she had at last put it behind her. The future was now where all threats lay, and she had no option but to meet them in the world where she was lying in a hospital room, watched and monitored, as well as in this world of her own making.

As she had recognized earlier in the night, when she'd yearned for Pax to find her, she was not dreaming. The shapen world of her extraordinary imagination was as solid as the quartz under her feet, as real as the hot pain that coruscated through the turnings of her damaged ear and throbbed in her bruised face.

This place lay between Heaven and Earth, and where she would wind up at the conclusion of her quest could not be imagined. It had to be achieved.

In spite of all her power, here in a world of her creation, she was not immortal any more than in the first world. She was not a god, merely a gifted imaginer. A shot to the head would put an end to her and all that she had imagined. If she died here, she died also in the world where she'd been born. And she was not confident about her chances.

From her shoulder holster, she drew the pistol. Considered it for a moment. Then put it down on the black-granite reception desk.

One enemy remained. In this world as in the one where she had been born, the ultimate enemy couldn't be dispatched with violence.

In the wall behind the desk, three doors were paneled with the same white quartz that surrounded them. She chose the middle of the three, which stood under the red-and-black symbol of totalitarian power. Beyond the door lay a hallway that she followed to an elevator alcove. When she pressed the call button, one of six sets of doors slid open, and she boarded that car. According to the car-station panel, there were four above-ground floors and a basement. The 4 lit without her touch, the doors slid shut, and she was whisked upward.

In this world of her invention, she had imagined other people with power, and none more than he into whose lair she now ventured. She thought of Kelsey Faulkner, the silversmith and father of this man, half his face handsome, the other half ruined. She thought of Kelsey's wife, Beth, mother of the man now awaiting her, raped by her own son, stabbed twenty-three times, acid poured on her face. He took their money, unspecified items of value, and set out upon a new life, that teenage boy obsessed with Hitler and the occult.

In the end, after Bibi had endured four Taserings, once she had understood that she possessed the power, Chubb Coy had been easily edited away, his role truncated to five appearances. But he had been a minor character and rather poorly imagined, with no past other than a reference to having been a police detective. By contrast, Robert Warren Faulkner, alias Birkenau Terezin, had a vivid and twisted past, a violent pathology that made him memorable. Besides, since this had begun, all the others who obstructed her were either members of Terezin's cult or in some way allied with him, which made him the spider at the center of the web, the primary antagonist. She could not edit him from existence without collapsing this entire imagined world. Only the most formulaic authors always knew when they began a story what the fate of their lead would be. When writing organically, allowing characters their free will, the author could be surprised by who died and who lived in the final act.

The elevator arrived at the fourth floor. She stepped out of the alcove into a wide, dimly lighted corridor with closed offices on both sides. At the farther end, a door stood open. The light beyond shone somewhat brighter. She walked toward it.

She was afraid but not frozen by her fear. Wary, heedful, and prudent, yes, because Valiant girls were always wary, heedful, and prudent. She had come here to save the life of Ashley Bell, and she realized now that somehow, if she accomplished that, she would also save herself from the death by cancer that threatened her in the world that was not of her imagination, though she didn't understand why this should be so. If she failed Ashley Bell, she failed herself.

Beyond the open door lay a very long room with a barrel-vaulted ceiling thirty feet high and walls curving to the floor. Olympian. Not human in scale. Reminiscent of designs by Hitler's favorite architect, Albert Speer. The ceiling and walls were paneled in light cherrywood finished with multiple coats of lacquer, glossy, with the depth of colored crystal, softly but dramatically lit by gold-leafed wall sconces that cast narrow fans of light both up and down. Here were the windows that Bibi earlier had thought were glowing spheres, mysteriously hovering in the fog, seven-foot-diameter portholes, concave from this side, the panes captured in bronze muntins. Along the center of the wide chamber, the polished black-granite floor did not reflect any of the wall lights, and Bibi felt almost as if deep space lay underfoot, an interplanetary void where she walked without the pull of gravity.

At the farther end of the room, before a wall hung with a tapestry replicating the red circle and black lightning bolts first seen in the reception hall, was an immense stainless-steel-and-black-granite desk unsuited to anyone but a mythic figure. If behind it had waited the Minotaur, with a human body and the head of a bull, or a horned mongrel as much goat as man, or some beast with furled wings and luminous green eyes, the desk and its owner would have been properly matched.

Instead, waiting for her was a tall athletic man in a slim-cut black suit of superb tailoring, a white shirt, and a black necktie, with a red display handkerchief in his breast pocket. Seventeen years later, he was recognizable as the boy of sixteen who murdered his mother and left his disfigured father for dead. He still parted his coal-black hair severely and combed it to the left across his brow, though anyone unaware of his obsession with the

741

Third Reich would not interpret the style as an homage to Hitler.

To an extent, his good looks would insulate him from suspicion, for in this new century, image trumped substance and appearance often mattered more than truth. He had been a handsome boy, and he'd become a man with movie-star features and a glamorous aura. Hitler and most of the Nazi party hierarchy had been unattractive men, doughy and chinless like Himmler or brutish like Hess and Bormann, in some cases even macabre, and yet they had led a great nation into hell on earth and a world into chaos and destruction. Had they looked like this Terezin creature, perhaps they would have enraptured even more true believers and would have triumphed.

As Bibi approached, the elegant murderer came out from behind his desk and stood beside an office chair in which sat a young girl, her back to Bibi. The lustrous, champagne-blond hair was like that of Ashley Bell in the photograph found at Calida's house.

To Terezin, Bibi said, "Why do totalitarians — communists and fascists alike — favor the colors black and red?"

The timbre of his voice, a masculine resonance halfway between bass and tenor, was a weapon as useful as his good looks. "Black for death, the power of life and death. Red

742

for the blood of those who won't respect that power. Or maybe it's because they're the colors of the roulette wheel, the colors of fate. Our fate is to rule, your fate is to be ruled. We are agents of fate, enforcing its dictates."

"What a load of horseshit," Bibi said, stopping ten feet from him.

"Yes, isn't it? But, lovely Bibi, horseshit is the preferred language of our times."

He swiveled the office chair, turning his captive into view. Ashley Bell's right wrist was handcuffed to the arm of the chair.

"The girl you named by divination," Terezin said, "spelled out with Scrabble tiles."

"I'll take her from you now," Bibi assured him.

The long blade flicked from the knife that she had not been aware he held. He put the razor-sharp cutting edge to Ashley's throat.

In the creation of this quest, there had been two authors: the Bibi Blair who wrote fiction and thought she understood herself, and another Bibi Blair, the shadow Bibi with paranormal talent, who was cloaked from her twin by the memory trick. For both of them, the one medicine that had always relieved their pain and healed their sorrow had been stories. In the creation of the search for Ashley Bell, Bibi had sought the full truth of herself, because the truth included the power to edit some things in the real world as she could edit them here — the power to edit away her cancer. But Shadow Bibi had been determined to keep the knowledge of that power in the memory hole where Captain had sunk it, because it was the cause of the greatest traumas of her life. To prevent Bibi from realizing that her real adversary was her alter ego, Shadow Bibi had to invent an antagonist, Terezin, who seemed to be her only enemy. But now Bibi and Shadow Bibi were one, united by the collapse of Captain's trick, by the restoration of memory. An antagonist was no longer needed.

Lightly sawing the flat of the blade, not the cutting edge, back and forth across the child's throat, Terezin said, "If I kill her, I kill you."

For a moment, Bibi didn't fully process that statement, didn't realize what it meant that Terezin should know such a thing. She was intent upon the need to edit him out of this world of her shaping, applying her metaphorical eraser to him as she had applied it to Chubb Coy.

He smiled and shook his head. "That won't work, lovely Bibi. And if you think about it, you'll know why."

126

THE DANGEROUS ART

As she sensed the story slipping out of her control, Bibi felt oppressed, claustrophobic. The architecture supported that reaction. The long cylindrical room and porthole windows suggested a vessel, a submarine, fog churning like a murky sea at the wedges of bronze-framed glass. Indeed, considering the grandness of this chamber and the megalomania expressed in its every detail, the vessel could only have been Jules Verne's *Nautilus,* and Terezin a stand-in for Captain Nemo with a measure of Ahab.

He had said, *If I kill her, I kill you.*

The meaning of his words suddenly detonated, and Bibi stood shaken as if by a psychic concussion wave. He knew the true purpose of her quest: to save herself, to free herself of cancer by some as yet not fully understood interaction with Ashley Bell. But if he was only a character of her creation, devised for her narrative purposes, he couldn't know anything about her other than what had happened in scenes that he shared with her. He could not know that to kill the child would be to kill her.

"The cancer's eating your brain," Terezin said. "Day by day, if not even hour by hour, your creative power as a writer will diminish, until soon you won't be able to construct so much as a short-short story let alone a long quest. If I kill this girl, your exhausting journey to this moment will have been for nothing. You'll have to start over — all new characters, all new incidents, cobble together another story to save yourself. And you don't have time for that."

Perhaps the cancer had already metastasized to the extent that her thinking was less clear than it had been. She knew what he said was half true, but she couldn't reason her way to an understanding of the other half. Her confidence declined, and apprehension stole upon her.

In the chair, the beautiful child maintained the expression that she'd had in the photograph: a hard-won serenity, a mask to deny her captor the pleasure of seeing her true emotions.

"Tell me," Terezin said, "in the swoon of writing, haven't you at times created a character who seems as real to you as anyone in your daily life?"

"Of course. But you're not one of them."

"And have you ever been surprised when a

character evolves such a degree of free will that he repeatedly does things that you don't see coming, that you don't plan, but that seem truly in character?"

"Every writer who trusts her intuition has that experience. It's when you know a character is working, is true and right."

Even a superior smirk could pass for an amused smile on his appealing face. "And has there ever been a time, during your writing, when you've had the uncanny feeling that one of your characters seems almost aware of your hand in his life, of being imagined and shaped, and he rebels, makes you struggle to keep him as you want him?"

"No," she lied. "That doesn't happen."

"Fiction is a dangerous art, Bibi Blair, creating new worlds populated by people as real as you can make them. Do you know how scientists explain the universe?"

She tried again to remove him, this time by the expedient of an aneurysm. Then by imagining him dropping dead of a heart attack.

He regarded her with an infuriating expression of forbearance, a smile tart with pity. When enough time had passed to make it clear that he would not succumb to editing, he repeated his question. "Do you know how scientists explain the universe?"

"What do you mean?"

"They *don't* explain it. Oh, after the Big

Bang, they can explain why and how it expanded as it did. But as to where it came from — that defeats them. Some say it came from nothing. They concoct grotesque unprovable theories that purport to show not only that something can come from nothing but that it happens all the time. Happens without reason, is an effect without a cause."

In the chair, Ashley Bell closed her eyes in resignation, as though she detected some clue in the cadences of his speech by which she knew he would soon arrive at a crescendo that he intended to emphasize by slitting her throat.

"Quite a few philosophers," Terezin continued, "including some of the most respected and enduring, say the world was *imagined* into existence. The scientists who insist something can come from nothing will ridicule the philosophers. But at least imagination suggests a cause and a power behind it. Considering that I exist by virtue of the story you've been telling yourself, I come down on the side of the philosophers."

"What's your point?"

He took the knife away from Ashley's throat, allowing the light to wink off its point. "Fiction is a dangerous art," he said again. "Creating worlds involves risks. Not risks just to readers who may be influenced toward darkness instead of light, evil instead of good, despair instead of hope, but also to the author."

As long as the knife was not pressed to Ashley's throat, Bibi could rush Terezin, bowl him off his feet. He might hit his head on the granite desktop, drop the knife. She could see how it might be done. Surprise him by going for the office chair in which the girl sat. Use her momentum and all her strength to wheel it backward into him. Imprudent, heedless of consequences. But considered action was always better than considered inaction. Yet she hesitated.

"When the author creates her characters," Terezin said, "she may think she knows what suffering should and will befall those who, like me, choose power over anything else. However, with your imagination, linked as it is to paranormal abilities, you empowered me in ways you couldn't anticipate."

With his left hand, he gripped Ashley by her brow and pulled her head back and put the point of the blade against the skin behind her chin bone. The opportunity to attack him was lost.

"Another way to do her would be to thrust the blade straight up through her mouth, through the soft part of her palate, and into her brain. That would be quite a moment, don't you think?"

Behind her closed lids, the girl's eyes rolled. Terezin's eyes, which met Bibi's and challenged her, were lustrous but absent all warmth, black ice.

Hitler had established the policies that led to the systematic extermination of millions, but he had never visited a death camp to watch whole families being shot or gassed and sometimes conveyed into crematoriums while half alive. He'd never visited a slave-labor camp to watch political prisoners, captured enemy soldiers, and Christian activists being starved and worked to death. When his cities were bombed, he did not once walk the ruins to encourage his citizens and improve their morale. He could order savage violence, but he was too fastidious to witness it.

If ever Terezin and his cult came to power, he would without compunction order mass murder, but he would also participate in it with pleasure.

"If you mean to kill this girl no matter what," Bibi said, "you would've done that by now. You want something from me. What is it?"

"I'll let you save her and save yourself. All I want in return is, when you walk out of this story of yours, you leave this world intact. You leave it to me as my playground."

She thought he must be toying with her. "But this is all . . . imagined."

"Somewhere Huck Finn lives in his world, having adventures Twain never dreamed of.

Sherlock Holmes is solving new cases even now."

Bibi hesitated to answer, afraid of saying the wrong thing.

He was a megalomaniac, insane by any standard, though capable of functioning — and succeeding — in society, not unlike Hitler. If he truly believed that a fictional world continued to exist when the book ended, that on some mystical plane it was real and eternally rotating on its axis, there might be a way out of this impasse.

"Leave all this intact?" she said at last, playing along with him, indicating the grand room and the fogbound world beyond. "How does that work?"

"Finish the story. Publish it."

"You want me to sit down and write —"

"No. You've already imagined most of it. It's in your head, just imagine it being on your computer, the computer in your apartment, in the world you were born into."

She almost protested that he had confiscated the computer in her apartment and that she had thrown away her laptop, tossed it into the back of a landscaper's truck, when she was being sought by his men in the helicopter. Then she realized that those things had happened in *this* world, in this *story,* not in the real world, where she was dying of gliomatosis cerebri.

Her confusion, even if brief, seemed to be

evidence that the brain cancer was corrupting her intellectual capacity.

"I could jam this shiv into her brain through an eyeball," he said. "I could cut off her lips first, and her nose, and you couldn't stop me."

"You can have this world," Bibi said, certain that he would not be this easily deceived, that violence was coming no matter what she said or did.

His stare was glacial, but his voice contained a suggestion of childlike delight. "You'll publish the full story as a novel?"

"Yes."

"And this world will be all mine?"

"If it works the way you think."

"Of course it does. You surprise me, lovely Bibi. You should have more faith in fiction. It lets you come sideways at the truth, which is the only way anyone ever gets near it."

He closed the knife and tossed it on the desk. The weapon slid across the black granite and came to rest, spinning lazily like the indicator on some game of chance.

When he came toward her, she prepared to dodge a punch, another knife. But he only smiled and walked past and continued toward the open door at the farther end of the room.

She imagined him dead of a cerebral thrombosis. Imagined a lethal aortal blockage in his heart. Imagined with great intensity spontaneous combustion, Terezin consumed by fire, a lurching figure from which seethed blue-white flames as hot as the core of the sun, his body showering into glowing coals and ashes.

He pivoted, drawing a pistol from under his suit coat. Stepped close to her. "Sometimes a character understands the author as well as she understands him." The muzzle of the gun, an empty eye socket in a fleshless skull, eternity rimmed in steel. He waited while she considered it and finally raised her stare to meet his. "Somehow, each time you target me and fail, I grow stronger. Do you sense that, lovely Bibi? I do. I sense it clearly." When she said nothing, he took her silence to be confirmation. He holstered the gun, turned his back on her, and walked away once more.

She still did not believe that he was finished with her. Perhaps she should have said nothing. There was one question she felt sure that he expected her to raise, however, and if she didn't ask it, he would conclude that her promise must be insincere.

"How do you know I'll really do it?" she called after him. "How do you know I'll leave this world intact for you?"

Halfway across the room, he paused and looked back. "You're a girl who tries her best, who values truth, who keeps her word. You're my creator, aren't you? Well . . . if we can't trust our gods, who can we trust?"

She thought of a piece called "The Creative Life" by Henry Miller, in which he had written that madmen "never cease to dream that they are dreaming." She was surprised that those eight words should come to mind just then, so apropos to Terezin. But after a moment, she thought perhaps they cut too close to home, and she did not dwell on them.

She watched Terezin until he left the room and walked the corridor to the elevator alcove.

127
BIBI TO BELL

The impossible Mojave fog, a ghost of the sea that had existed there millions of years ago, washed against the portholes. Deep in the whiteness, gliding shadows passed, immense and strange, as though Bibi's busy imagination could not resist supplying those intimations of the behemoths that plied the ocean of an earlier creation.

Approaching the lovely girl, who sat with eerie equanimity, Bibi did a small editorial revision involving the manacle that cuffed her to the chair, and it clattered to the floor.

Ashley Bell stood and stepped forward. She wore black patent-leather shoes, white stockings, a white pleated skirt, and a crisp white blouse with pale-blue embroidered butterflies on the cuffs and collar.

They met face-to-face, no more than a foot apart. Her skin was flawless, as in the photograph, her features in exquisite proportion. Those wide-set eyes, the singular violet shade of certain hyacinths, were remarkable not solely for their color but also because they were unusually pellucid, her stare direct and piercing, as if she didn't merely see Bibi but also read her soul.

"You're thirteen and I'm twenty-two, but we're the same height," Bibi said. "How can that be?"

Ashley Bell smiled and said, "How, indeed?"

Bibi was surprised to hear herself say, "I know you. We've met before."

"Yes. Eight years ago."

"Where?"

"In a book," said Ashley Bell.

Wonder rose in Bibi. "You survived Dachau."

"Yes. And wound up in America."

"Those are the clothes you were wearing when the SS came for your family."

"My mother and father resisted. They were murdered, and I was dragged from the house."

Astonishment of the emotions. Amazement of the intellect. And wonder growing. "That's where I saw the house before. In Toba's first book," Bibi said. "Toba Ringelbaum. It was a house in a German city, not in the middle of nowhere in the Mojave desert. How could I forget you, Toba's wonderful book, Toba herself?"

She had taken from fact only what she had needed to craft her fiction, and blocked from memory anything that might have made her realize that she was in a dreamlike state of creation, anything that would have allowed her to understand that she remained cancer-riddled and unable to go on any real quest for a cure.

"You grew up to be a surgical oncologist," Bibi remembered. "Specializing in brain cancer."

"You don't need an oncologist, Beebs. Don't need me anymore," Ashley said. "I was never really in danger. How could I be, with my story told and finished long ago, in a book now out of print? It was you who needed to be saved." Her voice changed. Now she spoke with Bibi's voice. "And you needed to overcome Captain's memory trick, so that you could discover that you had the power to cure yourself."

"Do I really? Do I have such power?"

"If you can imagine Jasper so vividly that one day a Jasper comes to you . . . Well, surely then you can imagine yourself free of cancer."

As she spoke, Ashley Bell underwent a metamorphosis, her blond hair darkening nearly to black. Her hyacinth eyes darkled as well, and her features became a mirror image of Bibi's.

The Bibi who had been Ashley put a hand on Bibi's brow and then reached into her head as though flesh and bone presented no obstacle, her fingertips blindly tracing the surface of the brain, the gyri and sulci, the folds and fissures. This was an intimacy beyond Bibi's experience, and she stood breathless, for the brain was the throne of the soul. Some said that the soul did not exist, and we all wondered from time to time if the skeptics might be right, if we might be only animals. But the Bibi who had been Ashley not only traced the gyri and the sulci, peeling away the web of cancer, but she saw what her fingers felt, saw the brain in all its complexity, and Bibi saw it as well, a masterpiece of gray matter and within it a soft light that wasn't merely the current of brain waves, but the shining and eternal essence of the girl whom Paxton loved.

When the other Bibi withdrew her hand, tangled in her fingers were black skeins of tissue, alien and foul, which could be nothing other than the hideous threads of gliomatosis cerebri. She worked her fingers, rolling the spiderweb filaments into a glistening bundle as big as a golf ball before throwing them aside. She leaned forward, embraced Bibi, and whispered, "Let's finish this, Beebs. Close your eyes. Let's finish this and go home."

When Bibi opened her eyes a moment later, there was only one of her — as should always have been the case.

Alone, she moved slowly through the colossal room in a condition of purest awe, as she might have felt if she had been born and raised in a deep cavern and had come above-ground after nearly a quarter of a century to see the starry night sky for the first time.

She did as Terezin asked, imagining the entire quest onto her home computer and her laptop, though not for his benefit, only for her own, that she should never forget all that had happened. She harbored no intention of publishing the story. And she would not leave this world that she had imagined for the mother-murdering monster to use as his playground. Let him perish with it. She was no god; she was a mortal liar.

No need to walk the corridor or take the elevator, now that she understood the true nature of this place. She imagined floating like a haunting spirit down through the higher floors of the building, down-down-down into the reception hall, and a moment later she found herself there.

When she raised her eyes to the big red circle with twin bolts of stylized lightning, the inlaid stone melted as if it were wax and streamed to the floor. Around her, the white quartz walls began to lose their opacity, until they became as transparent as sheets of glass, while at the same time Room 456 appeared like a heat-veiled mirage and began rapidly to solidify, though it was without patient or visitors.

She didn't walk but floated across the

disintegrating reception-hall floor toward the hospital bed, as the transparent walls of the building could no longer hold back the sea of fog. Billowing white mist flooded across the scene, claiming forever what had been the future headquarters of Terezin, Inc., as it would claim the rest of this world that she had imagined into existence during the past four days, which for her had seemed to be only two. By the end, even the fog would cease to exist.

The bedrail was down. She climbed onto the mattress. Put her head upon the pillow. Closed her eyes.

And opened them to the sight of the four people whom she loved most in all the world.

128
GOD BLESS YOU, ERICH SEGAL

What can you say about a twenty-five-year-old girl who died?

That she was three years older than Bibi Blair. That she was the ill-fated heroine of *Love Story* by Erich Segal. That she never had a chance, and she broke millions of hearts in her dying.

When Bibi opened her eyes, she saw four hearts waiting to be broken. She at once gave them a reprieve by saying, "Wow. I'm not going through *that* again. Brain cancer sucks."

As Bibi pulled the electro cap off her head, Nancy said, "Honey, wait, no, what're you doing?"

"My hair's a mess," she said, as the EEG went into alarm mode, "and it stinks like stale sweat. I stink all over. Yuck. I can't wait to take a shower."

When she sat up in bed and examined the catheter taped to the crook of her left arm, wondering if she might be able to remove it herself, Murphy went a bit nuts, seized simultaneously by tentative joy and trepidation, hands shaking and mouth trembling as he hovered, babbling, "You're awake, you're talking, baby, don't get up, chill out, Beebs, you can't get up, you're talking, look at you, I love you, you're scaring me."

To Pax, Bibi said, "Hi, hunk. I love you more than oxygen." And to Pogo she said, "You were there when I needed you, dude, loaning me your car. No, wait. I invented all that. But if it had been real, you would have lent it to me, wouldn't you, sweet boy?"

"*Mi* jalopy *es su* jalopy," Pogo said.

Pax and Pogo seemed to be riding with her abrupt recovery much better than were her mom and dad, almost as if they understood and had internalized a little of what had happened, though she couldn't figure out how that could be possible.

In response to the EEG alarm, a nurse arrived. Recovering quickly from the shock of seeing her formerly comatose patient so animated, she tried to calm everyone and explain that the catheter could not come out until the doctor ordered it removed. "You still need to be hydrated, Bibi."

"What I need," Bibi replied, "is two cheeseburgers and a pizza. I'm starving. A glucose diet sucks. Sorry I smell so bad."

"You don't smell bad," the nurse assured her.

"Well, see, I still have a nose, so while it's

762

kind of you to say I don't smell, I really do. By the way, I don't have brain cancer anymore. We need to do all those tests again, so you can let me go home." She winked at Pax and said, "You look delicious. What are you grinning about?"

Just then a night-duty intern arrived, as did another nurse, and a discussion ensued about whether or not Bibi still had cancer, who had the authority to order the tests, and whether they would have to wait until morning. Technicians were on duty to do everything from X rays to MRIs; they had to be there for the ER, which never closed. Murphy and Nancy somehow got the idea that the problem was related to insurance-company reluctance to pay for off-hour tests, and they declared that they would pay cash, to hell with the insurance company. Pax said he would pay for the tests, and Pogo said he would sell his damn car to pay for them. But finally everyone was made to understand that the insurance-company thing was a misunderstanding and that no one would have to pay cash. The head nurse on that shift reached Dr. Sanjay Chandra by phone. He expressed doubt that Bibi could know that she was cancer-free, doubt that it was even possible for gliomatosis cerebri to go into remission, but he ordered the catheter removed and the tests performed after Bibi spoke with him and told him she was symptom-free.

When she got out of bed, her mother grabbed her, embraced her with the ferocity of a Realtor who never let a client get away. Nancy was crying and laughing, and her kisses were wet, and she said, "How can this be, how can this happen?" And Bibi said, "After all, it *won't* be what it'll be," and into her mother's confusion, she said, "I love you so much, Mom, I always have, I always will." Murphy was there, it became a group hug, and he was a bigger mess than Nancy. In spite of all his thrashing the waves, lacerating and shredding and riding the behemoths with no fear, Big Kahuna of his generation, he was nonetheless a softie, all heart and as tender as a kitten. He couldn't speak, except to say her name, over and over, as if he had thought he'd never say it again to her alive. Pogo, too, looking at her with those blue eyes that melted other women, but with a love as pure as any that anyone had ever known, her brother from another mother, adoring her as she adored him. "Beebs," he said, and she said, "Dude," and he held her just long enough to convince himself that she was as real as she had always been.

In sweaty and rumpled pajamas, hair wild and tangled from being scrunched under the electro cap, certain that her breath could put a coat of rust on polished iron, Bibi nevertheless fell into Paxton's arms, and he folded her to him so that the hospital room seemed almost to disappear. She said that she was a mess, and he said that she was the best thing he'd ever seen, and she said she stank, and he said she smelled like springtime, and damn could that man kiss.

When an orderly arrived with the gurney and Bibi was transferred to it, along with her IV rack, she said to him, "I'm sorry I stink," and he said, "No, hey, I've smelled a lot worse."

Pax and Pogo and Nancy and Murph violated hospital rules by accompanying Bibi to every test venue, although they couldn't all fit in the same elevator with the gurney and the hospital personnel. Without asking permission, the four of them gathered with the MRI technician and watched through the big window as Bibi was conveyed into the ominous tunnel, waving at them as she disappeared headfirst.

Everything went pretty much this time as it had when she had *imagined* being cured by the night visitor with the golden retriever and had *imagined* being retested with astonishing results. When Dr. Chandra came to her room past midnight with a retinue of fascinated physicians, he said nearly the same thing he had said when she had imagined this meeting: that nothing in his medical experience had prepared him for this, that he wasn't able to explain it, that it wasn't possible, but that she was entirely free of cancer.

She hugged him as she had done before, though this time she apologized for reeking like a pig. He told her that given her impossible brain-wave patterns and now this miraculous remission, all manner of specialists would want to study her. Although she knew the reason for her cure, and though she intended to keep it secret within her little family, she agreed to make herself available in the weeks ahead. After apologizing in advance, she hugged him again.

Dr. Chandra looked happy and wonder-struck when he said, "On Wednesday, when I told you that you had at most a year to live, you said, 'We'll see.' Do you remember?"

"Yes. Yes, I do."

"It's almost as if you knew then that you'd be going home soon."

A post-midnight discharge was not unprecedented, but nearly so. Nevertheless, by 2:25 in the morning, Bibi was at her parents' home in Corona del Mar and in the shower, the water cranked up as hot as she could tolerate. Bliss.

No one was sleepy, least of all Bibi, who'd had days of sleep or something like it. Pax and Pogo had stopped at a twenty-four-hour market on the way, to buy ground sirloin, hamburger buns, tomatoes, lettuce, and Maui onions. Because she'd been without solid food for more than four days, Bibi had been warned to start with a soft diet, but she refused to think that gastric distress could lay her low when cancer couldn't. By the time she came downstairs to the kitchen, her parents, her beau, and her best friend were singing along with the Beach Boys, drinking Corona, and grilling monster burgers with all the trimmings.

Pax was the first to realize that Bibi's facial bruising was gone, that her crushed and abraded ear was as good as new, that she apparently had healed herself. As they regarded her with something akin to reverence, she said, "Yeah, I have some big news, and I don't know where all this is going in the days ahead. But wherever the hell it goes, compadres, if any of you ever looks at me again like you're looking at me now, like I'm something too precious for words, I'll kick your balls up past your gizzard. You, too, Mom."

They ate on the roof deck, with the night sea black to the west, and talked until the sky pinked in the east, and then longer still, and for most of that time she sat on Pax's lap, and touched his face from time to time, and marveled.

129
WHERE SHE GOES FROM HERE

The shingled bungalow had not been torn down by the people who bought it from Bibi's parents. She had imagined its destruction to facilitate the plot, themes, and atmospherics of her life-or-death quest. The house stood much as it had been in her childhood. On a sunny Tuesday afternoon, less than forty-eight hours after Bibi had been released from the hospital, she rang the doorbell, but no one responded.

The new owners were nice people, not the suspicious Gillenhocks who claimed to be retired investment bankers in the alternate world of Bibi's fancy. They wouldn't mind if she enjoyed their porch for a while. The rocking chairs were gone, but she sat in one of the patio chairs, looking out at the street, where the tresses of the palm trees rustled in a shifting breeze and the ficuses seemed to twinkle as their leaves — dark green on one side, pale green on the other — flickered this way and that in the changeable air.

In the weeks after Captain died, she had sat here to write some of her stories about Jasper, and here on a rainy day, a Jasper had come to her. As much as she loved her parents, they had not been able to understand her the way that Captain had understood her, and if she hadn't eventually imagined sweet Jasper into her life, she might have imagined the captain alive again. She had desperately needed a dog, a dog suitably mysterious. To her, nature wasn't merely a beautiful engine that powered fate. She didn't believe in coincidence. Neither did Captain. Neither did dogs. In their constant joy and bottomless capacity for love, dogs were in tune with a more complex truth.

This place would always be home to her, and perhaps one day she and Pax would own it. *Home is where the heart is.* No, nothing quite as simple as that. Home is where you struggle, in a world of endless struggle, to become the best you can be, and it becomes home in your heart only if one day you can look back and say that, in spite of all your faults and failures, it was in this special place where you began to see, however dimly, the shape of your soul.

On Wednesday, she and Pax sat on a bench at Inspiration Point, watching the sea as it carried to shore millions of fragments of the sun and cast them, cooled and foaming, on the sand.

With only three months to go on his current re-up, he had arranged to spend them stateside, assisting in the training of new recruits. He had given the Navy SEALs ten good years, and he would give to Bibi what years remained.

As pelicans flew in formation low along the coast and sandpipers worked the wet beach for lunch and a couple of hundred yards offshore schooling dolphins arced in and out of the water, she and Pax talked about how cautious she must be in the exercise of her imagination. This was not her world to change even if she thought that she could change it for the better. Considering how disastrous might be the unintended consequences of her actions, her greatest flights of fancy were best kept to the pages of books. If they had children — and they would — and if one terrible day cancer or some other hateful ailment threatened to cut short a precious life, she would have to risk those unintended consequences, as she might have to do as well in other extreme circumstances. Valiant girls, however, were always judicious and prudent. Pax wondered if she might be unique in all the world or if perhaps everyone possessed latent powers of imagination equal to hers. She thought the latter must be true, because she didn't believe that she was special. She said, "If we were imagined into existence with a universe of wonders, then the power to form the future with our imagination must be in our bloodline," and out in the sun-spangled sea, the dolphins danced.

On Saturday, Bibi had a lunch date with Pogo at Five Crowns in Corona del Mar. She arrived half an hour early and left her car in the restaurant parking lot.

At the corner of Pacific Coast Highway and Poppy Avenue, she stood remembering the two teenage girls as she had last seen them, Hermione and Hermione, one blond and one brunette, walking south to the corner and then west, not yet grown into their grace, leaning against each other, perhaps laughing, so alive. Bibi had known them only a short while, yet she had felt a remarkable affection for them because of their gameness and vulnerability, their combination of knowing-ness and innocence. That day, as they had faded out of sight in the fog, she had said to herself, *There go two dead girls,* and had been distressed by that surprising thought.

Now she understood the full meaning of those words. Hermione and Hermione, daughters of Harry Potter faniacs, had not been walking toward their murderer or any-thing as dramatic as that. They were two dead girls because they had never been living. They had been citizens of Bibi's imagination, who had never drawn one breath or laughed one laugh that anyone could hear.

Now she walked the length of tree-shaded Poppy to the sea, and back again, past houses that she'd seen a thousand times. She studied each dwelling with greater interest than before, half hoping that she would glimpse those girls passing a window, discover them lounging on a deck, coming out a door. This casual search could end only as had the search for Ashley Bell: an encounter with no one other than herself. Nevertheless, she entertained a little hope anyway, as an antidote to the sadness that shadows every writer's heart. For all the effort of creation, for all the hours at the keyboard and the intellectual exercise and the emotion expended, all of a writer's creations are but a ghost of the Truth, as ephemeral as are all the works of humanity in this world within time.

Later, over lunch, when she shared that thought with Pogo, he said, "Yeah, but just like me, you've got today. You've got today, and there's all of time and all the world in today. Walk the board, dudette."

130

She Hears the Song in the Egg of the Bird

At sunset he came to the shop on Balboa Peninsula, near the second of the two piers. It was not a jewelry store named Silver Fantasies; and of course it never had been. Newport Beach had never been home to a silversmith named Kelsey Faulkner, and no child named Robert Warren Faulkner had ever murdered his mother here. The space was occupied by a souvenir shop that sold items made of seashells and driftwood and chunks of driftglass smoothed into sinuous shapes by the ceaseless action of the sea.

He had no past except the one that she had invented for him, but it was a past he liked, and it portended a future that excited him. He could document a past for himself with ease, one that would be without blemish, designed to withstand scrutiny. He didn't even mind starting from scratch, so to speak. He had only the black suit he was wearing and the cash he'd had on him when last he had seen her. He possessed certain strengths and talents, however, and would surely make rapid progress.

As the sky caught flame across the west and purpled in the east, he returned to the car that he had stolen that afternoon. He drove to the head of the peninsula, and then a short distance south on Coast Highway, finally turning inland, abandoning the vehicle on a side street that he had selected earlier.

This was such a rich world, with so many prospects for a man of his good looks, charm, sharpness of mind, and determination. With all due respect for her extraordinary powers of imagination, the woman's world was a thin soup compared to the thick stew of this reality. Her mistake had been to craft a narrative in which he had become aware of her true nature in the imagined world that they had both left behind; he had then realized the existential danger that he faced — and the opportunity.

In the ruby and sapphire twilight, as he walked to the nearby high-end supper club that he had scoped out earlier, he cautioned himself not to underestimate the spunky Ms. Blair. Her imagination was such that she could hear the song of the bird when it was still but a yolk in an egg. Sooner or later, she might wonder if she had opened a door for him by imagining her entire quest for Ashley Bell onto her computers in this world. Once that thought rooted in her, she would be forever on the watch for him and, if she recognized him, dogged in pursuit. He would need to change his appearance, lose the current haircut for starters; the homage to Adolf was a childish touch, anyway.

When he built a power base — when, not if — and when the time came to move boldly and publicly against his enemies, which were the same in this world as in the previous one, he would start by burning the books. Those of lovely Bibi would be in the first pyre. She would appreciate the irony. She had created him with a hatred for books and bookish people, and she would reap the consequences of that hatred. Just as her books would be among the first set ablaze, she would be on the first train to the first death camp.

Overlooking Newport Harbor, the supper club was elegant in the extreme, luxurious, sensuous, decorated in shades of blue and gray, with black and silver accents. Large windows offered views of yachts at anchor and smaller boats cruising the twilight as dock lamps and house glow began to glimmer romantically across the darkening water.

The bar was large and well attended, clearly a gathering place for the well-to-do, especially singles of all conditions — divorced, widowed, never married, and single for the night only — hoping to hook up with those just a step below or above their station. He ordered a martini, pretending not to notice the women who were interested in him even as he surreptitiously cataloged and evaluated the qualities of each.

The quickest way to acquire a fortune, a network of valuable social contacts, and a respectable position in society would be to marry a woman who already possessed those things. In the other world, Bibi imagined him a cult leader, then a young high-tech billionaire. But with money and position, he would more quickly achieve his goals through politics, whether he was the golden-boy candidate himself or the manipulator of such a one; he didn't care which.

The woman would need to be beautiful but not too sexy. Not flashy. Elegant. Stylish. Cultured. Ideally, she would be several years older than he was and not quite as attractive, so that she would be flattered by — and grateful for — his interest in her. He spotted her across from him at the horseshoe bar. A cool blonde who might have been forty, forty-two. A single exquisite diamond pendant and a forefinger ring of the highest caliber were all she needed to declare her unmarried status and the depth of her wealth.

Their eyes met a few times. When the barstool next to hers became available, she looked boldly at him and, with a coquettish glance, indicated the empty seat. Carrying his martini, he moved with self-assurance to her side. Her name was Elizabeth Barret Radcliffe, but friends called her Beth.

If he were to avoid drawing Bibi Blair's attention in the years ahead, as he became an increasingly prominent person, he could not, of course, call himself Robert Faulkner or Birk Terezin. He needed a simple but solid name, a name of substance; and one had occurred to him earlier. Quite a lot of time would pass before he would realize that this name had been a literary allusion that Bibi made in her first novel, which she had imagined him reading after she had come to his attention in that other world of her invention. He introduced himself to Beth, but it was not then, at that early stage when he might have avoided the error, that he discovered the trap into which he had stepped. Beth was not a bookish person, and as her elevated social circle was not very bookish, either, the former Birk Terezin established his new identity with impeccable forged papers.

A few years later, he was fast on the rise with that new name before he discovered it was also the name of a sociopathic murderer in five novels by Patricia Highsmith: Thomas Ripley. By then his picture had been in many admiring newspaper articles, his name in headlines, and he could only suppose that she had become aware of him, had recognized him even with his new look, as she might not have done if he had been named Bob Smith. He could not decide how worried he should be until that same night he woke in terror from a dream involving assassins. After leaving bed and hurrying to his home office, he searched the Internet for a photograph of Bibi Blair's husband, who had been a Navy SEAL. Ripley could not help but be alarmed to discover that the spouse of such a famous author seemed never to have been photographed. Paxton Thorpe's photo was also missing from the public archives of former SEALs. And what of the men with whom he had served, all of them special ops veterans? What did they look like?

Without quite knowing how he'd gotten there, Thomas Ripley found himself at a window, peering out at Newport Harbor, at his private dock, past his impressive yacht, to where reflections of the moon trembled on black water. Only the moonlight, rippling. Nothing else. All seemed as it should be. As it would until . . . He stood there waiting in a torment of imagination.

ABOUT THE AUTHOR

Dean Koontz, the author of many #1 *New York Times* bestsellers, lives in Southern California with his wife, Gerda, their golden retriever, Anna, and the enduring spirit of their golden, Trixie.

www.deankoontz.com
Facebook.com/Dean Koontz Official
@deankoontz

Correspondence for the author should be addressed to:
Dean Koontz
P.O. Box 9529
Newport Beach, California 92658